PRAISE FOR

"[A] history myst

ber's spirited debut mixes classic country house mystery with a liberal dash of historical romance."

—*New York Times* bestselling author Julia Spencer-Fleming

"Riveting. . . . Huber deftly weaves together an original premise, an enigmatic heroine, and a compelling Highland setting."

—*New York Times* bestselling author Deanna Raybourn

"[A] fascinating heroine. . . . A thoroughly enjoyable read!"

—*USA Today* bestselling author Victoria Thompson

"Romance, suspense, mystery . . . add up to a fine read."

—*Kirkus Reviews*

"Gripping. . . . Fans of C. S. Harris's Regency mysteries will be pleased." —*Publishers Weekly*

"[Huber] designs her heroine as a woman who straddles the line between eighteenth-century behavior and twenty-first-century independence." —New York Journal of Books

"[A] must read. . . . One of those rare books that will both shock and please readers." —Fresh Fiction

"Anyone who enjoys historical mysteries, atmospheric settings, and strong female investigators should have Huber on their automatic-buy list." —Criminal Element

"One of the best historical mysteries that I have read this year." —Cozy Mystery Book Reviews

Titles by Anna Lee Huber

THE ANATOMIST'S WIFE

MORTAL ARTS

A GRAVE MATTER

A STUDY IN DEATH

A PRESSING ENGAGEMENT
(an enovella)

AS DEATH DRAWS NEAR

A BRUSH WITH SHADOWS

AN ARTLESS DEMISE

A STROKE OF MALICE

A WICKED CONCEIT

A PERILOUS PERSPECTIVE

A FATAL ILLUSION

A DECEPTIVE COMPOSITION

A TARNISHED CANVAS

A BITTER CUT

A Bitter Cut

ANNA LEE HUBER

Berkley Mystery
New York

BERKLEY MYSTERY
Published by Berkley
An imprint of Penguin Random House LLC
1745 Broadway, New York, NY 10019
penguinrandomhouse.com

Library of Congress Cataloging-in-Publication Data

Names: Huber, Anna Lee author
Title: A bitter cut / Anna Lee Huber.
Description: First edition. | New York : Berkley Mystery, 2026. |
Series: A Lady Darby mystery
Identifiers: LCCN 2025053060 (print) | LCCN 2025053061 (ebook) |
ISBN 9780593955284 trade paperback | ISBN 9780593955291 ebook
Subjects: LCGFT: Detective and mystery fiction |
Historical fiction | Novels | Fiction
Classification: LCC PS3608.U238 B58 2026 (print) |
LCC PS3608.U238 (ebook)
LC record available at https://lccn.loc.gov/2025053060
LC ebook record available at https://lccn.loc.gov/2025053061

First Edition: June 2026

Printed in the United States of America
1st Printing

The authorized representative in the EU for product safety and compliance is Penguin Random House Ireland, Morrison Chambers, 32 Nassau Street, Dublin D02 YH68, Ireland, https://eu-contact.penguin.ie.

For my family.

For my parents, grandparents, great-grandparents, in-laws, 4 brothers, 1 sister, 5 brothers-in-law, 7 sisters-in-law, 8 nieces, 7 nephews, 7 aunts, 6 uncles, 16 cousins, and all of their partners and children.

I have had the privilege to grow up with you, and get to know you, and to continue to spend time with you. We are loud and rowdy and rambunctious and at times contentious, but we love each other, and we want to know one another. It's from you that I've learned what family is and how to write about them in all of their dramatic glory, both the highs and lows, always knowing that it comes back to one single truth—love.

Thank you for shaping me into the person I am.

And thank you for just being so darn awesome!

A
Bitter Cut

CHAPTER 1

When I was sick, you gave me bitter pills,
And I must minister the like to you.

—WILLIAM SHAKESPEARE

JULY 1833
WARWICKSHIRE, ENGLAND

Perhaps it was my own fault for allowing my mind to wander rather than fully focusing on the task before me. But when the door burst open, causing me to nearly snip the tip of my finger off along with the stem of the rose I was trimming, I was more inclined to blame the intruder. Especially when I discovered it was my sister. I opened my mouth to berate her, but she actually had the temerity to shush me. So I glowered instead, ready to ignore this order. That is, until the oddity of her behavior stopped me.

Alana now stood with her back pressed to the door as if to hold it shut in preparation of a siege. Her chest rose and fell with each swift inhalation as she turned her ear to the wood, presumably listening for noise on the other side. I ascertained that I had not, in fact, amputated a digit, and lowered my pruning shears to the table, before puzzling over her conduct.

Clearly, she was hiding from someone. My first guess was that it might be her own children. She was known to play games like hide-and-go-seek with her brood from time to time. However, the last I'd heard, all the children had tramped out to the gardens with their nursemaids to enjoy the lovely weather we were having.

It was hard to imagine my fierce older sister hiding from anyone else. As the Countess of Cromarty, Alana often outranked everyone. Though she'd also faced down duchesses and society's starchiest matrons with ease. But it seemed, in this instance, she might have met her match. And I had a sneaking suspicion of just who had driven her to seek refuge with me in the dining room.

After a tense few moments, she must have decided the coast was clear, for she released the door handle and pressed a hand to her chest. Stepping away from the door, she smoothed a stray strand of chestnut brown hair back into place. She fluffed her lilac and pale rose muslin skirts, before offering me a wide smile, for all the world as if she hadn't just appeared to be running for her life.

"Ah, Kiera. Here you are," Alana declared breezily.

I arched a single eyebrow to let her know that I didn't believe for an instant that she'd actually been searching for me.

"Arranging flowers for dinner tonight?"

When my sister began stating the obvious, it was a clear indication she didn't wish to discuss something. So like the good little sister I was, I called her to account.

"Hiding from Mrs. Birnam, are you?" I remarked, adding

the pale cream shrub rose I'd just pruned to the cut-glass vase at the center of the long oak table. Various smaller sprays of blooms were arranged down the length of the runner interspersed with candlesticks, baskets of fruit, and crystal vessels waiting to be filled.

A faint furrow etched Alana's brow. "Don't tell me you're not doing the exact same thing. It's perfectly obvious why you're in here arranging flowers when you have members of your staff who are capable of the task."

I didn't attempt to deny it, but unlike Alana, I also didn't try to pretend otherwise. Instead, I focused on pruning the thorns from another rose before finding a place for it between a soft pink peony and a lavender phlox.

Alana rounded the table to stand next to me, picking up a coral daylily to examine it. "I thought you hated floral arranging."

"I don't hate it." I tilted my head, scrutinizing my work. "Though I admit it was never my favorite pastime." If given the choice, I'd always preferred painting and sketching or, barring that, practicing my viola or embroidery to anything gardening related. But our mother and later our governess had made certain my sister and I were educated in all the feminine arts, not just the ones we favored, and that included arranging flowers.

"It does provide a convenient excuse to escape the drawing room." Alana sighed. "I wish I'd thought of it."

My lips quirked. "But as hostess, I would never dream of asking such a thing of one of my guests."

She narrowed her eyes at my teasing before picking up a stem I'd discarded earlier. "Perhaps you should if you're using larkspur in the dining room. You do know it's poisonous."

Her imperious tone pricked my irritation. "That's why it's over there and not in this vase. It must have gotten mixed in with the other blooms when the gardener was selecting them."

The hum of her voice sounded unconvinced.

I snapped up the daylily she'd set down. "Now you're beginning to sound like Mrs. Birnam," I needled.

She scowled, but her annoyance at me quickly gave way to vexation at the woman in question. "That woman is insufferable. Have you ever met anyone who thought so highly of their own opinion? Not even the patronesses of Almack's are so puffed up with importance. Without cause!"

I shushed her. "Someone might overhear."

"Oh, let them. She'd probably think I'm complimenting her."

"Maybe. But think of Miss Birnam. She seems a kind girl, and Trevor is awfully sweet on her. You know what he intends."

When our brother had told me three months prior that he'd met the woman he wished to marry, I'd been overjoyed for him. However, he'd also been nervous to confess that her father was in trade. I'd personally not cared a fig about this fact, though I knew many among our class looked down on tradesmen and self-made men, no matter how wealthy they'd become. But Alana, who was far more of a stickler to society's rules—not entirely without reason—had voiced concerns. It was she who'd suggested I invite the Birnams to the house party I proposed to host at Bevington Park so that we might have a chance to get to know them before Trevor took any irreversible steps.

I'd had to concede that this was a wise proposal and a reasonable request. After all, I was well aware that marriage was not something to be entered into lightly. My first marriage to Sir Anthony Darby had turned out to be the worst decision of my life and a complete nightmare. Of course, Sir Anthony had been deliberately duplicitous. I knew my father would never have arranged the marriage had he known Sir Anthony's real intentions. But the fact remained that if the courtship had lasted longer and we'd all spent more time with my first husband before our wedding, there was a chance we might have realized his true nature sooner.

I trusted that Matilda Birnam wasn't being similarly deceitful, but one couldn't always be certain. Thus far, Alana's and my plans to get to know her better had been foiled by her abrasive and overbearing mother. I didn't believe I'd managed to exchange more than half a dozen sentences with Matilda before being interrupted by Mrs. Birnam. Given that, we'd hardly progressed beyond the state of cordial acquaintances.

Alana cast me a long-suffering look as she handed me another rose. "Miss Birnam is aware of her mother's deficiencies. It's writ all over her face every time Mrs. Birnam utters one of her vainglorious platitudes."

"That doesn't mean she should be subjected to your ungracious complaining," I stated as I adjusted the position of some of the flowers. "If, as you say, she already knows, I should hate to subject her to further pain by overhearing our complaints."

My sister grumbled under her breath before relenting. "I suppose you're right." She crossed her arms and turned away from the table, allowing her critical gaze to sweep over the arrangement on the sideboard behind us. "But I'm not sure this is going to work."

I glanced over my shoulder, trying to follow her stare, until I realized she wasn't speaking of the decorations but a union between our brother and Matilda Birnam. "Maybe they're nervous. You know how terribly awkward I am at social events, particularly with people I don't know."

"You've improved markedly," she said in my defense.

"Yes, but only because I've gotten better at emulating what everyone expects even if it seems ridiculous to me." I shrugged one shoulder. "And I feel more at ease with Gage by my side."

Alana's face softened. "Love has a way of doing that."

"Yes, plus I figure more people are looking at him than me."

It was in no way an exaggeration to say that my husband, Sebastian Gage, was an attractive man. Combined with his legendary charm and competent bearing, he was rather difficult to overlook.

"But the Birnams don't have someone like Gage to ease their way." I pressed my point. "Perhaps they're just awkward, too. After all, they haven't grown up in this world like us."

My sister's voice turned biting. "Kiera, there's a difference between awkward and a trifle . . . unwitting . . ."

I assumed this was her delicate way of describing my inadequacies.

". . . and being consciously gauche and downright rude."

It was difficult to dismiss some of the Birnams' behavior as merely bumbling. Perhaps one or two of the vulgar remarks Mrs. Birnam had made about money could be ignored, but not her constant comparisons. Mr. Birnam, for his part, was almost belligerent in asserting his opinions. I'd feared that he and my father-in-law might actually come to blows more than once over the way Mr. Birnam preferred to dominate the conversation. The younger Mr. Birnam—their son, Jemmy—was quieter but no less snide in his facial expressions and commentary. Of the four of them, only Matilda appeared versed in how to conduct herself pleasantly.

"And don't pretend you don't know the difference," Alana charged when I didn't respond. "Or pretend that they're not the reason why you haven't given us a tour of the finished dower house yet."

I frowned at the floral arrangement before me, making unnecessary adjustments to some of the blooms so that I wouldn't have to meet my sister's eye. She was correct, of course, but I'd thought I'd done a better job of concealing my motivations. Truthfully, I *was* a bit irked and disappointed that I'd not been able to show Alana and some of the others our newly renovated dower house yet. But having been subjected to enough of Mrs. Birnam's daggered criticisms, I was not about to invite her to direct it at my new home with which I was so pleased.

Bevington Park was, in actuality, my father-in-law's estate. And Bevington Hall, the manor house, was more than large enough for Lord Gage, my husband—his only son and heir—as well as me and our daughter. It was more than large enough, in fact, for the six dozen guests that would be arriving by the end of the week. We feared, however, it was *not* large enough for us to coexist peacefully for long.

Truth be told, before the events of the previous summer,

I could not have imagined living in such close proximity to my father-in-law. He'd not only held me in contempt, but he'd been harsh and demanding with his son. However, a brush with death and the birth of his first grandchild had wrought a number of changes in him, and he and my husband had begun to heal their contentious relationship. There was more mutual respect and understanding between them than ever, but Gage and I knew his father would never entirely abandon his manipulative nature. So we'd decided it would be in *all* of our best interests not to be caught living in one another's pockets.

Still, Bevington Park was Gage's birthright. He would inherit it upon his father's death, and I knew he already felt a responsibility to it. The future prosperity of the estate and all who relied upon it would, to a great extent, lie on his shoulders, so it behooved him to become familiar with the land, its workings, and its tenants while the current Lord Gage was still living. Consequently, when Gage's father had suggested we refurbish the dower house and make it our country home, after a brief deliberation, we'd agreed.

An estate's dower house was normally utilized by the dowager—the current lord's predecessor's widow, often his mother—but that didn't mean it couldn't be used for another purpose. Bevington Park's dower house had sat empty for a number of years, but most of it remained in good condition, if outdated. The cottage was situated in a wooded glade, perhaps a mile and a half's distance from Bevington Hall itself, down a charming path. There was also a broader lane that led to it, which had recently been improved upon so that carriages wouldn't become stuck in the ruts.

I was proud of the alterations we'd made to the cottage, particularly my art studio, and I'd been excited to show my family and friends. But not if that meant I must also invite Mrs. Birnam, as politeness would dictate. Any tour would likely have to wait until the end of the week when the bulk of the guests arrived at Bevington Park, swelling the number of guests to over fifty. Then our absence would not be so conspicuous.

In any case, for the duration of the house party, Gage and I, and our young daughter, had been forced to move back into the suite of rooms we'd formerly occupied at the hall. Lord Gage was a widower, and as his daughter-in-law, the duties of hostess had fallen to me. Duties I couldn't perform properly from across the park. While we'd only been here three days, I was already missing the comforts and solitude afforded to us at the dower house.

"A number of Lord Gage's political friends and their wives will be arriving this evening," I told Alana, striving to keep the nerves that fluttered in my stomach from showing. "Perhaps we'll have a chance tomorrow for a tour."

This was doubtful. Only two of the six men were currently married, and I would be expected to entertain their wives. A task that I suspected was going to be made even more difficult by Mrs. Birnam.

Alana reached up to touch my shoulder, stilling my fidgeting with the flowers. "They look lovely." She offered me an encouraging smile before glancing about us. "Everything looks lovely."

I dropped my arms, fussing instead with the fabric at the sides of my white skirt patterned with wavy blue dots. I should have known better than to think I could fool my sister. She'd been caring for me since our mother died when I was eight years old, and she was adept at reading my moods and idiosyncrasies. "Do you think so?" I asked, unable to stop myself from seeking her reassurance and approval.

She grasped my hands, quietening them again before adjusting the gold broach at the center of my scalloped lace collar. "I do."

I nodded, trusting she wasn't lying. Alana didn't do that. Not even to placate me.

I inhaled past the tightness in my chest. "Then I suppose it's time we rejoined the Birnams and Lorna for tea." I gasped. "Oh dear! Lorna. Have you left her alone with them all this time?"

Lorna was Gage's cousin Alfie's wife and hence the Viscountess of Tavistock, but her upbringing had also been rather unconventional. She was the illegitimate child of a viscount, and her mother had raised her in an isolated cottage on Dartmoor. I preferred to judge a person on their character and not the happenstances of their birth, but I was well aware that not everyone was so rational. Society's gossipmongers had certainly enjoyed chewing on this tidbit when Lorna and Alfie married, but had discarded it swiftly enough in favor of tastier morsels. Two years had passed since their hasty wedding, and I'd been somewhat surprised that Mrs. Birnam was even aware of Lorna's past. Apparently, she read the gossip rags. She'd felt no qualms about displaying her censure of the viscountess.

"No, Lorna had already gone out to the gardens to check on her sons." Based on Alana's sly smile, I guessed this was meant to imply that Lorna had also been escaping the Birnams, as the nursemaids undoubtedly had all the children in hand. Lorna's elder boy, Rory—named in honor of Alfie's deceased younger brother—was just eighteen months old, and her younger, Sherry, barely four months.

"When are the men due to return?" Alana asked, moving toward the window through which one could glimpse the stables beyond a small copse of trees.

"Soon, I suspect."

All of the men had ventured out that morning for a spot of hunting, but I knew it was Malcolm, Alana's oldest child, she was chiefly thinking about. He was on summer holiday from school, having recently completed his first year away. Though she tried to hide it, I knew Alana had missed him terribly and was struggling to adjust to the changes in her son. Malcolm was growing up, in more ways than one, and this was the first time he'd been deemed mature enough to join the hunting party of men rather than remaining in the schoolroom and nursery.

I linked my arm with my sister's, towing her toward the door. "Come. If I know anything about men, it's that as soon as the refreshments are brought out, they'll arrive at the door, having smelled them from halfway across the park."

Alana smiled faintly at my jest. "Malcolm will. I vow he's grown another two inches just in the fortnight since we collected him from school."

"Soon he'll be taller than you."

"And you," she retorted. We were almost identical in height.

I grinned, not being ruffled by this fact. Not when my firstborn had only recently begun toddling.

"You just wait," my sister warned.

I patted her hand where it rested against my arm. "I know, dearest. I'm sure I shall get my comeuppance."

Alana narrowed her eyes, recognizing I was appeasing her.

"Until then, you can enjoy my being chastised by Mrs. Birnam for abandoning her."

CHAPTER 2

True to my expectations, when we joined them in the red saloon, Mrs. Birnam managed to slip in plenty of barbs and complaints about our leaving her and her daughter, Matilda, to their own devices. Even though it had been less than half an hour, I didn't attempt to counter her, deciding it would be simpler to allow her to gripe while we waited for the staff to arrive with tea.

True to the room's name, the saloon's predominant color was red. From the silk wallpaper to the upholstery on the furniture to the trim of the drapes, there was no shortage of the vibrant hue. Even the woodwork was stained to a reddish tint, while gold accents shimmered in the picture frames, the gilt outlines of the medallions on the ceiling and the Baroque ornamentation above the three sets of tall double doors leading out onto the terrace. The ceilings on this level of the house were all at least fifteen feet high, with the great hall at the center being a full two stories.

Despite the warmth of the day, per Mrs. Birnam's request, a fire had been lit in the hearth. Though I noticed she was now seated on a settee ten feet away from it, her woolen shawl discarded. Matilda, on the other hand, sat with flushed cheeks in a chair near the flames. While clearly miserable, she seemed determined that someone make use of her mother's earlier demand.

I strolled toward one of the sets of French doors, which were propped open to allow a breeze to waft inside, saving us all from slowly roasting, as Mrs. Birnam harrumphed.

"I cannot imagine what is keeping Lady Tavistock so long. When my children were young, I would never have allowed them to place such demands on my time, especially not whilst attending a house party. Honestly, I cannot imagine why she even brought them with her. What else are nurses and governesses for?"

"Oh, I asked her to bring them," I replied artlessly. "To see how much Rory has grown since November, and to meet dear little Sherry."

"Sherry." She tsked. "What sort of name is that for a child?"

"His full name is Sherracombe, after his late grandfather," Alana reminded her, though I doubted Mrs. Birnam was unaware.

"A connection better left unadvertised, if you ask me."

Anticipating Alana's terse response, I called over my shoulder to Matilda before she could speak. "Miss Birnam, will you come closer? I should like your opinion on something."

"Of course," she said, immediately rising to her feet to join me at the window.

Outside, beyond the terrace, lay the parterre garden set-out in a circular design. It was too regimented for my taste, but I knew my father-in-law favored it. Since Lord Gage had spent more than twenty years of his life in the Royal Navy, it was not a surprise that he preferred neatness and order to the more chaotic, natural gardens which appealed to me. In any case, plants and gardening were not my forte. But Matilda had confessed an interest in such things, and Trevor claimed that the roses she had cultivated at Twizel Hall—Mr. Birnam's recently acquired estate—were a sight to behold.

"Do you see the flower beds around the outside of the central path of the circle?" I asked in a voice soft enough that I hoped Mrs. Birnam wouldn't overhear and interject. Alana—bless her—seemed to infer my intent, for I heard her address the other woman as I continued. "His lordship is not happy with their current appearance, and I must agree. Though I'm not sure what to advise him."

The plants that had been chosen for that patch when the house and gardens were refurbished three years prior, when my father-in-law, Lord Gage, was granted this property as well as his title by the king for services to the Crown, had not thrived. While most of the beds were bright with color and flush with growth, the vegetation in those beds appeared almost dead.

"Do you have any suggestions?" I asked Matilda.

She bit the corner of her lower lip, giving the matter her serious consideration before answering.

Upon first being introduced to Matilda, I could tell why my brother had taken an initial interest in her. She was a lovely girl with hazel eyes lively with good humor and a button nose. Her soft brown hair was remarkably fine, struggling to hold the curls about the temples that were so fashionable, but she had no need of them. Not when her skin was so creamy and smooth. I was relieved to see that the red in her cheeks appeared to be fading in the cool draft gently billowing the drapes on either side of us.

"It could be the soil or the type of plants," she replied. "I believe the ones embedded there thrive in a shady environment rather than full sun. But I would have to examine them more closely to say for sure."

"Would you do so and then give us the benefit of your guidance?"

Her smile brightened. "I would be happy to."

"Excellent," I declared. "That is one less thing for me to worry about."

Matilda seemed to read more into this statement than intended, for her eyes dimmed. "Is there anything else I can assist you with, my lady?"

"Oh, thank you. But truly, it's nothing to concern yourself with," I hastened to assure her. "Though won't you please call me Kiera. Under the circumstances, it seems rather unnecessary to be so formal."

"I should like that," she confessed almost shyly, the crests of her cheeks pinkening again. "And you must call me Matilda."

"*Why* are you conversing by the door?" Mrs. Birnam's strident voice demanded to know. "Matilda, come away from there. You'll catch a chill."

"It is plenty warm, Mother," Matilda answered evenly,

though she complied with her request. "We were just admiring the garden and planning to take a stroll through it after tea."

"Not without your pelisse, you won't."

The doors opened then, saving Matilda from needing to make a response, and two footmen strode inside carrying enormous silver trays. The first was laden with three teapots as well as cups and all the other accoutrements necessary for tea. The second contained tiered plates piled high with sandwiches, biscuits, and patisseries of every variety. I directed the footmen to set the trays on the table at the center of the room beneath the crystal chandelier so that we all might serve ourselves, then excused them.

Mrs. Birnam scowled as they bowed and departed, perhaps having expected them to remain to attend us. However, I knew the staff was already at sixes and sevens preparing for that evening's dinner, not to mention the extra work required to ready the manor for the eventual arrival of fifty more guests. I did not require footmen to stand about pouring tea and passing out sandwiches when Bowcott, the butler, could put them to better use elsewhere.

"May I pour for you, Mrs. Birnam?" I offered, hoping to stave off another snide remark.

"That's not necessary," she answered as she fluffed the enormous apple green gigot sleeves of her gown, which were currently so *en vogue*. Frankly, their width over the past three years had grown from simply annoying to beyond absurd. She nodded to her daughter. "Matilda will see to it."

I was prepared to argue when Lorna wafted into the room like a petal on a breeze. Her long blond hair was plaited into an elegant knot threaded with a gold cord and a pale pink ribbon which matched her dress as well as the shade of her lips.

"Oh, I must have impeccable timing," she declared with a tinkling laugh as she saw the mountainous spread. "For I must confess, I'm famished."

"The needs of young children will do that to you," Alana told her with a knowing smile.

"Impeccable timing, indeed," Mrs. Birnam drawled with arched eyebrows. "And here, I feared you might have gotten lost."

I frowned, displeased with her relentless disapproval of my friend, but I took my cues from Lorna, who seemed entirely unruffled as she began selecting food for her plate.

"Well, of course, the children were also being served their tea, so it was no great work of deduction that we would soon be as well." This effectively squashed any implied notion that Lorna had been anywhere other than where she'd said she was. "Though, on the subject of impeccable timing, I do believe Alfie's stomach has proved itself infallible yet again, for I understand the men have just returned to the stables."

Alana and I shared an amused glance, having made a similar prediction of the hunting party's imminent arrival.

"Then I suggest filling our plates before they join us or risk there being nothing left," my sister jested.

"Mr. Birnam does work up a ferocious appetite whenever he goes off on one of his rides," Mrs. Birnam commented, her florid features softening in a brief but genuine smile. It offered me my first glimpse of the pretty woman who still lurked beneath her mask of steely propriety and discontentment.

She wasn't the first matron I'd met who had transformed herself into such a figure. For some, it was the result of life's accumulated disappointments, while for others, it seemed to be caused by a particular rigid sense of Protestant religiosity in which anything that one took pleasure or enjoyment in was by default suspicious and should therefore be shunned. As if joy and happiness were an anathema to Christianity. Based on some of her comments, I suspected Mrs. Birnam's motivation was due to the latter, but I was leery of assuming that the first couldn't also be true. Many people had silent tragedies and hardships they were loath to speak of that had shaped them irrevocably. I knew this intimately.

"Jemmy, on the other hand, picks at his food like a bird rather than a grown man of four and twenty," Mrs. Birnam added, her brow furrowed as she spoke of her son.

Matilda eyed her mother over the cup of tea she was preparing for her. "That's because he doesn't like outdoor pursuits. Or killing things," she murmured softly.

Her mother stiffened. "What nonsense! All men enjoy killing things."

I found this a puzzling sentiment, for I knew plenty of men who didn't enjoy harming living creatures. For all that Gage had been to war and been forced to injure or kill culprits in the course of his duties as a gentleman inquiry agent, I knew that he didn't *enjoy* such violence. Just as I knew he didn't precisely *enjoy* hunting as sport, no matter that it was a staple activity of the country gentleman.

Both Alana and Lorna also seemed troubled by this attitude, perhaps thinking of their sons. As such, I searched for a safe change of topic.

I crossed the room toward one of the cabriole-legged

chairs set near the cooling draft of the windows, noting that Mrs. Birnam was fluffing her sleeves again. Either she was uncomfortable, or she wished someone to remark upon them.

"Such exquisite material," I told her. "And the color complements your eyes." Which were a soft shade of brown.

"Thank you. I'm told it's the latest fashion from Paris." She smoothed a hand over the satin fabric across her lap. "With Mr. Birnam's enhanced position, I find it is important that I dress to reflect his status." She accepted her cup of tea and a selection of small sandwiches from her daughter. "But perhaps not everyone shares this view. Or maybe the extra fabric is too costly."

Despite her brief but pointed stare at my attire, I didn't realize she was criticizing my appearance until I heard Alana choke on her tea. Matilda's expression was horrified.

"Oh, no. It's not that," I replied, resigned by now to my unfashionableness. "I simply don't like the style."

Mrs. Birnam blinked at me as if I'd grown a second head. "You simply don't like the style?"

"No," I said with a light shrug of my shoulders before taking a bite of cucumber and watercress sandwich.

"But . . . why?"

It was my turn to stare back at her in bemusement, unsure what was so confusing about what I'd said. "The sleeves. They're cumbersome, and they interfere with my painting." And painting was my passion, in particular portraits. I spent as many hours in my art studio each day as I could. Which, given my demands as hostess of this house party, would be very few over the next fortnight. The thought was enough to make me stifle a forlorn sigh.

I tilted my head, considering the extreme proportions of Mrs. Birnam's à la mode gown. "They also distort the natural human figure, making the silhouette ungainly."

Mrs. Birnam bristled.

"She's speaking in terms of artistic aesthetic, Mother," Matilda hastened to say.

I halted before taking another bite of sandwich. "What else would I be speaking in terms of?"

My sister made another sound at the back of her throat, but this time I could tell she was smothering laughter, though I didn't know exactly what I'd said to cause her such amusement. Even Lorna was hiding a smile behind the brim of her cup. She rolled her heavily lashed green eyes at me playfully, as if I was in on the jest.

A jest that Mrs. Birnam appeared to believe was being made at her expense. "Yes, I'd forgotten that Mr. St. Mawr warned you about his sister's peculiar proclivities," she stated slyly to her daughter.

My chest grew tight, and I felt my expression begin to fall, though I knew I shouldn't let her see how this comment had distressed me. The trouble was, I'd been fending off malicious remarks about my awkward demeanor and unnatural tendencies for what seemed my entire life. Society, in particular, was most unkind to those who did not conform. And when the scandal that had broken after my involvement with the work of my first husband, the anatomist Sir Anthony Darby, had become known—heedless of the particulars and my enforced participation—it had only made matters worse.

That being said, my second marriage and my role assisting Gage to bring murderers, thieves, and other criminals to justice had gone a long way to preparing my reputation. My family's and friends' love and support had also helped heal many of my old wounds. Which was why it was so hurtful to hear that Trevor had felt it necessary to warn Matilda about me. Perhaps I shouldn't have been upset, for my brother had undoubtedly meant well, but I couldn't halt the sickening swirl of shame that filled my stomach all the same.

And I couldn't hide it from him when he was the first of the returning men to stride through the door.

"Hail your conquering heroes," Trevor announced, a jovial smile splitting his face. One that began to die as he first caught sight of Matilda's countenance and then glanced at me and our sister, who appeared ready to spit fire. She had always been protective of me.

Mr. Birnam followed soon after, clapping Trevor on the back. "And would ye look at this fitting feast they've prepared in our honor." His broad barrel chest shook as he chuckled, the bushy red hair going to white at the sides of his face catching the light.

"I hardly think these ladies were in any danger from a deer and a few pheasants," Alfie drawled, his dark hair in artful disarray. He went straight to his wife, wrapping an arm around Lorna's waist and pressing a kiss to her temple before whispering something in her ear that made her smile and pinken, uncaring of what others might think of this public display of affection. Truth be told, it made me like Gage's cousin all the more for it.

"Dinna dampen our spirits, lad," Mr. Birnam countered in his loud brogue. "'Twas a fine bag. Especially for this lad's first attempt."

Malcolm smiled shyly as Mr. Birnam and the others

cheered him. At the sight of her son, Alana's anger swiftly died, and she moved forward to greet him and Philip, my brother-in-law, who stood behind Malcolm, a hand on his shoulder. As the trio drew to the side to confer, I could tell that Alana was relieved to find them both hale and whole.

Just as I was when Gage entered after them.

Even after two years of marriage, my heart still fluttered whenever I saw him again after we'd been separated for any length of time. His skin was bronzed and his golden hair bleached from the hours he spent in the sun every day at the estate. This made the pale winter blue of his eyes all the more arresting when they landed on me. I could tell from the tiny furrow that formed between his brows that he'd noticed something was amiss, just as I could tell from the hard line of his jaw that the hunt had not proved as enjoyable for everyone. When his father failed to join us, it wasn't difficult to figure out who.

I stifled my grimace by taking another bite of sandwich, though the flavor had lost its appeal.

My father-in-law had already made it clear how much he resented my subjecting him to Jeremiah Birnam, whom he deemed a trumped-up tradesman. He'd made it crystal clear what a disaster he believed Trevor was courting by pursuing Matilda's hand, no matter how large her dowry. I'd ignored this pronouncement. Hadn't he also opposed me and Gage marrying? Vehemently. But his dire predictions for this house party were harder to ignore, especially now that they seemed to be coming true. If Lord Gage's political cronies were lords after his own mold, then they were not going to appreciate Mr. Birnam's blustering presence either.

I could sense the unasked query in Gage's gaze and

minutely shook my head. There wasn't time to confer now. Not without drawing unwanted attention. So he turned to the tea table instead, but only after offering me a sympathetic smile.

"And how have you ladies been entertaining yourselves?" Trevor asked after pouring himself a cup of tea and moving to stand next to Matilda. This was obviously asked out of politeness. He had no way of knowing he was potentially setting light to a powder keg.

I braced myself, waiting for Mrs. Birnam to rattle off her list of complaints, only to be surprised when she kept her counsel. It was Matilda who had to speak up, answering somewhat obscurely. "Oh, with this and that. We've been admiring the gardens." She glanced about as if searching for someone, and I realized she'd meant to compliment Lord Gage. Her smile fell a notch when she realized he wasn't present. "We were planning to take a stroll after tea."

"Delightful." Trevor leaned toward her. "And may I join?"

Matilda twinkled up at him. "But of course."

"Where is Jemmy?" Mrs. Birnam suddenly demanded to know. This was why she'd remained quiet, then. She'd been focused on her son. "He must have returned with you."

The men all turned to look at one another as if someone else held the answer.

"I sent him to fetch Miss Whitlock," Mr. Birnam finally responded around a bite of something. He didn't even bother to look up but continued filling his plate while alternately stuffing morsels into his mouth.

Judging from Mrs. Birnam's ferocious scowl, this was not favorable news. Even Matilda seemed startled by his pronouncement. Yet Mr. Birnam appeared all but oblivious to his family's reaction.

It could not be denied; this was a bit of an odd turn. I had been introduced to Miss Portia Whitlock the day of the Birnams' arrival, but then she had been indisposed, so I'd had no chance to offer her more than that initial greeting. In truth, I'd not anticipated interacting with her more than that, for she was not a guest in the traditional sense, but rather an employee of Mr. Birnam—his private secretary.

While it wasn't all that unusual for men of importance to travel with their secretaries, it *was* uncommon for them to be female. In fact, it was practically unheard of. Not that I necessarily disapproved. For I believed a woman could do just as good a job as a man, especially at such an endeavor. But her presence raised questions, particularly when the women in his family reacted in such a manner.

It was also rare for a secretary to be invited to associate with the guests. After all, they were employees brought with the gentlemen to do a job. But their status fell into the hazy realm between traditional staff and social equal, much like governesses and stewards. As these people were often individuals of a genteel and well-educated upbringing who simply did not possess the means required not to hold employment, they were at times asked to step in to help round out uneven numbers at a dinner party or such, but usually as a last resort. In all my time at Bevington Park, I'd only eaten a meal with Lord Gage's private secretary, Mr. Thorndike, once.

It was under this pall of uncomfortable silence that the younger Mr. Birnam and Miss Whitlock arrived. The tension must have been obvious, for they both halted in their tracks as if hitting a wall. Jemmy recovered more quickly than Miss Whitlock, albeit with little grace. He darted a sullen look at his father before retreating to a chair in the far corner, ignoring his mother's request for him to join her on the settee.

Miss Whitlock, for her part, seemed on the verge of turning tail and running, but then she straightened her spine and slowly advanced into the room. She was young—certainly no older than Jemmy's four-and-twenty years and perhaps several years shy of that. Her coloring was fair, her clothing demure, and while she would never be called a great beauty, she was more than passingly pretty.

Recognizing my duty as hostess, I crossed the room to smooth matters over and reassure her of her welcome. Though I was forced to wait as Mr. Birnam urged her to fill the plate he thrust at her, even going so far as to plunk several sandwiches onto it unbidden before striding off.

"I am glad to see you are much improved," I told her with a smile. "Long carriage rides can be quite trying, can't they?"

Her gaze scoured my face, seeming to search for any evidence of anger or displeasure, and finding none, her shoulders relaxed. "Thank you, my lady," she replied in a well-modulated voice. "I'm ever so grateful for your kindness and that of his lordship's staff."

"This is why we need to get these steam locomotive railways built," Mr. Birnam declared loudly. "'Twill shorten the journey cross-country by half."

"The Liverpool and Manchester Railway has reduced the trip between the two cities from nearly a full day to just two hours," Trevor supplied, and then the pair of them were off again, absorbed in their growing passion for the machines. For in addition to his highly profitable mills and factories, Mr. Birnam was heavily invested in efforts to transform transportation across Britain. Trevor was fascinated by the locomotives and had invested, to a lesser degree, also convincing Philip and Gage to purchase stocks. However, that did not mean they shared the other men's enthusiasm for the topic.

"Have you been able to acquire everything you need?" I asked Miss Whitlock, unused to providing for the requirements of a secretary.

"Yes, thank you. And I was introduced to Mr. Thorndike this morning and told he could assist me, if necessary."

There was a note in her voice that was overly bright, and being acquainted with Lord Gage's personal secretary, I suspected it might have something to do with him. Having been subjected to his condescending view of women who *dabbled* in art, I could only imagine that his reaction to a female secretary had not been as congenial as one might wish.

"Well, please do not hesitate to ask if he is unable," I told her, striving toward an evenhanded approach.

She hesitated but for a moment before nodding. "I will."

I found myself wanting to ask her a number of questions. Who was her family—for it was obviously genteel—and where did they come from? How did she come to be employed as Mr. Birnam's personal secretary? And what was her relationship like with the other Birnams, for there was definitely some strong undercurrent between them? But I didn't know how to politely broach any of these queries.

And then Alfie was standing on my other side, jostling

me with his elbow like an annoying brother as he selected a few tea cakes. Though I had not liked him when we first met, finding him petulant and spiteful—and I'd been prepared to never fancy him considering how he'd tormented Gage when they were boys—a tragic and terrifying incident out on the moors had forged a bond between us that had transcended all that. Of course, it also helped that he and Gage had made their peace and his marriage to Lorna seemed to have tamed him. Somewhat. Now he treated me more like a little sister, alternately teasing and pestering me and then turning overprotective.

As such, by the time I'd finished badgering Alfie about taking all the fairy cakes, in response to which he'd merely flashed a roguish grin and popped another into his mouth, I discovered that Miss Whitlock had glided away. I noted she'd chosen a seat near the windows, far from any of the Birnams. Lorna went to join her. A move that, while kind, seemed to invoke a rather strong reaction from Mrs. Birnam, whose flushed face and tight lips suggested she was withholding an outburst.

Given her continued disparagement of Lorna, I couldn't help but wonder if she was reacting to something she saw as being similar between the two women. Was Miss Whitlock also illegitimate? Or were Mrs. Birnam's suspicions more insidious? I didn't like to nurse the thought, particularly when it was rather an unworthy one and there was no proof of anything untoward. But Mrs. Birnam's glacial stare could not be ignored.

Alfie, on the other hand, had no such qualms.

"I wouldn't have thought the mushroom had it in him. Do you think he's tupping her right under his wife's nose?"

Gage, who was standing on his other side, and I both turned to glare at Alfie not only for the rude comment but for the reluctant admiration we detected in his voice. His saving grace was that he'd spoken softly enough that no one else appeared to have heard him.

"I'm sure that is none of our affair," Gage uttered quellingly.

Alfie was undaunted. "I'm just saying what we're all thinking."

"Yes, but would that not be a curiously bold move on his part?" I couldn't stop myself from asking, even though it earned me a glare from Gage also. "Foolish even."

Yes, gentlemen and other men of means were known to keep mistresses, but they did not normally flaunt them in front of their wives. Such things were simply not done. And Mr. Birnam was here to court political favor from Philip, Lord Gage, and his political connections. That much had been made very clear over the past two days. Surely, he would not jeopardize that by foisting his mistress upon us in such a thin guise.

My eyes trailed over the assemblage toward the corner where Jemmy still sat, arms crossed morosely. For the most part, he kept his attention directed at the floor, but periodically he shot a scowl in the direction of Miss Whitlock.

"Maybe Mr. Birnam's designs lay in a different direction," I posited. After all, he had sent his son to collect Miss Whitlock. Perhaps that was intentional. If so, Miss Whitlock's connection to the Birnams must be more than coincidental.

I wondered if Trevor knew. At the moment, he seemed oblivious to everything but his conversation with Mr. Birnam.

Even his near-fiancée and the daggered look Jemmy sent his way when Mr. Birnam praised Trevor for something clever he'd said escaped his notice. Clearly, there was some animosity and jealousy there as well. Perhaps my brother should tread with more care.

CHAPTER 3

Gage found me some hours later standing before one of the tall windows of our bedchamber staring broodingly out at the lake at the edge of the southern lawn. By all rights, I should have been preparing myself for dinner, but I'd delayed Bree McEvoy, my lady's maid, asking her to return in a quarter of an hour. There was someone I needed to speak to first.

My husband rested his hands on my shoulders, lightly kneading them as I watched a family of ducks waddle down the hill toward the water. The evening sky was painted with shades of azure, mauve, and apricot. The clouds almost appeared tipped in gold. I began sifting through various pigments in my mind, trying to decide which I would combine to recreate each color. It soothed some of the frayed edges of my temper.

"You did not expect him to be any different, did you?" Gage murmured gently, pressing a kiss to my temple.

I'd known better than to think my husband would be unaware of the main source of my discontent. "No. Your father behaved precisely as I thought he would," I replied stiffly. "But . . ." I broke off, too vexed to even finish the thought.

"That doesn't make it any easier," Gage construed.

I heaved a sigh, knowing part of my impatience was directed at myself for nursing even the smallest hope otherwise.

As fellow hosts, we had joined Lord Gage earlier in the soaring great hall to greet his political cronies as they arrived one by one or in pairs. The first was Baron Foley of Kidderminster, a young and promising Whig, who had been taken under the wing of the second arrival, Lord Melbourne, who currently served as home secretary. Another Whig, Baron Brougham and Vaux, and his wife clattered up the drive next followed by a man I'd believed to be his rival—the Tory Lord Lyndhurst—and his wife. Last to arrive was a pair of Tory Conservatives, the Scottish Earl of Strathblane and his young protégé Lord Milngavie.

While not overtly frosty, Lord Gage's treatment of me during these receptions had not been warm. Not as it had been in recent months. I tried not to let this bother me, though I couldn't deny it stung to feel his disdain directed at me once again. However, his warnings about Mr. Birnam's intrusion into his home and the reason for his being there grew ever more biting with each recitation. All of the guests had reacted with either resignation or sangfroid, none being so impolite as to visibly recoil at the Birnams' presence, but I'd been forced to grit my teeth when more than one had chosen to praise Trevor's shrewdness in nabbing a girl with such an immense dowry.

I knew how marriage was viewed by the aristocracy. Most matches were arranged to either bolster familial connections, increase wealth, or consolidate power, irrespective of the compatibility of the couple. As the grandson of a baron and the great-grandson of a duke, with a minor estate and no title of his own, Trevor would not be expected to capture the hand of a nobleman's daughter. This meant he should either aim to secure a bride of equally genteel lineage or a woman possessed of a large enough dowry as to overlook her ancestry.

But Trevor, Alana, and I had not been raised to view marriage in such a transactional fashion. Our parents had been a love match, as had our maternal grandparents and a number of our aunts and uncles. It was true, most of them had not strayed far beyond the boundaries of expectation, but that had not been their chief consideration. Alana and Philip had also married for love, or else my sister might not have been deemed to be of sufficient rank to secure a powerful earl.

In truth, among our family my first marriage had been the exception, for it had decidedly *not* been a love match. I could only believe this had contributed to the fact that it had been a complete and utter disaster. Fortunately, my second husband, Gage, and I were wholly devoted to each other and far happier. I knew Trevor had been searching for something similar. So to hear his courtship and any possible affection he might feel for Matilda reduced to such mercenary terms set my teeth on edge. It was a refrain that was undoubtedly to continue.

Suddenly weary, I allowed myself to lean back into Gage's embrace. "If this afternoon was any indication, it's going to be six very long days."

"Yes, but then the rest of our friends and family and neighbors will be joining us just in time for the ball. And they will be remaining while Father's cronies return to London."

"That's true." I was looking forward to seeing them all. It had been several months since I'd laid eyes on many of them. But we still had the intervening days to endure.

I heard a rap on the outer door to our suite of rooms and then the voice of Gage's valet, Anderley, bidding my brother to come through. I'd been expecting him and turned to make my way toward our private sitting room, where I'd intended to receive him, but Trevor met me at the door to our bedchamber, looking harried in his dark evening wear.

"I know why you asked to see me," he announced before I could speak. "Please, allow me to explain."

I blinked at him, surprised he'd inferred as much, and wary of what his agitated state meant. I advanced past him into the sitting room, gathering my composure and forcing him to turn and follow. The chamber boasted a lovely wallpaper of twining roses, and furniture upholstered in a shade of pink that strongly resembled the gemstone thulite recently discovered in Norway. As in most of the rooms at Bevington Hall, as well as Lord Gage's London town house, there was an ample number of gilt accents to be found in the picture and mirror frames, surrounding the fireplace, and decorating the chandelier.

Sinking down on a chair angled toward the southern-facing windows, I gestured for Trevor to speak while he claimed the seat opposite.

He leaned toward me, his hands spread wide and his deep lapis-lazuli blue eyes, so like my own, imploring. "I do not know why Mrs. Birnam spoke of my guidance to Matilda in such an unpleasant manner, but I was not *warning* her about you. Or rather, I was . . ." He grimaced as he broke off, raking his fingers through his chestnut brown hair. "But not *because* of you."

I stiffened, for this was not what I'd expected to hear. Gage had remained in the connecting doorway, leaning against its frame, and I could feel his questioning gaze, but I remained focused on my brother. He appeared to be struggling to find the right words as I waited, hoping he would say something to soothe the old wounds Mrs. Birnam had reopened.

"I warned her because . . . Matilda can at times be a trifle self-conscious about other people's opinions of her." His eyes lifted to meet mine, pleading for understanding. "And I did not want her to leap to the wrong conclusion if you did not respond as . . ." he seemed to search for the right word before settling on ". . . *effusively* as she hoped. She wants so much for you and Alana to like her, and I worried she might misunderstand."

The knot in my stomach loosened upon hearing this explanation, for I knew that there were times when I did not react as expected. That there were times when the social cues that everyone else seemed to read so easily eluded me. I had improved in the years since my awkward first attempts to mingle with society, but I suspected I still missed at least half of the innate inferences that others caught.

Of course, this also enabled me to observe things that others ignored. Things that enhanced the quality and lifelikeness of my portraits. Things that had proved invaluable to Gage's and my investigations. Things that had made me realize that given the choice between being like everyone else and being myself, I would choose the latter, regardless of the frustration. Though it had been a long road to this acceptance, and the occasional twinge of shame and jealousy still struck me when my differences were pointed out.

"I'm terribly sorry, Kiera." Trevor reached for my hands. "When Matilda told me what her mother had implied, I was horrified. I never meant to hurt you. You must know that."

I did know that. Losing our mother when we were both so young, just ten and eight, had forged a bond between Trevor and me that was stronger than most. We had been each other's fiercest allies and friends. Particularly, when Alana took it upon herself to interfere as only an older sister could, albeit with good intentions.

I owed my brother for so much, including protecting me when the scandal of my involvement with my first husband's anatomical practice broke following his death. Sir Anthony had forced me to sketch the dissections he performed for a definitive anatomical textbook he was writing, intending to claim the artwork as his own. Except his poor draftsmanship had been well known, and upon his death, when the manuscript had been passed into his colleagues' hands to be completed, they'd instantly suspected the truth and had me taken before the magistrate's court, accused of all sorts of heinous crimes. The notion that a gentlewoman could be exposed to dissected corpses and not collapse under the strain or go mad from the horror was impossible for them to believe, never mind that I'd had no choice in the matter.

If not for Trevor and my brother-in-law, Philip, I shuddered to imagine where I might have ended up. If not the gallows, then possibly the same lunatic asylum where Sir Anthony threatened to send me during our marriage if I did not comply with his orders. I squeezed my brother's hands in return, assuring him I understood.

His shoulders drooped in relief, but a deep furrow cut through his brow as he proclaimed, "I'm afraid I'm going to have to have a difficult discussion with Mrs. Birnam." He shook his head. "I don't know why she's been behaving in such a confrontational manner. She's never acted this way before."

I suspected I knew, but it was a lengthier discussion than we had time for.

"Her remarks aren't why I asked you here," I informed him. "Though I am glad you cleared that up."

The corners of his eyes crinkled in confusion as I looked up at Gage still lounging in the doorway with his arms crossed, wondering if *he* was even aware.

"Oh. Then . . . ?"

"Miss Portia Whitlock," I pronounced briskly, conscious of the clock ticking on the mantel and the time passing. "What can you tell me about her?"

From the manner in which his pupils widened, this was not a question he'd been anticipating. He stared at me speechless, but rather than prod him, I waited with strained tolerance to hear what he would say.

"I . . ." He shifted uncomfortably. "I suppose I don't know what you mean."

I scowled, his prevarication making me more suspicious by the minute. "Trevor, I invited these people into my father-in-law's home to dine and socialize with our family and his guests. If you have brought some sort of disgraceful tomfoolery into our midst . . ."

His hands lifted in defense. "Now, wait just a moment." His eyes darkened with anger. "You can't actually think I would do such a thing?"

"I don't wish to think it," I snapped. "But when I ask you a perfectly reasonable question and you hem and haw, what am I to think? Especially when all the Birnams, save Mr. Birnam, react to Miss Whitlock's presence as they do. And now Mr. Birnam has cornered me into including her at the dining table this evening."

Trevor groaned and even Gage straightened in surprise, for I'd not yet had time to inform him of my most recent interaction with Jeremiah Birnam.

"So forgive me if I should like the matter made crystal clear to me," I enunciated, barely restraining my temper. "Who is she?"

"Not what you fear," he hastened to assure me, before swiping a hand over his handsome features and settling deeper into his chair. "I'm not familiar with all the particulars, but I can tell you what I do know."

I gestured impatiently for him to continue.

"Apparently, Miss Whitlock's father was an old friend of Mr. Birnam's. One who invested his money poorly, losing his entire fortune before he died just a year after his wife, leaving Miss Whitlock an orphan. Mr. Birnam was named her guardian, and for a time she was raised in his household alongside his own children. Matilda recalls sharing a governess with her for several years." He frowned. "But then one day Miss Whitlock was suddenly separated from them."

"Why?"

Trevor shook his head. "Matilda doesn't know." His brow furrowed. "Or she wouldn't say. Only that Miss Whitlock was sent away to school, and when she returned a few years later, she became her father's private secretary."

"An odd arrangement, surely," Gage remarked, finally advancing farther into the room.

"It's certainly not the norm," I conceded. "In such a situation, it's more common for a young lady in Miss Whitlock's circumstances to be gifted a small dowry and a suitable match arranged. Or barring that, for her to be found a post as a governess or a companion."

I wasn't certain if it spoke well of Mr. Birnam or not that Miss Whitlock had not taken either path. I supposed it depended upon whether she'd been given a choice. If she had, and had opted instead to become his private secretary, then that said something rather different about the players involved than if she'd been given no alternative.

"How long has she served as his secretary?" I asked.

"I couldn't tell you for certain," Trevor said. "Several years at least."

"Then it's not a recent development," Gage summarized.

I tapped my fingers against the arms of my chair, trying to grasp the dynamics of this unusual arrangement. "Does Miss Whitlock often dine with the family?"

"On occasion. I've dined at their table twice when she was present." His gaze was troubled. "Though, I confess, I thought she was included to even the numbers. But perhaps not."

"And how did Mrs. Birnam treat her?"

He tugged at his sleeves. "I didn't witness much of their interactions, but what I did was polite but strained."

"And Matilda?" I asked.

His lips twisted unhappily. "She confessed to me once that, given their history, she doesn't know precisely *how* to act around Miss Whitlock. Are they friends? Is she supposed to treat her like the staff? And I gather her mother doesn't make the situation easier."

"What of Jemmy Birnam?"

Trevor crossed his arms—further evidence of his discomfort with this topic—and turned toward the window. It was clear my brother was grappling with something, and his next remark made me think it was his loyalty to Matilda and whether to share the things with us that she might have told him in confidence.

"Matilda told me that her father is always trying to manipulate her brother and Miss Whitlock into proximity with one another."

"He wants them to wed?" Gage queried as his gaze met mine over Trevor's head. The intimation was obvious. If Mr. Birnam wished for Miss Whitlock to become his daughter-in-law, it was unlikely he had designs on her himself, either in the past or the present.

But Trevor hedged. "Maybe. If so, Matilda says Jemmy is categorically opposed to the match."

I supposed that explained his behavior toward her in the saloon. "And Miss Whitlock? How does she feel about it?"

"Matilda didn't say." He frowned. "I don't suppose she knows."

I nodded, suspecting Miss Whitlock probably kept most of her thoughts to herself. Though, considering her position, I imagined she felt she had little choice in the matter.

Regardless, if Mr. Birnam was trying to encourage his son to marry his secretary, and Jemmy and Mrs. Birnam were both opposed to the match, then that could explain a great deal of the tension we'd witnessed earlier.

"Then, should I be concerned about Miss Whitlock dining with us?" I pressed Trevor. "Will it cause difficulties with Mrs. Birnam and Jemmy?"

"Contrary to what you experienced today, Mrs. Birnam does know how to behave with decorum." He frowned. "Especially when her family's reputation and her husband's business dealings are on the line. I can't imagine she—or Jemmy—would create a scene."

"But perhaps you should warn them," I suggested.

He considered this and nodded. "Yes, I probably should." He rose to his feet. "It can't hurt."

"I've already sent word to Mr. Thorndike," I said as I joined them in standing. "It seems wrong to exclude Lord Gage's secretary if Miss Whitlock is being included."

His presence might also mask the peculiarity of her being there from the others. In this case, two secretaries dining with us was less conspicuous than one.

Gage agreed. "I imagine Thorndike is quite pleased by the invite." He arched a single eyebrow. "Though it's doubtful he'll tell you so."

I'd noticed that my father-in-law's personal employees tended to adopt his worst tendencies. His valet, Lembus, for instance, had perfected his scornful glare, and was well known among the staff to be "a mite too high in the instep," as my maid Bree described it. Mr. Thorndike was no different. Though I'd mostly been shielded from any display of the secretary's contempt because of Lord Gage's and my recent amicableness. However, that closeness had been altered by Mr. Birnam's visit, and I suspected Mr. Thorndike was well aware of it.

"I'm not holding my breath," I conceded before turning to my brother. "Thank you for confiding in us what you know," I told him earnestly. "I understand why you perhaps hesitated, and I appreciate you trusting me." I sighed. "I can't say I'm any happier with Mr. Birnam for cornering me into this arrangement. I would much rather he have made his request quietly upon their arrival." My brow furrowed. "Or at an earlier hour. But at least I now know it's unlikely I'm courting an enormous scandal by allowing Miss Whitlock to dine with us."

"You're not," Trevor assured me, though the hesitance in his gaze told me he still held at least a sliver of uncertainty. One I didn't want to see.

I glanced at the clock, surprised to discover the hour was even later than I'd expected. "I need to dress for dinner," I said, hurrying toward the bellpull to ring for Bree.

Trevor slipped quietly from the room as Gage followed me into our bedchamber. "Perhaps I should warn my father as well."

"After you change," I agreed, noting he'd already tugged loose his cravat.

Bree came bustling through the dressing room door, my gown of cerulean and gray silk draped over her arm. Anderley was, no doubt, waiting to assist Gage in the adjoining bedchamber. My maid all but ignored my husband's presence, hanging the dress on the outside of the wardrobe before spinning me around to begin on my fastenings. This, more than anything, told me how little time we had.

But before taking the hint to begin his own ablutions, Gage grasped hold of my hands, urging me to look up into his wintery blue eyes. "All will be well."

I appreciated his attempt to ease my concerns, but I was all too aware that he couldn't know that. Nonetheless, I squeezed his hands in return and offered him a grateful smile before shooing him from the room. Only Bree saw it fall as the door shut behind him.

CHAPTER 4

As it turned out, Miss Whitlock proved to be the very least of my concerns.

While Miss Whitlock had garnered more than her fair share of curious looks upon her introduction prior to dinner, any suppositions about either her origins or her unorthodox presence were soon forgotten in the face of several other contretemps.

First, Lady Lyndhurst protested in the feeblest and most apologetic manner possible that she couldn't stomach anything planned for the evening's menu. Her long face did look pale and her soft features rather listless, as if she was still recovering from an illness, but the fact that she'd waited until this very moment to inform me left me wondering if the move was not calculated to gain attention from her fellow guests. But in the end, it didn't matter that even an hour's notice would have prevented the problem. Lady Lyndhurst was our guest, and so her needs must be attended to regardless.

Fortunately, Lord Gage's butler, Bowcott, was more than equal to the task of finding out her dietary restrictions and communicating them to Lord Gage's most excellent cook. Within a few minutes, Lady Lyndhurst was presented with a comparable first course and then something supplemented for each course thereafter. The fact that Lord Gage's most excellent cook also possessed an ego the size of his employer's, and a temper which far surpassed his, was never discussed, though I suspected the blameless kitchen staff belowstairs were all feeling his wrath at these last-minute alterations.

Then Lord Milngavie clutched a handkerchief to his nose, insisting that daylilies made him ill. This prompted the removal of the floral arrangement at the center of the table I had worked on earlier that afternoon, as well as several of the smaller vases interspersed about the room. Bowcott came to the rescue again by transferring a simpler arrangement from the saloon into the dining room—this one sans daylilies.

There was a draft from the side door that Lady Brougham didn't like, so her shawl had to be fetched. Baron Foley complained that a glare from the window was striking him in the face, though he wouldn't dare impose upon us by being moved. He also wouldn't stop mentioning it. Not until the drape was pulled partially closed. And it appeared Jemmy had begun tippling early, for he was already three sheets to the wind when we sat down at the table and was steadily drinking his way to four.

So when Mrs. Birnam proceeded to grumble under her breath about her placement at the table, I had little empathy left to offer her. Especially when someone had altered my carefully planned seating arrangement at the last minute. Artfully interspersing the eight women present amid the fourteen men had been no small feat. Yet someone had presumed to change it without my permission. And I had a strong suspicion who.

Lord Melbourne, the home secretary, was supposed to be seated near the head of the table next to my father-in-law, but he had instead been moved to the seat next to me near the middle of the long table. It took everything within me not to aim a glare past him toward the man seated on his other side—Mr. Birnam. Considering the smoldering heat of the glares Lord Gage kept sending my way, perhaps it would not have been remiss. Clearly, he blamed me, and this only made me angrier. He should know by now that, despite my social ineptness, I would never make such a bumbling mistake.

Between dealing with Lady Lyndhurst's dietary requirements and Lord Milngavie's incompatibility with daylilies, Bowcott managed to catch my gaze. The normally merry twinkle in his eyes was dimmed, though his unflappable demeanor remained unchanged. However, it was evident that he was just as surprised by the switches made to the place cards. Short of causing a scene, there was little that could be done about it. But I anticipated Bowcott would have some stern questions later for the footmen assisting him in serving dinner. Whether one of them had aided and abetted Mr. Birnam—likely because of a bribe—or the tradesman had maneuvered matters more directly remained to be discovered.

There was nothing for it at the moment but to make the best of it. Though this proved difficult when Mr. Birnam proceeded to talk the hind leg off Melbourne's horse, practically bludgeoning him at times with his words. For Melbourne's part, he appeared to take the matter in stride, perhaps accustomed to such fervent attempts to sway his opinion or garner his favor. However, I was deeply embarrassed that he should be treated in such a manner while receiving our hospitality. But while I and others made every effort to redirect the conversation, Mr. Birnam would not cease yammering on about the changes to the Factory Act being debated before parliament.

"But come now, good sir," Melbourne retorted, finally managing to slide in a word edgewise after Birnam's most recent speech. "Surely, you must see that the establishment of a proficient Factory Inspectorate is beneficial for all. Why, if you're already following the laws, as you assure me you are, then they'll protect *you* as much as the laborers in your mills." He swirled the Bordeaux in his glass before taking a drink.

"O' course, I'm followin' the laws," Mr. Birnam insisted.

Which only made my suspicion that he wasn't all the greater. I glanced toward Trevor, who was seated across the table and two seats away, but he kept his own gaze trained on his plate, a troubled furrow marring his brow.

"But ye must see that havin' these inspectors traipsin' through the factories, askin' questions o' workers, gettin' in the way, will only slow production. 'Tis an insult to think such a thing is needed." Birnam pounded the table. "That our word isna tae be trusted."

"While I can tell that your honor is very important to you," Melbourne replied without a hint of irony, "what of your competitors? What if they are not being so diligent? Shouldn't they be held to the same standard?"

"Weel, yes . . ."

The viscount nodded. "Good, then we're agreed that for

the sake of fairness, and the well-being of the children and a future workforce, an inspectorate is needed to ensure the laws are enforced."

"The bairns are better looked after in the factory than rovin' hungry in the streets . . ." Mr. Birnam began to protest again, but Melbourne had turned his head resolutely toward me.

"Now, I've neglected my other dinner companion for far too long," he stated firmly before offering me a determined and charming grin. "Lady Darby, my apologies." Though I much preferred to be addressed as Mrs. Gage, he used the title my marriage to my first husband had bestowed upon me. Since Sir Anthony Darby had been higher ranked than my second husband, many in society continued to call me Lady Darby out of courtesy rather than right, but I was perfectly happy to be stripped of the honor.

"None are needed, my lord," I answered softly, responding with my own apologetic smile. How much he read into this, I couldn't be sure, but I hoped he understood. At least, unlike my father-in-law, he didn't seem to hold Birnam's remarks against me.

I'd first met Lord Melbourne when Gage and I had helped Lord Gage solve a rather fraught and complicated inquiry for the home secretary. I'd found Lord Gage's friendship with Melbourne astounding at first, considering my father-in-law had been a staunch Tory, and the viscount was one of the most important Whigs. But then I'd realized that Lord Gage was, by some necessity, a Vicar of Bray, changing sides to ally with those in power when required in his roles as advisor to the king and the nation's premier gentleman inquiry agent.

Intelligent and well-connected, Melbourne had likely received dozens of invitations to house parties during this brief parliamentary recess, but he'd chosen to accept Lord Gage's. As such, I was savvy enough to recognize he wasn't here just because he enjoyed our company. And judging from the other men seated around the table, that ulterior motive had much to do with upcoming legislation, most notably the Factory Act and the Slavery Abolition Act. Both important bills.

But Birnam's presence threatened to disrupt that.

I wanted to berate myself for thinking that inviting the Birnams was a good idea. I recalled how Trevor had confided in me that one of the reasons Mr. Birnam even considered him a worthy suitor for his only daughter's hand was because of his social and political connections. Now I wondered if part of me had wanted—in a misguided manner—to prove that to be true. If so, this had been a spectacular blunder.

"I understand your daughter recently turned one," Melbourne inquired. His thick dark hair had largely gone to gray, particularly the large swathes of facial hair at the sides of his face, but he was still a striking man.

"In April," I confirmed.

"Then she must be walking now." His bushy eyebrows arched expressively over his twinkling eyes. "And exploring everything."

"Indeed." I laughed lightly. "You cannot turn your back for a moment."

He chuckled. "When George began toddling about, Lady Caroline suggested he needed a second nursemaid just to keep track of him."

I was surprised to hear him speak of his son and now

deceased wife, for he rarely did so. As such, I decided to tread carefully, gentling my voice. "And how *is* your son?"

His response was tempered. "George is much the same as always."

While I didn't know all the details, I was aware that George had been born with mental complications, including the falling sickness. But contrary to most noble families, who sent relatives with such ailments to institutions, George had always been cared for at home. Having intimate experience with the barbaric treatment of patients at some of these types of asylums, I felt myself disposed toward Melbourne and his late wife for protecting their son, no matter the other scandals that lay in their pasts.

As if intuiting my thoughts, Melbourne ruminated, "Children are precious creatures, are they not, my lady?"

"They are," I agreed, recalling then that Melbourne and his wife had lost numerous children to miscarriage, stillbirth, and premature death. It was a heartbreaking reality for many. One I couldn't help but fear facing someday myself.

I'd believed our conversation to be too low to be overheard, but I was wrong.

"Right you are," Mrs. Birnam declared with a decisive nod of her head across the table. "Such a blessing, children are."

"Aye, but if they've no' the wages from the factories to fill their bellies, then how are we tae care for 'em," Mr. Birnam interjected. "Many o' their families rely on it tae help feed the younger ones."

I frowned, both repelled by Birnam's arguments and the exploitive system it laid bare, and exasperated by his refusal to be swayed from the topic. His chief tactic seemed to be to wear down his opponents with pure obstinance. In such instances, it seemed the only recourse was to meet rudeness with rudeness. And fortunately, Gage's cousin Alfie was up to the task.

"So dull," he groused after heaving a loud sigh. "We heard you both the first and fifth time. We've grown tired of that topic, old chap." He flashed a grin meant to disarm. "I would much rather hear the latest gossip from London," he told Lady Lyndhurst and Lady Brougham, before turning to Lord Gage on his left. "Or barring that, hear what our host has planned for us over the next few days."

I could tell from the glint in my father-in-law's eyes that, while he didn't normally countenance Alfie's irreverence, he'd rather enjoyed his setdown of Birnam. But that didn't stop him from scowling at Jemmy on his other side when he tittered into his glass.

"Tomorrow, I thought we'd take a ride about the estate before doing a bit of fishing on the River Arrow," Lord Gage proclaimed, and his gaze swept around the table before returning to me. "Where, I believe, the ladies—and anyone who prefers to ride in the carriages—intend to join us for a picnic." He peered at me almost in challenge, causing me to stumble over my response.

"Er, yes. Then, in the afternoon, some archery, for those inclined."

Many at the table murmured their eagerness as the next course of pike in meunière sauce with lemon and parsley was laid before them. I was pleased our plans met with most of their approval.

"Weel, noo, that sounds like a fine activity for the ladies," Mr. Birnam remarked as he lifted his fork and knife. "Though I warn ye. My Matilda is quite the keen shot."

She blushed prettily at the compliment, and Trevor's face brightened upon seeing her happiness.

"Though Miss Whitlock is also a dab hand."

He seemed oblivious to the effect of this offhanded remark as he dove into his fish. The table quieted in discomfort and Mrs. Birnam's smile turned brittle. Matilda's expression grew taut, and her gaze dropped to her plate. Trevor's hand lifted as if to reach across the table toward where she sat at an angle from him, only to realize that such a move would be both impractical and indecorous. However, Miss Whitlock's response proved the most arresting, for she had suddenly stiffened as if turning into a block of ice.

I recognized this for what it was—an attempt to mask any and all of her emotions. For there was no single correct response to her employer's remark. Each of the conceivable reactions she might exhibit would draw criticism from someone. I perceived this because it was what *I* had so often attempted to do. And what had so often earned me disapproval anyway because I'd failed to display proper feeling. It certainly didn't shield me from snide remarks, just as it didn't shield Miss Whitlock.

"It seems Miss Whitlock is a 'dab hand' at many things," Mr. Thorndike, Lord Gage's secretary, quipped in a voice that wasn't loud enough to carry to the ends of the table, but that Miss Whitlock two seats over undeniably heard. Her shoulders tensed, but otherwise her gaze remained trained on her plate.

This gave everyone sitting near the center of the table ample time to scrutinize her and draw their own—possibly wrong—conclusions. Having been subjected to similar looks all of my life, I refused to allow it to last for long.

"Lord Milngavie," I stated, leaping at the first person I saw to Miss Whitlock's left. This was said perhaps a trifle too loudly, for he startled at the pronouncement, though it did at least divert his narrow-eyed gaze from Miss Whitlock's profile. "I understand that both you and Lord Strathblane . . ." I nodded to the white-haired gentleman farther down the table ". . . boast estates north of Glasgow. Have you had occasion to make Mr. Birnam's acquaintance before?"

Mr. Birnam might have recently acquired Twizel Hall in the Borders, bringing him into contact with Trevor, but he also owned a lavish town house in Glasgow where many of his manufacturing businesses were located. Cotton mills and linen mills, and factories which manufactured products useful to both, such as bleach and oil of vitriol used for dying. They were how he'd made his fortune.

"No. I can't say I've had that pleasure," Lord Milngavie answered with what could only be termed strained politeness, carefully enunciating each of his words as a proper British nobleman. My brother-in-law, Philip, the Earl of Cromarty, also adopted a formal tongue, all but losing his Scottish Highland accent whenever he was among society. But while Philip's sounded natural, Milngavie's seemed purposely attuned to point out the differences between him and Mr. Birnam. "But the estate hasn't been mine for long."

Lord Strathblane—perhaps because of his age—was less affected, merging his Scottish roots and proper British tones. "Aye, and we met . . . at the St. Enoch's Church benefit, wasn't it?"

"And the opening of the Royal Exchange," Mrs. Birnam supplied helpfully.

Lord Strathblane nodded. "Aye."

Mr. Birnam appeared on the verge of launching into another verbal attack on the upcoming legislation, so I hastened to continue the conversation. "What of Lady Bearsden?" The estimable lady was my dear friend Charlotte's great-aunt, and an incorrigible delight. "You must be near neighbors."

"Indeed," Strathblane agreed after dabbing sauce from his lips. "An excellent woman," he added with relish as he reached for his glass. "Such wit."

"She'll be joining us on Saturday."

"Jolly good. Why, when I think of all the house parties we've both attended down the years . . ." He broke off, chuckling to himself. "Yes, her ladyship is always up for a spot of fun. Jolly good, indeed."

I could only guess at the past fun he was alluding to, for I'd already heard stories aplenty about Lady Bearsden's younger days. She possessed an impish streak, and it was nearly impossible to shock her.

I glanced at Lord Milngavie, but he didn't seem to have anything to add to Strathblane's remarks about their neighbor. Perhaps he was not conversant with her. There was an age difference between him and her ladyship of about forty years, if I recalled correctly, and, as Milngavie had alluded to, he'd only recently ascended to his title. It had been quite unexpected, at that. For he'd inherited from a distant cousin. One of those sad instances when all the relatives closer to the line had passed without producing an heir.

Milngavie had sat rigidly through the earl's and my exchange, rather like a schoolboy waiting to be dismissed. Turning away, I released him from the conversation and watched out of the corner of my eye as he lifted his utensils to resume eating. This, as much as anything, was an indication he'd not been raised amid the world of careless competence that noblemen inhabited. He'd likely come from a less genteel background, probably the professional class of physicians and solicitors and such.

I wasn't the only one taking note of him. Miss Whitlock also appeared to be observing her neighbor peripherally, her brow puckered in speculation. What concerned her, I couldn't tell, unless she recognized in him a person of similar upbringing. Lord Milngavie, undoubtedly, had expected to work most of his life for his keep. I was curious what he'd been trained in, though I knew that to ask him outright would be considered impertinent. No matter. Someone at this table would know.

As I considered who was most likely to possess such information, Miss Whitlock suddenly shifted her consideration to me. I met her gaze openly, waiting for her to speak. For there was something in her eyes, a hint of an emotion I struggled to name. Uncertainty? Apprehension? But she merely offered me a reserved smile before turning back to her food.

She'd been reticent all evening, though polite. Her soft jonquil gown, I suspected, had been chosen to blend in as much as possible, and her pale brown hair had been twisted into the simplest of styles. She spoke only when spoken to, which wasn't often. She certainly wasn't eager to put herself forward. In fact, I had a feeling she'd been maneuvered as much into dining with us as I'd been maneuvered into including her.

If that was true, I was more baffled than ever as to Mr. Birnam's motives for such behavior. Matchmaking certainly hadn't seemed his aim, for he'd orchestrated to have his son moved to the opposite end of the table, farther away from Miss Whitlock. So why had he all but forced me into setting a place for her at the table?

Or was I overthinking the matter? After all, I knew quite well that sometimes there *was* no reason behind powerful men's actions. When the world was structured to cater to your every whim, thoughtless expectation became your normality, regardless of how it affected or inconvenienced others. And if Mr. Birnam's actions over dinner were any indication, he had become accustomed to having his way.

The remainder of dinner passed pleasantly enough, though Mr. Birnam did try once more to return the topic to the revision of the Factory Act. When he was categorically ignored, he grumbled a bit to himself but otherwise accepted the rebuff. As the guests finished the last course, I rose to my feet to withdraw to the mauve drawing room with the ladies, leaving the gentlemen to their port and cigars for a short time. Before I'd even reached the door, Miss Whitlock appeared at my side.

She didn't say anything at first. At least, not until we'd exited the dining room and crossed in front of the less grand—at least when compared to the south staircase—but still opulent north staircase. Then she spoke in a soft voice I almost had to strain to hear. "My lady, might I have a private word?"

Strolling on Miss Whitlock's opposite side, Alana's gaze shifted to meet mine, telling me she'd also heard her. Interest gleamed in the jewellike lapis-lazuli depths of her eyes, and she nodded, letting me know she would temporarily assume my role as hostess.

"Of course," I replied, redirecting my steps to the great hall while my sister urged the others to follow her.

The two-story great hall at the heart of Bevington Hall had been built in the late seventeenth century to resemble its medieval predecessors, albeit with Baroque flourishes. Lavish Rococo plasterwork competed with busts and vases on brackets on the walls and a forty-foot-high coved ceiling. Here and there, clusters of furniture drowned in the expansive space.

Truthfully, the great hall was my least favorite room in the manor, chiefly because much of the time it seemed utterly useless. It was far too large, dim, and drafty to be utilized comfortably. But also because it was trying to be too many things at once. Medieval with its enormous roaring fireplaces, Baroque with its elaborate pillars and molding, and Regency with its blush wall color. It was overdone.

Something my father-in-law, for once, could not be blamed for, as he'd not touched it since inheriting the estate. I suspected that, like everyone else who stepped foot inside, he was flabbergasted as to what to do with it. And so the great hall sat, largely ignored, except when passing from one end of the house to the other.

I paused next to a wall sconce and the bust of some stern historical figure, waiting for Miss Whitlock to speak. She first peered wide-eyed around the vast chamber and then upward toward the balcony which crossed over the great hall along the western end, connecting the north and south staircases. I couldn't tell whether she was worried about someone eavesdropping or simply overawed by the room, like so many before her.

"Is there something I can help you with?" I prodded her, conscious of my need to return to the other guests.

Her gaze lurched back to mine and she nibbled her bottom lip briefly, seeming to gather her courage. "Is . . . is it true? Mr. St. Mawr . . . he said you and your husband conduct discreet . . . inquiries . . ." she swallowed ". . . for people in trouble."

"Yes, it's true," I replied, stifling my surprise. I certainly hadn't expected such a query from Mr. Birnam's secretary. I could only guess what exactly my brother had told her about us.

She stared back at me with wide hazel eyes which sported a gold ring at the center, nibbling her lip again.

"Are you . . . in trouble?" I guessed.

"Maybe," she whispered, glancing around anxiously. "I'm not sure. But . . ." She broke off, inhaling a sharp breath. "Will you meet me later? Somewhere more . . ." her eyes traveled up to the balcony ". . . private." Her gaze abruptly returned to mine. "I know you must return to the drawing room. But I . . ." She inhaled again, and this time her breathing was ragged. "Will you meet me?"

I wasn't sure what had so unsettled Miss Whitlock, but one thing was clear. She was afraid. But of what? Of whom?

It was also clear she was not going to reveal anything more. At least, not here, not now. So while I felt a stirring of unease in the pit of my stomach, I knew there was only one answer I could give her.

"Yes."

She nodded judderingly, visibly relieved by my agreement. "Where?"

I paused to consider. "Do you know the morning room?"

"Where breakfast is served?"

I wasn't sure if she would know this, given her recent illness. Trays had been taken to her in her bedchamber until earlier today. "Yes. There are two smaller chambers beyond it. I'll meet you in the one on the right." It served as a small office and storage space. "At midnight?" That should be late enough that most of the guests would have retired after a long day of travel.

She reached out to grasp my hand rather impulsively, squeezing it. "Thank you."

I was struck by the fervency of her words, barely managing a short nod before she released me.

Backing away, she pressed two of her fingers to her temple. "Will you tell everyone I have a headache. I can't . . ." She broke off, trying vainly again in a shaky voice. "I'm not . . ."

"I will," I assured her.

She nodded and then turned and fled toward the door through which we'd entered, only to reverse course, moving instead in the direction of the south staircase with a taut grimace. Presumably, she didn't wish to meet anyone as she made her escape. I watched as she disappeared through the open passage, listening to the light patter of her footsteps until she passed beyond hearing.

I wished there was something I could do to ease her palpable distress. But then, I supposed I already had by agreeing to meet her later. I just hoped the hours 'til then would not prove too fraught for her.

It was a hope that would turn out to be tragically forlorn.

CHAPTER 5

I stifled a jaw-cracking yawn as I reached the bottom of the staircase, wishing instead I was crawling beneath my warm covers rather than venturing back downstairs to meet Portia Whitlock. Had I realized how soon most of the guests would choose to retire, I would have suggested an earlier hour for our private conference. I'd tried sending Bree to notify her, but there'd been no answer to the knock on Miss Whitlock's bedchamber door.

The evening had gone as well as could be hoped, especially after Mr. Birnam's ill-mannered behavior at dinner. Upon joining the ladies in the mauve drawing room, I'd realized that a laissez-faire approach to hosting was not adequate. If I didn't take charge, Mr. Birnam certainly would. As such, I requested that each of the ladies who played pianoforte take a turn at the keyboard. Then when the gentlemen joined us, I coaxed everyone into playing a few rounds of charades, before dividing those who were interested into pairs for cards.

Mr. and Mrs. Birnam grumbled a bit at this maneuvering, but everyone else seemed satisfied with my benevolent administration. Well, everyone except Lord Milngavie and Lady Brougham, who ended up being Mr. and Mrs. Birnam's partners, respectively. But they would soon discover I intended to alternate partners and dinner companions throughout the week and hopefully be content with that.

However, the players at the tables began to dwindle as guests retired, wearied from their travels that day, the earlier hunt, or Mr. Birnam's pontificating. Shortly before eleven, I'd gone upstairs to see to my daughter, Emma, leaving the few gentlemen who remained to my husband's and his father's care. I hadn't heard Gage enter our suite when it was time to leave for my appointment with Miss Whitlock. I'd not had a chance to tell him about my midnight rendezvous, but Bree was aware of my plans should he return before I did. Even so, I elected to take the grand south staircase down to the passage which led past the library and study, suspecting the men might have retreated to these cozier environs.

The house was quiet, both upstairs and down, though the wall sconces lighting the corridors had not yet been doused. However, I spied a footman in the library extinguishing the lamps there. Save him, I saw no one else in the other chambers I swept through. At least, Miss Whitlock and I wouldn't be interrupted.

As I passed from the plush Aubusson rug outside the study onto the black-and-white marble tile floor of the great hall, my footsteps echoed off the high ceilings, sounding overloud to my ears. I turned my head to peer down the length of the room now wreathed in heavy shadows. I'd never been in the great hall this late at night, and I had to admit the chamber had an eerie quality to it. The high windows over the main doors above me allowed hallowed moonlight to filter into the space, but it failed to penetrate even halfway into the chamber's enormous depth. Someone could be standing at the opposite end, watching me, and I might have no idea they were there.

I shook my head at the absurd thought. Clearly, I was allowing the unnerving atmosphere to run away with my good sense. Even so, I tightened the paisley shawl I'd draped over my shoulders against the night's chill and hastened my steps.

I could see the door to the blue room which led directly into the morning room stood ajar. I suspected this meant that Miss Whitlock had arrived before me and so pushed it open to announce myself. However, I'd taken no more than two steps into the room before I stumbled to a halt, my heart stuttering in my throat.

Miss Whitlock lay crumpled on the floor with Mr. Birnam leaning over her. He'd not yet noticed me, and I watched as he bent to pick up a glass bottle lying beside her. It was as he shifted that I got my first look at Miss Whitlock's face and gasped in horror. The burns were appalling, peeling away or dissolving skin, muscles, and sinew. As I inhaled, I could smell it. The scents of singed hair and flesh. It was enough to make my stomach lurch.

There was only one thing I knew of that could have wrought such damage, and it wasn't fire.

My gaze jerked to Mr. Birnam's hands, now lifting the bottle. "Don't touch that!" I shouted too late.

He inhaled a sharp breath through his lips, releasing the

bottle so that it thudded against the carpet, rolling toward me. I stepped gingerly around it, urging Mr. Birnam into the water closet beyond. "Rinse your hands with water. Do it immediately."

He hurried to do as he was told, cursing foully in pain as he went, and I turned back to Miss Whitlock. She didn't appear to be breathing, but I had to be certain. The trouble was, how to go about doing so without exposing my own skin. I knelt carefully beside her, examining both arms. The left sleeve of her blush gown seemed less damaged, so I reached for that wrist. It was still warm and pliant as I felt for a pulse, though the fingers appeared to have stiffened. There was none.

Lifting my gaze once again to Miss Whitlock's face, a sob escaped my lips. The poor woman. Who would do such a thing? Why?

I'd heard of acid attacks before, but I'd never seen one—had *hoped* never to encounter one. But here the evidence was all too obvious, including the bottle that winked up at me in the lamplight, the words "Birnam's Oil of Vitriol" stamped in the glass.

I could hear Birnam still blaspheming in the smaller chamber beyond, frantically trying to rinse the acid from his hands. Inhaling a shaky breath, I forced myself to my feet. I needed help. Now.

Stumbling from the chamber, I dashed back across the great hall and through the study. There I encountered the footman just departing the library. He startled as I came hurtling down the corridor toward him.

"Fetch Mr. Gage or Lord Gage. Whoever you can find. I need them in the blue room. Now!"

His eyes wide, he hastened in the direction of the stairs, and I retraced my steps.

Discovering that Mr. Birnam was still in the water closet, I halted just inside the doorway, forcing myself to take a few slow deep breaths so that I could better assess the situation. After all, there was nothing I could do now for Miss Whitlock. Nothing except catch the monster who had done this to her.

The obvious answer seemed to be Birnam. After all, I'd found him standing over her body. But he might just as easily have come along after the fact. And if he'd thrown the oil of vitriol in her face, then why had he reached for the bottle, burning his own hands in the process?

I couldn't dismiss the possibility that this had been a ploy. That upon my arrival, he'd panicked and taken drastic measures to divert suspicions from himself. But if the acid attack had just happened, then why hadn't I heard Miss Whitlock scream, as surely she must have? It would have been terribly painful, and her death would not have been instantaneous even if she'd inhaled or ingested some of it. It seemed far more likely that the attacker would have fled rather than stand and watch.

Birnam had also appeared to be genuinely in shock, and my observations of him thus far had not led me to believe he was a good actor. No, his thoughts tended to be writ large across his every feature. But that didn't mean I was ready to rule him out entirely, or to be alone with him for longer than necessary. I trusted the footman would send help quickly, but in the meantime, there were a couple of tasks better off completed before they arrived.

I slid open the top drawer of the console table against the

wall next to the door, knowing I would find a steel-point pen. Then, inching forward, I avoided all the spots in the Axminster medallion carpet which had been damaged by acid. A spot on the silk upholstered settee near Miss Whitlock's body also now bore a ragged hole. Otherwise, the furnishings in the chamber, which functioned as a receiving room, appeared undisturbed. It was evident that the assailant's aim had been true, and the victim had borne the full brunt of the attack.

I forced myself to look more closely at Miss Whitlock's ravaged face, cataloging her injuries. In the course of our inquiries, I had examined a fair number of victims' bodies endeavoring to uncover clues. They were each of them disturbing in their own way, but not since some of Gage's and my earliest investigations had I been this rattled by the state of a corpse. The wounds were gruesome. Had Miss Whitlock survived, she would have been severely scarred, with no nose, one ear, and likely the loss of sight in both eyes. But it was the viciously personal nature of the attack that was most alarming. The killer hadn't aimed just to harm her, but to obliterate her.

I swallowed hard, forcing the bile that had risen back down my throat, and lowered my gaze to her neck and then torso, using the pen to shift aside clothing when needed. Then I moved on to each of her hands. The right was badly damaged, making me suspect she'd either lifted it to shield herself or reached up to swipe the vitriol from her face before she'd realized it was acid. The left was less burned, but I found no marks to indicate self-defense. The attack must have been a surprise. She probably hadn't even seen it coming.

Anger coursed through my veins that someone should do

something so ruthless and dastardly, and while under my father-in-law's roof! What on earth could Miss Whitlock have possibly done to provoke such a thing?

My scrutiny returned again to her fingers, which I'd noted earlier seemed stiff. I was well aware that rigor mortis usually began in the face and small muscles of the hand. The rigidness of her fingers would seem to indicate that she'd been dead for some hours, but the state of the rest of her body and the corresponding damage to the surroundings said otherwise. I puzzled over this for a moment. The eyelids and most of the face had been too damaged by the acid to assist me in figuring out time of death, but the jaw might still be enough intact. Carefully, I used the pen to press on the corresponding tissue, able to open and close the jaw easily enough to tell that rigor had not set in.

So why were her fingers so stiff?

Leaning close to her left side, I gripped her still-warm wrist with one hand and used the pen with the other to examine her fingers. It was then that I realized some of her digits were either naturally missing their top joints or that they were unusually rigid. Not inflexible enough to hinder her work as a secretary evidently, but sufficient enough they might have caused her discomfort when gripping a pen or fork if the joints of her right hand were similarly stiff. But while a curious anomaly, I couldn't see how this discovery had any bearing on her death.

"My lady?"

My head jerked toward the door. In my preoccupation, I hadn't heard Bowcott arrive. The butler's brow creased with concern, taking in the scene before him as if in one glance as I straightened. Of all of Lord Gage's servants, I was glad it was Bowcott who had found me, for his congenial nature stood in marked contrast to the haughty behavior of the other male members of my father-in-law's staff.

I inhaled a shaky breath, the sight of his kind face suddenly making me want to fall to pieces. But I couldn't. Not yet.

"Please, send someone for Dr. Clarke." I nodded toward the doorway to the morning room and the water closet beyond as I retreated from the body. "Mr. Birnam has injured himself."

"Of course. Shall I . . . ?" He broke off before finishing his sentence, glancing behind him. Then he bowed and backed away as I heard footsteps fast approaching. A moment later, Gage burst into the room followed closely by his father.

At first, Gage's eyes were all for me, scouring my face and figure for signs of injury, but they swiftly dropped to the body on the floor behind me, his features transforming in alarm.

"Good God!" Lord Gage exclaimed, finding his voice first as he recoiled from the sight of Miss Whitlock. After a moment, he recovered his self-possession, moving closer. "Is she . . . ?"

"Dead?" I finished for him when he failed to utter the word. "Yes." He'd not seen the bottle on the floor, and I lifted a hand to halt him before he stepped on it. "Oil of vitriol," I explained, motioning to the vial. "Presumably the cause of death." I turned to indicate the chambers beyond. "Mr. Birnam picked it up and burned his hands."

Both men paused to listen, noting the muttered cursing coming from the water closet for the first time.

"Birnam was here?" Lord Gage clarified, his eyes sparking with anger.

"I found him standing over her," I replied scrupulously. "He appeared shocked, and he seemed to grab the bottle without thinking, but . . ."

"He may have been trying to mask the burns he'd already received," he was quick to point out.

I nodded, albeit reluctantly, for I was not so quick to want to cast the blame on Birnam. Though Lord Gage was correct. Whoever threw the acid in Miss Whitlock's face might have been splashed, particularly if they'd not been wearing gloves. We would have to be on the lookout for burns and damaged clothing.

My father-in-law bent over, closely examining the bottle. "It's one of Birnam's own, isn't it?" His mouth twisted almost in cruel satisfaction. "Rather damning."

"Not really," Gage said. "Birnam's factory in Glasgow is one of the largest producers of oil of vitriol in the country. It's widely available. In fact, I wouldn't be surprised to find one used by your staff in the cupboards belowstairs." He paced in a wide circle, taking in the scene before him from a different angle. "If anything, it might be more indicative of motive."

"Using Birnam's own product to disfigure and murder his secretary in a sort of retaliation?" I extrapolated, trying to follow his thinking.

He shrugged. "At this point, it's hard to tell."

At that moment, Mr. Birnam rejoined us, holding his still dripping hands in front of him. His face was a rictus of pain.

I went to him, guiding him toward a chair far from Miss Whitlock's body. "I've sent for our local physician," I told him. "I'm sure he will hurry. In the meantime, try not to touch anything."

He bobbed his head woodenly, though I wasn't certain he'd heard me.

I peered over at Gage, uncertain what to do with him. Birnam was stunned and in distress. His body trembled as if chilled. I pressed a hand to his shoulder, offering him what comfort I could. If he wasn't the murderer, he deserved all our sympathy for what he'd witnessed and the agony he was feeling, but even if he was, he was suffering for it, and I could not turn away.

However, Lord Gage plainly didn't believe Birnam should be handled with such kid gloves. "What happened?" he demanded of him, and when that didn't earn a response, he leaned into Birnam's face. "What happened?!"

Birnam blinked up at him for several seconds before attempting a fumbled response. "Portia, she . . . I got a note. Asked me tae meet her. She said . . ." He swallowed loudly. "She said 'twas important."

"She left you a note, asking you to meet her here about something important," I clarified in a gentle voice. If he was telling the truth, Miss Whitlock must have had a reason for requesting he join us. One she'd not chosen to share with me.

He turned to me, seeming relieved I understood. "Aye."

"Did she regularly request such assignations?" Lord Gage asked.

I noted the snide tone of voice, though Birnam seemed to miss the unsavory implication. "Nay. 'Twas no' like her. But then I remembered she'd no' been in the drawin' room after dinner, and I thought . . ." He broke off, shaking his head.

"So I came." He exhaled a long breath, and I wondered what he'd stopped himself from saying and whether it was relevant. But before I could speak, he shuddered. "And found her." He flicked one of his raw and ravaged hands still held before him toward Miss Whitlock. "Like that."

Gage opened his mouth to ask a question, but Lord Gage spoke over him. "Are you sure it wasn't the other way around? That *you* didn't lure *her* to this clandestine tête-à-tête. One with an entirely different purpose."

Birnam blinked back at Lord Gage as if he was struggling to comprehend, but then his brow crinkled in outrage. "Nay! *She* summoned *me*. I have the note . . ."

"And where is it?"

He scowled. "I put it in my pocket." He began to reach into his coat but halted abruptly upon recalling his injuries.

"May I?" I asked.

He nodded, a puzzled frown settling over his features as I lifted aside each flap of his frock coat to search the pockets inside, careful not to cause him further pain. I found a pocket watch and several other bobs and bits, but no paper.

"Then I must have left it in my room," he supplied, his voice turning barbed. "Didna ken I'd be facin' an inquisition."

"Did you see anyone while you were making your way here? Did you hear anyone?" Gage queried, attempting to soothe his ruffled feathers.

He considered this. "Passed Foley upstairs outside his chamber, but I dinna think that's what ye mean." He squinted one eye. "There might o' been a footman in the dinin' room, but other than that . . ." he shrugged "nay one."

I presumed he was speaking of the room we'd dined in

earlier that evening but sought clarification. "Then you came down the north staircase?"

"Aye."

Remembering something, I turned toward the door set into the wall paneling across the room. I pointed. "Not through there?"

"Where?"

"That door."

"Nay."

Gage's gaze met mine, recognizing what I had. There was a stairway just behind that door, and a matching one on the opposite side of the house. They were utilized mostly by the staff, but I couldn't help but think what a convenient escape route it would have made for the assailant. Philip and Alana's suite was situated in the pavilion at this corner of the house above. We would have to ask them if they or their personal servants had seen anyone.

I looked up as Bowcott appeared in the door to the south corridor.

"Dr. Clarke is being summoned," he informed us, carefully keeping his eyes averted from the gruesome sight on the other side of the room.

I straightened. "Thank you. Would you escort Mr. Birnam to his bedchamber and help make him as comfortable as possible until the good doctor arrives?"

Gage gently clasped Birnam's elbow, helping him to his feet as Bowcott stepped to the side, waiting for the tradesman to proceed him. I watched as they disappeared down the corridor out of earshot before turning back to face the calamity at hand. Instead, I found myself under the scrutiny of two unhappy gentlemen.

Standing side by side, the resemblance between father and son was easy to see. They both possessed the same cleft chin, the same strong jawline and sculpted cheekbones, and the same twist of curls at the forehead, though Lord Gage's hair was now gray, while his son's was golden blond. Their eye shape was also similar, but Lord Gage's irises were granite gray, while Gage's were the pale blue of a winter sky the morning after a snowstorm and almost as piercing in clarity. Their skin was bronzed—my husband's recently from his frequent rides about the estate, while his father's was perpetually so from the years he'd spent on the quarterdeck of a ship as a captain in the Royal Navy. I suspected the iron stare he fastened on me now had also been perfected in the same capacity.

"And just what were *you* doing here?"

CHAPTER 6

Lord Gage arched a single sardonic eyebrow. "Did Miss Whitlock send you a note as well?"

Gage turned his frown on his father.

"No, she made her request in person."

This surprised both men.

"When?" my husband asked.

"After dinner. Before the gentlemen joined us in the drawing room," I explained, crossing to the console to return the pen to the drawer. "She wished to speak with me in private and was afraid we might be overheard. She asked if I would meet her later in the evening." I crossed my arms, huddling into myself. "I agreed and suggested the office next to the morning room."

"Then she must have been intercepted here on her way to your meeting place." Gage pulled me close to his side. "Did she tell you she was going to ask Birnam to join you?"

"No. That revelation was unexpected."

"If it was even true," Lord Gage muttered under his breath.

I couldn't deny I'd wondered the same thing.

Gage's brow furrowed with puzzlement. "Did she give you any indication *why* she wished to speak with you in private?"

"She asked if it was true that we conduct inquiries, and when I confirmed that we did, she intimated she might be in trouble, though she didn't say why." I frowned. "But one thing was quite clear. She was afraid." I cast a fleeting glance toward where her body now lay. "Rightfully so, it seems."

Guilt stirred inside me. Perhaps I should have dismissed my responsibilities as hostess and insisted we find someplace more private to speak when she first approached me. Maybe if I hadn't been wrapped up in performing my duties to perfection, I would have recognized the danger sooner.

I knew this was an illogical thought. How could I have known the matter was so urgent? How could I have known that it might lead to her death? But the guilt remained anyway.

As if sensing this, Gage rubbed his hand up and down my back. "Did *you* see anyone?"

"I came down the south staircase. I thought I might find you or your father in either the library or study, but the only person I saw was a footman extinguishing the lamps. He was still there when I went for help." I focused on Miss Whitlock's feet, shaking my head. "If only I'd not dawdled. If only I'd gotten here sooner."

Gage pulled me tighter to his side. "Then you might have been attacked as well."

"Sebastian is right," Lord Gage agreed, his demeanor

softening. "Whoever did this was clearly consumed by rage. A rage that was probably stoked over some time. After all, an acid attack requires some degree of premeditation and planning. It's not as if he simply picked up an object to hand."

Gage eyed the empty bottle. "We'll need to speak with your staff to see if any oil of vitriol is missing from the manor stores or if the killer planned far enough in advance to bring it with him."

"Or her," I countered. Such an act could have just as easily have been committed by a woman.

"Yes."

My gaze returned to the blush skirts spilling across the carpet and then up reluctantly to the once lovely face still staring sightlessly up at the ceiling for I'd not wanted to risk touching her. "But first, what is to be done with Miss Whitlock?"

Neither seemed to know how to answer at first, nearly as affected as I was by the tragedy of what had been done to the secretary. Her life had been snuffed short in such a horrifying way.

Finally, Gage inhaled a taut breath before addressing his father. "What officials need to be informed?"

"Wixford is the local magistrate. I'll speak to him. He's a fair man, and not one to cut off his nose to spite his face. I imagine he'll be more than happy to leave the investigating to us, considering our reputations and the rank of many of our guests." His features settled once again into a fierce scowl at the reminder of all that was at stake. "Though, of course, there will still need to be a coroner's inquest. With any luck, Wixford and his constable won't insist on dragging any of our more illustrious guests into it."

It was implied that Birnam was not one of those he considered "illustrious."

Unlike in London and Edinburgh and other large cities where metropolitan police forces had been established, crimes in rural areas were still regulated by the old system of peacekeeping, under the authority of a local magistrate. Not that any of Britain's police forces were particularly well equipped to investigate crimes after the fact. They had been established to keep the peace and prevent crime. That was their primary function.

This was why agencies like the Bow Street Runners in London still thrived, because they specialized in detection. Or they were supposed to. But corruption was rife, and witnesses were sometimes intimidated or outright fabricated. Consequently, the wealthy, noble-born, and even royalty often preferred to turn to Lord Gage and his son. In their minds, rank conveyed trustworthiness, though our previous inquiries had proven this to be a prejudicial and patently false assumption. Those who were to the manor born were just as capable of violence and perfidy. They were simply more likely to get away with it because those with the power to do something about it looked away.

"I suppose you'll want to make an announcement to the other guests," Gage said.

"Yes, but not tonight." My father-in-law's shoulders bowed, his face appearing fatigued. "Tomorrow morning is soon enough."

I wanted to urge him to take a seat, but I knew he would not thank me for my concern. He was a stubborn man. Even more so than his son.

Gage glanced over his shoulder at the console table.

"You've seen everything you need to?" Evidently, he'd recognized the reason I'd been holding the steel-tipped pen.

"Yes." I hesitated to continue in front of Lord Gage. Though he was fully aware of and now empathized with my past, and while he even recognized the usefulness my knowledge brought to our inquiries, I preferred not to remind him of it, lest he revert to his previous disgust over the matter. But then I realized he would have to be told what I'd discovered. "She had no defensive wounds. At least, none that were visible after the . . . burns." I stumbled over my words as I pictured in my mind the painful injuries I'd examined. "It's clear she lifted her hand to shield her face when the acid was thrown at her. But I don't think the killer actually got that close to her."

Gage's eyes glinted with compassion. "He wouldn't have needed to, would he?"

"No."

He could have stood several feet away and still managed to throw the acid accurately in her face.

"What of her other injuries?" Lord Gage asked, eyeing Miss Whitlock's body as if it were a snake that might leap up and bite him.

Grateful that he at least wasn't looking at me in the same way, I replied, "They are, I imagine, as to be expected." I shrugged. "To be honest, I'm not familiar with the wounds caused by burns, particularly acid burns. But given how quickly she succumbed, I suspect she must have inhaled or ingested some of the vitriol. Enough that it proved fatal."

It was difficult not to think this might have been a blessing. Otherwise, she might have lived in constant agony for days or even weeks before expiring. For as severe as the burns were, the likelihood of her recovering from them was minuscule. Even then, she would have been severely impaired and continuously at risk of deadly infection. It would only have ever been a matter of time.

"Do you wish to be sure?"

I turned to meet my husband's gaze, knowing what he was asking. Did I want to perform an autopsy, or a partial one?

Though it might have been better not to, I couldn't help but glance at Lord Gage's face. But rather than the contempt and disgust I'd anticipated, he merely returned my gaze with one that was attentive.

"No," I said after a moment of consideration. "It's true, an autopsy might tell me precisely how she died, but we already know what caused her death. Further examination of her nasal passages and throat is not going to help us figure out who did it or why."

Gage accepted this answer with a nod, trusting in my greater expertise in this area. This was something I knew from experience that few men would do, and just one of the many reasons I loved him. "Then why don't you go on up to bed. It's been a long day."

"For all of us," I chimed in to say, darting a look at his father, who stood staring down at the floor, rubbing a hand over the back of his neck.

"Yes, there's nothing more you can do until tomorrow. The killer has long fled, and short of dragging everyone from their beds and insisting on searching their rooms . . ."

Lord Gage aimed a sharp look of displeasure at his son, letting him know he was not about to insult his guests, particularly men like Lord Melbourne and Lord Brougham, in such a manner.

". . . we'll simply have to wait until morning to do more." He raised his eyebrows at his father, telling him he should have known better than to think he would attempt such a stunt. "The footmen and I will remove Miss Whitlock's body to the cellar."

I opened my mouth to caution him about the vitriol, but he held up a hand to forestall me, now arching his eyebrows at me.

"*Carefully*. I'll also speak with Dr. Clarke after he's finished with Birnam and ask Bowcott to secure any additional oil of vitriol that may be on the premises and check the manor's supplies." His mouth firmed. "If the murderer got it belowstairs, we'll know soon enough."

I had to admit, he had everything well in hand, and I was tired. My emotions were all a jumble in my breast, and I knew it was only a matter of time before I could no longer suppress them. I would prefer that happened in private. So I agreed with a weary sigh. "If you're sure?"

He offered me a gentle smile. "I am." Then he pressed a kiss to my brow before turning to his father. "Father, would you escort her? I'd really rather she not be traversing the corridors alone just now."

I recognized this request for what it was—an attempt to convince his father to retire as well. But I also couldn't help but wonder if he was right to worry. Could the murderer be concerned I'd seen them or that I'd witnessed something damning? Might they try to silence me before I realized it?

The thought sent a chill down my spine. I couldn't help

but recall the unnerving sensation I'd felt when walking through the great hall earlier. *Could* someone have been watching me from the opposite side of the chamber? Could it have been the killer?

Lord Gage had been on the verge of quarreling with his son, but the words died on his lips as he caught sight of my face. Clearly, I'd not done an adequate job of masking my alarm.

"Yes, of course," he said instead, reaching for my arm. "But then *I'll* check on Birnam. With any luck, Clarke will have already arrived, and it will give me a chance to ask for this alleged note he received from Miss Whitlock."

Gage didn't argue, and Lord Gage swept me from the room.

Rather than take me by the route I'd chosen earlier—a fact I was grateful for—he led me down the corridor past the dining room and up the north staircase, affording me little opportunity to peer into the shadowy great hall. With that room now behind us, the fog of my apprehension began to fade, and my faculties were better able to focus on the rest of my surroundings. Namely, Lord Gage. With each step we climbed, I could sense his indignation rising as the arm beneath mine turned more rigid and his gait—still slightly hampered from the gunshot wound he'd suffered to his left leg the previous summer—grew stiffer.

Perhaps the wisest course would have been to remain quiet, but after all the progress we'd made in the previous year, I did not want to revert to the chilled silences and strained politeness of before. That was, when my father-in-law was not being outright contemptuous. I knew it would fall to me to bridge the divide, because he was not good with complicated emotions. He preferred to deny them or wrangle them into submission, glossing over them with anger or disdain. At one time, I'd believed he would rather burn his entire house down than admit to any tender feelings, but I'd since learned that wasn't true. He simply had to be shown the way, even if sometimes that meant dragging him kicking and screaming.

So I offered the first olive branch. "I know this house party means a great deal to you, and it has not exactly gone to plan."

He scoffed. "You think?"

"I believed I was acting in my brother's best interest, but I see now that I was too hasty. That I should have met the Birnams in another setting before inviting them here. Had I known . . . well, I would have proceeded differently."

"*I* could have told you what a disaster it would be to invite Jeremiah Birnam, *had you asked.*"

"You told Sebastian and me we could invite whomever we liked. You made *no* stipulations."

"I didn't think you would invite a jumped-up mushroom like Birnam. I thought you would have more sense and taste than that." He sniffed. "My cork-brained nephew is one thing. Birnam is quite another."

"Alfie isn't cork-brained," I protested, latching on to the thing I could most easily dispute. "He's annoying at times, yes, but he's certainly not a fool. And as for Birnam . . ." I exhaled forcefully through my nose. "I'm more concerned with his daughter. *Who is perfectly lovely,*" I stated in challenge, lest he attempt to dispute it. "And may soon become my sister-in-law."

"But not without her father's approval."

I turned sharply to look at him. The keen glint of cynicism in his eyes made my stomach pitch. "What are you suggesting?"

"I'm suggesting nothing, only pointing out that Birnam is the type of man who expects to get his way, and when he doesn't, he's not above retaliating."

It was on the tip of my tongue to make a quip about other men I knew like that—including the one in front of me—but the ramifications for Trevor's future were too startling. I'd thought giving Birnam access to Philip and Gage and their connections would appease him, but it had become clear that he was after something else. His strident efforts to dominate the conversation, his manipulation of the place cards, even his smug attitudinizing all seemed aimed toward one goal—stymieing the revisions to the Factory Act. If he didn't get what he wanted, would he refuse Trevor's suit?

Lord Gage watched as I struggled to reconcile with these implications, but he wasn't finished. "And I'm not just talking about your brother."

"You mean Miss Whitlock?" I frowned. "You think she didn't give him what he wanted." I recognized immediately what he meant. "But Trevor told me that Mr. Birnam doesn't . . ." I stumbled over the word ". . . *didn't* want her for himself, but for his son. I demanded he explain Miss Whitlock's relationship with the family after Mr. Birnam all but forced me to have her dine with us."

"And presumably he heard this from Miss Birnam, who as the daughter of the family is the least likely to know the truth." His biting voice made it clear how naïve he thought I was being.

"You think young ladies aren't attuned to what's going on

in front of them, especially when it has to do with their father and a woman nearly their own age?" I countered, letting him know I thought *he* was the one being credulous. I lowered my voice as we reached the upper landing, nearing the bedchambers. "But I admit, it's possible Miss Birnam lied for her own reasons." Shame. Embarrassment. Willful denial.

"Regardless, Mr. Birnam could have had other motives for attacking Miss Whitlock—motives we're not yet aware of—and note or not . . ." He narrowed his eyes. "I don't trust him."

I didn't disagree. I didn't trust him either. Though that didn't mean I was prepared to accuse him of throwing oil of vitriol in his secretary's face. I felt it more likely he was the *cause* of the attack, that his actions had either directly or indirectly led to it, rather than the attacker himself. It was as yet just a suspicion, but I sensed Birnam would somehow play a part in the guilt that should be meted out.

"Birnam's reputation isn't exactly angelic," Lord Gage continued.

"What do you mean?" I asked in interest.

"Let's just say, there's a reason he doesn't want a Factory Inspectorate established. There have been a number of accidents in his factories and mills, and a number of violations reported. If the law was enforced by a professional inspectorate—one less inclined to be bribed—he could face some very serious fines."

My eyes widened at his mention of bribes.

"Just as he bribed a member of my staff to move place cards before dinner."

My gaze darted to his harsh gray one in surprise before I could stop myself.

"Yes, I figured out what happened. You may be a trifle graceless, but you're not so witless as to put Melbourne next to Birnam."

The comment stung, though I guessed Lord Gage thought it was a compliment.

"It was obvious he bribed someone to switch Melbourne's and his bottle-headed son's cards."

I was trying to find a way to persuade him to allow Bowcott to deal with the issue without actually confirming his suspicions, when he pivoted subjects.

"Though your handling of matters in the drawing room after dinner was quite expertly done. I'd feared Birnam would attempt to dominate the entire evening." He smiled with fierce delight. "But you neatly waylaid his plans without being obvious you were doing so."

I couldn't halt the warm glow his approval gave me, though I was careful to temper it. After all, I'd not acted just in his interest, but that of the entire party. I also suspected he was more pleased by the fact that Birnam had been foiled than any skill I had shown in doing so.

By then we'd reached the door to Gage's and my suite and I bid him a muted good night. He waited until I'd closed the door before presumably haring off to further harass Birnam. I pivoted to find both Bree and Anderley standing in the doorway between the suite's sitting room and dressing room. The anxiety writ across their faces told me they were at least aware of my urgently summoning my husband.

"Miss Whitlock is dead."

Bree crossed herself, I suspected without even realizing she was doing so, for she normally preferred to keep her Catholicism private.

"How?" Anderley asked. I could read in his eyes that he already knew we were dealing with more than a simple accident.

"Oil of vitriol. Someone threw it in her face."

Bree gasped in horror, pressing a hand to her mouth. Even steadfast Anderley appeared a little shaken, his olive complexion turning waxen, but he rallied swiftly.

"Does Mr. Gage need my assistance?"

"He may," I said. "You'll likely find him somewhere between the blue room and the cellar."

Anderley nodded, moving toward the door.

"While you're at it, see what you can learn from the footmen who were on duty," I instructed him. "They may be more comfortable revealing something they saw to you rather than the master's son."

The valet nodded again, though he'd probably not needed this reminder. He and Gage had been working together on inquiries long before Bree and I came along. He knew what was expected of him.

As did Bree, I realized, when I turned to face her as the door shut behind Anderley. "Let's get ye oot o' those clothes, m'lady, and intae somethin' more comfortable."

I allowed her to guide me into the bedchamber and undress me as I succinctly relayed the events of the evening. By the time I'd finished, I was nestled beneath the thick ivory counterpane. I fell silent, tracing the gold-threaded embroidery with the tip of my finger while my maid fussed about the chamber, straightening and gathering my clothing. A deep furrow pleated her brow.

"Bree," I said softly, waiting until she paused to look at me. I almost couldn't force the words out. "It was *awful*." The tears I'd been withholding began to fall, and I pressed a shaking hand to my forehead. "Truly awful," I hiccupped. "That poor woman."

Bree perched on the edge of the mattress, taking my other hand in hers while I quietly wept. After a few minutes, I inhaled a ragged sniffle, and she passed me a handkerchief.

"Dinna worry, m'lady. We'll figure oot who did this."

I eyed her warily as I blotted my eyes and nose. "I thought you might object."

She turned to me in surprise, and I could see the weight of the memory of our past conversations settle across her shoulders. The last few inquiries we'd undertaken had proven to be tremendously dangerous, particularly for Bree and Anderley, and I'd belatedly begun to realize the hazards we all but forced our staff to undertake. We never asked them to do more than they were willing, but when one was a servant, how much of a choice did one truly have?

Her frown eased, and a sheen of tenderness briefly washed over her features before she set her jaw in determination. "This is different. Miss Whitlock. She . . . well, she was one o' us. A member o' the staff. Mayhap, she was a bit higher ranked than some o' us, but she was staff, all the same."

I understood what she was trying to convey. Most of our clients were aristocrats or well-to-do. The times we had investigated the deaths of a lower-ranked individual had been at our own impetus because it directly touched someone we cared for. The same could be said for Miss Whitlock, given the fact the murder had occurred in my father-in-law's home and her employee was the man my brother hoped would one day be *his* father-in-law, but this didn't change the sentiment behind what she was saying. She might willingly assist us with all of our investigations when asked, despite the dangers they posed, but in Miss Whitlock's case, she would have *insisted* on it.

Bree tucked a loose strand of her strawberry blond hair behind her ear as she considered her next words. "Though ye havena said as much, I gather from what ye *have* said that ye dinna think Miss Whitlock did anything tae inspire such anger."

"It's early days . . ." I qualified ". . . but no." I exhaled heavily. "I don't think Miss Whitlock incited the attack. Unless . . . it was to keep her quiet." I explained in greater detail how the secretary had asked me earlier to meet her in private.

"In private. Yet she asked Mr. Birnam tae join ye?"

I could hear the skepticism in her Scottish brogue and wondered if I'd been too quick to try to dismiss Birnam as the culprit. "Lord Gage is collecting the alleged note."

"If he does, I s'pose that'll tell ye somethin'." Bree studied me with her whisky brown eyes. "What do ye think she was afraid tae tell ye?"

I shook my head in bewilderment. "I don't know. But the fact she referred to our reputation as inquiry agents makes me think it must be something criminal. And considering she works for Birnam . . ." I met Bree's troubled gaze. "I can't help but wonder if it's something to do with him."

"How did she act at dinner?"

"Quiet. Reluctant." I frowned. "I got the impression she would rather not have been asked to join us."

"Maybe she was embarrassed?"

"I wondered the same thing," I admitted. If she'd known Birnam had all but forced me to include her that might explain why. "She comported herself well, but I could sense her discomfort."

Unless it was for a different reason. Birnam had been nearly belligerent in expressing his opinions and dominating the table topic. Perhaps the views he'd expressed were what had rattled her. Lord Gage had suggested Birnam wasn't complying with the existing Factory Act. If that was true, and Miss Whitlock knew it, she might have felt agitated by his blatant lies.

But would she truly have been afraid to speak of it?

Maybe.

"I'll ask aboot her tae the other staff," Bree said. "Should be easy tae get 'em tae talk. Though I can tell ye she was generally well-liked. Knew her place, but didna lord it o'er nobody. Spoke kindly." Her fair eyebrows ruffled. "Near as I can tell, the only person who had a problem wi' her was Mrs. Birnam's maid. But given hoo little Mrs. Birnam liked Miss Whitlock, 'tis nay surprise McClintock took her mistress's side."

She pushed to her feet, gathering the pile of soiled garments into her arms once again. "Get some rest, m'lady. Ye ken the wee one'll be up wi' the dawn."

And wanting me.

I glanced at the clock, estimating how many hours of slumber I might be able to get before then. When I turned back, Bree was nearly out the door. I halted her by calling her name.

"Thank you," I said as our eyes met, knowing she would understand what I meant. That I was aware that she was setting aside any reservations she might have once again because Miss Whitlock deserved justice, and the surest and quickest way to get it for her was with Bree and Anderley's help.

She didn't reply, but there was a light of genuine solidarity in her eyes. One that I had sorely missed.

CHAPTER 7

I had been certain I wouldn't be able to sleep until Gage joined me, but it turned out I was more tired than I'd thought. The long days of preparation and then hosting duties, ensuring I was the last to retire and the first to rise, at least among the ladies, had made it impossible for me to keep my eyes open once my head touched the pillow. When I was awakened the next morning by Mrs. Mackay's light tapping against the door, it was all I could do to roll myself out of bed and don a wrapper.

I noted that Gage was sprawled out across the other side of our bed, his arms above his head, still oblivious to the world. It was difficult not to watch him as he slept, with his features softened and his golden curls tumbled about his head. He wore no sleep shirt, and the musculature and sinew of his bare torso was something to be admired, both as an artist and a wife smitten with her husband. I might have stared longer, but I heard Emma's voice raised in demand.

Dragging myself into the adjoining sitting room, I offered my daughter and her nanny a weary smile. Emma's face split into a wide grin, her cherubic golden curls so like her father's already escaping from their cap. My heart melted instantly.

"Aye, there ye are," Mrs. Mackay crooned to Emma. "I told ye that ye'd see yer mam soon enough." She passed her to me. "She woke half an hour early, but after the evenin' I heard ye'd had, we decided 'twould be best tae wait tae wake ye. So we've been watchin' the birds from the terrace." Her eyebrows arched in gentle question, asking after my well-being as much as the night's events.

"Yes, another murder," I replied resignedly. "I know this isn't what you joined us for."

"Och!" She waved away this comment, as unflappable as ever. "I ken exactly who ye and Mr. Gage were afore I accepted the position. Didna I tell ye I wanted a wee bit o' excitement in my old age?" Her eyes twinkled at her jest. Though silver-haired with wrinkles and gently sagging skin, Mrs. Mackay brimmed with the energy of someone half her age. "I spent enough uneventful years buried away on Scottish estates wi' my previous charges." Then her expression dimmed. "Though I am sorry for the lass who was killed." She shook her head. "And with vitriol, no less."

"Did you meet Miss Whitlock?" I asked, curious if she had any impressions of the young secretary.

"I'm afraid no'. But as always, I'll keep my ears open. There's bound tae be much discussion o' the young lass o'er the next few days, considerin' her fate."

I could only hope some of that gossip proved fruitful to our investigation.

"Thank you," I said.

She nodded and turned to depart, aware that I would ring for her when I needed her to return for Emma.

I settled into one of the chairs near the window to nurse and cuddle my daughter, a ritual I normally found soothing. Unfortunately, today it gave me too much idle time to think. A decision would have to be made about how to handle the guests. We couldn't allow them to leave, but precautions would also have to be taken to ensure they felt safe.

Though it seemed callous to continue with our plans for the house party, we still had more than a dozen guests to entertain, and dozens more arriving Saturday. We couldn't very well insist they stay and then fail to offer them any diversions. However, we also now had an inquiry to undertake, and balancing our time could prove complicated.

That morning, the men were touring the estate on horseback and then fishing, which might allow Gage and his father to question the other men alone or in pairs as they straggled out along the trail and the riverbank. I, on the other hand, was going to find it more difficult given the nature of activities planned for the women. Perhaps with Alana and Lorna's help, I might manage a brief tête-à-tête or two.

Such was my distraction that Emma seemed to finish almost moments after she'd begun. It was a jarring reminder of how much she'd grown. Soon enough, she would no longer require me for sustenance—a day I both longed for and also dreaded. At times, it seemed my child and I were bound together by a series of invisible threads, and with each new milestone, each step into independence, a thread was snipped, until one day there would be no threads binding us left. It was the goal of motherhood and yet also terrifying to contemplate. I wondered if other mothers ever felt the same.

She lay pliant in my arms for a few minutes longer, babbling back at me and giggling when I tickled her chin. She had learned a few words, but most of what she said was a delightful baby gibberish. Too soon for my liking, she demanded to be let down, and I watched as she toddled about the room, exploring. She no longer needed the aid of chairs to help her maintain her balance, but at fifteen months her stride was still far from steady. Much of the time she staggered about like a sailor who had yet to adjust to dry land. It was comical.

I was just about to ring for Mrs. Mackay when the door connected to our bedchamber opened to reveal my sleep-tousled husband now clothed in his merlot red dressing gown. Catching sight of him, Emma immediately reversed course, nearly tumbling onto her bottom. Gage smiled and scooped her into his arms as she drew near.

"Did we wake you?" I asked apologetically as he turned to look at me. My heart warmed as it always did at the sight of father and daughter together.

"I needed to rise anyway," he said with a yawn. "And I can't think of a more adorable way to do so," he added, pressing a kiss to his daughter's chubby cheek.

She giggled and then insisted on being let down again.

"Done with me already?" he jested good-naturedly before setting her back on her feet. Then she was off, waddling about the room.

Gage closed the bedchamber door before crossing the room to greet me more properly with a kiss before flopping down into the chair opposite. He peered distractedly out the window where morning mist still shrouded the land and much of the sunrise. "It seems you were just sitting here with Trevor." He propped an elbow on the arm of the chair, cradling the side of his face. "What a difference twelve hours can make."

I understood what he meant. Twelve hours ago, Miss Whitlock was alive and my chief concern was preventing a scandal.

"What time did you finally retire?" I asked.

Another yawn cracked his jaw. "Sometime after two." One corner of his lips twisted. "Father caused a bit of a brangle with Birnam."

"Oh, dear. Over the note?"

He nodded.

"I take it that it couldn't be found?" If Lord Gage and Mr. Birnam had quarreled, that seemed the likeliest reason.

"Birnam swore he must have left it on the writing desk in his chamber, and his valet—a chap named Paget—claims he saw his master pick it up off the floor, read it, and place it on the desk." He arched his eyebrows. "Or he saw him do that with some sort of piece of paper, in any event. He didn't read it."

"I take it from your expression that there's something about this story that you don't find credible," I said, watching Emma as she banged on the surface of one of the side tables. All of the small breakable objects had been moved to the mantel over the fireplace days ago.

"It's this Paget fellow I don't find credible." He glowered. "There's something evasive about him. I'm not sure his origins are entirely respectable. Which doesn't preclude him from making a good valet. But his shifty eyes and misleading comments make me think he still might not be entirely reputable. Anderley agrees."

This last remark added a great deal of credibility to his impressions, for Anderley himself had a bit of a checkered past. He'd been born in northern Italy, where much of the region was struggling to rebuild after years of occupation by Napoleonic France. Believing there was little future for him there, his family had sold him to a padrone, hoping he would gain valuable experience in a troupe of traveling actors. However, the padroni who preyed on such desperate families had far more nefarious intentions in mind, instead forcing these Italian Boys—as they were called in London and other cities throughout Britain—to perform on the streets and beg for money, which was then all handed over to their padrone master. They lived in cramped houses under horrendous conditions, and were often malnourished and mistreated, left with little hope for their future.

Anderley had run away from his padrone and made his way to Cambridge, where he'd scrabbled out a rough existence until the day he saved Gage from a pair of thieves and tended his wounds. Gage had seen the potential in Anderley and decided to hire him, first as an errand boy and later his valet. For Anderley was a quick learner and a skilled mimic, able to adopt the mannerisms of just about anyone, including a toplofty valet to an aristocrat, men who were often even more snobbish than their employers. But most importantly, he was fiercely loyal—to Gage and now his family.

At any rate, given Anderley's past, I trusted his judgment when he deemed that someone or something wasn't entirely aboveboard.

"Mr. Birnam hasn't always been wealthy. Maybe he knew Paget before he made his fortune and brought him along with him," I suggested.

After all, much like a lady's maid, valets were privy to the most sensitive details of their employers' lives. A gentleman needed to be selective about who he placed in such a position.

"Yes, Anderley and I suspect something similar. Which could account for his accent and lack of polish, but not his dubiousness." He drummed his fingers against the arm of his chair. "Unless Paget's prior service was dubious in nature. That's why I've asked Anderley to uncover what he can about the man."

Emma moved along the wall, passing behind her father's chair before emerging on the other side and ambling toward the window.

"So at this point it's unclear whether Miss Whitlock left Birnam a note or not," I clarified. "Though your father evidently believes it's fabricated. What do you think?"

Gage exhaled a long, exasperated breath. "Honestly, I don't know. On the one hand, it seems a ridiculous fabrication. One that can be easily disproved if he fails to produce the foolscap she wrote it on. But to believe she did write it and that the note is now lost, we must also accept that someone entered Birnam's room and took it from his desk."

"I see what you mean." Any other explanation didn't make sense. None of Lord Gage's staff would have ventured into Birnam's chamber at that hour, and if they'd had cause to be there, they wouldn't have taken or discarded any papers, even if they had fallen to the floor. They were too well trained for that.

I didn't know what the answer was to this conundrum, so

I pressed on. "What of Birnam's hands? Did Dr. Clarke see to them?"

Emma stood at the window, reaching up toward the sill, but she wasn't tall enough to see out. "Up, up!" she demanded, and Gage rose from his chair to lift her so that she could look out at the pond. It was one of her favorite places on the estate, and she was soon quacking in her own peculiar way like the ducks that swam there. I couldn't help but smile.

"Clarke covered Birnam's hands with some ointment and wrapped them," Gage said in answer to my question. "But he warned that lesions may form, and the damage could take considerable time to heal."

I watched my husband with our daughter, grateful that Emma could not comprehend what we were talking about and that she would never remember it. The day was coming when that would no longer be true.

Soon enough, she grew tired of looking out the window and demanded to be put down. Gage complied and then glanced at the black ormolu clock on the mantel. The morning was already advancing rapidly, and there was much to be done.

"Before I ring for Anderley, you should know that, as far as Bowcott and the rest of the staff could tell, there was no oil of vitriol missing from Bevington Hall's stores."

I straightened. "Then the killer must have brought it with them."

Gage's voice was grim. "Which means he—or she—must have planned this."

For why else would someone have traveled with a bottle of sulfuric acid? It served no practical purpose except industrially and as an ingredient in some cleaning agents or as a replacement for sour milk when bleaching cloth.

I shuddered at the thought of someone plotting to disfigure Miss Whitlock, for we couldn't be certain that their objective had been murder. More often, oil of vitriol maimed and defaced. Rarely did it actually kill. Though the victims had to live with the pain and scars the rest of their lives.

"If it was premeditated, then we might be able to eliminate a pool of suspects," I ruminated, though I didn't like where my thoughts were leading me. "Not everyone would have known Miss Whitlock would be here." In fact, only the Birnams, for Lord Gage's political cronies hadn't known the factory owner would be present, let alone of the existence of his female secretary. The notion that any of the Birnams might be capable of such an act left me cold, especially knowing how Trevor felt about Matilda.

"That's assuming Miss Whitlock was the intended target."

I blinked up at Gage. "You mean . . . ?"

He nodded. "It's possible Mr. Birnam was the original target, but something made the attacker alter his plans."

The image of Miss Whitlock's frightened visage swam to the front of my mind, the way her gaze darted about the great hall and up to the balcony, wary of eavesdroppers. *Had* someone been listening? Had they feared Miss Whitlock knew something and was going to reveal it? If Gage was correct, there had to be some sort of catalyst to convince the attacker to change his target.

I shook my head, for casting Mr. Birnam as the original victim still presented the same obstacle. "But no one but my family and the Birnams themselves knew they would be here. Surely, your father didn't alert . . ." I broke off, able to tell from Gage's strained expression that this assumption was also incorrect. "You mean, he did?"

"He may have informed some of his political friends." He turned to the side, watching Emma arch up on her tiptoes as she tried to grasp the fireplace tools stored out of reach behind the strategically placed screen keeping her away from the dormant hearth. "In fact, I think it very likely he did."

I knew nothing should surprise me about my father-in-law at this point, but this was unexpected. However, matters were never straightforward when it came to Lord Gage. "Yes, but will he confirm he did so?" I queried pointedly. For we knew from past bitter experience that Gage's father was not opposed to protecting his high-ranked friends.

The pleat that formed in Gage's brow told me my husband was also skeptical about his father being forthcoming and that it wounded him to even have to consider the possibility. Their relationship had progressed far during the last year but not far enough for him to be entirely certain when all was said and done where his father's loyalties would lie.

Wanting to shift the direction of his thoughts, I crossed to the bellpull and tugged. "If you finish dressing before I do, will you make sure Bowcott has closed off the blue room. Though I'm sure he has matters well in hand, I forgot to direct him to do so last night."

"It's already done," Gage said. "And breakfast is to be served in the dining room."

I exhaled a sigh of relief. "Oh, good."

"I also secured the empty bottle found next to Miss Whitlock's body in the cellar with her remains and ordered the door to her bedchamber locked until we've had a chance to search it."

"You seem to have thought of everything," I replied as he drew near. "Thank goodness one of us kept their head."

"From what I could see, you never lost your good sense, though you had every reason to do so. It was quite the shock." He searched my face now in concern, but uncomfortable with his regard, I turned to watch Emma, who had returned to the window.

"How will we tell the others?" I asked softly, more comfortable focusing on the logistics of the day than the emotions stirring within me.

His hands clasped my arms gently. "I suspect most of them will already know by the time they come down to breakfast. The staff is useful in that regard."

"Except that they deprive us of the opportunity to observe everyone's reactions to the news."

"In this instance, I don't know if that would have done us much good. Given the severity of the injuries and the fact that death might not have been the intention, I imagine the culprit would not have much difficulty feigning distress." His voice was stark.

I lifted my hand to his unshaven cheek, feeling the bristles that had grown overnight against my palm. He took this as the invitation it was meant to be and lowered his head to press his lips firmly to mine. But he didn't deepen it, for this kiss was one of comfort rather than passion. All too soon, we were interrupted anyway, by Emma tugging at our legs and then a rap on the door undoubtedly from a member of our staff.

We shared a tender, long-suffering smile, prolonging the moment a few seconds more before he bent to pick up Emma and I called out for the knocker to enter.

CHAPTER 8

Normally at country house parties, the guests were slow to rise, making their way down to the breakfast room at their leisure, or if one was a lady, asking for a tray to be brought to her room. The gentlemen were expected to appear earliest so that they could set off on whatever the day's pursuit was to be, in this case, riding and fishing. While the ladies enjoyed a much more languid start to their day, sometimes not even bothering to make an appearance until after noon.

However, this morning, the servants' gossip had done its work, as predicted, and by half past seven everyone was gathered in the dining room demanding answers. I was doing my best to alleviate their fears without revealing more than we wished, but with little result. Fortunately, when Lord Gage finally appeared, he chose to use his authoritative manner combined with his legendary charm to good effect. By the end of his concise but dynamic speech, even I felt calmer and ready to comply. Though I wasn't sure whether his claim that we had a strong suspect we were close to apprehending was a part of the ploy or if he was ready to blame Mr. Birnam even as our investigation had barely begun.

Unsurprisingly, Mr. Birnam was the only one absent—somewhat conspicuously, considering how ponderous his presence had been the evening before. This might have given the other guests the wrong impression—or rather the right one, if that was Lord Gage's true intent—but he was fair-minded enough to mention Birnam's injuries. Something that most reacted to with concern and pity rather than suspicion. How long this would last, only time would tell, but I couldn't help but think that Birnam's case would be better served by his absence.

I also learned along with the others that, apparently, Lord Gage had already spoken to Lord Wixford, the local magistrate. Or at least he maintained that he had. Whether this had been done in the middle of the night or early this morning, I didn't know, but Gage's expression suggested he'd also been unaware of it. Whatever the truth, I was beginning to have the sinking suspicion that my father-in-law was up to his old tricks.

Considering the appalling nature of the attack, it wasn't surprising when most of the men wished to postpone the morning's ride in order to remain with the women. So it was decided that rather than arriving separately, the entire group would set out together for the River Arrow shortly after mid-morning. This afforded Gage and me several unexpected hours to conduct our investigations here at the hall, though I feared most of that time would be eaten up by further queries from guests, particularly my family, who were eyeing me rather insistently. Foremost among them being Trevor.

No sooner had I risen from the table than I found him beside me with Matilda hovering at his elbow. "Is it true . . . ?"

I pressed a hand to his arm to halt his words, offering him a calm smile that I was far from feeling. "Come with me."

Leading them from the room, I hesitated for a moment, uncertain where to go. The blue room would have been the natural choice, but not after last night's events. The mauve drawing room and red saloon would be put to use by other guests, and the green drawing room connected to the billiards room, where some of the gentlemen might gather. I entered the great hall but knew immediately it would not do. It was too exposed, and I would not risk someone overhearing us as the attacker had possibly done with me and Miss Whitlock the previous evening. The library, then, I decided, crossing the great hall to the southern side of the manor.

The library was a long room with two tall windows at one end, allowing in natural light. It was perhaps the least ornamented room in the house, with simple crested bookcases lining two of the walls and carved swags over the doors. Even the white marble fireplace boasted little embellishment. Once inside, I closed all three doors before allowing my brother to speak. He seemed unnerved by my precautions.

"Is it true? Was Miss Whitlock attacked with oil of vitriol?"

This was a detail we'd not shared directly with the guests, but considering it was not something we'd been able to hide from the servants, I suspected most of them already knew about it anyway.

"Yes. And before you ask, yes, it was a bottle of Birnam's."

Trevor turned to Matilda who stared at him with wide, anxious eyes. "But that . . . ?"

"Means nothing," I finished for him. "Because Birnam's is perhaps the most widely available." I nodded. "We know."

My brother's gaze searched mine for reassurance. "Then I'm simply misreading the situation. Lord Gage didn't mean to imply Mr. Birnam is the culprit."

Though my hesitation was slight, it was long enough to alarm both of them. "At this point, we're still gathering information and must reserve judgment."

"But it can't be Father," Matilda blurted in horror at the same time Trevor protested, "That's ridiculous! Why would Birnam injure his own secretary? And with his own factory's vitriol."

I could sense my brother's rising anger, but I couldn't allow myself to be swayed by it. "There are facts that you are not aware of," I replied evenly.

"Then enlighten us," he demanded.

My eyes bore into his, urging him not to press, not in front of Matilda. "Facts I am not at liberty to discuss. But we are still investigating, and neither Gage nor I are ready yet to pinpoint a specific suspect."

"It's not my father," Matilda stated even louder, drawing our attention. Her face was flushed, and her chest heaved beneath the primrose and coral print of her bodice. But for all her adamance, she couldn't continue to meet my gaze as I scrutinized her.

"Are you saying that as a loyal daughter, or do you know something?"

When she failed to answer my question, failed to even lift

her head, allowing the silence to stretch, Trevor took a step toward her uncertainly. "Matilda?"

She released the piece of ribbon trim she'd been fretting and paced several steps away before pivoting to return. "As a loyal daughter . . . but . . . He thought of Portia as practically a daughter, too. He *couldn't* have done this to her."

I narrowed my eyes, unable to help the impression that there was something Matilda wasn't saying. Something that had held her immobile as if in the grip of fear until she'd deliberately turned away to regain her composure. It was startlingly akin to Miss Whitlock's behavior in the great hall the previous evening. I looked at Trevor, whose expression seemed to suggest he'd seen it, too. But Matilda interpreted this in a different manner.

"I know Trevor has informed you about Portia's connection to our family," she said. "That he had no choice but to do so after Father cornered you into including her at the dinner table yesterday evening."

My brother's lapis-lazuli eyes glinted with apology. Evidently, he still felt guilty about that, believing he may have betrayed her trust in doing so.

"That may be, but he only informed me of the bare minimum," I told her. "Enough to ease my fears that in complying I wouldn't risk insulting your mother, but not enough to explain why someone would do something so malicious to her."

Matilda paled.

"Do you have anything you can add to what Trevor already explained? Anything that might help us better understand."

"I . . . I don't know," she stammered.

Trevor reached out to take her hands, offering her comfort.

"You said she was practically like a daughter to your father," I said.

"Yes," she replied weakly.

"But it was obvious yesterday that there was some sort of rift between her and your mother and brother."

She looked up in alarm.

"Can you explain why? Did something happen? Something that made your parents send Miss Whitlock away?"

"No," she exclaimed before rethinking her words. "I mean . . . I don't think so. I believe it was always the plan that she should go away to school."

This hadn't been what Trevor had seemed to convey to me earlier, though I supposed it wasn't surprising that she was now attempting to temper the matter. She was clearly afraid I was about to blame her mother and brother for Miss Whitlock's murder next.

"There was no rift between them," she insisted, her eyes flicking back and forth between me and Trevor. "Only . . . Father's clumsy attempts to promote a match between Jemmy and Portia."

"Jemmy wasn't interested?" I attempted to verify.

She frowned. "Didn't you hear me? She was like a sister!"

I *had* heard her, and she hadn't mentioned anything about her brother's feelings about Portia. This was also not the impression I'd gained from seeing them together. His animosity toward her had been obvious. It wasn't the impression Trevor had gained either, if his puzzled attentiveness to her was anything to judge by. But I decided there was nothing to be gained at the moment from disputing this. Not when she was obviously protecting her family and I needed more information.

"And you have no idea whether any of the other guests have a connection with Miss Whitlock?" I tried again. "You have no idea why one of them might wish her harm?"

She paused, appearing to consider the question, but then shook her head. I glanced at Trevor, who seemed equally bewildered. I realized I would get nothing helpful from him while we were in the presence of Matilda. Any further conversation would have to wait until I could speak with him alone, so I turned to go.

"Perhaps it's to do with Father."

I stopped to peer over my shoulder, waiting for Matilda to elaborate.

"With his mills and factories." She worried her thumbs. "After all, Portia was his private secretary. Maybe . . . maybe it's an angry mill worker."

This comment captured enough of my attention to make me turn around entirely, resting my hands on a wingback chair. "Why would mill workers be angry at your father?"

"Because of the looms and machines." She turned to Trevor for support. "There have been recent attacks against several other mill owners and their foremen."

"She's right," Trevor confirmed, sliding a hand into the pocket of his trousers. "Vitriol has been used in a number of such incidents, particularly around Glasgow. Some of the workers are angry they're losing their jobs to industrialization and that their wages are being cut in some instances."

This wasn't the first time we'd confronted growing discontent with the country's increasing industrialization. For all the advances made, I couldn't help but feel empathy for the people whose skilled trades were being displaced. Trades that oftentimes entire communities were involved in, their families having performed the same roles for generations. Now they faced not only the loss of their livelihoods, but their very way of life as they and their family and neighbors were threatened with eviction and forced to seek employment elsewhere. It was little wonder why they protested, and why violence was sometimes the result.

But Birnam's factories and mills were in Glasgow, three hundred miles away from here. Not a short journey for anyone, least of all a poor mill worker.

"I see the merit of what you're suggesting, but would a mill worker actually have the means and wherewithal to follow your father all the way here?" Most mill workers were paid barely enough to feed and house themselves.

"Maybe," Matilda replied. "If they were determined enough."

I supposed. Except from a logistical standpoint, it seemed more likely they would wait until the Birnams returned to Scotland to mount an attack. Why squander the funds and effort traveling all this way and take the risk of breaking into a baron's country manor when they knew Mr. Birnam—and his secretary—must return eventually? No, it simply didn't make sense.

Though I could understand Matilda's desire to see the crime blamed on some nameless mill worker rather than face the possibility it might have been someone from her own family. But while anger and revenge against Birnam might very well have been the motive for the attack, there must be more to it. There must be a connection to someone here we weren't aware of.

Trevor would surely realize this as well. So rather than explain any of it to Matilda, I left the matter to my brother, hurrying from the library in search of Gage. I didn't make it far before being cornered.

"Here she is!" Alana exclaimed to Lorna, who was mounting the grand south staircase, presumably in search of me.

I stifled a sigh of impatience, knowing I would never escape my sister without making some sort of explanation. It was better to submit than to waste time deferring her.

"Kiera, what really happened? I know there must be more . . ."

I grasped my sister's arm, silencing her as I poked my head into the green drawing room. The sound of clacking balls from the adjoining billiards room told me it was being used. So I retreated, diverting to the great hall as I urged both ladies to follow me. But I wouldn't let either of them speak until we'd reached a point far enough from the balcony above to be able to see if anyone was lurking there. Then I spoke in a hushed voice that would not carry far, swiftly relaying the information I thought pertinent about the murder that Lord Gage hadn't already shared with everyone.

Their empathy as I stumbled over my words, struggling with the image seared into my brain of Miss Whitlock's disfigured face, was tangible. But for all that I appreciated their support, their compassion also undermined my composure. I shook away their kind tokens of sympathy, knowing I had to remain focused on the tasks at hand or else the swell of emotion that threatened would render me useless, not only to our efforts to unmask the culprit but also to coordinating the house party.

"What can we do to help?" Lorna asked as I pinched the bridge of my nose, stifling tears.

"I need you both to help me manage the guests. Their needs can't be ignored just because we now have an inquiry to conduct."

Lorna touched my arm, her large green eyes wide with concern. "Of course."

"What of Trevor?" Alana asked. "How is he weathering this? And Matilda?"

I glanced back the way we'd come. "I just left them and . . . they're both still in shock."

She nodded, but her eyes were alert, clearly sensing there was more I wasn't saying. "I suppose that's to be expected. How well did Matilda know Miss Whitlock?"

"I'm not entirely sure." I frowned, realizing this was one of the things that bothered me. "It seems she must have known her well once upon a time, but matters have changed in recent years." I shared what little Trevor had told me of Miss Whitlock's background, noting again with keener awareness the number of gaps. Perhaps in filling those holes we would discover something that explained why she was attacked.

"I wonder why she was sent away," Lorna ruminated, her brow furrowed. "Had that always been the plan or was there a sudden reason for it?" Given Lorna's background, I suspected she was even more sensitive than me or Alana as to the ambiguous nature of Portia Whitlock's situation. After all, she had lived a similar existence as both the beloved daughter and illegitimate offspring of a wealthy baron—cherished and yet unacknowledged by society.

"And then she was brought back," Alana pointed out. "Had that also been the plan or did circumstances change?"

I stared up at the bust of a middle-aged gentleman I couldn't identify positioned on the pedestal nearest to us—one of many that lined the room. "Both excellent questions, and ones I hope I can convince the Birnams to answer."

"You think they won't."

I could hear the surprise in Lorna's voice, so I answered honestly. "I think they'll tell me what they want to tell me and not much more." And unfortunately, they were our only immediate source of information about Miss Whitlock.

Alana and Lorna seemed to recognize this as well, or at least their faces conveyed the same displeasure I felt.

The half hour chimed in the tall case clock, telling me more time had passed than I'd realized. We were all still attired in morning dresses with our hair loosely arranged and would need to change before the party set out for the River Arrow. "I need you both to be prompt in meeting the guests who gather for the picnic," I told them, suspecting I might be running late considering the tasks I still needed to finish. "But before you go, tell me, what were the reactions of the other women when Miss Whitlock pulled me aside after dinner? Did any of them notice?" I'd not been there to witness them myself, but I strongly suspected at least a few of them had looked askance at what they might have perceived as boldness in the secretary. Considering this was the last time most of them had seen her alive, I felt it might be telling.

Lorna and Alana turned toward each other, engaging in an unspoken consultation.

"Well, Mrs. Birnam was visibly . . . agitated," Lorna said. "Is that the right word?"

"She was certainly irritated," Alana agreed. "Though she didn't say anything. She just kept darting peevish glances toward the door."

"When I joined you, I noticed she looked unhappy," I said. At the time, I'd figured her crossness could be attributed to any number of things that I doubtless didn't want to hear about. "What about Matilda?"

"She was agitated as well." Lorna tilted her head, causing the heavy braided cornet of pale blond hair to shift. She reached up to adjust the pins holding it in place. "But in a different way."

"Her mother's behavior obviously causes her a great deal of anxiety," Alana concurred.

"She doesn't like confrontation," Lorna said, speaking of Matilda. "But the rest of her family doesn't seem to care who they offend."

I silently agreed. "Anyone else?"

Lorna and Alana exchanged another look, but this time my sister was the first to speak. "Both Lady Lyndhurst and Lady Brougham seemed to notice your absence, but they didn't remark on it. At least not in my earshot."

"Or mine," Lorna said.

"And none of them left the drawing room?" I verified.

This made Alana's eyes narrow at the corners, but Lorna didn't appear to suspect anything as she answered for them. "No. You joined us just a few minutes later."

My conference with Miss Whitlock had seemed longer,

but I supposed it *had* lasted less than five minutes total. It had probably been closer to three.

I thanked them and then made my excuses, shaking my head slightly at Alana to deter the other questions I could tell she wanted to ask. Before she could stop me, I hastened off in search of my husband.

CHAPTER 9

I finally tracked down Gage in the corridor outside our suite. It appeared he'd been looking for me as well.

"Do you have time to search Miss Whitlock's room?" he asked as his gaze swept over my appearance, noting I'd yet to change for our excursion. He was already dressed in attire suitable for fishing, including dark breeches, tall boots, and a broad-brimmed hat.

"Yes. If we hurry," I replied, not wanting to be excluded.

"I saw your brother and Miss Birnam pull you aside," he said as we strode side by side down the corridor which spanned the western side of the house. It was lined with bedchambers. There was a question in his eyes.

I sighed, briefly recounting our conversation.

"I've heard a bit about these acid attacks on mill owners and masters. Though, as I understand it, sometimes the vitriol is also being thrown at the workmen, particularly when there are opposing factions of workers at odds in these disputes."

This was an angle I hadn't considered. "Do they think the mill owners are involved when it's the workers who are injured?"

Gage's pale eyes darkened with displeasure. "I think it would be naïve not to suspect that in some cases they're at least aware of what their foremen are planning. Now, whether that means Birnam is one of them, I can't say," he added, already anticipating my next question. "But it has to be considered."

"Particularly since he owns one of the largest factories in the country to produce oil of vitriol."

To say he had a readily available source was putting it mildly. Though just because he had the means didn't mean he'd done it. Still, the notion sent a chill down my spine, for this was the man Trevor hoped would one day soon be his father-in-law.

As if sensing the direction of my thoughts, Gage reached over to grasp my hand, squeezing it as I turned to look at him. "Don't leap to that conclusion yet. We've still got a great deal of evidence to gather before we can point a finger at anyone."

"I'm not sure your father would agree with you," I said, cautiously broaching the topic as we turned the corner.

His brow lowered. "Yes, well, there are a lot of things Father and I don't agree on. But I take your point."

For all we knew, Lord Gage might be quietly convincing his political cronies and the local magistrate of Birnam's guilt while allowing us to continue investigating. It would be the neatest solution and resolve a number of problems, not to mention having the added appeal of silencing a man he simply didn't like. But for all my father-in-law's faults, I struggled to believe he would actually be so heartless and vindictive as to allow a man to be convicted of a crime he hadn't committed, no matter how much he might loathe him.

"I'll speak to him," Gage assured me.

I squeezed his hand in return. "We'll speak to him together."

Our eyes locked in solidarity as we reached the end of the corridor.

"Here we are," he declared somewhat unnecessarily.

I realized we were near the northeast pavilion. The large suite of rooms at the corner had been assigned to Alana and Philip. The pair of doors before us led to two smaller bedchambers which overlooked the front drive. I'd nearly forgotten I'd assigned one to Miss Whitlock.

Interestingly enough, the staircase leading down to the blue room was situated but a few steps away. The one we'd theorized that the attacker might have taken to escape undetected. It was possible Miss Whitlock had also used the staircase to get to the blue room immediately below us.

Gage pulled the key from the inner pocket of his frock coat, but before he could insert it into the lock, the door opened under his touch.

"I thought you said the room had been secured," I murmured in shock.

His voice hardened with anger. "It had." He glanced around as if searching for something, perhaps a weapon. "Step back. If someone is still inside . . ."

I nodded, letting him know it wasn't necessary to finish that statement.

Cautiously, he pushed open the door. I was glad to hear it

was in good maintenance, issuing no squeaks. Then silently he edged his way inside, keeping the wall at his back. My heart pounded in my ears as I waited, wondering if I should go for help. I looked toward the door to my sister and brother-in-law's suite of rooms. Maybe Philip was inside. He might be able to assist.

Fortunately, Gage returned a moment later. "It's empty now, but it's evident *someone* was here before us."

I followed him inside, unable to perceive at first what he meant. The drapes were pulled shut against the bright day, but enough light filtered through the apricot fabric to allow us to see. The bed was still made, though there was an indentation on one side of the counterpane that indicated someone had lain there recently. The door to the wardrobe stood ajar, but that might have been Miss Whitlock's doing or even Gage's, for he'd undoubtedly been assiduous in his search, checking the furnishing for lurking intruders. But then I saw Miss Whitlock's writing desk.

It was a simple mahogany desk with brass details, a black leather inlay and an elevated sliding door compartment at the back. I'd not known the secretary long, but I'd developed the impression of a tidy woman, one who took her work seriously. However, the sliding doors were askew, revealing several crumpled pieces of foolscap, and the two small drawers below had been left open to show their contents of writing implements and supplies. Meanwhile, the writing surface was bare save for a single sheet of paper dropped at an angle.

"Someone took all of her papers," I concluded after turning over the lone piece remaining—an old invoice. Even the scraps of foolscap only contained arithmetic figures. "And did a thorough job of it. But why?"

"I think you know the obvious answer."

I turned to face Gage, who was standing with his hands on his hips, surveying the room. "They must have thought there was something incriminating in them. But incriminating for the attacker or incriminating for Birnam?" I glanced at the old invoice again. "I suppose we'll have to tell Birnam."

Gage's gaze met mine, his eyebrows arching. "Unless he's the one who took them."

I felt an initial pulse of surprise, but it swiftly faded. "Birnam doesn't seem the type to let a locked door or a murder investigation stop him. Though I imagine it was a member of his staff who did the actual pilfering." Probably his manservant, Paget.

Gage returned to the door, examining the lock. "Whoever picked it was skilled. I can't see any scratches. I suppose it's possible they got ahold of the housekeeper's copy of the key," he added as he straightened. "But if that was the case, why not lock the door when they were finished?"

"I think that's improbable," I said, joining him. "Mrs. Taylor keeps her set of keys together on one ring and she's rarely without them." I suspected she kept them close by even when she was at rest.

"Then they picked it, and they knew what they were doing."

I could tell he was thinking of Paget. He'd said that he thought the valet had a shadowy past. Hopefully, Anderley would be able to confirm this and find out more.

Gage closed and relocked the door, and we began to retrace our steps.

"Tell me," I said, threading my arm through his. "What did the men discuss over port yesterday evening?" I'd asked

Alana and Lorna what the women were doing while I'd conferred with Miss Whitlock, but I wondered about the men as well.

He slowed his steps, seeming to consider his words before responding.

My tone sharpened. "Or was the topic something not fit for a lady's ears?"

I knew men could sometimes be crass, even gentlemen, but I would not have expected my husband to stand for it.

He startled, turning to look at me. "No. That's not why I failed to speak. I was just trying to decide what might be relevant. Someone inquired about the local trout and that was discussed, and Strathblane asked about Stratford-upon-Avon. Apparently, he's a great admirer of Shakespeare." The village where the bard was born lay just a short distance to the east, close enough for a day trip by carriage.

"Then Birnam didn't attempt to turn the conversation to the subject of the Factory Act again?"

His tone deepened with wry humor. "He tried, but we mostly ignored him." He tilted his head. "Though I couldn't hear what was being discussed at the opposite end of the table."

"I could."

Both of us jumped at the sound of the voice directly behind us. We whirled about to find Alfie grinning back at us remorselessly.

"How long have you been following us?" I demanded to know, chagrined we hadn't heard him approach.

"Long enough to know that you're coaxing Seby to tattle on us."

I rolled my eyes.

He leaned closer to me, lowering his voice further. "And that *you* have a naughty mind."

I flushed, making his dark eyes twinkle brighter.

"What did you *think* we were discussing, Kiera, dear?"

"Don't tease her, Alfie," Gage ordered. "With *you* at the table she was undoubtedly right to be suspicious of the subject matter." He began to turn away but then aimed a scowl at his cousin. "And don't call me Seby."

"Apologies, *Sebastian*," Alfie replied, adding an extra syllable to my husband's name like his snobbish mother had the tendency to do. He fell into step behind us as we resumed our stroll toward the other end of the manor. "But I *can* tell you what was being discussed by the other men." He paused, clearly wishing for one of us to beg.

"And?" I finally appeased him by asking.

"Emeralds."

I turned to peer over my shoulder at Alfie, confirming I'd heard him correctly.

"And copper."

"Why emeralds and copper?" Gage queried, taking the bait for us this time.

"Apparently, young Birnam is straining at the bit, eager to escape his father's orbit. He was nattering on about mining interests in South America and the West Indies."

"Emeralds and copper," I confirmed.

"Yes. He's been lobbying his father to purchase an interest in one of the endeavors, but thus far his father seems disinclined. He wants to keep his son close at hand and under his thumb."

Gage frowned. "He told you all that?"

"Indeed," Alfie replied. "But then, he was deep in his cups. Had to excuse himself shortly after."

This led me neatly to my next question. "Did any of the other men leave the table early?"

"Thorndike departed almost immediately after the women," Gage answered. "But that may have been at my father's behest." The implication being that, while Lord Gage would tolerate having his secretary dine with us from time to time, he was not keen on allowing him to socialize more intimately with his guests of higher rank.

"Milngavie stole away early, too," Alfie supplied. His hands were clasped behind his back, allowing him to crowd in close behind us, almost looming over me. It was all done quite purposely, I was sure, but I refused to be riled.

"Did he give any indication why?" I asked.

"No," he chirped with perfect insouciance.

Nevertheless, that was three men we needed to speak to at the very least, even if I couldn't puzzle out a motive in harming Miss Whitlock, or Birnam for that matter, for two of them.

"Why are you asking?"

I turned to meet Gage's seeking gaze. It was a perfectly reasonable question, though I hesitated before answering, unsure myself whether Miss Whitlock's fear we'd been eavesdropped upon had been justified. However, contrary to my concerns, my husband seemed quite satisfied with my explanation. I supposed my instincts had proven themselves often enough in the past to temper skepticism.

"It's certainly worth questioning them," he agreed. "I don't anticipate any of them will admit to listening to your conversation, but their reactions might prove informative." He peered over his shoulder at Alfie. "Keep this . . ."

". . . to myself," he finished for him, a sarcastic sneer creasing his face. "Yes, I know. I'm not quite the dolt you believe me to be."

Gage scowled. "I've never believed you a dolt. Just careless and selfish."

I cringed at his words, despite the truth of them. Gage and Alfie had a complicated history; one they had mostly moved past. But that didn't erase the memory of the years Alfie had bullied him, nor did it eradicate the demons in Alfie's past that we could only guess at. I suspected Lorna was the sole person privy to the private pain that had made Alfie into the man he was when she'd first met him.

Notwithstanding, I didn't want the cousins' relationship going backward because of this small snipe. So I pressed a staying hand to Gage's arm when we reached the opening to the staircase and pivoted to face Alfie.

"Thank you for telling us what you observed," I told him sincerely. Then the spark of an idea came to me. "And if you should learn anything more from Jemmy Birnam . . ."

The cynicism which had constricted his expression eased and a sheen of amusement returned to his eyes as he comprehended my meaning. "I'll let you know." He turned to Gage, dipping his head once in a silent truce, which his cousin returned, and then departed.

My husband's jaw was tight, telling me he wasn't entirely happy with my decision to play peacemaker. I waited for him to speak, expecting an irritated retort, but he seemed to master his vexation. "I suppose Jemmy is more liable to speak openly to Alfie than you or me," he conceded with just a hint of resentment. I considered it a minor victory that he'd omitted the scornful words "someone like" before his cousin's name.

"Yes," I answered simply, arching up on my toes to press a kiss to his cheek before I also hurried away. A glance at the watch pinned to my bodice told me I had only ten minutes to change, and I would need every single second to make it downstairs in time to help herd everyone into the carriages.

The River Arrow flowed just yards from the gatehouse for Bevington Park, but the carriages drove us a short distance to the southeast, toward Wixford, to a place where it would be easier to hike to our picnic destination. The staff had gone before us, setting up blankets and chairs, and preparing the tackle for the gentlemen who wished to fish. The weather was lovely, if a bit warm. Though it had been warmer than average since early May, so I had grown almost accustomed to it. Fortunately, the riverbank was dotted with willows, alder, oak, and hawthorn trees, providing plenty of shade as well as perches for the local birds.

As we made our way through the meadow toward the trickling sound of the river, I could hear the songs of goldfinches who in winter feasted on the seeds of the prickly small teasel that lined the banks. It being early July, the teasel hadn't yet flowered, but the small white buds would bloom soon, joining the blossoms of purple loosestrife and great willowherb. A kingfisher took flight, flashing its bright blue–colored feathers as it glided down toward the riverbank.

Though I hadn't been certain Mr. Birnam would feel well enough to take part in the day's excursion, he'd been waiting in the entrance hall with all the other guests when I'd finally joined them. His hands were, of course, still wrapped in the bandages Dr. Clarke had applied the evening before, eliciting much sympathy from those not yet acquainted with his injuries. If Lord Gage had meant to subtly imply earlier that Birnam was our chief suspect in Miss Whitlock's murder, his appearance and the pain he seemed to be enduring did not aid in this insinuation.

Rather than approach him directly, I elected to observe Birnam's interactions with the others as unobtrusively as possible, trying to gain a sense of whether he was exaggerating his injuries. From what I could tell, the discomfort his hands caused him appeared to be genuine, as did the grief that bowed his shoulders. However, this didn't stop him from exhibiting anger at what had been done to his secretary. And much of that fury seemed to be directed at my father-in-law.

Though I hadn't been present the previous evening in Birnam's chamber, it was clear the argument between him and Lord Gage had been every bit as contentious as Gage had suggested. Word must have also gotten back to Birnam of his host's speech that morning, and he was determined to shift the blame. I'd been curious who he might point to as the culprit, but rather than choose someone from among his fellow guests or the staff, he seemed to favor the idea that it had been an intruder.

Watching Birnam, I couldn't decide whether he actually believed this dubious theory or if he was simply savvy enough to understand it was the notion most likely to obscure culpability from his family and gain him the support of the other guests. After all, if he named another guest, that might anger some of the peers, but an unknown intruder was an outsider, and so did not threaten the fiction so many of our social class chose to believe that only the lower orders were capable of murder. I knew from vast experience that a person's class and wealth had no bearing on their ability to do terrible things.

Blaming an intruder also had the added benefit of casting aspersions on Lord Gage. The implication being that he had failed to protect his guests by allowing an intruder to violate his home and harm one of them. This was not stated outright by Birnam, but rather subtly insinuated, countering his host's own inferences about him. I discerned in the derisive, almost mocking twist to my father-in-law's lips and the hard, calculating glint in his eyes the moment he grasped Birnam's ploy. I couldn't tell if this gave Lord Gage—who despised weakness—greater respect for the upstart tradesman or if it had made him his mortal enemy.

In any case, I hadn't long to contemplate it, being pulled away to deal with numerous other complications. Complications that didn't allow me much time to pursue my own agenda. Frustration bubbled up inside me at the realization that if I was to learn anything during that excursion, it would be haphazard and mostly by observation.

I would have liked to speak with Mrs. Birnam and Matilda, to ask them questions about Miss Whitlock's past and upbringing, but they and Trevor seemed determined to avoid me. I did notice that Mrs. Birnam was quieter than usual and more withdrawn. Whether this was because she'd genuinely been affected by Miss Whitlock's death or she was merely unsettled by the situation, I didn't get the chance to discover. But her behavior didn't stop the other guests from speculating.

"Looks like regret to me," Lady Lyndhurst remarked,

waving a fan before her face while holding her glass out to be refilled by one of the footmen.

"At the very least, shock," Lady Brougham concurred in the hushed but titillated voice of a born gossip taking delight in the trials of others. I knew the tone well, though, having heard it used in relation to me more times than I cared to count.

"My modiste told me the cousin of one of her clients threw vitriol in the face of her rival for a suitor's affections. Apparently, he'd seduced her and seemed inclined to discard her for the other woman." Lady Lyndhurst's eyes were bright as she tipped her head closer to her companion. "Of course, the entire matter was hushed up, given the families involved. But the rival was badly burned. They say she'll never take part in society again."

If it was true, my heart ached for the poor girl who certainly didn't deserve to be attacked, no matter if she was a rival or not. I wanted to ask what had happened to the jealous assailant and the unfaithful suitor, whether any justice had been done, but I'd long ago learned that the law was far from impartial and that families of high rank rarely suffered genuine consequences for their actions, especially when appearances were everything. Perhaps it was better not to know.

"She probably thought she'd merely disfigure the girl," Lady Brougham pronounced over the rim of her glass as she stared at Mrs. Birnam, returning to the topic of Miss Whitlock. "That it would discourage her husband's attentions."

Lady Lyndhurst seemed to approve. "A *vicious* plan, especially considering she used the vitriol produced in his own factory."

Evidently, I'd not been wrong that assumptions would be

made about Miss Whitlock's relationship with Mr. Birnam. Assumptions that were unfair if what Trevor had been led to believe was true. Was there some way to confirm it?

My gaze slid toward where Mr. Birnam stood along the pebbly shore of the river, watching the other men fish for chub and pike. His manservant, Paget, hovered a few paces behind him, ready to assist should he need it. The squat, balding man might be the only one who knew the truth, but reports were that he was loyal to Birnam. As such, it was difficult to believe that whatever he chose to tell us would be fact and not just what Birnam wished him to say.

Leaving the shade of the oak and the persistent chirping of a grey wagtail overhead, as well as the chirping women below the branches, I made my way toward the riverbank, curious whether any of the gentlemen were in a talkative mood. Most of them stood in clusters of two or three, casting their lines out over the place where the river twisted and widened to form a languid pool. Here and there, mallards and moorhens dotted the edges lined with fool's watercress, watching over the nests of their broods. Water boatmen and whirligig beetles danced on the sun-speckled surface of the water, twirling around the thin fishing lines.

The estate's gamekeeper had told me that otters swam in the river but cautioned me that they could be elusive. So while I kept my eyes peeled for any sign of their sleek bodies, I didn't expect to see them. Not with all the noise some of the men were making.

Melbourne, Baron Foley, and Lord Gage, in particular, were making no effort to be quiet. And Lord Strathblane was prattling rather loudly to Philip, but I suspected that was more to do with his being hard of hearing. Farther upstream,

Lord Lyndhurst kept aiming sharp glances toward the trio whenever their voices carried to him. It was clear he took his angling quite seriously.

I spied Lord Milngavie a short distance in the opposite direction downstream. He didn't have a fishing pole but seemed deep in thought. Or perhaps just deeply interested in the dragonflies wheeling through the air around him. Recalling that he was one of the men who had departed the dining room prematurely the previous evening, I began to make my way over to him.

Passing a patch of alder trees growing nearly right up into the river, I caught sight of Alfie with one foot propped against a large rock where Jemmy Birnam perched. They were tucked out of sight of most of the others. I was glad to see Alfie doing exactly what I'd suggested and so did not wish to disturb them. But as I began to move on, Alfie surprised me by beckoning me over.

Jemmy, who was staring perhaps unseeing at a patch of moss, didn't turn to squint up at me until I was almost upon them. His appearance was rather ghastly, and judging from his gray complexion and furrowed brow, he was crapulous and suffering for it. I noticed myself that young Birnam had already been three sheets to the wind by the end of dinner, and Alfie had suggested he had only gotten more intoxicated.

"I was just telling Mr. Birnam that you'd expressed concern about his illness yesterday evening," Alfie prompted, obviously wishing for Jemmy to repeat something he'd already told him.

I nodded, playing along.

Jemmy grunted. "Don't mind me, my lady. 'Twas my own doing. Nothing for you to be concerned about." He sounded melancholy and dejected, his usual surliness and unpleasant demeanor temporarily blunted.

"That may be," I said measuredly. "But you are our guest. And one who has suffered a great loss. So if there's anything I can do . . ."

His face screwed up as if he tasted something bitter. I allowed my words to trail away, hoping he would explain his reaction.

"'Tis no great loss." His dark eyes lifted, pinning me. "I saw Portia speaking to you yesterday evening, and while I don't know what she said, it was undeniably rubbish."

I stiffened in surprise, both at the vehemence in his tone and the fact he must have been referring to when Miss Whitlock and I were conferring in the great hall after dinner, for that was the only moment we'd spoken. The fact he'd so readily admitted to seeing us either spoke to his innocence or revealed stupidity and bravado.

"I learned long ago not to trust a word she said," he continued. "So whatever she claimed or complained about, it was pure fiction."

CHAPTER 10

This was the first time someone who had actually known Miss Whitlock had directly accused her of something unflattering.

"You didn't like her," I stated plainly.

He scoffed. "You've got quite the gift for understatement, Lady Darby," Jemmy sneered, using the title I'd asked all the Birnams to abandon upon their arrival at Bevington Park.

"No cause for that." Alfie reproached the younger man's insolence. His crossed arms were nonthreatening, but there had been enough steel in his voice that Jemmy reacted by mollifying his tone.

"No, I didn't like her. But my father did. Couldn't see the deceit in her." This bothered him. "And he treated her incredibly well. Better than she deserved," he grumbled.

"Because she was merely staff?" I asked.

His eyes narrowed. "Because she was a liar."

I opened my mouth to question this bald statement, but apparently Jemmy was finished talking. He pushed to his feet and strode off with a perfunctorily muttered, "Excuse me."

I turned to Alfie as Jemmy disappeared through the trees. "Did he tell you anything more?"

"Nothing except that he would sooner slash his throat than wed Miss Whitlock."

My eyebrows arched skyward. "He despised her that much?"

"Seems so. But I'm no closer to understanding why that is than you are." He frowned down at his feet. "Though I must say, it seems rather foolhardy for him to admit all of this if he was the person who attacked her. And for all young Master Birnam's youth and inexperience, I don't think he's this big of an idiot."

I peered through the screen of trees in the direction Jemmy had gone. "No, I don't think so either."

"For all his apparent hatred, it's obvious he was still conflicted about the matter."

I was struck by the astuteness of this observation. "You think he 'doth protest too much'?" I asked, quoting Shakespeare.

Alfie considered this. "No, I believe he genuinely disliked her. But for all that, he's still struggling with how he feels about her death."

"Just because you dislike someone doesn't mean you wish for them to be killed in such a terrible manner," I suggested. "Maybe it's as simple as that."

"Maybe," Alfic concurred, but I could tell he wasn't convinced. Neither was I.

"I'll keep close," he said after a few moments. "There's a chance he'll say more." One corner of his lips twisted wryly. "Especially if he continues sousing himself."

Strong drink did tend to loosen lips.

"By the way, has Lorna had a chance to ask you about the medications the doctor prescribed Birnam?"

I pulled my thoughts away from the lubricating effects of alcohol and the internal debate I was waging as to whether this was helpful or harmful. "She has not." I turned to face him more fully. "Does she think she might be able to concoct something better?"

As a gifted herbalist—or a hedge witch, as she'd been known on Dartmoor—Lorna knew more about plants and their attributes and healing properties than anyone I'd ever met. She'd learned from her mother, who'd passed down the knowledge from her mother, and so on, extending several generations farther back than that.

"She said she's willing to try. I believe she already has something in mind. That is, if Mr. Birnam would welcome it." Not everyone trusted the abilities of a woman, more the fool they. For all Dr. Clarke's competence, it was doubtful he'd prescribed anything but laudanum for the pain, which dulled the senses and at times caused nausea as well as a number of other complications.

"I'll speak with Mr. Birnam," I said. There was no use in Lorna wasting her time and efforts if the patient wouldn't even accept it.

Alfie escorted me back toward the river, where I hoped to still speak to Lord Milngavie. Unfortunately, he was nowhere to be found. However, I did spy my brother, and what's more, for a rare moment he was alone. He appeared lost in serious thought, much like Milngavie had been earlier, but whatever Trevor was contemplating seemed to be grim.

Reading my mind much like his cousin did, Alfie leaned close to murmur, "I shall leave you here."

I nodded my thanks and picked my way across the rocks and silt toward Trevor, hoping he wouldn't attempt to evade me and the conversation I was determined to have. It turned out I needn't have worried, for he stood waiting, his gaze trained on something on the opposite side of the riverbank. Only the tension in his shoulders told me he knew I was approaching. I realized as I drew closer that he was observing a kingfisher's burrow.

I stopped beside him, watching the brightly plumed bird clean the coppery brown feathers on its breast, and waited to see if Trevor would speak first. It would be far easier if he did. I didn't like the notion of having to interrogate my brother, but interrogate him I would if need be.

I had just begun to fret over how to begin when Trevor heaved a heavy sigh.

"This is a right guddle, isn't it?"

He surprised me by choosing the Scots word. I'd heard both Mrs. Mackay and Bree use it before, but I supposed Trevor might also have learned it from one of his farmhands—living in the Borders region as he did, with both Scottish and English influences. His home, where we'd all grown up, sat on English soil, but we could see Scotland through the rear windows just over the river. Wherever he'd picked it up, it aptly described the situation.

"You know what I'm going to ask you," I said softly, keeping my gaze trained on the brilliant blue feathers of the kingfisher's back.

"I do." He inhaled a shaky breath. "And the truth is . . . I just don't know."

Hearing the agony in his voice, my heart constricted. If he would have welcomed my compassion, I would have reached for his hand, but I knew my brother well enough to tell how tightly coiled he was. Any display of empathy and he would retreat rather than confront the emotions bubbling beneath the surface.

"Have you told me everything you know about Miss Whitlock?" I asked instead. "Did you hold anything back?"

"I didn't hold anything back." His mouth flattened. "Though I know there's more. I asked Matilda about it after you left the library, but she claimed she didn't know anything else."

"But you don't believe her."

He spread his hands helplessly. "How can I? Miss Whitlock lived with her for years, said she was like the sister she never had. And she's been in close proximity with her often enough since she returned from school for Matilda to have learned *something* about her."

"You mentioned that Matilda said something occurred to cause Miss Whitlock to be sent away. Did she at least tell you what that was?"

"She says she doesn't know. That she never has."

But he didn't believe this either. And frankly, neither did I.

I risked stating the obvious. "She's afraid."

He turned to look at me, his features suddenly guarded.

"I know you saw it in the library, too. Something has terrified her." I searched his eyes beneath the shaded brim of his hat. "And I think we both hold the same suspicion what."

Trevor turned away, unable to continue holding my gaze,

and rubbed a hand over the back of his neck. "Aye," he admitted. "Though just because she fears someone from her family killed Miss Whitlock doesn't mean they did."

The firmness of his tone and the glint in his eyes made me wonder if he was also speaking for himself. If in a roundabout way he was admitting to his own fear that Matilda might have been involved.

"You're right," I answered evenly. "But we still have to confront the possibility whether we like it or not." I turned away, observing the river as it flowed around the rocks, forming little eddies and currents. "Didn't you have to confront the possibility I might be guilty of all those things Sir Anthony's colleagues accused me of?"

Trevor seemed caught off guard by my harkening back to that dark moment—one of the most terrifying of my life—when I'd been taken before the Bow Street magistrates, accused of all sorts of despicable crimes. "No," he insisted, growing almost angry. "Not for a moment did I think my sister capable of what those morbid, overwrought men suggested."

I rather liked hearing them described as "overwrought," but there was a point to be made.

"But I did." I could tell I'd stunned him and then realized I should clarify. "Not the luring men to their deaths on my husband's anatomy table and feasting on their organs nonsense! But I did assist Sir Anthony with his dissections. I did make anatomical illustrations of the bodies laid open on his table."

"Because you had no choice!" Trevor's face was red fury, but I could also sense his rising alarm.

He was right. Had I refused, Sir Anthony had threatened

to break all my fingers and throw me into a lunatic asylum. And as my husband, he would have had every right to do all of it, and neither my family nor the law could have stopped him. I forced myself to breathe calmly as I recalled the terror of those years of my first marriage, of knowing Sir Anthony had such absolute power over me. The same could be said of Gage, but I had married a very different man the second time. Though even that knowledge didn't entirely impede the dread I sometimes felt creep over me that he could change, and I would have no recourse. However, I trusted Gage. I trusted in his love, honorability, and goodness. And I trusted in my ability to discern that he would never use any power he might hold to hurt me.

"But I still did it," I murmured to Trevor, allowing him no quarter.

He blinked at me.

"And you must have at least had to consider the possibility of my guilt."

His gaze was so stricken as he stared back at me that I trusted my point had been made.

"The fact of the matter is that each of the Birnams seems to have had a motive for wishing Miss Whitlock either silenced or out of their lives," I continued. "We don't know that murder was the actual intent or if disfigurement and impairment were the goal. In all likelihood, it was the latter, or else a method other than acid would have been chosen."

"What motive could Mr. Birnam have possibly had?" Trevor queried, recovering himself. "You heard Matilda. He treated Miss Whitlock very well."

"Yes, but how might he have reacted if he thought she was about to reveal something damning about his businesses?"

Trevor was taken aback by this. "You think . . . ?"

"Miss Whitlock asked me to meet with her in private. And she referenced Gage's and my work as inquiry agents. That's why she was near the blue room at that late hour. I'd suggested we meet in the small chamber off the breakfast room."

He rubbed a hand over the back of his neck again, struggling with these ramifications. "Did she tell you it was about Birnam's businesses?"

"No, but the possibility has to be considered. She *was* his private secretary, and she was anxious about being overheard."

He nodded.

"And I found Birnam standing over her dead body."

Trevor was not entirely shocked by this. Given the state of Birnam's hands, the guests already knew he had been present—just not the details. "But he picked up the bottle," he protested. "Why would he do that?"

"We have to consider the possibility that this might have been a ruse to cover up the burns he'd already received. After all, I'd entered the room before he could get away."

"Yes, but Birnam knows how corrosive oil of vitriol is. He owns the factory where it's produced, for God's sake! He would never have handled it without gloves."

"People do stupid things when they're in the heat of fury," I countered calmly. "Though I do admit, I struggle to believe it myself. But there are other factors to consider. Such as the note he claimed Miss Whitlock left him asking him to meet her. When we requested to see it, he couldn't produce it. And while she was speaking with me, she gave no indication that she wanted someone else to join us. Quite the opposite, in fact."

Trevor stared miserably back at me, his bewilderment evident.

"You understand our difficulty. I don't *want* it to be Birnam. Heaven knows, I don't. Or Mrs. Birnam, or Jemmy, or any of them. But someone did it. And we owe it to Miss Whitlock to find out."

His posture deflated. "Yes. Yes, we do. Even if the truth stings."

I reached for his hand then. I couldn't stop myself. "I'm sorry, Trevor. I know how you feel about Matilda. You were . . . *are* planning to propose, are you not?"

He hesitated but for a moment before nodding. "I'd planned to at the ball. But . . ."

I squeezed his hand when he couldn't find the words to explain, letting him know I understood. Whatever the truth—good or bad—he needed to know before he took such an irrevocable step.

"We need to know more about Miss Whitlock," I entreated him. "And unfortunately, the Birnams seem to be the only ones with that information."

"I'll keep trying to convince Matilda to confide in me." He didn't sound confident, and this troubled him. After all, Matilda was the woman he wanted to marry, but if she couldn't or wouldn't trust him, what did that say about their future together. "Otherwise, you might try Mrs. Birnam."

"We will," I promised, though I was even more doubtful that *she* would unburden their family's secrets.

We turned to watch as the kingfisher took flight, circling the river twice before landing on a perch overhanging the water.

"Jemmy made an interesting claim," I remarked almost

offhandedly. "He insisted that Miss Whitlock was a deceitful liar." I studied my brother for his reaction. "That his father was blind to it."

Trevor glowered. "But of course he didn't explain *why* she was deceitful."

I offered him a humorless smile. "No."

He shook his head. "I don't know what he's alluding to. Except . . . I don't find Jemmy Birnam to be the shrewdest judge of character."

"What do you mean?"

"Let's just say that if his father hadn't put a stop to it, he would have been bilked out of a considerable fortune by some prospectors from Cuba."

I couldn't withhold my surprise. This must be the copper mine Jemmy had told Alfie about.

Trevor removed his hat, swiping his forearm over his brow. Even in the shade surrounding the river, the rising heat was noticeable. "I tried to tell him about my own youthful follies with my finances, but he didn't want to hear it."

I gestured for my brother to join me as I made my way back along the shore toward the clearing where our picnic was laid out. "That was kind of you." I knew he was ashamed of his past mistakes with gambling and, as such, it wasn't his favorite topic of conversation. For him to admit to his own faults in order to try to help Jemmy was generous.

Trevor grunted, brushing it aside as if it was nothing. "All this is to say that Jemmy isn't the most insightful fellow. And one can be certain he doesn't view Miss Whitlock fairly."

"Because his father persisted in throwing them together?"

"I'm sure that's part of it." His eyes narrowed. "But there's more to it." His face fell. "If I can only convince Matilda to divulge what."

I wished I could offer him some consolation, but if he was to wed Matilda, they would have to work this out between themselves. My inserting myself in the middle would not help. The added pressure of the information she was withholding perhaps pertaining to a murder was enough without my piling on.

Of course, I wasn't sure our older sister would see it that way.

Alana caught sight of us as we emerged from the trees, striding determinedly toward us. Trevor glanced anxiously at me, and I knew without his saying a word what he was asking. I gave him a minute nod of reassurance. We had often colluded like this, much to our sister's vexation.

"There you are," she declared, giving us both a searching look. The taut quirk of her lips suggested she already knew we were conspiring against her. I struggled not to feel guilty. "Mrs. Birnam feels faint."

I began to move forward. "Oh, no. Then we should have a carriage . . ."

"Return her to the hall," my sister finished, falling into step with me. "It's already being prepared."

"I should go with her to be sure she's settled comfortably."

"No, you should stay with your guests. I'll go," Alana stated as if the matter had already been decided. And I supposed it had, for she was right. I needed to stay.

"Then perhaps . . ." I didn't need to finish this remark either, for my sister and I exchanged our own bit of silent communication. She would pry what information she could from Mrs. Birnam.

"Perhaps I should go," Trevor offered, misunderstanding. But Alana cut him off.

"No. You should stay." She arched her eyebrows at him meaningfully. "And make sure Matilda stays as well." She would get more from Mrs. Birnam without her daughter present, especially if the details were in any way sordid.

Trevor caught on. "I see. Then I'll stay." With this, he tipped his hat to us and went in search of his near-fiancée.

"What else should I know?" I asked Alana as we traversed the remaining yards between us and the others.

"Birnam nearly came to blows with Baron Foley."

My eyes widened. "What?"

"Apparently, he made a disparaging insinuation about Miss Whitlock."

"And Birnam took offense?"

"Told Foley that Miss Whitlock was a respectable maiden, and if he dared imply otherwise again, he would see him over pistols at dawn."

"A duel?" Never mind that they were illegal and rather old-fashioned.

"A duel," Alana confirmed.

"Mrs. Birnam couldn't have liked that." Which was perhaps the cause of her feeling faint as much as the warmth of the day.

"I imagine not."

We were nearly upon the others then, so I spoke in a hushed voice. "We need to know more about Miss Whitlock's past. We need to know why she was sent away."

Alana's jaw firmed. "I'll see what I can do."

CHAPTER II

The remainder of the picnic and fishing party passed rather sedately. The chief topic of conversation turned to the heat, which had forced us all to cling to the trees and the cooling shade they cast. Few could remember a summer more intemperate sprinkled with days like this one which were warmer than we were accustomed to. Those who had arrived from London commented on the stench that had enveloped the city as it did every summer, but usually not until August when much of society made their escape to the country.

Mr. Birnam, in particular, was suffering from the heat, as well as the pain of his hands, but he would not be swayed to return to the manor like his wife. Whether he thought this would make him look too delicate or he feared missing an opportunity to press his cause, I didn't know, but his weakened state proved to be an unwelcome distraction. Birnam and the men might have removed some of their clothing or even waded into the river for a swim to gain some relief by at least cooling themselves, but with the ladies present that option was not open to them.

Eventually, it was decided we should all return to Bevington Hall. So while I helped situate the guests back into the carriages, Gage had a word with staff, urging them to take their time cleaning up and not to overtax themselves. He also instructed them to enjoy any of the food left over that they wished—and there was plenty of it! The heat had blunted appetites and also made it unsafe to return many of the items to the larder. It had to be eaten soon or tossed out with the slop for the pigs at the estate farm.

By the time we'd seen everyone else off, Gage and I found ourselves the sole occupants of the final carriage.

"Now, isn't this a happy accident," Gage declared, draping an arm around me.

"Yes," I agreed, pushing against his chest. "But darling, can you scoot to your side of the bench? It's simply too hot."

He didn't take offense. "Quite right," he declared with a weary sigh, sinking into the opposite corner.

For several minutes, we lounged in blissful silence, enjoying the light breeze created by the movement of the carriage while Joe, our coachman, munched on the plate of sandwiches I'd passed up to him before we departed. But our current predicament soon intruded into my thoughts. Truthfully, the memory of Miss Whitlock's ravaged face was never far from my mind. I suspected it would be with me for some time. I hoped bringing her killer to justice might help lay her to rest, but the workings of the brain were a mystery, and the memories that haunted us were rarely so compliant.

"Did you have any luck?" I prodded my husband, trusting he would understand what I meant.

"Not much," he roused himself from his stupor to reply. "Lord Brougham trapped me for some time." His brow furrowed. "Scared all the trout away, too, with his angry prattle."

"What was he prattling on about?"

"The Slavery Abolition Act. He thought he was here chiefly to strategize and discuss its passage with some of the lords who are on the fence. But Birnam and this murder have rather impeded his efforts."

"He understands you support the act?" Which would abolish slavery throughout the British Empire. If anything, Gage and I both believed the act didn't enact reform fast *enough*, for emancipation was gradual and compensated the slave owners for the loss of human "property" to a filthy degree. We hadn't been entirely certain which side of the issue Lord Gage landed on, but I was encouraged that he also supported it given the assortment of noblemen he'd brought together at this house party as the crucial vote in the House of Lords approached.

He grimaced. "Yes, but that didn't stop him from practicing his arguments on me."

I couldn't halt a spark of amusement. "Well, Lord Brougham is lord chancellor and a rather celebrated legal counsel." After all, as Queen Caroline's attorney general, more than a decade earlier he'd successfully defended Her Majesty against her husband King George IV's attempts to see their marriage dissolved and her royal titles stripped from her, causing the campaign against her to collapse.

Gage grunted. "Perhaps we should put Brougham and Birnam in a room together and just let them pontificate at each other. I wonder who would outlast the other." A smile creased his face as he opened his eyes to find that, unable to contain my mirth at the image that sprang to mind, I'd dissolved into laughter. "You find that quite amusing."

I shook my head, struggling to regain control of myself. "I think . . . it's less the notion . . . and more . . . the heat and . . ." I stammered out before adding with one last gasp ". . . this murder." That word certainly had the ability to take the wind from anyone's sails.

My husband's pale blue eyes shone with empathy. "Did *you* learn anything?"

I briefly recapitulated my conversations with Jemmy, Alfie, and Trevor, and informed him that Alana had returned to the hall early with Mrs. Birnam.

"I wondered about that." He dipped his head out the window, either gauging the distance to the manor or simply trying to feel the wind on his face. "Upset about the row between her husband and Foley?"

"She claimed it was the heat—and it quite possibly was—but Alana and I also believe the confrontation played a part." I forced myself to straighten from my slouch, echoing Gage's movements. We must be close to the hall. "Hopefully, my sister was able to learn something from her during their drive."

Gage reached for my hand as I smoothed my skirts, lifting it to his mouth. He smiled apologetically over my knuckles after placing a kiss there. A smile which turned into a grimace. "Since it's too bloody hot for anything else." My husband rarely swore, and almost never on purpose, but this heat was tiresome to everyone.

Bowcott was waiting for us at the door as we climbed

from the carriage and mounted the left arm of the curved staircases constructed of rusticated stone up to the portico. Bevington Hall was Palladian in style, with four unfluted Ionic columns and pediments over the entrance at the center. Three round-arched French doors marched across the portico, the central of which was most used, and where Bowcott stood at the ready.

"Has everyone been settled?" I asked, only slightly out of breath after such a climb in this heat.

"Yes, my lady." He stepped back, allowing me to enter, but I could tell there was more. "His lordship asked that you both join him in his study when you returned."

And since the study was immediately to the left, overlooking the front drive, he knew we'd already arrived.

I shared a wary glance with Gage before nodding. "Thank you, Bowcott."

He bowed his head in acknowledgment before closing the door and retreating deeper into the house.

"I suppose there's nothing for it," Gage muttered, fastening a baleful glare on the study door. Apparently, he was no more optimistic about what his father had to say than I was.

He rapped perfunctorily but did not wait for Lord Gage to reply before opening the door. A fact his father noted with a scowl as he turned from the tall window he stood looking out of.

"I am not pleased," he stated without preamble, crossing toward his large oak desk. "This murder overshadows everything. And as much as I'd like to blame Birnam . . ." he gritted his teeth ". . . I don't think he did it."

My astonishment must have been evident, for a cynical smirk creased his lips.

"You seem surprised by this, but I can be a fair man." He arched a single eyebrow. "I changed my mind about Lord Drummond, didn't I?" he said, referring to a previous inquiry.

Only after the evidence I'd gathered—against his wishes—had *forced* him to.

Gage's scowl matched my own. "Let's not put forward that particular example."

Lord Gage ignored this in favor of his own agenda. "I want you to get to the bottom of this." He pressed his index finger into the center of his desk as if this would make his point stronger. "And I want you to do it as swiftly as possible."

My husband's rigid countenance tightened even further. "What do you think we've been doing?"

"For one, you let Brougham corner you," he criticized. "And that man could talk the clothes off a pauper's back."

Gage's face reddened. "Then, let's gather everyone together and have it out directly."

"Good God, Sebastian," his father snapped. "Have you lost your wits? You do realize the importance of the men we have gathered here. You cannot simply accuse them of murder or put your other suspects on display for them. There must be decorum. More than *my* future is at stake."

Before Gage completely lost his temper and said something he would later regret, I stepped in. "But surely you realize that one of those men might have done it. We haven't yet ruled anyone out." And given the hour the murder had occurred, I didn't anticipate there being many alibis. Wives might vouch for husbands, and friends for friends, but unless a member of the staff or someone from my family substantiated their claim independently, I wasn't certain I trusted it.

Lord Gage turned to me impatiently. "Yes, but until you have substantial proof of their culpability, we are not going to disturb them."

I wanted to know exactly how we were supposed to gather information to solve Miss Whitlock's murder if we weren't to "disturb" their lordships, but Gage was still focused on an earlier remark.

"When you say, 'more than my future is at stake,' I do hope you're referring to Emma's future marriage prospects." Gage's fists were clenched at his side. "Because we've been over this."

His father scoffed in irritation. "Stop being a fool, Sebastian. An overt appointment such as a cabinet minister might be beyond my reach, but with the right connections and your charm and pedigree, you could be home secretary or foreign secretary someday. Perhaps even prime minister." His voice had grown impassioned but then turned more measured as he glanced at me. "In spite of your wife's past and peculiarities."

The image he'd painted sounded like a nightmare to me. I already struggled as a hostess, and that was a politician's wife's primary role. I'd known that my brother-in-law, Philip, was considering a bid for such a high position, and as a powerful earl this was a genuine possibility. If so, Alana was well suited to her role, and as her sister I'd been prepared to endure greater public scrutiny. But not as the politician's wife myself!

Because of this, I didn't feel the slight of my father-in-law's words as perhaps I should have, but Gage clearly did.

"When will you listen to me?" he demanded. "Father, I have *no* political ambition. I will take up your seat in Lords when the time comes, but beyond that, I want nothing to do with it. And none of your machinations are going to change that!"

"I knew I would regret being swayed by your mother when she begged me not to send you to sea," Lord Gage retorted, his own temper getting the best of him, for I knew he didn't mean the cruel words. He'd admitted as much some months past, confessing he was glad he'd not forced the same life upon his son that he'd faced after being compelled to join the Royal Navy at the tender age of nine. "You have no aspiration, Sebastian. No initiative!"

"I do," Gage growled. "They're just not the same aspirations you desire for me."

"Gentlemen!" I stepped between them, raising my voice. "We are straying far from the matter at hand. Miss Whitlock's heinous murder." I turned to glower at my father-in-law. "A matter we have already been putting our utmost efforts into solving. Now, what of pertinence—if anything—have *you* learned today?"

Lord Gage fastened a black scowl on me but allowed himself to be redirected. "Lyndhurst claims he was seeing to his wife's comfort at the time the murder occurred. That his wife's maid can confirm this. As you may have noticed, Lady Lyndhurst has been struggling with poor health." Hence her dietary restrictions. "And Melbourne and Foley were playing billiards."

Except I'd already decided wives and husbands and friends were not sufficient enough of an alibi, and the word of personal servants could likewise be suspect, given their loyalty to and reliance on their current employer for their future prospects. However, I decided to pretend for the moment. "Did Melbourne or Foley hear anything or notice anyone else about?"

"No, and they expressed surprise that they hadn't."

"The billiards room is somewhat tucked away from the rest of the house," I conceded. I assumed this had been done on purpose to mute the noise of clacking balls carrying throughout the manor. Regardless, I couldn't decide whether the gentlemen's response spoke more or less in favor of the veracity of their story.

I turned to see if my husband had anything to add, finding he was still visibly riled from his exchange with his father.

"You might see what else *you* can learn from Birnam." I judged from my father-in-law's begrudging tone that he was speaking to me. "He seems to respond better to you than us."

Maybe because I hadn't treated him like a parasite and all but outright accused him of sleeping with and then killing his secretary.

Lord Gage's gaze flicked over my features. "And because you're a woman, he won't bother trying to change the topic to the Factory Act."

It was true, Birnam was rather like a dog with a bone when it came to the subject. But as a lady, I could not serve in parliament, and neither did my opinion count for much in the eyes of many men. Though presumably Birnam believed females had some intellect, or otherwise he would not have hired one as his personal secretary.

"Well, before I trot off to do that, I would like to look in on my daughter," I replied pointedly, knowing what a weak spot he held for his only grandchild. I pressed a hand to Gage's upper back as I turned to go, letting him know he had my support, and also conferring that he was free to walk away. He needn't continue this conversation until he was ready, or at all. He'd already communicated his intentions for the future. The fault for not listening lay with his father, and it was not Gage's responsibility to correct it.

Unfortunately, Emma was napping, her cheeks pink with slumber and the warmth of the nursery. I lingered for some minutes, chatting softly to Mrs. Mackay about my daughter's day, but since Emma had just drifted off, I decided not to wake her. She nursed just twice a day now, in the morning and evening, so we could be separated for the duration when necessary. However, as I was walking away, I suddenly realized how much I'd been looking forward to her smiles and snuggles. Only the sound of children's laughter coming from a room farther down the corridor that we'd put to use as a secondary nursery kept the tears that threatened at bay.

I peeked inside to find my nephew Malcolm entertaining his two younger sisters and brother, as well as Lorna's older son, Rory. I presumed her younger son, Sherry, was also napping or with Lorna. At four months old, he would still require more rest and more frequent attention from his mother. Alana was speaking with the nursery maid left in charge of this rowdy bunch, but at the sight of me, she excused herself to come over to me.

"I suppose you're looking for me."

"Not actually." I glanced back over my shoulder. "I came up to look in on Emma, but she's asleep. This is merely a happy accident."

"Well, I'm sorry to say, there isn't much to tell," Alana said with a shake of her head, making the pale chestnut brown curls at the side of her temples bounce. "Mrs. Birnam evaded every attempt I made to pry any information from her." Her face screwed up in displeasure. "Though she made certain to once again insult my modiste and my fashion sense."

"I would have thought she would leap at the chance to vent her displeasure at Miss Whitlock." I frowned. "Unless she's afraid to do so."

Alana turned to watch her children, who were now slithering across the floor as if they were snakes. "That's what I wondered. If perhaps she's afraid of saying the wrong thing, of revealing something she shouldn't."

And she would only be afraid of that if she thought she knew something related to Miss Whitlock's murder. Something that implicated either herself or a member of her family.

"She thinks she's protecting someone," I said, putting it succinctly.

My sister nodded. "The question is, who?"

"And how do we figure that out when she won't confide in us?" I sighed. Maybe Mr. Birnam would give me some hint.

CHAPTER 12

I arrived in the sitting room attached to Mr. Birnam's bedchamber just as Dr. Clarke was changing the dressings on his injured hands. The valet, Paget, had answered the door at my knock, his face a stony mask. I wasn't certain of the cause of his strained stoicism until the physician glanced up at me and called me over.

"Ah, my lady. Will you come assist me? This fellow . . ." he tipped his head toward Paget ". . . is all thumbs."

"Of course," I replied, hurrying over.

Birnam, for his part, appeared miserable. His hands now laid bare were an angry red as the skin peeled away and here and there lesions began to form. He'd closed his eyes, as if reluctant to look at them.

"Hold this," Dr. Clarke directed me, passing me a bandage. "And feed it to me while keeping it taut."

I did as directed, noting he'd smeared some sort of unguent over the skin.

"I know it doesn't look it, but thus far Mr. Birnam is healing nicely," Dr. Clarke remarked almost cheerily. "Blood is still flowing to each finger, and the nails have not died. However, it will be some days before we know the true extent of permanent damage."

"You mean, scarring?" I queried.

"At the least. If Mr. Birnam is fortunate, he will not have any lasting deep tissue damage or loss of dexterity."

Birnam did not react to this assessment, but I supposed he'd heard his prognosis earlier. It bothered me how pale he looked. Plainly, the man was in a great deal of pain. So much so that I moved him to the very bottom of my list of potential suspects. It was too hard to believe he would do this to himself in order to avoid suspicion.

Once Dr. Clarke finished the first hand, we began the second, all while the physician kept up a comfortable stream of chatter. I presumed it was meant to soothe the patient's nerves, and it undoubtedly worked for some, but it didn't seem to have any effect on Birnam.

"My lady, may I rely on you to handle changing these dressings if I don't make it here by this time tomorrow and possibly Thursday?"

I lifted my gaze to Dr. Clarke in surprise, not having anticipated such a request. Though we were barely acquainted, I was quite certain he was aware of my past and my scandalous involvement with my first husband's work as an anatomist. Some medical men viewed this with disgust and misgiving, while others seemed to pity rather than despise me. The rare few looked on me as not a figure whose knowledge was to be feared, but to be appreciated.

Apparently, I'd taken too long to respond, for his eyes shifted to meet mine over Birnam's half-swaddled hand.

"Of course," I finally managed to reply.

He nodded once, returning his attention to his work. "Mrs. Wright—over near Weethley—her youngest daughter is due with her first child. Her stable lad delivered a message as I was departing to come here to tell me her pains had just begun. Now Mrs. Evans . . ." presumably the daughter ". . . is a hardy lass, and I suspect she'll sail through with no issues. But a woman's labor with her first child always takes the longest." His gaze flicked to mine again. "As I'm sure you remember."

Much of my labor with Emma had happened while Gage and I had been trapped in the underground Edinburgh Vaults, so I hadn't exactly been focused on the time passing or urging my daughter to come more quickly, but rather for her to stay put until we were rescued. However, I remembered my physician accoucheur in Edinburgh warning me that labor with my first could be long.

"By the fourth child, I often barely make it in time to catch them." He chuckled. "I don't anticipate Mrs. Evans being ready to deliver her first until tomorrow afternoon at the earliest, but her mother will grow antsy if I don't arrive in the morning, though she knows from her own experience and her two other daughters that the wait will be long. So off I'll go to twiddle my thumbs 'til the time is ripe."

I didn't know why Dr. Clarke was confiding all of this to me—and in the hearing of Birnam and his servant—but it took a considerable amount of my self-control not to scowl openly at him. The favorable impression he'd made in accepting my medical experience so readily had all been undone, and I was now quite determined that I should never have my lying-in with any of my future children in Warwickshire, but instead put my care in Dr. Fenwick's competent and compassionate hands in Edinburgh.

Once the physician had finished—and not a moment too soon—and issued a few additional instructions to me for the morrow, I told Paget I would sit with Mr. Birnam while he showed Dr. Clarke out. The valet's pleated brow told me he wished to argue but knew better, so he complied.

After they departed, I turned to study Birnam's blanched face. He'd been assigned to one of the more masculine-decorated suites of rooms, boasting dark colors and heavy furniture. But the large man seemed dwarfed now by his surroundings, shrinking into himself as pain racked his body. I'd noted that the physician had told him he could continue to use the laudanum he'd left him to ease his discomfort, but it was obvious he'd not taken it. Even so, I pressed him.

"Shall I fetch you some of that tincture, Mr. Birnam?" I offered.

He blinked open his eyes, looking at me for the first time since my arrival. "Nay."

"Are you sure?" I asked, unable to keep the concern from my voice. "Or . . . if laudanum does not agree with you, Lady Tavistock has offered to fix you something milder. She's a gifted herbalist."

"Please thank her, but nay," he replied dully, lowering his gaze to his wrapped hands where they rested in his lap. "Nay, I deserve this. Every blindin' twinge and throbbin' ache."

For a moment I held my breath, wondering if he was confessing to something, but then he shook his head woefully.

"I was supposed tae protect her. Tae keep her safe. I promised her mam . . . her da." He screwed his eyes shut. "And I failed."

I'd not forgotten Miss Whitlock had been orphaned. "You must have been quite close to her parents," I prodded, hoping he would tell me more.

"Aye. Clive Whitlock was my best mate since practically the day we was born. And his wife, Ellie . . ." He heaved a sigh of almost yearning. "Aye, she was a fine woman." He looked at me directly. "They were the best o' us and not a day goes by that I dinna think o' 'em and miss 'em."

"You all grew up together?"

He nodded.

"Did your wife also?"

He rubbed a forearm against his chest, and I wondered if his heart was troubling him. "Nay. Maggie was from Port Dundas."

I didn't know anything about Glasgow's various neighborhoods, but I gathered this was different in some significant way than his own district.

"I haven't been able tae find the note," Birnam said suddenly. "That's why you're here, isna it?" His jaw tightened. "Tae ask after it for your father-in-law."

"I'm here to check on you," I corrected him, before cautiously adding, "though it would go a long way to convincing his lordship of your innocence if you were to find it."

His bloodshot eyes searched my face while I fought to keep my expression placid. "You dinna believe I did it, do ye?" he asked after a few intense moments.

"No, I don't," I admitted, hoping this would encourage him to trust me.

He sank back deeper in his chair with a harrumph. "Your brother said ye were a canny one. Speaks quite highly o' ye, he does."

For some reason this made my throat tight, hearing that Trevor was proud of me. I supposed I'd known it, but to hear it put so bluntly stirred something within me. I had trouble finding my voice.

"I hope he's right," Birnam continued. "Because it seems you're the only one wi' sense I have tae rely on tae bring Portia's murderer tae justice."

"I'll do my best," I managed to reply.

He harrumphed again as if this wasn't enough.

I scrutinized the barrel-chested man, disliking his arrogance. He might be a savvy tradesman, accustomed to ordering people about and demanding results, but I was not his employee, nor was this a mere business matter.

"However, my task would be much simpler if you and your family would answer my questions about Miss Whitlock," I pronounced sternly. "Remember, I made her acquaintance just three days ago. I haven't the slightest notion why someone would wish to throw acid into her face."

This wasn't strictly true. I had several notions, most of which implicated Birnam or his family in some way. But I was curious to hear his answer and witness his reaction to my deliberate use of such harsh words.

His face flushed nearly as red as his hair, bringing a bit of welcome color to his complexion. "Maybe ye dinna have the good sense yer brother ascribed tae ye, for 'tis perfectly obvious *she* was no' the target."

"You were." This was a statement, not a question, but Birnam answered it anyway.

"Aye!"

"And why would someone wish to throw acid in *your* face?"

This time his answer was not so quick, so I pushed harder.

"If you believe you were the intended target, then there must be a reason."

When still he didn't respond but sat ruefully chewing on the inside of his lower lip, I crossed my arms and glared at him.

"You just said you wished to see her murderer brought to justice. Was that a lie?"

"'Tis business," he groused. "Surely, you've heard o' the vitriol attacks that've been made on other mill owners."

I gave him no quarter. "And why would they target you specifically? And why here?"

"Opportunity. Obviously, Lord Gage's security is lax."

I raised my eyebrows, letting him know how absurd I thought his claim of an outsider causing such carnage was.

"As for why, some o' the workers always have a grievance. There are troublemakers in every lot. Men and women who dinna wish to work, who think life should be handed tae them on a plate instead o' laborin' hard for it."

Except from what I'd heard, their chief aims were simply to receive a living wage, to not be forced into debt to the owners by being compelled to live in company towns and company housing, and to toil in safer conditions.

"Why, when I started oot . . ."

But I had no desire to listen to him prattle on about how he'd gotten his start. I'd heard it all before. So I cut him off quickly. "Then why did they lash out at Miss Whitlock instead of you?"

This was something he'd evidently already been thinking about, for he answered readily. "They must've found her first. Must've realized hoo much it would outrage me. And . . ." He hesitated before continuing. "There are some who've no' taken kindly tae my hirin' a female secretary. Some who'd no' qualm to lash oot at her in spite, as well as tae get tae me."

"Can you think of anyone in particular?"

He shrugged one shoulder. "I dinna always ken their names."

This exasperated me, for he was giving me no information that I could use to find the culprit. "You should know, she asked me to meet her," I informed him crisply. This was not something I'd intended to divulge, but I decided that it might cut through some of his flimflam.

His brow furrowed.

"That's why she was there near the blue room at midnight. She'd asked me to meet her somewhere we wouldn't be disturbed." I could tell he was struggling not to react, and so I pressed on, determined to make him reveal *something*. "She didn't mention asking you to join us. In fact, I got the impression she didn't want *any* witnesses to our meeting."

"Hoo many times do I have to say it?" he erupted. "*She* slipped a note under *my* door, askin' me to meet her. I dinna ken why she asked me to meet her, only that she did. And 'twas no' in her character tae do such a thing, so I kenned it must be serious."

"Are you certain the note was from her?"

"She signed it, didna she?"

I huffed. "Yes, but was it in her handwriting? Was the wording her style?"

This, for once, seemed to give him pause.

"You said it wasn't in her character to ask for such a meeting, so what I want to know is, was it actually a note from her?"

He began to lift his hand but then lowered it. I could see it was shaking. "I dinna ken. I . . . I didna pay much attention."

I leaned toward Birnam, pleading with him. "The one thing I know for sure was that Miss Whitlock was frightened of something or someone. She wouldn't tell me then for fear of being overheard, but I assure you, her distress was palpable." I searched his frazzled features. "Why would she be afraid?"

"Afraid?" He seemed shocked. "But why wouldn't she have come tae me?" His voice was hollow with hurt as his gaze trailed away. "Surely, she must have kenned I'd look oot for her."

"Perhaps she was afraid *for* you," I suggested, attempting to refocus his thoughts. "What was she working on? Could she have uncovered something that put you at risk?"

"Just the usual invoices and correspondence," he muttered. "Nothin' extraordinary."

"Could we see it? It might help us understand."

His eyes returned to me, his fog of uncertainty clearing. "Nay."

"No?" I repeated in surprise, for I'd thought I'd made him understand.

He arched his chin. "What ye seek is no' in any o' my papers, and I'll no' risk them fallin' intae the wrong hands."

Instantly, I was suspicious, especially when I realized Paget had returned. A speaking look passed between the two men over my shoulder, and it was all I could do to swallow the accusation that sprang to my lips. For I was now almost certain it had been Paget who had broken into Miss Whitlock's locked chamber and confiscated the contents of her writing desk. However, without proof the allegation would only place more obstacles between us and Birnam, and we needed his cooperation if we were to uncover anything of import. I would have tomorrow and perhaps Thursday to try again while I changed the dressings on his hands.

Excusing myself, I left Birnam in Paget's care, wondering just who the valet was and what else he might do at Birnam's behest.

CHAPTER 13

It was still more than two hours until dinner, but weary beyond measure, I retreated to our bedchamber suite. Most of the other guests had likewise sought rest and respite from the heat, so I brushed aside any feelings of guilt that I might be failing at my duties as hostess. I heard voices coming from our sitting room and entered to find Bree and Anderley there conferring with Gage. They looked up as I entered.

I must have appeared as ragged as I felt, for Bree rose to her feet to pour me a cup of tea. Sinking into the soft cushions of the settee, I bent over to unlace my kid leather boots, heedless of whether it was impolite to do so while my husband's valet was present or not. Once my stocking feet were free, I sat up with a sigh, catching the smirk on Anderley's lips.

"Don't tell me you don't do something similar after a long day on *your* feet," I scolded him mildly.

"Sometimes he does it under the dinner table," Bree tattled

on him, crinkling her freckled nose as she handed me my tea. "Dinna ken why he thinks he can get away wi' it wi'oot our noticin'. His big feet stink somethin' awful."

"No worse than yours," he teased back.

Bree planted her hands on her hips. "You've never seen my feet."

He waggled his dark eyebrows. "That you know of."

I smothered my laugh with my hand as Bree narrowed her eyes at Anderley, as if ready to do him some violence. But there was also a glint of playful mirth in their depths, which told me she hadn't minded the jest.

"Enough, you two," Gage admonished them with a smile. However things had ended in the study with his father, he was now either sufficiently distracted or doing a good job of pretending it hadn't bothered him. "Tell Mrs. Gage what you just told me."

Anderley gestured for Bree to go first.

"I spoke wi' as many members o' the staff as I could," she said, sinking down on the settee a few feet away. "And as I anticipated, they all had nice, but fairly innocuous things to say about Miss Whitlock. Nothin' o' note." Her gaze sharpened. "Except Ann McClintock."

"Mrs. Birnam's maid?" I clarified, recalling our conversation during the wee hours of the night.

"Aye. She told everyone, 'The hussy got no more than she deserved.'"

I gasped aloud, a reaction which seemed to satisfy Gage and Anderley who had already heard this, for they nodded. "She actually said that?"

"Aye. Shocked everyone wi' in hearin'. And when she walked away, then I got an earful aboot *her*."

"McClintock?"

"Aye. Mrs. Taylor said she's a demandin' one. Tries tae bully the other maids tae get first go at everythin'. Tried tae elbow *me* aside the other day tae use the iron when I'd been waitin' for it tae heat. And she snatched Lady Brougham's breakfast tray straight oot o' her maid's hands just this mornin'."

"Well, that's no way to behave," I retorted, affronted for the rest of the staff.

"But then Elsie . . ." one of the upstairs maids ". . . told me she'd heard Mrs. Birnam screechin' at the woman fair loud enough tae wake the dead simply because she'd no' arrived wi' the hot water for her mornin' ablutions fast enough."

I paused to consider this. "Then maybe McClintock is acting as she is out of self-preservation." If Mrs. Birnam was that demanding and impatient, the maid's position could not be an easy one. "Have you thought to empathize with her?" Perhaps the maid could use a little kindness. Though I cringed at the knowledge I was asking Bree to do so in order to convince this McClintock to then confide in her. Such was the moral dilemma of some investigative work.

Bree affirmed she had and then grimaced. "Though I'm no' confident 'twill work. She's a suspicious one. And she does genuinely seem no' to have liked Miss Whitlock." She tilted her head. "Though maybe she was merely takin' her mistress's part."

That was possible. A willing ear and a bobbing head did often override any other faults for some people. It may be how McClintock stayed on Mrs. Birnam's good side.

I turned to Anderley. "What about you? I'm curious if you learned anything about the guileful Mr. Paget."

"Indeed," he replied, relishing his turn to speak. "It seems Paget does come from Birnam's early days, before he'd made his fortune." He flashed a grin. "Lachlan—the stable lad the Birnams brought with them—was full of information. Claims Paget often disappears at night or even for days at a time. And that he's a dab hand with a knife."

"Now that doesn't sound like a very reliable valet," I quipped dryly. "Who's to help Mr. Birnam dress and undress?"

"Certainly not a traditional one," Gage drawled in agreement. "It's almost as if his primary duties are something else entirely."

"So if Birnam is responsible for his secretary's murder, then there's a good chance Paget may have done the dirty work." I frowned, recalling what Anderley had said about Paget having known his employer before he'd made his fortune. "I wonder if he also knew the Whitlocks."

The others looked to me in question, and I quickly explained what I'd learned from Birnam.

"Then Paget took the papers from Miss Whitlock's desk," Gage surmised, coming to the same conclusion I had.

"It seems all but certain," I said, emptying my cup.

He shook his head angrily. "Does Birnam think no rules apply to him?"

It was a justified query. And one that made the tea in my stomach turn sour. For a man who believed the rules didn't apply to him might do just about anything with little or no remorse.

Trevor and I had once discussed the impact that one's in-laws might have on one's marriage. He had asked for my opinion because at the outset of Gage's and my marriage, his father and I were practically at daggers drawn. I had conceded that it had not always been easy—it still wasn't—but that if I had to choose all over again, I would still have married Sebastian.

But Lord Gage was a different man than Mr. Birnam, and there was Mrs. Birnam to be gotten along with as well. For all my difficulties with my father-in-law, at least he followed a code of honor. If Birnam followed no set of rules, then what would that mean for Trevor? What would that mean for his marriage if Birnam ever tried to pit his daughter against him? Would he ever resort to blackmail against those Trevor loved to get what he wanted?

These questions troubled me.

And they continued to do so, percolating at the back of my thoughts even as I bathed and dressed for dinner, and later made my way down to the mauve drawing room where the guests would gather. Called thus because of the shade of paint on the walls, it boasted tall western-facing windows that spilled ample light across the Aubusson rug. Pride of place had been given to a Broadwood grand pianoforte while various seating arrangements were sprinkled around the large room. When necessary, the doors to the red saloon next door could be propped open, or even to the green drawing room on the opposite side of that.

Earlier, I ordered that the windows on opposite ends of the house be opened, and the inner doors left ajar to promote a cross-breeze, and I was relieved to feel that the space was now blessedly cooler. Of course, everything on this level would have to be closed up tight overnight. Birnam's earlier implications that an intruder must have attacked Miss Whitlock would make this obligatory. Promoting an atmosphere of safety and security would be prioritized over comfort.

Being the first to arrive, I was able to steal a few moments to myself before the hubbub of the evening began. I considered returning to the nursery to see Emma, but I knew I had five minutes at most before the guests began to appear. I would have to wait to slip away to see my daughter once the gentlemen rejoined us following their port.

I perched on the edge of one of the rosewood sofas, wishing I could sink into its depths. I allowed my shoulders to slump and my posture to sag, only to be caught out by Lorna as she hurried into the room wearing an ethereal coral pink gown. However, she seemed to have little care for my breech of decorum, intent on something else.

"Kiera," she exclaimed. "Thank goodness I've caught you alone." She glanced about the room as if to verify this, before plopping down beside me. "I've thought of something."

I turned toward her, intrigued.

"Remember how Miss Whitlock was indisposed upon their arrival?"

"Yes. She claimed that long journeys don't agree . . . with her." My words slowed as I realized the query Lorna was about to make.

Her green eyes gleamed with awareness. "Could she have been with child?"

Yesterday I'd asked myself the same thing. Asked it and discarded it. But now, the answer was far more critical, far more pertinent. For if she was . . . if she was, that might provide us with a motive.

"And if so," Lorna continued on a whisper, sneaking a look toward the door, "who was the father?"

I began to question my decision not to perform an autopsy. Had I been too hasty in thinking I'd learned all I needed to know without making a single cut? A postmortem internal examination was never my first choice, but in some instances, it was not only useful but necessary.

I thought back over my recollection of the state of Miss Whitlock's body, trying to ignore the damages to her face, aware that their severity skewed my objectivity. I also thought back over her behavior and mannerisms during the hours leading up to her death. If she *had* been with child, she wasn't yet showing. There had been no telltale rounding of the abdomen or swelling of the breast tissue. She also had not yet developed the signature gait that expectant women exhibited due to the widening of their hips and the shifting of their internal organs. If I wasn't mistaken, this occurred fairly early during gestation.

It was true, she had been indisposed upon her arrival and her appetite over dinner had not been strong, but that didn't necessarily signal pregnancy. She could just as easily have been suffering from a stomach complaint or residual nausea from their travels. Her complexion had been wan, as one would expect in someone recovering from illness, rather than the typical glow of pregnancy.

I bit my lip in indecision. For the fact was, there was no way to be certain. Even an autopsy might not provide me with a definitive answer if the impregnation was within the past few weeks.

I'd performed a postmortem on an expectant mother just once before and had struggled mightily despite the fact that I hadn't needed to make the cuts. The killer had done that, monster that he was. I balked at doing one now, especially knowing it might not give us the answers we sought. And if it provided no answers, it could offer no proof to be brought against a suspect during trial. In fact, it might actually hurt the eventual case against whoever the culprit was if it turned out that a potential pregnancy had no bearing on the matter.

I spent much of the evening distracted by these ruminations, counting down the minutes until I could discuss them with Gage. Fortunately, most of the guests retired early again, claiming fatigue. When all but a few gentlemen had gone up, I felt it safe to excuse myself, leaving the fellows to my husband and his father's care. My lingering gaze as I departed must have done the trick in communicating my desire to speak to him, for Gage joined me in our bedchamber soon after I'd sent Bree off to seek her own bed. He found me standing before the long mirror turning left and right as I examined my figure through the fine lawn of my nightdress.

"What do you remember from when I was expecting Emma?" I asked without preamble. "Do you recall when I first started showing? When did my nipples and areolas start darkening?"

He seemed at a loss for words at first but soon recovered, closing the door to the adjoining sitting room before approaching. His hands fell lightly on my shoulders as he met my gaze in the reflection of the mirror. "Are you trying to tell me something?"

I stared back at him for the space of several heartbeats in incomprehension before realizing. "Oh! No. I'm not with child." But then I paused, tilting my head as I calculated the days since my last menses. I shook my head. "No."

I couldn't tell if his expression was relieved or disappointed. His mask of inscrutability was firmly in place.

"Then, am I to assume this has something to do with

Miss Whitlock?" His head reared back as he came to the realization Lorna and I both had. "She was indisposed."

"But I cannot decide if that's indicative of anything or not," I confessed in frustration before reiterating my thoughts on the matter. "So I've been trying to recall the changes my body went through when I was first expecting Emma. Was there something external that could give us the answer we seek without risking the invasion of an autopsy?"

"Well, I remember many of the changes you listed, but as to your . . ." he cleared his throat ". . . nipples, I'm afraid I don't recall exactly when they darkened. And as for Miss Whitlock . . ." He cleared his throat again. "If you don't know what color they were to start with, I'm not certain . . ." His words trailed off, but I recognized what he was attempting to communicate and the wisdom behind it.

I also couldn't stop a small smile from stretching my lips at the evidence of his discomfort with this topic. "You investigate grisly murders, but speaking of the anatomy of women's breasts makes you blush." For indeed, color had crested his bronzed cheeks.

He frowned.

I turned to face him, wrapping my arms around his torso. "Oh, now, don't get me wrong. I think it's quite endearing." Though I couldn't help teasing him just a little more. "Particularly since you seem quite without shame when it comes to lavishing attention on my anatomy."

"That's different," he growled.

I giggled. "That's true. Yes, point taken," I said, sobering. "None of this is a laughing matter." I inhaled a deep breath as apprehension flooded me again. "What should we do?"

Gage considered my question, seeming to realize what I was really asking. Should I have performed an autopsy? Should I do one now? Only a day had passed. The decay would not be far advanced since Miss Whitlock's body had been stored in the cold cellar. Though I still didn't relish the prospect.

He lifted his hands to rest them on my waist. "In this instance, I think restraint may be the wisest course. Especially if, as you say, an autopsy is unlikely to further our knowledge."

My shoulders sagged in relief upon hearing this. Something he noticed.

"And even if she *was* expecting, she might not have known it, let alone anyone else, since she wasn't far enough along for it to be noticeable," he added. "So its bearing on our investigation might be negligible."

That was perhaps putting it too mildly. I could only imagine how Mrs. Birnam would react to someone deeming the discovery that her husband had been sleeping with and had impregnated his secretary as negligible. But I understood what he meant to convey. There was no way to prove who the father was, and so without corroborating evidence, Miss Whitlock's being with child could not sufficiently indicate motive.

In any case, we agreed that performing a more in-depth postmortem was not the best step forward.

Basking in the comfort of his embrace, I forced myself to dwell on another topic. Though one that was perhaps not any more welcome.

"Did your father have anything else to say?"

He blew out a long breath. "Nothing worth repeating."

I pressed in close to him, offering him what comfort I

could. I'd considered the thought percolating in my mind a handful of times in the past six months, but this was the first time I'd dared to speak it. "Have we made a mistake?"

Gage drew back so he could see my face.

"Making the dower house our country residence," I clarified.

We had worried that, considering how Lord Gage was, proximity would breed contempt. Given his behavior over the past week, I feared that was exactly what we were reaping.

Gage pulled me close again, resting his chin on my head. "I don't know," he admitted, the aching honesty in his voice making my throat tight. "But for better or for worse, the house is finished, and to our specifications. So let's spend some more time there, dash the guests and the investigation and father. We're not automatons!" He grasped my long chestnut braid, tugging lightly so that my head was tipped back to look at him. "Let's collect Emma and take off for our house tomorrow afternoon, or barring that, the next."

I agreed, feeling cheered. "Yes, let's."

Arching up on my toes, I pressed my lips to his supple ones. His hand gripped a fistful of my nightdress at the back, anchoring me to him as he deepened the kiss.

Sometime later, once we were settled in bed with my head pillowed on his shoulder and my body draped along his side, skin to skin, he returned to the subject first raised when he entered the room. "You know, Emma is fifteen months old," he remarked almost idly, his fingers running up and down the length of my arm where it rested over his chest.

I waited to hear what he would say next.

"Should we be making a more concerted effort to have a second child?"

This made me chuckle. "I do believe you've been quite attentive enough." I ran my foot up his leg beneath the covers. "You do remember how it works?"

He smiled at my teasing. "I do. I just . . . wondered."

It was true, we hadn't exactly been *trying* to get pregnant. But we also hadn't been trying *not* to.

"It will happen when it happens," I said with a shrug. An answer he readily accepted. But then privately I began to wonder.

I'd not worried about it before, busy as I'd been with Emma and finishing my art exhibit and then completing the dower house as we prepared for this house party, not to mention our periodic investigations. I had also chosen to breastfeed my daughter myself, and I knew that could delay conception. But given Gage's regular amorous attentions, was it odd that I'd not gotten with child again?

I chewed my bottom lip, reluctant to admit my sudden concern. Plainly, Gage didn't know what was normal and what wasn't. But surely my sister would, and possibly Lorna. At least they'd both carried multiple pregnancies.

I tried to put the apprehension from my mind until I could broach the topic with either of them, but it was still a long time before I fell asleep.

CHAPTER 14

I overslept the next morning, barely making it down to the dining room to greet any of the gentlemen. I took some comfort in the report from Bowcott that all of the ladies had requested trays delivered to their rooms. All save Matilda, that is, who, as a single lady, was not yet granted the privilege. I would have broken etiquette to allow it, but she seemed content to take breakfast downstairs. Perhaps because it offered her the opportunity to spend time with Trevor outside the purview of her stringent mother.

Entering the mauve drawing room, I could see them now through the tall windows striding along a path in the garden taking a morning constitutional. I realized that I'd not yet had a chance to discuss with Lord Gage the changes Matilda had proposed to the plants. There had been more pressing matters occupying our time.

I turned away, content to leave them to their peaceful

promenade, only to find myself cornered by Lady Lyndhurst and Lady Brougham.

"We understand there is to be archery this morning?" Lady Brougham asked with an artful smile, her graying hair tucked neatly into a frilled cap.

"Yes, on the shaded south lawn in a little over an hour," I replied. It had simply been too hot the previous afternoon, and so the activity had been postponed until this morning. "There will be lawn billiards as well. And battledore and shuttlecock, if anyone feels up to such exertion."

"Perhaps the men," Lady Lyndhurst suggested, glancing at her friend. "Though I suppose Mr. Birnam won't be able to take part in any of it."

"No, I suppose not." I couldn't tell if her concern was genuine or if her point was to another purpose. "But he can still observe. I suspect there will be others who don't wish to participate."

Lady Brougham's gaze was bright with cunning. "Hmm, perhaps his wife. Though I would not like to test her aim. It seems deadly."

"Yes, indeed," Lady Lyndhurst agreed, turning to me expectantly.

"You mean to imply that Mrs. Birnam threw the acid in Miss Whitlock's face," I stated, following along with their game.

Lady Brougham's nose crinkled in irritation. "Blunt, as always, Lady Darby."

I felt the sting of her criticism but ignored it in pursuit of more information. "Do you have any evidence that is what happened? Did either of you witness anything?"

Lady Brougham scoffed. "What evidence do we need? If

disfigurement was the aim, then Mrs. Birnam is the obvious suspect. I can't say I even blame her, ghastly as the act was. It's bad enough that men must make mockeries of us outside our homes with their lovers. But if my husband dared have the gall to hire a girl more than half his age as his secretary, all in the guise of diddling with her underneath my nose, I might very well be tempted to an act as extreme as Mrs. Birnam."

I remembered then that Lord Brougham was not the picture of propriety. Rumors were that he'd fathered at least one illegitimate child and that he'd paid the infamous courtesan Harriette Wilson and her publisher to keep his name out of her memoirs. This could be coloring Lady Brougham's view of the matter. Though the Birnams' reluctance to confide in us and Mrs. Birnam's palpable hostility toward Miss Whitlock prior to her death made me hesitant to dismiss the possibility entirely.

However, I couldn't admit any of this to these women.

"But you haven't witnessed anything directly that might help prove it?" I pressed. Surely, they understood the courts couldn't base their judgments on mere opinion. Even the coroner's inquest, which was scheduled for the following morning, would be circumspect, undoubtedly finding Miss Whitlock had been murdered by a person or persons unknown and allowing the magistrate and constable more time to investigate. Or in this case, allowing the magistrate to allow *us* more time to investigate.

Lady Lyndhurst seemed almost offended by the query. "Of course not. Or else I would have told my husband immediately."

I nodded, allowing the ladies to depart and pretending

not to notice their falsely affronted looks. I would get nothing useful from them, and I felt a pulse of impatience with them for broaching the macabre subject purely for the purpose of exchanging tittle-tattle and then acting as if I was the morbid one.

My pique must have still been evident when I turned toward the terrace to find Trevor and Matilda entering through the doors leading into the red saloon. They hesitated, eyeing me warily. I did my best to smooth my features as I entered the saloon and greeted them a good morning.

"Good morning," Matilda replied, glancing up at Trevor as she explained unnecessarily. "We were just enjoying the gardens."

I realized she was nervous, though I wasn't certain why. "Yes, I saw you through the windows. I do think they are loveliest during the early hours of the day." I turned to my brother, silently asking for an explanation.

"Matilda has something that could be important to tell you," he prompted with an encouraging tone, his eyes warm with the promise of his support.

I rocked forward on the balls of my feet, eager to hear what she had to say, but I forced myself to ask if she'd like to be seated first. She shook her head as if she was simply ready to have it over with. Obviously, whatever she had to tell me about her family and Miss Whitlock must be upsetting.

But it was not about her family.

"Mr. Thorndike . . ."

She faltered, biting her lip, allowing me time to adjust to the unexpected direction of her confession.

"He said some rather inappropriate things to me about Miss Whitlock," she finished in almost a hush.

I frowned, glancing at Trevor, who was now struggling not to show his disapproval of Lord Gage's secretary. "What sorts of things?"

"He . . . he suggested Portia was applying to be my stepmother."

I failed to mask the surprise that I knew must have shown on my face. That Mr. Thorndike would make such a rude and improper remark to one of his employer's guests, particularly a young lady, was appalling. "When was this?"

She had folded her arms over her chest rather like a shield. "Before dinner the evening he joined us at the table."

The evening Miss Whitlock died.

She gestured with her head toward the chamber next door. "Here in the drawing room. We were among the first to arrive. I'd risked aggravating Mother by not waiting for her. I wanted to arrive when Trevor did."

It was clear from the apologetic look in my brother's eyes that he had not appeared early enough, likely because I'd delayed him with my questions.

"Tell her the rest," he urged.

Matilda swallowed. "He also said that Portia ought not be dabbling in men's work. That it was unnatural, and she was stealing employment from a man who needed it. That . . ." She faltered, inhaling a taut breath. "That someone ought to teach her to mind."

Anger stirred within me upon hearing many of the same arguments I'd heard aimed at me for daring to create the detailed illustrations for my first husband's definitive anatomy textbook. Never mind that these had been generated under duress and that I was not paid nor would I receive credit for them. Sir Anthony was determined to keep all the glory, which was why he hadn't hired a draftsman in the first place but rather married one, placing me entirely under his authority and all of our funds at his command.

I wasn't surprised to hear that Mr. Thorndike possessed such opinions. After all, I'd been aware of his disapproval of me without his ever verbally mentioning it. But I was shocked to hear him make such comments aloud to Matilda, specifically the veiled threat.

"We will speak with him," I promised her before turning to Trevor, hopeful there might be more. "Thank you for telling me," I added. "The more we know—about Miss Whitlock, about her past and the events surrounding her death—the better able we will be to figure out what happened."

But all Matilda did was nod, seeming determined to keep anything else she knew about the things I'd mentioned to herself. For his part, Trevor didn't press her.

I stifled a sigh, turning to go. If he could not convince her to confide in us, we might have to resort to a more direct confrontation. Because while Mr. Thorndike needed to be questioned and his whereabouts ascertained, I was all too conscious of the fact that Matilda—and even my brother—would have been looking for any motive outside her family to assign blame to for Miss Whitlock's death. This meant her interpretation and recall of her conversation with Thorndike might be skewed. Until we spoke to the pompous secretary, we couldn't know for certain.

As such, the sooner the interrogation transpired, the better.

Unlike my husband and his father, Mr. Thorndike was not difficult to track down. He was hunched over his desk in one of the smaller chambers behind Lord Gage's study. Another of the rooms belonged to the steward, while the third was utilized for storage. The complex of offices boasted a separate entrance leading to a servant stair or alternatively the library, as well as the door into my father-in-law's study.

When Lord Gage opened this last door to request that Mr. Thorndike attend him, I spared a moment to wonder if the secretary had overheard any of our conversation the previous afternoon when we had returned from the banks of the River Arrow. There had been nothing to stop him from eavesdropping except his own compunction unless my father-in-law had sent him away on another task.

Mr. Thorndike strode promptly to the door that had been left ajar for him. "Yes, my lord." He drew up short at the sight of me and Gage, either not realizing we were present or pretending not to.

"Close the door and have a seat," Lord Gage directed from his chair behind his broad oak desk. Gage and I occupied the two Rococo-inspired Chippendale armchairs—a match to the Rococo-style plaster ceiling and frieze below the cornice—forcing Thorndike to sit in the ladderback chair Gage had brought in from the library.

Lord Gage did not spare his secretary's feelings. "Some troubling information has come to my attention." He arched his chin sternly. "Did you indelicately imply to Miss Birnam—a gently bred young lady, regardless of her father's origins—that Miss Whitlock was applying to be her stepmother?"

Thorndike's face paled and his throat worked to swallow as he attempted to formulate a response that would save him from being sacked. To his credit, at least he didn't try to lie. "I have no defense, my lord. I used poor judgment in making such cruel and unconscionable remarks to the young lady. I . . . I do know better."

"What were you thinking, man?" Lord Gage demanded furiously.

"I . . . I wasn't," he stammered, clasping his hands together so tightly in his lap that the knuckles turned white. "It was only that I'd heard others make similar remarks and I thought . . ." He shook his head. "It doesn't matter what I thought. Or that I did not care for Miss Whitlock. I should never have said it. Particularly to Miss Birnam."

Though I had been convinced of his remorse until this point, there was something in the way he mentioned that he had not cared for Miss Whitlock, almost in an offhanded way, that made me scrutinize him more closely. For all that he appeared repentant, there was something in the creases at the corner of his lips or perhaps the shiftiness of his eyes that made me suspect he'd dropped in that remark quite deliberately, as if it was bait.

And Lord Gage snapped it up. "Why did you not care for Miss Whitlock?"

When he hesitated before responding, I was more certain than ever that he was acting with calculation. And if my husband's expression was anything to judge by, he suspected it as well.

"I do not wish to speak ill of the dead . . ."

I nearly snorted at this.

"But she was not the most conscientious of individuals." His lips tightened in disdain. "It was quite clear to me how she attained her position."

"Pretty, wasn't she?" I needled casually, hoping for a reaction.

He glowered at me. "I suppose to some." He sniffed. "But not really to my taste."

Except that was a lie. Even Lord Gage recognized it.

"How exactly wasn't she conscientious?" he asked.

Thorndike rolled his neck and shoulders, playing for time. "She was lax at her duties, for one. Took an *entire* day to recuperate from their journey." His voice conveyed his doubts about this. "And what I could see of her paperwork, it was slapdash at best."

"And what exactly did you see of her paperwork?" I queried. The documents might have been removed from Miss Whitlock's chamber, but if Thorndike had some inkling of what they'd contained, it might help us.

But this also appeared to be a lie. "Not much content. I would never stoop to prying in another man's business."

I couldn't tell if this was meant to be insulting or not, but he seemed to recognize his error, hastening to correct himself.

"They were Mr. Birnam's private papers, after all, but it was riddled with sloppy penmanship and skewed numbers."

Lord Gage seemed to find this as implausible as I did, for his voice lowered as if he was near the end of his patience. "We also understand that you suggested Miss Whitlock was unnatural and unfit for her position." He arched a single eyebrow. "That someone ought to teach her to mind?"

His shoulders stiffened, and this time the reaction was more genuine. "I realize in light of everything that's happened how that sounds, but I never meant to imply that *I* would be the one to do so."

Hadn't he? I narrowed my eyes. I wasn't so sure about that.

"I simply meant . . ." He paused to swallow, another

delaying tactic. "That there are many men who wouldn't take kindly to her holding such a position when it rightly belongs to a man. Her place should be at home rather than taking a good livelihood from a man, perhaps one with a family to support."

"And if she's an orphan with no family to keep her?" Gage interceded, his voice pitched with disinterest, almost as if he didn't truly care about the answer. However, I had learned long ago that when my husband was suppressing the inflection of his voice, he was more invested than ever in the response. Especially when he adopted the stance he now took with his fingers laced together over his flat abdomen. "Or she's of the inclination that she wishes to support herself? Should she still be forced to wed?"

"Of course. It's simply the lot God gave her. She can't change that." Thorndike leaned forward. "She *shouldn't*."

"And if there's no suitable man to marry? Of acceptable station, temperament, good standing? What then?"

He scoffed. "Then she's too fussy."

I had no doubt Gage was working toward pinning the secretary with some important point. Perhaps that, still unwed at a score and ten, Thorndike was not exactly an authority to speak for women. And I was content to allow Gage to continue. Truthfully, I was rather relishing the prospect of my husband skewering the fellow. But for whatever reason, his father elected to spoil it, though he was as aware of his son's tactics as I was, for they were also his own.

"Maybe, Thorndike. But there are men who are simply not fit for marriage." His eyebrows arched, seeming to communicate something specific. "Just as there are men who are not fit for fatherhood, and it is their wives, just as it is their children, who are the ones who suffer for it." He shook his head sadly. "You cannot blame a wise woman for thinking twice."

My ire at Lord Gage for interrupting turned to astonishment. For I couldn't help but think that he was speaking of Sir Anthony when he mentioned men unfit for marriage. It left me feeling a bit like I'd been punched in the stomach, albeit not with malicious intent. Still, I struggled to draw my next breath.

Gage obviously sensed this, for he glanced at me in concern, though he did not reach out and risk exposing something so personal to Mr. Thorndike's prying eyes. Though I was also certain Lord Gage had just revealed something equally personal about his secretary. For the remark about fathers and children had plainly been aimed at him.

Thorndike's response was to glower at the rug. He was clearly battling strong emotions, one of which was undoubtedly shame similar to what I still struggled to shed about my own failed marriage. Whether he would have conceded his employer's point, I didn't know, but there was more behind his mindset about the issue than the typical ignorance and almost willful denial that left so many women and children vulnerable.

"Why did you depart the dining room early on the evening you were invited to dine with us?" Gage asked, both rescuing the man from any unpleasant memories that had been raised by Lord Gage's remark and also returning to a point on which we still needed clarification. "Why didn't you remain for port?"

Thorndike's gaze sharpened briefly at my husband in dislike before shifting to his employer.

Lord Gage cleared his throat. "I asked him to leave. I didn't think it . . . advisable for him to remain."

Then Gage's earlier speculations about the matter were correct. It was his father's fault that Thorndike had departed early, not the secretary's own behest. But that didn't mean something useful still couldn't be gleaned from it.

"Did you notice anything unusual?" I queried. "Which way did you go?"

Thorndike didn't hide the fact that he found these questions odd. "Through the blue room and across the great hall to here. I collected my things from my office and left through the side door." For when in Warwickshire, he lived in a cottage a few hundred yards north of the stable block—one of half a dozen such homes utilized by a select number of staff members. "And no. I didn't see anything . . . unusual."

I couldn't tell if he was mocking me, but regardless, Gage took offense on my behalf.

"It's a perfectly legitimate question, Thorndike. Or do you have something to hide?"

The secretary straightened, smoothing away any trace of disrespect from his expression. "No, sir. Apologies, my lady."

I decided it was best to carry on as if his insolence had never occurred. "So you didn't notice anyone in the great hall or up on the pass-through balcony?"

This query seemed to give him pause. "Not in the great hall, no. But I don't think I took any time to note the balcony."

This sounded like an honest answer. The length of the great hall was immense, and as he was passing along the end farthest from the balcony and the place where Miss Whitlock and I had stopped to confer, it was feasible that he'd seen nothing. He might have even passed through before we entered. Because of this, I didn't press him further.

Lord Gage waited as if to confirm neither his son nor I had any more questions before addressing his secretary. "Understand this, Mr. Thorndike. You are on thin ice. I expect you to be obliging and respectful from this moment forward, and I shall let you know at the end of the week whether I shall still require your services. Is that understood?"

"Yes, my lord."

He was dismissed by a wave of Lord Gage's hand and hurried back to his office.

Gage waited until the door shut and his footsteps were heard receding before turning to ask me, "Do you believe him?"

I considered my response. "Yes. But only because I find it difficult to believe he would resort to such drastic measures. It would also seem out of character for him to throw actual oil of vitriol in a woman's face simply to teach her a lesson."

"He does seem more the type to use the vitriol of his words." Gage's voice sharpened with censure. "Or barring that, petty bullying."

"Agreed." Lord Gage's gaze was still trained on the door through which Thorndike had fled. I didn't like the man's chances of keeping his position. Not that there was anyone else to blame but himself.

"Now then," Lord Gage declared, turning to his son. "What was it you were saying about Birnam's manservant?"

This must have been the conversation I'd interrupted when I'd found them earlier standing next to the sideboard in the dining room.

"Anderley and I wish to question him," Gage informed his father. "But it will need to be done while Birnam is otherwise occupied. Can you manage that?"

Lord Gage rubbed his chin as a smile crossed his lips of which I was instinctively wary. "Leave it to me."

CHAPTER 15

My father-in-law did not deem to share his intentions with us, but he promised Gage he would ensure Birnam never left the south lawn where the amusements we had planned were to take place.

"We'll try to corner Paget near the northwest side entrance, if you'd like to listen in," Gage murmured as we made our way along the corridor toward the back terrace. "However, if I read the man correctly, I don't recommend speaking up." His expression turned stony. "He's more likely to respond to a show of force."

I realized what this meant, though I hated the necessity. Having witnessed Gage and Anderley work together to interrogate a suspect before, I trusted they wouldn't actually use violence, merely the threat of it. But it wasn't my favorite tactic. I knew it wasn't my husband's first choice either.

Arriving on the terrace, we discovered a number of the

guests already gathered. Many of the ladies were dressed in similar attire to my own, which would accommodate a freer range of movement for wielding a bow or swinging a mallet. Truth be told, I wished I could wear gowns like this archery dress every day, for it was also devoid of the voluminous sleeves I so despised. The gentlemen wore loose trousers and sporting coats in earthen hues.

Gage and I led the party down into the garden and then along the path around to the side of the house where a slope led to the south lawn. Beyond it lay the sparkling pond that Emma so adored. I noted a few fishing poles had been propped along the shore for the gentlemen's amusement. Targets had been erected along one end of the lawn, at the edge of the western woods, while the lawn billiard court had been laid out on the other. Between them, at the base of the slope rising to Bevington Hall, a white canopy had been erected and chairs and tables set out beneath it for spectators.

While warm, a cover of clouds had staved off the worst of the heat, and a cooling breeze from the southwest provided some relief. If we were fortunate, we might have rain later.

Lord Gage was slow to join us, but I soon realized why when I saw him leading Mr. Birnam down the slope. I wasn't certain what his plans were to keep the man distracted while Gage spoke to his manservant, but evidently, he intended to enact them immediately.

He called for our attention as they reached the canopy where we'd all gathered. "We shall begin our archery tournament shortly, and Mr. Birnam, here, has agreed to be our fair and impartial judge."

Some of the guests began to clap, and we all joined in, much to Birnam's delight. His color was improved, and I was curious if he'd finally taken some medication to ease his pain or if it was the fresh air and the chance to direct his thoughts to something else.

"Ladies, you will go first, so select your bow carefully." Lord Gage swept his hand toward the area where all the equipment had been laid out.

Alana and I jostled each other playfully in our haste to choose the best bow.

"What is the record? My one hundred thirteen to your one hundred twelve," Alana taunted as we began sorting through the available options.

"Not for long, dear sister," I quipped in return.

There had been a time when Alana, Trevor, and I had indulged in a fierce rivalry over our archery skills, shooting practically every day on the back lawn of Blakelaw House. But that was long ago, and our opportunities to compete against each other since had been few and far between. Though that didn't mean we weren't all quite aware of the current standing score.

"Oh, how quaint," Lorna interjected. "Though there's no need to squabble over second place."

"You think you can best us?" Alana turned to demand.

"Oh, 'best' is such a modest word," Lorna stated, patting her pale blond plaited hair to ensure it was still in place. She flashed her white teeth. "Decimate is more like it."

Alana scoured her figure with a derisive glare. "We shall see about that."

I couldn't restrain a smile as the two hurried off ahead of me still trading barbs. It widened when I turned to find Matilda staring at us wide-eyed as if we'd lost our minds. "It's all in good fun," I told her, looping my arm through hers to lead her toward the field of battle after pausing long enough to collect a quill of arrows for both of us. "Didn't you and your brother ever tease each other?"

"No . . . Well, a little." A pleat formed between her brows. "Actually, when we were younger, Portia was the one most likely to tease me."

I turned to search her face, recalling that she'd said Miss Whitlock and Matilda had almost been like sisters. "In fun, I hope?"

"Oh, yes. Portia was never deliberately cruel." But her response only seemed to trouble her more.

"You miss her," I said gently, suspecting it was the truth, whether she would admit it or not.

"Oh, no." She laughed nervously. "Why would I? Even though she was my father's secretary, we've barely spoken in years."

But that didn't mean she didn't still miss her, didn't still miss the friendship they'd once had. I wondered who had been at fault for their not having rekindled it upon Miss Whitlock's return. Had Matilda, perhaps under the influence of her mother, felt the social gulf too wide and a friendship inappropriate given Miss Whitlock's new position? It would admittedly have been awkward. Or had Miss Whitlock established the boundary, knowing the complications that could ensue?

Had we been alone, I would have pried deeper, but I had no desire to expose her tender emotions to the scrutiny of those around us. So instead, I squeezed her arm where it linked with mine. "I confess, I cannot recall the last time I fired an arrow." I'd lowered my voice as if confiding a secret.

"It is likely my sister will trounce me," I added with a laugh. "Are *you* any good at this?"

"Only adequate," she demurred.

But this proved to be a lie. Matilda was far more than adequate. She was quite good. Good enough to advance to the final round against Lorna. I had to settle for third, and the happy knowledge that at least I'd bested Alana. A fact I made sure to crow about.

"We're tied, dearest. *Tied*," Alana retorted with a sniff. "You still haven't bested me overall."

"She's a terrible loser, isn't she?" her husband, Philip, leaned over to mock whisper, earning himself a swat on the arm.

"Used to fill my bed with acorns when I bested her," Trevor declared.

Alana glared at him, but I could only gasp. "You never told me that? How did I not know that?" After all, I'd lived in the same house with them.

"I was but too honorable," Trevor replied with a false solemnity he ruined by grimacing. "And our governess threatened to tan my hide if she found any unwarranted forms of nature or wildlife in my room."

Gage erupted into laughter.

"And you knew that, didn't you?" I accused Alana.

She merely shrugged, though the brief curl at the corner of her lips revealed the truth.

"That's my girl!" Alfie shouted as Lorna let fly her first arrow of the final round.

We all turned to watch, cheering for both women. It was a tight contest, but in the end, Lorna emerged the victor, much to her husband's delight. Alfie even proposed to lift her up on his shoulder and parade her about. She countered that if he did, she'd slice his favorite coat to ribbons.

Meanwhile, Trevor consoled Matilda, who was grinning, accepting the loss with good cheer.

"Now, that's the way to lose," Philip continued to tease, and I thought for a moment Alana would do him true violence. Fortunately, whatever he murmured to her next made her snort with laughter.

I turned to Gage with a smile, but his attention was diverted elsewhere. I then noticed Anderley along the path toward the house, sending him a discreet signal.

"Follow me after a few moments," Gage urged.

"You're not going to shoot?" I asked.

"Not if the timing doesn't coincide." With this, he slipped away.

The men were already jostling each other over the bows, preparing for their turn. There would probably not be a more perfect time when most of the party was preoccupied either by participating in or watching the men's archery contest. Philip, Alfie, and Trevor, in particular, were filled with high jinks, and I wondered if Gage had hinted to one or more of them that a distraction was required. However, Jemmy, Baron Foley, Lord Brougham, Lord Milngavie, and even old Lord Strathblane appeared to be getting into the spirit of the contest. I was almost sorry to steal away.

As I neared the corner pavilion of the manor and the side entrance that led into the billiards room, I heard voices coming from the western face. Realizing Gage and Anderley must have cornered Paget there rather than inside the vestibule, I stopped with my back to the wall to listen.

"We already know about your past, Paget," Gage stated coldly. "Quite the criminal record."

I didn't know if this was something Anderley had since uncovered for fact or merely speculation, but Birnam's valet didn't attempt to deny it.

"In fact, if I were to identify someone here with the experience and mindset to commit such a deed, it would be you."

"I ain't never killed nobody," Paget growled. "That's no' in my *experience*," he retorted.

"Maybe you hadn't before," Anderley chimed in. "But we know you've pulled other nasty tricks. That you've pulled them for your employer. What's to say he didn't put you up to this one, too?"

But Paget only responded with a harrumphing noise. Or perhaps it had been a muttered curse, for Gage tsked. "He may have told you something to the contrary, but I don't imagine he'll be quick to step in to save you, should you be arrested. Not when he's determined to sway the gentlemen here to his view of the Factory Act revisions. Not when those gentlemen would all too readily believe us should we decry you as the culprit and reveal your criminal history."

"I ken that bumptious lass would cause me grief one day," Paget groused. "Warned Birnam the same, but would he listen? Nay!" Gravel crunched as someone shifted their feet. "She was a troublesome one. Always stickin' her nose where she shouldn't. Tourin' the mills and factories. Talkin' tae the men." His voice was gruff with harsh disapproval. "But Birnam said, 'let her,' so I did."

"Isn't that part of her job?" Anderley asked.

"Nay!" Paget retorted sharply. "She's himself's *personal*

secretary. She's no cause tae have anythin' tae do wi' the factories."

"But surely even a personal secretary would have dealings with his businesses?" Gage pointed out.

"But she was a lady!" Paget countered, apparently of the same opinion as Thorndike. "She had nay place there. No' unless she was one o' the lasses workin' the looms."

"Is that why you doused her with acid? Because she wouldn't mind her place?" Anderley pressed.

"Yer a bloody fool if ye think it was me," he snapped icily. "A bloody fool!"

"But you couldn't have been happy your employer was going to meet her under such odd circumstances," Gage interjected silkily. "You said you'd seen the note she left him," he reminded him.

"I said I'd seen it, *not* that I'd read it."

"Oh, come now. Not even a word or two?" Anderley baited.

"Nay!"

"A likely story."

"I canna read, ye lummox."

I straightened. Well, this changed matters.

"You cannot read," Gage clarified. "So you don't, in fact, know what this note Birnam allegedly received said?"

"I never claimed tae have read it," Paget protested. "Only that I'd seen himself pick up a paper that'd been slipped under his door, read it, and set it on the desk. That's all!"

This much at least seemed to be true, for he'd not altered his story even under circumstances that might have easily tripped him up.

"Did he tell you where he was going?" Anderley continued to push.

Paget's tone was withering. "Perhaps yer employer is different, but most do no' bother tae give their servants an accountin' o' their whereabouts. Mine certainly doesna."

He was right. Most didn't, even Gage.

"Noo, if there's nothin' more . . ." Paget slipped away before either of them could stop him, charging past the spot where I was concealed without looking back.

I waited a few moments before approaching the corner where Gage and Anderley stood.

"I wondered if you were listening," my husband admitted. His brow was furrowed in frustration. "What do you think?"

I turned to watch Paget as he continued down the slope toward where the other members of the staff were clustered, ready to assist. "He's clearly loyal to Birnam, but how loyal?"

Gage agreed with a sigh.

"What did you make of what he said about Miss Whitlock touring the mill and factories and speaking to the men?" I asked.

Gage exchanged a glance with Anderley. "It could mean nothing."

"Or it could mean everything," the valet supplied for him.

And that was the trouble. We still didn't know what information was pertinent and what was not. Not until we were certain of who the intended victim was.

"Let's rejoin the party before we're missed," Gage advised, offering me his arm to help me navigate down the slope. Anderley followed behind us, peeling off toward the group of staff like Paget had. The maids and footmen present seemed just as invested in the men's contest as the guests were, laughing and groaning and cheering along.

"Sad you missed out?" I asked my husband as we drew near.

"No," he answered blithely before flashing me a smug smile. "Besides, it's best I let someone else win from time to time."

I couldn't help but laugh. A sound that was nearly drowned out by the raucous shouts of the others over some contested feat. However, Gage heard me, and his smile warmed with genuine pleasure and then tender regard, making me flush with delight. Had we not been surrounded by several dozen people, I was quite certain he would have kissed me. Thoroughly.

I turned away, inhaling a deep breath to still my heart, and pressed a hand to the top of my head as a gust of wind threatened to dislodge my bonnet. This was just in time to hear a series of wild squawks coming from the direction of the pond.

"Good heavens!" one of the women exclaimed as the flock of ducks which had been swimming serenely across the surface of the water suddenly burst into panicked flight, with the result that two of them appeared to have collided into one another.

"Look, your terrible aim has even frightened the birds away, lest they be winged," Lord Melbourne called out to everyone's amusement.

It was only as the laughter died away that we became aware that something else even more alarming had occurred. A woman, who I later discovered was Mrs. Birnam, screamed, and we all turned back from the distraction, attempting to discover the source of her distress. It was Mr. Birnam. He lay sprawled across the ground at the opposite end of the archery range, though it wasn't immediately apparent why. Had he fallen?

Gage and his father began to make their way over to him, slowly at first and then with more haste when it was realized that an arrow stood with its tip either buried in the ground very near Mr. Birnam or within his body itself.

"Someone fired at Birnam," a guest gasped in outrage just as Gage broke into a run, with Anderley and Paget following close behind.

CHAPTER 16

I moved to follow, worried that Birnam might require medical attention. Turning to scrutinize the archers as I loped forward, I noted their dawning realization and confusion, each of them glancing left and right at the men next to them.

Reaching Birnam, I spotted Paget grasping the shaft of the arrow. "Don't pull it out!" I ordered him. "He could bleed to death."

But once the people surrounding Birnam separated enough for me to see fully, I could tell that the arrow had not struck Birnam but the ground.

"Oh, thank God!" I panted, pressing a hand to my pounding heart. "Are you injured anywhere, sir?"

Birnam appeared stunned, but with Gage and Anderley's aid was helped to sit upright. "I . . . I don't think so." He blinked rapidly, his bandaged hands held out in front of him.

"Your jacket, sir," Paget cried.

He was right. There was a tear on the sleeve. I knelt to examine it, relieved to see it had not caught the shirt or skin beneath.

"It only tore the fabric," I reported. "But still, too close for comfort," I added worryingly.

"Who fired the arrow?" Lord Gage demanded to know as we all turned to gaze across the field, but the archers were still looking at one another in bafflement. "Who fired the arrow?" he yelled more loudly. Still, no one stepped forward.

I exchanged a concerned glance with Gage. Had this not been an accident? Had it been a second attempt on Mr. Birnam's life?

Gage rose to his feet, gesturing for Anderley to follow him. "Had they all fired the same number of arrows?"

"It was the end of the round," Alana replied, joining us.

Gage nodded and lengthened his stride, presumably intending to speak to the archers and collect their quills. Though I wasn't sure that would tell us anything definitively. The archer who fired the arrow might have taken it from another contestant's quill.

Paget was now helping Mr. Birnam to his feet. It appeared he'd recovered his wits, for he aimed a venomous glare at my father-in-law. "Was this your plan, Lord Gage? Silence me once and for all."

"Don't be absurd," he replied scornfully.

"Is it? *You're* the one who asked me tae judge."

In order to keep Birnam busy so that Gage could interrogate Paget.

But Lord Gage mentioned none of this. "Because in your

current state, you can't hold a bow. It seemed logical to ask you to be the judge." His lips curled with derision. "I thought you'd relish it."

"Weel, I dinna relish bein' shot at!"

"Gentlemen," Alana interrupted. "This isn't helping. Let's return to the spectator area so that Mr. Birnam might have a seat and we can discuss this more rationally. Surely, it was an accident, and the culprit is simply too ashamed to come forward. Barring that, someone must have seen *something*!"

But no one had. Or at least, they wouldn't admit to it. We'd all been too distracted by the ducks and Melbourne's jest. We'd turned away from the archery range. Even the archers denied knowing who'd fired the arrow. They'd also been diverted.

Even after questioning each of the eight men individually, I could not sense artifice in any of them, though I'd never truly considered Philip, Trevor, or Alfie to be suspects in the first place. Most of them seemed genuinely shocked, bewildered, and outraged—more so that someone would attempt such a thing than that they were being quizzed about it. Collecting the quills ended up being a pointless endeavor, for the staff that had gathered the arrows after the ladies contest had not ensured each quill held the same number of arrows. Considering it was supposed to be a friendly competition, this had seemed unnecessary. As it should have been! Except for someone's reckless actions.

I found my temper fraying the longer the day wore on and the more the heat climbed. We had released most of the guests long ago, allowing them to return to the manor to escape the sun, which had emerged from the clouds, and to partake of the cold luncheon laid out in the dining room. I, on the other hand, had been subsisting on tepid tea, for I could not stomach it hot.

Paget had been ordered to stay close to Birnam's side until we figured out what had happened. It was the best we could do.

Trevor insisted on being the last archer interviewed. I suspected this was as much about lingering to overhear what he could of the other discussions, but we did not argue. Now it was just him, Gage, and me left, with Anderley lingering in the background. Like all the others, he was baffled as to how he could have failed to see anything, but he had an important question to ask.

"Does this mean that Miss Whitlock was killed by mistake? That Mr. Birnam was the intended victim?"

I noted the glint of hopefulness in his eyes that he failed to hide. For if Mr. Birnam had been the target, then it was unlikely that any of the other Birnams had been the killer.

Gage turned to me, allowing me to respond to my brother.

"It would seem so." I frowned. "And yet, I'm not entirely convinced."

"But someone fired an arrow at Birnam, presumably trying to kill him, as close as that shot was," Trevor contended.

"Yes, but . . . how did *no one* witness who fired the arrow?" I asked all three men. "Could the shot have come from a different direction?"

"Maybe?" Gage hazarded. But that would mean we were looking for a suspect outside our current list. The only person currently under consideration who had *not* been present was Ann McClintock, Mrs. Birnam's maid. I supposed it was possible she'd fired an arrow at Mr. Birnam from the shelter of the western woods, but the idea still seemed slightly mad.

Though the fact remained, *someone* had fired an arrow at Birnam.

"Maybe there *was* nothing to witness," Anderley said, speaking up for the first time.

I turned to him in confusion. "What do you mean?"

"Maybe the arrow wasn't actually fired," he explained. "Maybe Birnam ripped his own coat with one of the arrows littering the area near the targets and plunged it into the ground as he pretended to be knocked down." He shrugged.

I turned this new notion over in my mind, examining it for flaws.

"It would explain why no one heard or saw the shot," Gage conceded. "Just like no one saw him being hit."

"But his hands," Trevor argued. "He's in too much pain to have managed such a thing."

"You'd be surprised what the human body can endure when it or a loved one is threatened," Gage declared, and I knew he was speaking from experience. "If he thought one of his family members might be guilty of attacking and killing Miss Whitlock and afraid that they would be discovered, he might attempt something drastic."

"I'd noted his pain seemed better managed today," I confessed. "Though I don't know what he used to numb it."

"Probably whisky," Gage suggested. "Did you not smell it on him?"

"You cannot genuinely believe that Birnam would stage an attack on himself," Trevor exclaimed. "I know he can be a bit . . . difficult, but that's madness!"

"I'm not saying he did." I lifted my hands, attempting to soothe his agitation even as mine grew. "And right now, for his safety and that of the rest of the guests, I think we must operate under the assumption that he genuinely *was* attacked. But I also don't think we can dismiss the possibility that he feigned it in order to divert suspicion away from himself and his loved ones."

Trevor appeared as if he'd still like to dispute this, crossing his arms hostilely.

For me, this was suddenly the final straw. "Think whatever you want," I huffed, pushing to my feet. "I'm going to eat."

I strode furiously up the slope, growing a bit lightheaded by the time I reached the top from the exertion and the heat, and the fact I'd barely eaten that day. So much so that I had to pause to catch my breath, pressing my hand to the wall in much the same place Gage and Anderley had interrogated Paget earlier.

"Birnam thinks Lord Gage is behind it."

At the mention of my father-in-law's name my ears perked up.

"That's balderdash," a second older male voice responded.

"Maybe. But where was his son? He didn't take part in the competition."

I'd heard Birnam make his allegation against Lord Gage, but I'd thought it would go no further beyond that. However, here it was being discussed by these two men, who if I was not mistaken were Lord Milngavie and Lord Strathblane. My irritation returned, particularly at hearing my own husband implicated.

Fortunately, Strathblane seemed sensible. "He was standing in the crowd of spectators next to his wife. Came running as soon as anyone realized something was wrong." He paused and I heard a wheeze of an exhale that suggested the men had been smoking. Now that I'd noted it, I could also smell the faint tang of cheroots. They must have been standing in the vestibule of the side entrance, just outside the billiards room. "Can't very well have fired an arrow out of that crowd with no one noticing."

Lord Milngavie seemed to give this some consideration. "What of his manservant? I've heard rumors he's quite the capable fellow."

"He came running from the area where the staff was congregated." He made another puffed exhalation. "You don't truly believe our host is behind it, do you?" Strathblane sounded aghast.

"No," Milngavie answered easily after only a moment's hesitation. "But I can't seem to work out how anyone else did it either."

He was clearly frustrated by this fact, and I listened more closely in case he had any further insights.

"You were nearest the spectators, so it's understandable you wouldn't have seen anything, but I was at the opposite end, Strathblane. Farthest from the crowds. I can't help but think I would have *noticed* had one of the archers raised their bow and fired despite all the distractions. It just doesn't make sense."

"Then you think the arrow came from a different direction?" Strathblane queried.

"Maybe."

I could hear the consternation in Milngavie's voice, the tension, and I wondered if his mind was formulating the same suspicion Anderley's had. If so, I found it interesting that a third party had come to the same conclusion.

Truth be told, I'd not known what to make of Milngavie's behavior when we'd questioned him. He'd been one of the archers who'd seemed angry. But now I could tell the emotion he'd been struggling with was more a sense of exasperation and bewilderment.

Someone called to the men inside the billiards room, so I moved on before I was caught eavesdropping. But their conversation stayed with me as I went to seek my own luncheon.

Refreshed and restored after having a tray sent to my room and a brief respite before the window where the sharp breeze from an incoming storm had cooled my cheeks, I set off for Mr. Birnam's chamber to change his bandages. I could have waited a few more hours to complete the task, but after the morning's excitement, I'd decided a friendly chat would not be out of order. A rumble of thunder crackled in the distance as I turned the corner, and I spared a moment to wonder if Emma's nap would be interrupted by the storm.

Reaching Mr. Birnam's door, I rapped and then turned to scrutinize a watercolor hanging on the wall opposite while I waited for Birnam or Paget to answer. There was a long lull in which I heard nothing but the rumble of thunder, and I'd begun to wonder if Birnam was elsewhere, when the vibration of a heavy tread reached my ears.

Paget scowled at me as he opened the door.

"Good afternoon," I said politely. "I've come to see how Mr. Birnam is faring and to change his dressings."

"'Tis already done," he stated hostilely even as he allowed me to enter.

"What do you mean?" I asked in confusion before focusing

on Mr. Birnam where he was seated on the same settee as the day before. I crossed the room in dawning dismay and vexation as Paget scoffed.

"I can change a bandage, m'lady. 'Tisn't so very hard."

"Except it's not merely a matter of wrapping the wounds in a fresh dressing," I snapped. "The wounds must be examined to ensure they're healing correctly, and the pressure and tautness of the bandage adjusted to account for variations."

"The wounds looked the same tae me," he replied, his face pale, and I recalled the squeamishness Dr. Clarke had alluded to.

"You might think, but do you know the signs of necrosis? Are you able to recognize the slight variations in tissue coloration and inflammation that might allow us to act swiftly to save a part of Mr. Birnam's hands?" I gestured furiously toward the appendages in question as I pinned Paget with my gaze. "What of the smell? Did you make note of it?"

He stared at me as if I'd grown a second head.

"It's a pertinent question, Mr. Paget. Necrosis has a stench. Yet, you didn't bother to notice, did you?"

"Enough, Mrs. Gage," Birnam interrupted blearily. "You've made yer point. Paget will no' change my dressings wi' oot the doctor's approval. Ye may change them. But tomorrow. I canna stomach it again taeday."

And no wonder why. He reeked of whisky and, if I wasn't mistaken, was already foxed. Judging from his greenish hue, he was close to casting up his accounts, and I did not wish to be present when he did so.

"Very well." I turned to point my finger at Paget. "But I shall hold you to your word or else not be accountable when your employer's fingers rot."

Paget's scowl hadn't abated, but he nodded in acceptance.

"You may want to fetch him the chamber pot," I added in parting as I marched past him and out the door.

Evidently, Mr. Birnam was either in more pain than he dared to admit or even more agonized over Miss Whitlock's death than he wanted us to know. Perhaps both. I wished he would allow Lorna to prepare him an herbal tincture. It would be far better for his constitution than whisky. I sighed. But we could not force the stubborn man to see reason.

The thunderstorm continued to growl overhead as rain lashed the windows. Knowing this would keep everyone inside, I strolled through the chambers where everyone was most likely to have gathered, ensuring they were all well settled. Most of the men had congregated in the billiards room and adjoining green drawing room. The windows there had been thrown open to the covered terrace, and several of the men stood conversing and watching the storm.

Leaving behind the clack of the billiard balls, I entered the adjoining red saloon to find it empty except for Lord Lyndhurst, who sat reading. Not wishing to disturb him, I nodded in greeting and continued on through to the mauve drawing room. Here the windows to the terrace were shut save for one that was cracked to allow a slight breeze. Alana was playing the pianoforte while Lady Lyndhurst and Lady Brougham were bent over their needlework, idly chatting. Lorna was nowhere to be seen, but I suspected she was upstairs in the nursery, where I was bound next.

That is, after a stop outside Mrs. Birnam's door. I'd not failed to notice that she and Matilda were both also absent. However, no one answered my summons when I knocked.

Clearly, they were still unwilling to confide in us. One

would have thought after the incident with the arrow they would be more eager to speak with us, lest Mr. Birnam be attacked again. For it was doubtful that, if he'd feigned the attack, he'd informed anyone of his intentions save Paget, who must have riled the ducks somehow to distract us all.

Frustration bubbled up inside me, for we needed them to talk to us, or else we might never get to the bottom of Portia Whitlock's murder.

I hated to think that was exactly what they wanted, but the longer they refused, the more guilty they looked.

CHAPTER 17

The storms forestalled Gage's and my plans to retreat to the dower house with Emma that afternoon, but they didn't stop me from spending more than an hour in the nursery with my daughter. We read books and played with her doll Rosie, and then curled up together in the window seat, watching the rain while she chattered away and I pretended to understand. I would have stayed longer, but a maid from the kitchens came looking for me. Duty called.

Once a snaggle over the evening's menu was sorted, there were queries from Mrs. Taylor about the rooms being prepared for the additional guests arriving on Saturday. Then Bowcott needed instructions for the ball. It was to be held in the great hall, which meant rearranging most of the furnishings. We debated the merit of positioning the small orchestra in a corner versus the balcony overhead, ultimately deciding on the balcony.

Gage, his father, and I had briefly conferred about urging the new guests not to come or, at the very least, canceling the ball. But we'd swiftly realized that many of the guests were even now en route, and if we were already going to have a house filled with people, what difference would a few dozen more arriving for a ball make? All things considered, our only course seemed to be to forge ahead. And hope we apprehended Miss Whitlock's killer before anyone else reached Bevington Park.

By the time I retired to my bedchamber to switch gowns, I had only moments to exchange the briefest greeting with Gage, who thankfully was already dressed in his dark evening attire, before sending him down ahead of me to greet the guests in the mauve drawing room before dinner. I must have appeared as ragged as I felt, for he gripped my hand when I would have turned away.

"Tomorrow morning after breakfast," he promised. "We'll collect Emma and slip away."

To our home in the dower house, he meant. I smiled up at him in gratitude, and he leaned forward to steal a kiss before haring off to shoulder our responsibilities.

Dinner that evening was a fractious affair. Clearly, the day's events had proved universally unsettling, for many of the guests behaved either irritably or giddily. It was not the most conducive combination, particularly to the group's harmony. Before the last course was served, I was so frazzled from smoothing over tiny squabbles and deliberate misunderstandings that I was considering leaving the table without a word and fleeing into the night, heedless of the gossip that would arise from such an act. Gage appeared as if he wanted to join me.

I was only too glad when it became time for the ladies to adjourn to the drawing room. I deliberately slowed my steps as we processed, hoping to speak with Mrs. Birnam, but she seemed determined to avoid me. At the doorway to the drawing room, I glanced back to find her turning toward the staircase while Matilda advanced toward me.

"Mother isn't feeling well," she said, her voice soft with nerves. "She asked me to make our excuses."

In other words, she expected her daughter to retire as well, to attend to her. Perhaps I should have been more charitable. Perhaps I should have accepted this flimsy pretext with a gracious nod. But Mrs. Birnam certainly hadn't seemed indisposed at dinner, and I was tired of her rude dismissals and the domineering way she treated her daughter.

Matilda's eyes widened in surprise as I marched past her toward the base of the staircase.

"You really must speak with us, Mrs. Birnam," I called up to her as she slowly mounted the steps.

"No, I really must not," she replied, not even bothering to turn to address me.

I ground my teeth and turned to Matilda, who shrank back a step at the ire in my eyes. "You are all making this much worse for yourselves. Your silence only communicates callousness and guilt. The truth will out, Miss Birnam. It always does. And when it does, you may find you've forfeited the opportunity to explain."

With this, I whirled away, striding around the corner into the great room in order to take a moment to collect myself. Rarely did I speak so harshly to anyone, and the memory of Matilda's wounded expression made it worse. But truly, someone needed to make her see reason. Her mother might be compelling her to remain silent, but she was the one ultimately choosing to obey.

I closed my eyes, pressing my hand to the tight cornflower blue bodice of my gown as I tried to slow my breathing. I would linger a few more seconds, allowing Matilda a chance to make her escape. Her mother would be waiting for her at the top of the staircase, making sure she obeyed.

Feeling my pulse slow, I returned to the corridor to rejoin the other ladies but was brought up short by the sound of raised voices. They were coming from the dining room, and they seemed furious. Though I couldn't make out every word being said, they seemed to be discussing the Factory Act.

". . . You're only concerned with profits!"

"Those bairns' families need their extra wages tae survive. Refusin' 'em work or shortenin' their day only creates greater harm." That was Mr. Birnam, presumably making an argument for why children under the age of nine should be allowed to work in his factories and why children between the ages of nine and thirteen should be able to work longer than nine hours in a day.

The second man, whom I now recognized as mild-mannered Lord Milngavie, hurled a few insults at Birnam before addressing the point from a different angle. ". . . then ye should pay the workers ye *do* have more, so that they're no' reliant on sellin' their weens oot as slaves!" Such was his anger that the Scots brogue he strangled in order to speak like an Etonian-educated nobleman broke through.

Birnam retorted with a few insults of his own. Ones so vile that even I was shocked, and several of the other men spoke up to object. A woman behind me gasped, and I turned to see that the shouting had even captured the attention of the other ladies in the drawing room.

"What would ye ken aboot it?" Birnam flung out at the last.

"I ken plenty," Milngavie snapped just before he thrust open the dining room door with a bang, startling most of the ladies listening. He stumbled to a halt, clearly not realizing the audience they'd garnered. His cheeks flushed before he offered us a penitent bow. "Apologies, ladies," he murmured and then retreated up the stairs.

I ushered the women back into the drawing room, hardly knowing what to say. That had been an unexpected and rather disconcerting altercation.

When the gentlemen joined us, they seemed to deliberately avoid discussing it. I could tell from Lord Gage's face that these latest developments were not to his liking. I could also tell that he felt Gage and I were not working fast enough to resolve the matter of Miss Whitlock's murder. But truly, I didn't know what miracles he expected when we were thwarted at every turn.

"This was not the house party you were hoping for, was it?"

Recognizing my sister's voice, I straightened more slowly from the slouch I'd adopted, perched on a bench hidden amid the rose arbor the following morning. I'd come out here looking for Matilda, who I knew preferred the gardens, and not finding her, decided to steal a moment to myself.

I couldn't have known for sure that Alana had been searching specifically for me. She might just as easily have been taking a stroll among the beauty of the flowers. But somehow, I knew she was there for me.

"No," I admitted, not even bothering to put on a brave face. "Now I know how you felt when Lady Godwin was murdered," I commiserated, harkening back to the house party Alana had hosted nearly three years ago to reintroduce me to society after my scandal. One of the guests had been murdered, and because of my macabre reputation, I'd been pinned as the likeliest suspect. Of course, I had also met Gage, and we'd embarked on our first inquiry together, so it wasn't all bad. My life had certainly changed irrevocably since that moment.

"Yes, well, everything turned out well in the end." She sank down beside me, her brow lightly furrowing. "For most of us."

I guessed she was thinking of Lady Godwin and her murderer, who had ended up dead himself. It was a morbid topic for such a beautiful morning. The storms and rain had moved on, leaving behind cooler temperatures and sunshine.

"I suppose this is at least partially my fault," Alana said. "After all, I encouraged you to invite the Birnams."

"I would have done so without your encouragement," I admitted. "And that doesn't make any of this our fault."

"No, but you definitely can't describe them as restful company."

"No," I said with a sigh. "And I don't know what that means for Trevor," I dared to admit, though I felt disloyal to our brother doing so.

Alana turned to look at me. "I also have serious reservations," she admitted and then grimaced. "But will Trevor listen to them?"

"I'm more interested in the quandary of whether we should even voice them."

"We have to," she insisted.

I frowned.

"No, I'm serious. There's no need to be hurtful. But if we don't speak up now, we may be dooming him to a life of unhappiness."

I didn't know that it was as grave as that, but then maybe it was. After all, one of his in-laws might have murdered someone. Still, I had faith in my brother's good sense. "He won't do anything rash."

Alana was less credulous. "So you think, but love makes you do rash things." She arched her eyebrows, urging me to remember.

I had to admit she was right. After all, I'd done my fair share of rash things, all for the sake of love. But that didn't mean I believed she was right about Trevor.

After reaching over to pat my hand, she pushed to her feet, plainly believing the matter was settled. "Philip took Malcolm for a ride, but they should be back any moment now and . . ."

I grasped her hand before she could set off toward the stables. "Have a care, Alana," I warned her. "If you say the wrong thing, Trevor might not forgive you as easily as you think. Not about something this important." I knew I couldn't stop her from doing what she as our elder sister thought best, but I prayed she would at least take a little guidance from me.

She frowned down at me before trying again to stride off, but I tugged once more on her hand.

"I'm serious, Alana. If our inquiry proves one of Matilda's loved ones killed Miss Whitlock . . ." My voice dipped to an agonized whisper as I dared to say one of the things I feared most. "Trevor might never speak to me again." I swallowed, blinking back a sudden wash of tears. "Trevor . . . Trevor will need you."

I was grateful when she didn't try to deny that our brother would be hurt or that he might take Matilda's side against me. Instead, she squeezed my hand, offering what comfort she could. I sniffed and looked away.

"Surely, it won't come to that," she finally said, but I could hear the uncertainty in her tone.

Releasing her hand, I urged her to go. "I know your time with Malcolm is short." Before they knew it, he would be headed back to school for the autumn term. When still she hesitated, I flapped my hand harder. "Go!"

She bent to press a kiss to my brow and then hurried off, lifting her skirts.

I exhaled a long breath, dabbing at the corners of my eyes with my fingers before rising to stroll deeper into the gardens. A line of topiaries marked the edge of the gardens proper. I passed through them and veered left to join one of the charming little forest trails that wove beneath the trees at the edge of the woods. Here and there, wildflowers sprouted among the roots and shrubs, lending their color and scent to the scenery.

Another such trail formed a shortcut from Bevington Hall to our dower house. Gage and I had coordinated to make our escape in a few hours, after he and his father returned from the coroner's inquest in Alcester, so I didn't venture far. Although I'd been one of the first people to discover Miss Whitlock, I'd not been required to attend, allowing my husband to provide my testimony. However, Mr. Birnam had been summoned to appear, as well as Bowcott, the butler, and the footman I'd first notified.

With so many crucial people absent, I knew I should return to the manor and my duties as hostess, but the very thought made my footsteps drag. Then I spied someone up ahead, making their way toward me. Their head was down, so it took me a moment to realize it was Lord Milngavie. He must have been very deep in thought, for he didn't notice me until he was nearly upon me.

"My lady," he remarked, straightening in surprise. "My apologies. I didn't see you there." He touched the brim of his hat. "'Tis a beautiful day, isn't it?"

"It is," I responded agreeably. "I'm pleased to see you enjoying it."

His blue eyes warmed as he smiled, improving his looks considerably over the dour expression he often wore. But just as swiftly his happiness faded, replaced by a worried frown. I suspected I knew the reason for it. "I am glad I have a moment to speak with you alone. For I must apologize for my behavior yesterday evening. I'm afraid I let my temper get the best of me." He spoke with great care, and I did not doubt his sincerity.

His gaze dipped to the forest floor by the path which was populated with enchanter's nightshade and lavender herb Robert. "It is perhaps my besetting sin, letting my rage overcome my sense." He looked up imploringly. "I do most heartily apologize for my behavior and my . . . my language. That I should have shocked the ladies so . . . why, I feel ashamed."

I looped my arm with his. "Think nothing more of it, my lord. We all stumble at times. And I take it that none of the men realized your voices were carrying so far."

"No!" He sounded aghast as we began to stroll back toward the manor. "Or else I hope I would have better controlled myself."

"You were discussing the Factory Act?"

"Yes." He heaved an aggrieved sigh. "A matter that Mr. Birnam and I do not see eye to eye on in any way."

That much had been obvious.

I followed the flight of a butterfly as it crossed our path, deliberately keeping my voice light. "You passionately believe these revisions and the establishment of a professional Factory Inspectorate are needed."

"I do. Or else the laws are all but unenforceable and the owners will continue to do as they please, exploiting their laborers." The ferocity I'd heard in his voice the previous evening was back, albeit more restrained.

"If I may ask, what inspired your interest in this particular issue? Are there mills and factories located in your barony?"

Though I'd tried to phrase the question delicately, he knew what lay behind it.

"You, no doubt, have heard I inherited my title from a distant cousin. 'Twas not entirely unexpected, but startling, nonetheless. For you see, much of my branch of the family had fallen below the distinction of gentlemen, being forced to work for our living."

"I do not believe that to be such an anathema," I assured him. "Not like some members of society do." My lips twisted as I dared to voice a thought I often had. "In fact, I daresay, a bit of proper employment would do a number of gentlemen I know a bit of good."

This made Milngavie grin, however briefly. "Aye, well, some of my family members cannot even cling to the edges of the genteel professions."

I turned to him, realizing what he was saying. "Some of them work in mills or factories."

He nodded. "Some of my cousins work in a cotton mill, and the conditions I've been told of . . ." His face flushed with anger. "And the number of children who work there, the injuries some of them have suffered . . ." He inhaled deeply, trying to squelch his fury. "It would turn your stomach, my lady."

I'd heard some tales. Enough that I could well imagine. I pressed my hand against his arm, letting him know that I understood, that I empathized.

"Yet men like Birnam insist it's good for them." His Scottish brogue had begun to creep into his accent again, and I took that as a sign he was growing comfortable with me.

A house sparrow sang in the branches overhead as we neared the end of the path and the line of topiaries emerged. Soon we would be in the gardens, and the opportunity to converse in private would be over, so I slowed my steps and then stopped. He looked at me in query.

"I know you said you'd never met Mr. Birnam before three days ago, but what of his secretary, Miss Whitlock?" My tone hopefully conveyed this was not an accusation but rather a bid for information.

He clasped his hands behind his back, turning to survey the upper façade of Bevington Hall rising above the topiaries. Seeming to come to some sort of decision, he lowered his voice before confiding, "I had not met her, but I knew *of* her." The manner in which his mouth had set in a grim line made my stomach dip.

"I heard she was touring the mills and factories, speaking to the workers."

"She was gatherin' information," he confirmed. "Information I'm not certain her employer wanted her tae know."

"Was she planning to . . . *expose* something?" I murmured.

He shook his head. "I dinna ken. Once I realized Birnam was here, and her wi' him, I'd hoped she'd speak wi' me and Strathblane. Obviously, we never got the chance. But I *can* tell ye that if Birnam had suspected she meant tae betray him . . ." He grimaced. "Weel, you witnessed his temper."

This information corroborated some of our suspicions, but it was far from proof.

"But what of the arrow fired at Mr. Birnam yesterday?" I asked, curious if he would go farther in his theories than he had yesterday with Lord Strathblane. "Doesn't that suggest that Birnam is also in danger? That perhaps he was the intended victim rather than Miss Whitlock?" I didn't mention the note Birnam had allegedly received or Miss Whitlock's request that I meet her.

"I must confess, I've been pondering what happened yesterday. In fact, I've thought of little else. And I simply *cannot* comprehend how another archer could have fired an arrow without my noticing." His jaw firmed. "Indeed, I would go so far as to say that I think it impossible."

I nodded. "Then you think it came from the woods?"

I couldn't tell whether I'd given my intent away or he was trying to decide how much to entrust me with, for he hesitated, scrutinizing my features intently. "*Or* . . . Birnam planted that arrow." It was spoken carefully . . . as if the suggestion might be snapped back in the next moment.

"I admit," I said, equally as hesitant, "the thought crossed my mind." The sound of voices in the distance drew my attention toward the gardens beyond our view. "The trouble is proof."

"Aye." I could hear the deep disgruntlement in this acknowledgment.

I began strolling toward the house again, trusting him to follow. "That first evening," I broached after a few steps, "you left the dining room while the men were still taking port." It wasn't a question precisely, but I hoped he would answer it.

"I did. I . . . needed a moment to myself."

I recalled how Birnam had tried to dominate the conversation and how agitated Milngavie had seemed. Now knowing his history, I could understand why he would wish to escape Birnam.

"I stepped into the blue room. The one that's been closed off since . . ." He didn't finish that sentence but frowned to himself.

Then Mr. Thorndike had undoubtedly departed before him, and Milngavie was unlikely to have witnessed whether someone was standing on the balcony over the great hall or to have seen Miss Whitlock and me conversing. I was beginning to think that Miss Whitlock's anxiety about being overheard was just what I'd initially believed it to be—nerves. Perhaps no one had been eavesdropping on us after all.

But then how had the attacker known about our planned meeting? Had Miss Whitlock informed someone else? Either someone she trusted for support or someone she thought should also hear what she wanted to tell me? Or had she been followed?

I was beginning to think we might never know.

CHAPTER 18

"Anything I should know about the coroner's inquest?" I asked Gage.

It was the first time we'd broached the subject since he'd returned to Bevington Park and found me conversing with Mrs. Taylor. We'd been finalizing the room assignments for the guests arriving in two days when he'd grasped my hand and quietly drawn me away. Mrs. Taylor had only smiled, as charmed by my husband as everyone else, and promised she had the matter well in hand.

I'd been sorely pressed not to burst into laughter and ruin our escape as we'd stolen down the corridors and up the stairs, darting around corners and stepping into doorways so as not to be seen. We'd only been spotted by one maid, who tittered to herself as we scuttled past and Gage murmured, "Nothing to see here."

"They'll think we're balmy," I'd protested, breathless with suppressed mirth.

"They'll think we're in love," he corrected. I had to concede; he was probably right.

We collected Emma from the nursery, inducting her into our little game. She was terrible at it. Far too giggly for a prison escapee. But we made it clear of the house and set off down the shortcut to the dower house at a gentle run, with Emma in her father's arms. I'd only made it a few hundred yards before we had to stop because of the stitch in my side from all my suppressed amusement. Now that we were out of sight of the manor, we could slow our steps to a walk anyway, strolling hand in hand toward our country home.

Jeffers, our butler, was delighted to see us, and I him. He along with a handful of staff had been maintaining the cottage while we were staying up at the hall. Though he and most of our staff would also be transferring to the manor in anticipation of the other guests' arrival. It would be all hands on deck for the extra staff would be needed, in particular Jeffers. Fortunately, he and Bowcott cooperated well with each other, for I'd known other butlers who became territorial and more consumed with who outranked whom than the success of an event when forced to work with others of a similar rank.

We'd gone immediately to the long room at the back of the cottage we'd dubbed the solar. It had swiftly become our favorite place. After throwing open the two sets of French doors leading out to the veranda and the garden beyond, Jeffers retreated to the kitchen to ask our cook to prepare tea and sandwiches. Gage had set Emma down so that she could toddle around while we'd promptly collapsed side by side onto the mint green upholstered settee.

For a long time, we simply sat in silence, listening to the birds twittering, the tick of the clock on the mantel, and Emma babbling and grunting to herself as she explored. There were no stairs from the veranda into the garden, so as long as she remained in sight she was free to roam. I felt my heart settle into a slower rhythm and turned my head to rest my ear over Gage's heart to hear if his had done the same. His hand lowered from the back of the couch to idly play with the curls at the side of my head.

Though somewhat loath to bring up the subject of the inquest, I'd decided it was better dealt with sooner rather than later.

"No," he replied evenly. "It was exactly as we expected."

"Then they're content leaving the matter in our hands?"

"They're content leaving the matter in Father's hands, who is leaving it in ours." He frowned. "For the most part."

I decided not to ask what he meant by that, not wanting to discuss his father during our idyll.

"And we can begin making arrangements for Miss Whitlock's burial."

I wondered if the Birnams would wish to manage that. Transferring her back to Scotland would be impossible, especially in the heat of summer, so she would undoubtedly be laid to rest here.

Emma was just beginning to venture out to the veranda when Jeffers returned with tea. She immediately reversed course, offering him a slobbery grin as she staggered toward him.

"Why, Miss Gage, you are walking steadier than when I

saw you a week ago," he declared as he set the tray down on the high table near the door, lest Emma be able to reach it and burn her fingers. The slight curl at the corner of his lips, which was all the smile he allowed himself, told me he returned her regard.

"She's quick, too," Gage boasted like the proud father he was. "Almost too quick."

I chuckled, rising to my feet to pour myself a cup of tea. "Weren't you the one who couldn't wait until she could walk?"

"Yes," he admitted with a grin, able to derive amusement from his own foibles.

"Ah, well, she needs to be quick," Jeffers said with a chuckle. "One day it'll be her chasing after her younger brothers and sisters rather than you."

I smiled over the rim of my cup as I took my first sip, but inside my stomach did a little flip. *If there were any younger brothers and sisters.* I pushed the worrying thought away, refusing to dwell on it now.

Having been sufficiently admired, Emma veered toward the statue of a cat which was meant to be utilized as a doorstop. She bent over to pat its head. It was too heavy for her to tip over and too sturdy to be damaged by her hands.

Our mouser cat was smart enough not to allow himself to be caught by a fifteen-month-old, and he wasn't really of a temperament suitable for children. It made me miss Earl Grey, the cat I'd adopted from my brother's home—or had he adopted me?—and taken to my sister's home in Edinburgh. Where he had promptly ingratiated himself to my nieces and nephews, convincing them to sneak him food. The last time I'd seen him, he'd been twice the size as when he'd shown up in my art studio, and none of the extra pounds were due to mice.

I'd hoped my sister might bring Earl Grey with them, but the extra weight had harmed his health. So he'd been left in the staff's care at their town house in Edinburgh and placed on a strict diet of scraps. Without the children there to aid and abet him, Earl Grey would no doubt slim down rapidly.

"We heard about what happened at the hall," Jeffers said, adding with a shake of his head, "what a tragedy."

I'd expected word to carry here quickly from the main house, so this wasn't a surprise. The staffs were friendly with one another and often traded gossip.

"Have you heard anything *else*?" Gage asked. Anything that might prove useful to us, was what he meant.

"Nothing that Miss McEvoy and Mr. Anderley haven't already communicated with you, I'm sure. But I shall keep my ears pricked."

With this, Jeffers departed, and I prepared Gage a cup of tea before settling back down beside him. I couldn't help but shake my head in amusement as Emma plopped down in front of the cat statue and proceeded to pat its carved cheeks while she jabbered away.

"Perhaps we need a dog," Gage proposed.

"A mild-mannered one," I observed. The sounds of our daughter's hand smacking the stone cat were audible. I winced, fearing she would hurt her hand, but her happy chattering never stopped.

Hearing the sound of approaching footsteps, I thought Jeffers was returning to ask if we would like luncheon prepared. Instead, he was followed by five impatient individuals.

Jeffers cleared his throat. "You have callers." His expression was aggrieved, clearly having realized we'd come here seeking a bit of respite, but also fully aware of my family members' tendencies to barge in unannounced.

"Very good," I said, letting him know that I understood.

"We're here for that tour you promised," Alana proclaimed, stepping forward. "And perhaps a bit of a confab," she added with a glance over her shoulder at the others.

"I'll bring more tea and sandwiches," Jeffers announced before slipping away.

"Emma, love," Alfie exclaimed. "What did that cat ever do to you?" He turned to his wife, muttering under his breath, "Our boys better learn quickly never to cross their cousin."

Lorna rolled her eyes while Alfie grinned. He then sank down on his haunches to encourage Emma as she rose to her feet to toddle toward him, the statue all but forgotten.

Philip ushered my sister inside, allowing Trevor to enter the room behind him. I peered past my brother's shoulder, hoping to see Matilda. He shook his head. The stoop of his shoulders and the sadness that glinted in his eyes told me all I needed to know.

I made room on the settee for Lorna while Alana settled in one of the armchairs. Philip carried over two chairs from the table across the room so that everyone would have a seat. Pleased as I was to see them and to have the opportunity to show them our new home, I couldn't help but worry that the other guests couldn't have failed to miss seven people leaving the manor.

"Have no fear," my sister consoled me, evidently reading my mind. "We slipped away almost as unobtrusively as you did." Her lips pursed in amusement, telling me that she must have caught sight of our stealthy antics. "We'll return in pairs and trios, and none will be the wiser."

"Now, update us on this inquiry," Philip said, the cane-back chair he'd set beside his wife creaking as he settled deeper into it. "The inquest was this morning, was it not? And now there's been an attempt on Birnam's life."

Gage and I shared a speaking look. One in which we silently conferred about how much to share. For while many hands made light work, it was also true that too many cooks spoiled the broth. And now I was jumbling together my proverbs. Maybe we truly did need help.

For the truth was, we were currently at a standstill. Without the Birnams confiding in us, without more information about Miss Whitlock's past and her intentions in asking me to meet her, without some proof of where the bottle of vitriol had come from, we could not move forward. So what would be the harm in sharing what we knew? We trusted the five people before us. Trusted them with our lives, with our daughter's life. Perhaps they could help us to untangle this Gordian knot.

Taking turns, Gage and I relayed the facts as we knew them, sparing no details, even from Trevor. Meanwhile, Jeffers entered and took on the task of pouring tea for everyone and passing around the plates of sandwiches. Once we'd finished, there was a lull of silence while everyone processed the information. There had been a great deal of it.

Philip was the first to speak, obviously trying to use his experience as an earl and a member of the House of Lords to confront the problem. "Let's break it down into separate, but related issues. You said Miss Whitlock was agitated when she asked to speak with you in private, that she referred to your work as inquiry agents. But she gave no hint of what she needed to tell you. Your only guess is that it might have had to do with Birnam's mills and factories."

"And that's based on the knowledge that she'd toured them and spoken to the workers," I said. "Paget and Lord Milngavie both confirmed this." I noted how my brother's brow had furrowed. He was not finding any of this easy to hear. "Paget also said she was meddling where she didn't belong, and he'd known she would one day cause them all grief. But none of that is proof that whatever she needed to tell me was to do with the factories. It might have been something entirely different."

"No," Philip agreed. "But it does make sense. And I can attest that there has been a rash of attacks on mill owners, as well as scuffling between different factions of workers." He rubbed his chin. "So it's possible it was as much to do with that as Birnam's business practices."

"Birnam *has* received threats," Trevor interjected.

Gage and I both shifted in surprise.

"He has?" Gage demanded sharply.

My brother eyed us in confusion. "Yes. Or so Matilda told me."

"He mentioned the attacks on other owners, but he failed to tell us outright that he himself had been threatened." My voice was wry. "And I can't help but wonder why."

Unless Matilda had lied to Trevor. I supposed we would have to ask Birnam directly.

Alana smoothed the floral muslin of her skirts over her lap. "So one theory is that Miss Whitlock intended to reveal something presumably unsavory or criminal about Birnam's businesses, and either Birnam or Paget threw acid on her in order to prevent her. Which means Birnam picked up the bottle of vitriol to cover his actions and later faked the arrow shot to try to throw suspicion off himself further." The same doubt I felt was written on her features.

"It could have happened that way," Alfie said from his position now seated on the floor with Emma in his lap. She was quietly entertaining herself by examining his pocket watch and chain. "But acid seems an odd choice in that instance."

Lorna spoke up. "Perhaps if it had happened on the streets of Glasgow, where most of the other attacks have occurred, but here . . ." She shook her head. "It simply doesn't make sense. No one in their right mind would blame such a thing on a vengeful mill worker who'd come all the way from Scotland."

My gaze shifted to Trevor, recalling that it had been Matilda and her father who had separately made such suggestions. However he felt, he didn't react.

"Why would someone choose oil of vitriol as their weapon?" Alana posited.

"To maim and disfigure," I supplied. "Not necessarily to kill. Such instances are rare."

"Because Birnam manufactures it," Alfie added.

Alana returned to my point. "Then the attacker may not have expected her to die. In which case, how did he expect to get away with it?" She glanced around at us. "Wouldn't she have been able to identify him?"

"That's a good point." Philip tapped his fingers together. "Why would he risk such a thing? Did he believe she *wouldn't* identify him? Did he think himself above the law?"

Lorna arched her eyebrows. "Or was he—or *she*—so

overcome by anger or jealousy or righteous indignation that she just didn't care?"

She was right. The attacker could have been a woman. Jealousy or anger or righteous indignation could have been the motive. Perhaps all three. And if Mrs. Birnam had committed the act, she might have believed herself above the law, especially if she'd been convinced her husband was keeping Miss Whitlock as a mistress. Maybe she'd seen the note Miss Whitlock had slipped under her husband's door, and assuming the worst, decided to put an end to it once and for all.

"Maybe she even intended to be caught," Lorna pressed on. "Until she saw how severe the wounds were. Until Miss Whitlock died. Then the attacker panicked and fled."

Trevor was leaning forward now with his elbows braced on his knees. He knew who this theory implicated, and he could be no happier with it than the previous one.

"You said no oil of vitriol was missing from Bevington Hall's stores?" Philip verified.

"Correct." Gage raked a hand back through his hair. "Which means whoever attacked Miss Whitlock brought the acid with them. Suggesting premeditation. Which does not match the notion that this was a crime of passion."

Philip's warm brown eyes narrowed as if trying to see his way through the problem. "It's seemingly a dichotomy."

"Precisely." Gage scowled. "And yet there must be some solution that reconciles that fact."

Having lost interest in Alfie's watch, Emma now noticed we were eating without her. I urged Alfie to hand her to me and then sat her on my lap to feed her small bites of my cucumber and watercress sandwich. Her tiny face screwed up at first at the taste—much to all of our mirth—but then she began contentedly consuming it, opening her mouth like a baby bird whenever she wanted another bite.

Lorna chuckled. "Rory does the same thing."

"They'll grow out of it," Alana advised.

"I don't know," Gage proclaimed doubtfully. "Alfie still does it."

Hearing this teasing remark, Alfie tipped his head back and opened his mouth, tossing in the last bite of roast beef and horseradish, earning himself a great deal of laughter. Even Trevor cracked a smile. I wished I could make all of this go away for him.

For perhaps the first time in the course of one of our investigations, I felt the impulse to turn a blind eye. But one could never really pretend something this heinous hadn't happened, and not knowing what exactly the Birnams were capable of would surely eat at Trevor, would surely consume me. Not to mention the injustice it would be to Miss Whitlock, and the abject failure it would be to the principles Gage and I strived to uphold.

"Trevor, you said that Matilda told you that her father was trying to convince her brother to wed Miss Whitlock?" Alana queried.

He frowned. "No. Matilda told me that her father kept forcing them into proximity to one another."

"*Implying* he meant them to wed," Alana pressed.

But Trevor wouldn't agree. "Maybe."

She scowled.

"Perhaps he was forcing them into proximity for another reason," Philip said, playing the peacemaker.

"Such as?" she challenged.

"When Miss Whitlock was sent away," Gage interjected, "maybe the cause was a rift between her and Jemmy. Maybe Mr. Birnam wanted it healed."

"But Jemmy wasn't interested in mending any rifts," I reminded them. "He called Miss Whitlock a deceitful liar, and he was angry with his father for not seeing her that way."

Trevor shifted uncomfortably in his chair.

I turned to Alfie, who now sat in the second cane-back chair. "Has he told you anything else?"

He grimaced. "Not worth repeating."

Which was saying something if Alfie was the one who didn't wish to repeat it.

"You've been ingratiating yourself with Jemmy?" Trevor demanded to know. He sounded outraged.

"It's not like that," Alfie protested. "I've simply been bending an ear to listen to his sorrows. Of which he has many," he quipped wryly, earning a scowl from me.

"And *you* asked him to do it?" Trevor accused me.

Emma began to fuss because I'd stopped feeding her.

"Jemmy was already speaking to him," I countered in my defense. "I merely asked him to pass on anything pertinent that he might share."

Trevor pushed to his feet. "That's underhanded, Kiera."

"How do you think an investigation works, Trevor?" I snapped, struggling to tear the cucumbers into small enough bites. Gage took the plate and sandwich from me, assuming the task while Emma continued to grunt. "We're not forcing him to incriminate himself or anyone else."

"No, but you're tricking him!"

I blinked back at him in shock, struggling to understand why he was riled. "You've sat here with us listening to all the evidence. You comprehend how guilty the Birnams look." He shrank back from me, but I would not let him retreat. "I know you do. I can see it in your eyes. Yet they will not talk with us. They will not attempt to explain. So what are we to do?"

"Do you know something, Trevor?" Alana's gaze was probing in the way only an older sister's could be. "Something you haven't yet shared with Kiera and Sebastian?"

"No!" Trevor denied. "No, I've shared everything of *pertinence* that I know." He plopped back down in his chair, mocking my earlier choice of words. "But I still think what you're doing is dishonest."

Maybe it was. After all, this wasn't the first time I'd worried about the morality of such an action. It wasn't the first time one of our inquiries had required us to do something I wasn't entirely comfortable with. But I knew, without a doubt or hesitation, that the intentions behind those acts had always been good, and the response measured.

Just as I knew without a doubt or hesitation that Trevor was lying.

I had always been able to tell when my brother was fibbing, even as a child. He simply wasn't good at it. This was something I'd always taken comfort in, but now I was conflicted. Should I confront him now or give him time to decide to confide in me later?

When Emma suddenly demanded my attention, asking for a drink of my now cold tea, I accepted my choice had been made for me. But that didn't mean I didn't keep one eye trained on Trevor.

CHAPTER 19

Now, how about that tour?" Alana declared.

The others expressed their interest, so Gage and I conceded graciously, rising to our feet to join them. Gage took Emma from me so that I could lead them through the house, awkwardly at first and then with more excitement as I explained the changes we'd made.

Stepping out onto the veranda, we showed them the small garden, which I hoped to continue improvements to the following spring. Then we moved into the adjoining conservatory-type space which we had added to the cottage for my art studio. It boasted two glass walls and a glass ceiling to provide ample light, as well as a customized ventilation system to rid the space of noxious smells and the toxic fumes that arose from some of my pigments.

Much of the rest of the main floor had required little renovation, though I was perhaps a bit overly pleased to show them the artwork I'd inherited from Gage's grandfather and finally been able to hang. If Alfie was at all disgruntled that the late Lord Tavistock had left the paintings to me, he didn't show it. But then he readily admitted he didn't know a thing about the subject.

I elected not to take our party of seven—eight including Emma—traipsing through the servants' domain, though the kitchen had been given a significant refurbishment. However, several of the bedchambers had been altered and a water closet had been added as well as a bath with running taps, the water for which was collected in a cistern on the roof.

We ended our tour in the nursery, admiring the new furniture and fresh paint, and the charming view from the windows. Lorna and Alana expressed more interest in this child's domain than the men, so we became separated as Gage, Emma, and the others drifted back downstairs. A short time later, I heard the faint clack of balls, telling me they'd returned to the study where the carom billiard table was located.

Lorna was admiring the tent Bree and I had constructed in one corner from bent rods and gauzy fabric so that the light could filter through. We'd tossed a number of large pillows inside along with a cozy blanket. "It's enchanting," she said, bending down to peer inside. "Does Emma like it?"

"It's her favorite place in the nursery. And mine as well," I admitted with a laugh. "I may or may not have nearly fallen asleep the last time we were playing 'bears in a cave.'"

"Like I may or may not have once fallen asleep after being taken captive by Malcolm while we were reenacting the Battle of Waterloo," Alana admitted with a chagrined smile.

"You did?" I gasped. "Oh, I imagine he still hasn't forgiven you for that." I turned to Lorna to explain. "He takes his reenactments very seriously. Particularly when they involve Wellington."

"I was able to convince him I was merely attempting to personify a French soldier worn down by the might of the British troops." Her smile broadened in the face of our amusement. "In actuality, I was expecting my third child and desperate for a nap." Her expression turned shrewd. "Are you . . . ?"

Though she didn't complete the question, I knew what she was asking. My hands lifted involuntarily to press to my abdomen. "No."

She nodded, but didn't press for more information, turning instead to examine a simple charcoal sketch I'd made of her children that I'd framed and hung on the wall above Emma's cradle.

"But perhaps it's time," I admitted hesitantly, unsure how to ask the question I wanted to.

"Are you trying?" Lorna inquired.

"We haven't *not* been trying."

Her lips quirked, knowing what that meant. After all, she'd conceived Sherry when Rory was just five months old.

"And Emma is fifteen months old now. Which I suppose makes me wonder . . ." I didn't know why I couldn't utter the rest of the words. Perhaps it was because they were both looking at me with such kindness.

"Why you aren't with child again?" Alana finished for me.

I bit my lip and nodded.

My sister draped her arm around me, heedless of how it rumpled the wide gigot sleeves of her chartreuse morning dress. "Oh, dearest. Don't worry. Certainly not yet. Sometimes it simply takes the time it takes. I didn't conceive

Philipa until eighteen months after Malcolm was born, and that wasn't for wont of trying," she finished on a chuckle. "And Philipa was well over three years old before I realized I was expecting Greer."

I dabbed at the corner of my eye with my finger as relief stole through me. "I hadn't thought of that."

"It's early days," she declared with a wave of her hand. "It happened readily enough with your first. It will happen again. Just be patient."

"Alfie and I didn't even realize it could happen again so quickly," Lorna confessed. "You should have seen his face when I told him." She fluffed her primrose printed skirt. "And to tell you the truth, I sort of wish we could have waited a little longer." She flushed as if this might be a shameful admission. "Rory had barely turned one and then Sherry was born. And you know how much of your time and vigor a newborn consumes, even with a nursemaid. I fear I'm missing out on so much with Rory. And then when I'm thinking about Rory while I'm caring for Sherry, I fear I'm missing out on my youngest as well!"

Alana stepped away from me to embrace Lorna.

"I guess there is no perfect timing," I confessed, never having considered Lorna's perspective. "Not that we have much control over the matter in the first place."

"Oh, wouldn't that be a comfort!" Alana proclaimed longingly. I knew she was thinking of her own difficulties. She'd almost died giving birth to Greer and had been warned that another pregnancy could be dangerous. But in spite of all of her and Philip's precautions, she'd gotten with child again. I remembered the anxiety of those months, the worry that she might not survive the birth of her fourth child. Providentially, she and wee Jamie had both lived, though there had been a few terrifying hours when that had been uncertain. I knew that she and Philip were doubly cautious now, but at the back of their minds, they must always be aware that no precautions were foolproof.

She shook off the thought, refocusing on Lorna. "But Rory knows you love him. Sherry, too."

I nodded eagerly in agreement. "You can see it in their faces when you walk in the room."

"Really?" she asked, blinking back tears.

"Yes," I said with quiet conviction, sensing she needed it. Honestly, I wondered that she *couldn't* see it and then wondered if my sister couldn't either. I turned to her. "It's the same with Alana's children. They've always adored her."

Alana's mouth opened and closed without making a sound, though I caught sight of a suspicious glimmer in her eyes. I supposed we were to all take our turns being emotional.

"Thank you, Kiera," she finally managed to murmur.

I clasped my hands together and glanced at the door. "I suppose we should rejoin the men."

But before I could take a step toward the door, I was unceremoniously hauled backward into an embrace by both women. Alana smelled of the French perfume our mother had always favored, while Lorna's scent hinted of thyme, rosemary, and lilacs. I melted into them, absorbing their warmth and reflecting it back to them. But I also couldn't help remarking, "This would be much easier if you weren't both so enamored with these gargantuan sleeves."

Lorna laughed while Alana scolded me affectionately. "Kiera."

"What?" I protested, batting at her sleeve now that they'd released me and I could breathe again. "It's rather like being smothered by a buckram cloud."

Alana shook her head, but she couldn't hide her smile.

I'm not sure what I'd expected, but when Gage and I emerged from the forest path into the parterre garden a short time later with Emma, there were no irritated guests waiting for us. Even when we stepped through the French doors into the red saloon, there were no angry glares or accusations. Rather, everything seemed to be carrying on as usual. I could hear ladies' voices coming from the left in the mauve drawing room and male voices coming from the right in the green drawing room.

The tension I'd been holding in my neck and shoulders released as we crossed the saloon toward the great hall. There we were intercepted by Bowcott.

"Mr. and Mrs. Gage," he declared, sounding a trifle winded. "I'm glad I've found you." He took a moment to regain his normally unflappable composure, lowering his voice so as not to be overheard. "Your maid and your valet are looking for you."

Gage and I shared a look of misgiving, for if they were looking for us, and Bowcott was this ruffled, it must be something important. My fears instantly centered on Mr. Birnam. Had there been another attempt on his life? But the second after I entertained this thought, I dismissed it. If Birnam had been attacked, surely the other guests would be at sixes and sevens. Whatever had happened had been kept quiet. So far.

"They are requesting that you join them in Mrs. Taylor's sitting room," the butler explained.

"Of course," Gage replied, but halted mid-step, realizing he still held Emma, who was asleep on his shoulder.

I glanced behind us to see if my sister or Lorna, or even Trevor had entered behind us, but true to their resolve, they'd lagged behind, so that it wouldn't seem we had been together.

"I can take Miss Gage up to her nanny, if you'd like," Bowcott offered.

"If it's not too much trouble," I said.

"Not at all," he assured me, and some of the merry twinkle returned to his eyes.

Gage carefully transferred Emma's sleeping frame to the butler. She snuffled softly but then fell back asleep.

We opened the door leading to the servants' stairs to descend belowstairs while he ascended up toward the nursery. Almost directly across from the base of the staircase was the entrance to the servants' hall, where we could hear several voices conversing. From our left issued the usual bangs, sizzles, and thwacks associated with all the racket of a manor's kitchen, while to the right lay a corridor with a series of bedchambers designated for mostly the female staff. The housekeeper claimed the suite of rooms at the corner nearest us while the butler was given the suite at the opposite end. The bedrooms for the cook and footmen were located on the other side of the building, between the kitchens and the various other workrooms.

Upon reaching the housekeeper's suite, we found the door to the neat and tidy sitting room ajar, but rapped on it nonetheless before pushing it open. Anderley straightened from his position leaning against the wall near the door while Bree rose to her feet from a wooden bench where I imagined Mrs. Taylor made recalcitrant maids sit when they required a reprimand. As they approached us, I could see the housekeeper beyond them sitting in one of her chintz floral upholstered chairs, her hands clasped in her lap as she observed the proceedings with an expression of placid indifference.

More intriguing, a second man claimed the matching chair next to her. As he was not dressed in Lord Gage's livery, but the clothing of a conservative gentleman, I suspected he was valet to one of the guests. A gentleman's gentleman, as it were. Albeit a young one. He'd broken off from whatever he was saying to wait for our personal servants to explain matters to us.

"This is Mr. Armstrong, Lord Milngavie's valet," Anderley explained.

"He witnessed somethin' that we think you'll find *verra* interestin'." The tone of Bree's voice and the glint in her eyes left no doubt what *she* thought.

Mrs. Taylor seemed to take this as her cue, rising to her feet. "I shall leave the matter in your hands, then," she said, a similar glint in her eyes. "But let me know if you should require any further assistance."

I thanked her and she nodded, closing the door softly behind her. I trusted that she would keep whatever she'd heard to herself, for in the past I'd found her to be the soul of discretion. Also, traditionally, servants' gossip moved up or parallel to the chain of command, not in the other direction.

Gage approached Mr. Armstrong. "You have something to tell us?"

"Aye, sir," he replied, fidgeting in his chair. "M'lord . . . Lord Milngavie," he clarified. "He said I should inform someone straightaway, and Mr. Anderley, here, had been askin' if anyone had seen anythin'." He paused, his eyes widening uncertainly. "I . . . I would've spoke up *straight*away, but it seemed I should ask his lordship first, seein' as he's, ye ken . . . m'lord."

His brogue was thick and his meaning a bit garbled, but we were able to work out what he was trying to say. Watching his eyes dart between us all nervously, I found myself revising my estimate of his age. He must be even younger than I'd first thought. Perhaps someone Milngavie had brought along with him from his former life before he inherited his title and estates. In that way, Milngavie and Birnam were similar, considering Paget's origins.

"Of course," Gage replied as if everything the valet had said made perfect sense. He gestured for me to take the chair Mrs. Taylor had vacated while he perched on the matching tufted footstool. "So what did you witness?"

Mr. Armstrong swallowed, seeming to settle once he saw how equitable Gage was being. "The afternoon we arrived, a few o' us was in the laundry, chattin' while we waited our turn with the box irons. Gettin' our lords' and ladies' garments ready for dinner, ye ken?"

Gage nodded in encouragement.

"Weel, there we was, actin' friendly, takin' turns wi' the starch and iron, and in walks this maid. I learnt later her name was McClintock and that she works for Mrs. Birnam. Anyway, in she walks, skirtin' round the room, no' sayin' anythin' tae anyone. I may o' only noticed 'er cause I was facin' the door. *And* cause she was actin' all sleekit, like my younger brothers do when they're up tae no good."

I was sorely tempted to smile at this description, but I refrained, not wanting him to falter.

"So I watch 'er from the corner o' my eye." He tapped his face there. "And I see that she's holdin' a bottle."

My hand closed around the arm of my chair as I strained not to react, though I could feel Bree's gaze on me. Clearly, she'd recognized I already knew where this was leading.

"I didna ken o' what, but it was like she didna want us tae mark it." Mr. Armstrong frowned. "Then durin' a moment o' distraction she slipped it ontae a shelf and left the room. I didna see when she actually did it, but I noticed where the bottle was when next I looked up," he confessed. "And curious, I went tae see what it was once I finished wi' his lordship's shirt."

"And what was it?" Gage prompted even though it was evident he also already knew.

"Oil o' vitriol. A bottle wi' *Birnam's* mark." His face crumpled in worry. "At the time I didna ken that it meant anythin'. I just noticed she was actin' odd. Even later, I wasna quick enough tae put it taegether, but then I realized . . . the young lady that was murdered . . ." He swallowed again, struggling to finish the sentence.

"Thank you for telling us," Gage said, sparing him. His eyes met mine briefly, stark with the knowledge of what this meant for our inquiry and for my brother. The likelihood that the Birnams were involved had just increased tenfold.

I grasped the arms of my chair even tighter, trying to ignore the sour taste that had flooded my mouth, and ordered the contents of my stomach to stay put.

"You said there were other people in the laundry with you?" Gage glanced back at Bree and Anderley with a nod to tell them they'd done well. "Do you mind telling us who they were?"

He designated them by their employer's name, correctly deducing that we would not know their personal names. "Let's see, there was Lord Tavistock's valet, and Mr. Birnam's . . . the younger Mr. Birnam, no' the older."

My heart sank further.

"And Lady Brougham's maid." His eyes were narrowed in thought. "Ah, and Lady Cromarty's maid."

Gage turned to Anderley and Bree again, and they moved toward the door, anticipating that he wanted them all to be located immediately. "Keep Mrs. McClintock separated from the others. Ask Mrs. Taylor or Bowcott for assistance, if needed."

Mr. Armstrong's eyes had widened in alarm. "I dinna ken if they saw anythin'," he protested, obviously concerned he may have gotten them into trouble.

"We realize that, but it's important that we verify it," Gage reassured him. "There's a chance that one of them did see something that could prove pertinent and simply doesn't realize it."

The young valet still appeared doubtful, but he seemed to recognize there was little he could do to change our mind.

"Did you happen to notice if the bottle is still there?" I asked, realizing we might be putting the cart before the horse. Was it too much to hope that the bottle we'd found next to Miss Whitlock's body had been a different one?

"I'm afraid I didna think tae look again 'til today," Mr. Armstrong admitted with a small shrug. "But it's no' there noo."

This wasn't proof, of course, that this bottle of oil of vitriol was the one that had been used to attack Miss Whitlock, but it was certainly suggestive. We had been unable to locate where the acid had come from, but here was a bottle, seen just hours before Miss Whitlock was killed, which seemed to match the one found next to the victim.

Though I was baffled as to what exactly Mrs. McClintock was doing with it. If her actions in bringing it to the laundry were innocent, surely there would have been no need for stealth. To be fair, this was just one person's interpretation of events. Perhaps Mr. Armstrong was only reading sly intention after the fact, now that he knew vitriol had been used against Miss Whitlock. We would need to ask the other servants who were present that afternoon their impression of events.

Gage thanked Milngavie's valet and warned him to keep quiet about what he'd told us for the time being before dismissing him.

"Do you think he'll listen?" I asked my husband once the young man was out of earshot.

"I think he's worried the others will be angry with him for involving them in the matter."

"He doesn't realize you'll be circumspect."

"As much as possible." He turned to look at me, a deep furrow forming between his brows. But whatever thought had caused it, he didn't have a chance to share, because the first of our witnesses had arrived.

I recollected Alfie's valet, Mr. Cooper, from our visits to Langstone Manor on Dartmoor. Anderley disliked the fellow intensely, calling him a repugnant toad, and I couldn't say he'd given me any more favorable an impression. From the moment he entered the housekeeper's sitting room, his pompous demeanor was on display, with his neck arched as if to look down his nose at us even though Gage towered over him. Mr. Cooper was no good at hiding his thoughts, so it was abundantly clear that he found our questions to be a waste of his time, but he answered them, nonetheless.

Yes, he'd been ironing clothes in the laundry on Monday afternoon. No, he hadn't noticed anything unusual. Yes, he remembered Mrs. McClintock joining them. She'd been returning something. A bottle of some sort. No, he didn't know what of.

The last remark was said with such derision that I thought Gage might be driven to wring the man's intricately tied cravat. I certainly wanted to. But at least Cooper had corroborated Mr. Armstrong's claim that Mrs. McClintock had placed a bottle on the shelf in the laundry. Though he'd read nothing sly or sinister in her actions, merely that she was replacing it.

Both lady's maids—Lady Brougham's and my sister's, Jenny—recalled being in the laundry room and seeing Mrs. McClintock enter, but neither had seen the bottle. I was rather disappointed that Jenny had not seen more, for I trusted her. But she'd been focused on treating a stain on a delicate piece of lace and so had not been paying particular attention to her surroundings.

Last was Jemmy's valet, a man rather in the mold of Mr. Cooper, though it was evident this fellow at least did not wear a corset. There wasn't enough meat on his bones to require one. I found myself most interested of all the witnesses to hear what this Mr. Simpkins would say, but his responses were disinterested at best. At least until it came to

Mrs. McClintock. Then it was evident he was suspicious of our curiosity about her. He claimed not to have seen a bottle, but by that point, I thought he might have baldly lied if it meant protecting someone he either admired or considered a friend.

Once we'd finished, Gage insisted on conferring with Anderley outside the door before he released Mr. Simpkins. I guessed that he wanted to ensure Mrs. McClintock had been secured elsewhere so that Jemmy's valet couldn't forewarn her. Once Gage had dismissed him, I joined my husband in the corridor, learning that Mrs. Birnam's maid was waiting with Bree in the butler's sitting room.

"First," Gage instructed Anderley, "show us the laundry."

He led us through the servants' domain, and I did my best to ignore the inquisitive glances cast our way by those we passed. There were two maids in the laundry when we arrived—one of them Lady Brougham's—but they both obeyed Gage's request for them to step out for a moment without complaint. I surveyed the room, finding it much like any other laundry, except perhaps a bit larger than most. I could easily imagine the staff conversing with each other as they worked at the tall tables. Meanwhile, Gage and Anderley shuffled through the bottles stored on a long shelf above the sinks. There was no sign of the bottle of oil of vitriol, and nothing that might resemble it.

"Where is the manor's oil of vitriol stored?" I asked.

"With poisons and other caustic substances in a locked cabinet off the kitchens," Gage replied. "My father insisted on it. And Mrs. Taylor has the only key."

I suspected he'd adopted such precautions because of his experiences as an inquiry agent. Gage and I had resorted to similar measures in our homes, not because we didn't trust our staff and guests, but because we understood how often mistakes occurred. One white powder might look like any other, except that it could kill you.

But Miss Whitlock's death had certainly been no accident. And I felt a terrified surge of both hope and dread that we were finally about to find out who had done it and why.

CHAPTER 20

I had estimated Mrs. Birnam to be close to two score and ten years old, and I guessed that Ann McClintock was of a similar age. However, the maid had not had the benefit of decades of being waited upon. So where Mrs. Birnam was round and soft, McClintock was thin and hard. Her hair had gone almost all iron gray and was scraped back severely from a face with not enough flesh to temper the sharp wrinkles etching the corners of her eyes and mouth and the broad swathe of her forehead.

We had been warned that she was loyal to her employer, and this bore out to be true when we attempted to question her, for she abjectly refused to answer. She stared at the square of floor in front of her, only acknowledging our presence in the minute tightening of her lips. I had been prepared to be convinced that Mr. Armstrong might have been mistaken in what he'd seen, but Mrs. McClintock said not a word in her defense, neither explaining what the bottle had been nor denying that it had been oil of vitriol.

With each query she ignored, my heart sank further, until with leaden feet I followed Gage from the room, standing just outside the doorway with Bree.

"Has she been like this since you brought her here?" Gage asked.

"Aye," Bree confirmed, her arms crossed before her. "She's no' even coughed."

"She does understand us, doesn't she?" I wanted to verify. "She does speak?"

"Oh, aye. She's just choosin' no' to."

I turned to Gage, anxious to discover if he had some other explanation, but it was clear he found her silence as incriminating as I did. After all, if there was an innocent explanation, why not give it?

"Keep her here," Gage instructed Bree before meeting my gaze. "Meanwhile, I think it's time you and I spoke with Mrs. Birnam." His voice hardened. "Whether she wishes to or not."

We both knew it would be the latter. So when Matilda opened the door of her mother's sitting room in answer to our knock and attempted to deny us entry, Gage merely pushed the door wider.

"Not this time," I told her quietly in response to her shocked expression.

Gage allowed me to be the first to enter. Inside, I found Mrs. Birnam attempting to sit upright on the sofa where she'd been lounging.

"How dare you!" Her face flushed red. "Barging in here. Is this the way you treat your guests? I demand you leave." She pointed toward the door. "I demand it now."

"Mrs. Birnam, we have detained your maid," Gage pronounced.

Behind us, Matilda gasped while Mrs. Birnam's eyes bulged in their sockets.

"How dare you!" she exclaimed again once she'd recovered. "I demand that you release her. Release her at once!"

"We can't do that, Mrs. Birnam," Gage continued calmly. "She was seen with a bottle of oil of vitriol in the hours before Miss Whitlock's murder. The same bottle that was used in the attack."

We did not have proof of this yet, but I did not fault him for stating it as fact. It was the only explanation that made sense.

Matilda whimpered behind us, and I turned to see her shoulders crumpling as she pressed a hand to her mouth to contain her sobs.

"Matilda, leave us," her mother ordered, and when she did not comply fast enough, she shrieked, "Go!"

I watched as Matilda turned to flee the room. I considered going after her, but then Mrs. Birnam spoke.

"*If* McClintock was seen with a bottle of vitriol, I'm sure she had a perfectly legitimate reason for having it." She twitched her skirts, straightening her appearance. "But I had no knowledge of it. As I'm sure she's told you."

"She hasn't told us anything, Mrs. Birnam," Gage said sternly. "And that is very damning. You *must* see that."

"What I see is that you are prepared to condemn her . . ." she arched her eyebrows ". . . and *me*, if I don't mistake the intention of your barging in here for a minor coincidence. So McClintock was seen with a bottle of vitriol hours before the attack on my husband's secretary. She *wasn't* seen around the time the crime was committed. She couldn't have been, because she was with *me*."

"Then she should explain that and tell us what she was doing with the vitriol in the first place and where it is now," Gage countered, struggling with his temper.

"Why should she? She's not beholden to you. She's done nothing wrong."

"Because we are attempting to solve a murder! The horrific murder of your husband's secretary, *Miss Whitlock*." He emphasized her name, evidently having also noted how Mrs. Birnam avoided saying it. "One would think you both would wish to see the perpetrator brought to justice."

"We do." She patted her hair, affecting an air of unconcern, but I could see the way her hands shook before she returned them to her lap. "But that's *your* task to see to, not ours."

"Then why won't you answer our questions?" I interjected.

She turned to glare at me. "Because we had nothing to do with it."

"But your family knew Miss Whitlock best."

She scoffed. "I would hardly say that."

I frowned, trying to understand why she was being so difficult. What was she afraid of?

"Mrs. Birnam, was your husband sleeping with Miss Whitlock?" Gage surprised me by asking. I supposed he'd decided the direct approach was now our only option. At least this way, we could attempt to judge from her reaction.

As predicted, she was outraged. "How dare you insult me

in this manner! My husband is a good and faithful man. He would never . . ." She stumbled over her words, but they were inconsequential anyway. For I could already tell that something in her statement was not strictly truthful. It was evident in the way her jaw tightened, and her eyes slid away. But which part was a fabrication?

"Was he attempting to convince your son to ask for Miss Whitlock's hand in marriage?"

Her head reared back as if I'd slapped her. "Absolutely not! Of all the notions."

This declaration I believed. Her almost disgust of the idea was written in every fiber of her body. It puzzled me, for I would have thought she would have been more appalled by the suggestion her husband was having an affair.

"Then why did you dislike Miss Whitlock so much?" I inquired.

Mrs. Birnam began to fidget with her garments again. "I liked her just fine."

I tilted my head in disbelief. "Come now, Mrs. Birnam. It was obvious to everyone that neither you nor your son approved of Miss Whitlock. Why, you can't even say her name."

"What nonsense!" she insisted. "Jemmy and I liked Miss Whitlock just fine." Her lip curled. "Despite the gossip that was stirred up over my husband hiring her for such a position. It certainly didn't do us any favors. Especially Matilda." Who would have been entering the marriage market at about that time.

Perhaps this was the source of her animosity, perhaps it was nothing more. But the fact she so readily admitted it when she acknowledged nothing else made me skeptical.

"Whose idea was it?" I asked.

"I'm sure I don't know," she retorted before giving the query a moment's consideration as she worried the chain of her pendant. "Probably Mr. Birnam's. He was rather resistant to the notion of her being married off at such a young age."

Yet she hadn't been enfolded back into his household as his ward. Instead, she'd been forced to take up employment under him. I could see that Gage was puzzled over the same thing.

"What did you think of Clive and Ellie Whitlock? Were they good parents?" I was curious about her impressions.

She seemed startled at first by the question. "Attentive enough, I suppose. Clive was a good man, if a bit gullible, and sadly too reckless. Lost all his fortune through bad investments, you know. He had pretentions to greatness. He named his daughter Portia, for heaven's sake. But he'd not half the wits Jeremiah possesses." A frown marred her brow. "And Ellie was sweet, I suppose. Pretty, in a blowsy sort of way. A bit crude, but as you'd expect from a woman growing up where she did."

I'd recalled that Mr. Birnam had said that he and Mr. and Mrs. Whitlock had all come from the same neighborhood, while Mrs. Birnam had come from a perhaps more genteel part of Glasgow. I couldn't tell if this was the reason for her disapproval of Ellie or if the woman's daughter had inspired it retroactively.

"It was kind of you and your husband to care for her when her parents died," I complimented, hoping this would convince her to share more.

Her expression was troubled. "He'd made a promise."

A promise she wished he hadn't. At least, that was the impression I received. Peering into the past had distracted her, so I decided to risk asking the question I knew she would never answer otherwise. "What happened when Miss Whitlock was sent away to school?"

But she wasn't nearly as preoccupied as I'd hoped, pausing her fiddling with her necklace to peer up at me in suspicion. "I don't know what you mean."

"Something happened that made you send her away," I stated, refusing to back down.

"What nonsense! Now who told you that?" She arched her chin. "It was always the plan to send her away for finishing. Weren't you and your sister?"

Alana was prepared for her debut into society by our Aunt Cait, while I was more interested in art than securing a husband through the marriage market. However, I didn't tell Mrs. Birnam this. Not when she was attempting to divert attention from herself.

"But Miss Whitlock wasn't finished off in the traditional sense. She undertook employment."

Mrs. Birnam scowled. "Yes, well. That was not the plan."

This, I believed.

"Will you speak to Mrs. McClintock and tell her that it is important she cooperates with us?" Gage requested, perhaps thinking we'd strayed far from the aim of our visit. "For her own sake and yours."

Mrs. Birnam gave this minimal consideration before rising to her feet. "No."

It was Gage's turn to stiffen in shock. "Why not?" he demanded as she turned to walk away.

"Because her reasons are her own." She spoke over her shoulder, not even affording us the courtesy of addressing us directly. "And I would not wish to exert undue influence on her." She paused at the door leading to her bedchamber just long enough to add, "You can show yourselves out."

Short of manhandling her or breaking down the door she locked behind her with a snick, there was little we could do. Though judging from the look in Gage's enraged eyes, that didn't stop him from considering it. "Undue influence? What rot," he snarled.

I had to agree. "Obviously, McClintock knows something. Something Mrs. Birnam would prefer she not reveal."

The problem was, what? Did she suspect her maid was guilty and preferred to avoid the scandal of her confessing? Or was the maid protecting her employer, or perhaps her employer's son?

I thought of the arrow that had been fired at Mr. Birnam. Jemmy had been among the archers. Could he have made the shot undetected? Or had Mr. Birnam feigned the attempt on his life, hoping to avert suspicion from him? Or from his wife?

I grunted in frustration. "We need to convince Mrs. McClintock to speak to us."

"Perhaps Mr. Birnam might have some *influence* over her," Gage proposed, evidently still irked by Mrs. Birnam's remarks.

I could think of no better suggestion. "It's worth a try."

Exiting Mrs. Birnam's sitting room, we moved just a few steps down the corridor to Mr. Birnam's door. But before we could knock, Trevor called out for me to wait. I turned to find him hurrying toward us with a tearful Matilda trailing behind him.

My first reaction was disappointment, thinking he was about to upbraid me for upsetting Matilda. But as he drew nearer, I realized the source of his agitation wasn't me or Gage but the woman beside him.

No, not beside him. She was just behind him, partially cowering from the trio we'd formed.

I looked from her tear-streaked face to his rigid one in question.

"Can we speak somewhere private?" He appeared to struggle for control of his façade as he turned to his almost-fiancée. "Matilda has something she needs to tell you."

"Of course." I scrambled to decide the best place to take them. "Follow me," I said, opting to lead them toward Gage's and my private sitting room. It was nearby and we were certain not to be interrupted there.

I didn't know precisely what had happened between Trevor and Matilda, but it was serious. I could only think that it had something to do with whatever I'd sensed Matilda was keeping from us. She'd clearly been anxious about something since Miss Whitlock's death. I'd believed she suspected someone in her family of being involved, but maybe it was more than suspicion. Maybe she knew something that until now she'd been afraid to reveal.

Whatever the case, our discovery that Mrs. Birnam's maid, McClintock, had been seen with a bottle of oil of vitriol had altered matters. At least, that seemed to be the catalyst for Matilda disclosing to Trevor whatever she was about to tell me and Gage.

I led them into our suite and through the door into the sitting room, gesturing for them to take a seat. But neither Trevor nor Matilda accepted the offer to sit.

Matilda waited just long enough for the door to close behind us, holding her hands out toward me as if in supplication. "It was mine!" She hiccupped on a sob. "Tha-tha-that bottle of vitriol," she stammered. "It was mine."

I stared at her in shock before turning to see that my brother's expression was one of anguish. It was clear from the anger and hurt raging in his eyes that he'd not known about this until minutes before.

"*I* asked Mrs. McClintock to get rid of it for me," Matilda continued. "I thought she would dispose of it in the rubbish, but she said it was dangerous to just throw out acid. She promised to see to it." Her voice took on a note of pleading. "So you see, it's my fault she ever had it. She's protecting *me* by refusing to talk, not Mother."

"But why did you bring a bottle of oil of vitriol with you in the first place?" I asked in confusion. It wasn't something people would typically travel with, and I couldn't think of any justifiable reason why Matilda would have required it.

She backed away, seeming to shrink into herself, and I realized this was the real crux of the matter. For if she'd had any legitimate reason for having it, she wouldn't have needed her maid to get rid of it or been so afraid of telling us.

My chest tightened in dread as I looked to my brother to see if he was already aware of the answer to this question, but his eyes bored into Matilda with something akin to dawning horror, making it clear he'd not yet heard this part. Gage observed us both with empathy.

"Matilda," I prodded gently but firmly even as she bent her head and wept, her chest rising and falling with each sob.

"I . . . I don't really know what I was thinking," she finally managed to say. "I was just . . . so *furious* with Father . . . and Portia." She sniffed, wiping her nose. "I heard all the reports of the mill workers using . . . *it*. How most of the time the damage was minimal. And I thought, I thought maybe if Portia wasn't so pretty . . ." Her face crumpled and she covered it with her hands as if to shield herself from the horror of the admission she'd just made.

Trevor's features were stricken with agony and disbelief.

Matilda inhaled a ragged breath, lifting her head to implore us. "But I didn't use it! I . . . I *couldn't*." It was clear she wanted to believe this. "After arriving here, I realized what a terrible, awful, *despicable* thing it would be. And I just wanted it out of my sight. Which was why I asked Mrs. McClintock to dispose of it."

I wondered if she'd feared she might change her mind if the option was left open to her.

"So it wasn't me who attacked Miss Whitlock," she asserted primarily to Trevor. "I couldn't have done it. I just couldn't." When he didn't respond, her voice cracked. "*Please*. You have to believe me."

My brother was struggling with these revelations. *I* certainly was, and I could only imagine how much greater they'd affected him. To think that sweet Matilda had actually considered doing such an appalling thing to another person, that she'd even gone so far as to procure the weapon to do it, made my heart stutter in my chest. And while she'd claimed she'd not gone through with it, I now held doubts. There were definitely further questions to be answered. When Trevor turned away from Matilda, pacing toward the window, I pressed for them.

"You said you were furious with your father and Portia. Why?"

She was slow to respond, distressed by my brother's response. "I was furious because . . . because Father seemed to prefer her to me. He never seemed to have time for me. But with Portia . . ." Her face twisted not just in scorn but also pain. "There was no one cleverer, no one kinder." She sniffed sorrowfully. "I sometimes wondered if he wished Portia was his daughter in truth rather than me."

From my vantage, I could see Trevor's shoulders tense as he stared out the window. I wondered if he was fighting the compulsion to comfort her or the desire to throttle her father.

"His only use for me seemed to be in marrying me off," she added in a voice throbbing with heartbreak, and I watched the way the words caused the muscles in my brother's back to ripple with his own silent despair.

But Gage seemed to decide this was enough self-pitying talk. "You do realize it was that bottle of vitriol you brought that was likely used in the attack on Miss Whitlock," he told Matilda severely. "That the killer seized on the opportunity *your* malicious jealousy presented them."

Matilda paled, eliciting a gasping wheeze as if she'd been punched. While Gage's harsh remarks provoked Trevor to pivot back toward the room, offering us his quarter profile, he didn't speak.

"I've half a mind to take you down to the cellar and show you what damage your acid caused."

Until that moment, I hadn't realized how very irate my husband was. And he wasn't wrong to be. I suspected my own anger had been blunted by astonishment and concern for my brother, but it was still there, simmering deep in my belly.

Silent tears tracked down Matilda's cheeks as Gage continued.

"All of you Birnams!" he stated in disgust. "You profess to have cared for Miss Whitlock, and yet all you're worried about is yourselves. Not a one of you has been entirely honest with us."

"You're right," Matilda ventured in response, her voice quaking. "But that doesn't mean I don't care. I know it may not seem like it, but I do. Portia and I . . ." She crossed her arms as if to insulate herself from the chill of his glare or to squelch the pain of her admissions. "Once upon a time, we were so close. And she wanted to be again." Her lower lip trembled. "But Mother said it was inappropriate. And I listened to her." She turned her head to the side. "Oh, why did I listen to her?"

Gage all but ignored this confession. "Is there anything else you're keeping from us?"

Matilda blinked rapidly, her eyes gleaming with unshed tears as she shook her head.

"What of your mother?" he pushed. "She purports to have cared for Miss Whitlock in her own way, but the animosity she felt toward her was crystal clear." He arched a single eyebrow in challenge. "Perhaps McClintock told her about the vitriol. After all, her loyalty is ultimately to your mother, isn't it? Perhaps your mother decided to put the acid to use."

Matilda gasped, shaking her head. "No. My mother could never . . ."

Gage's second eyebrow joined the first, daring her to finish that statement.

"I don't *think* she could," she amended.

"But you weren't with her during the time frame the attack occurred?"

"No," she admitted in a small voice.

"And what about your father?"

She scowled. "I just told you that Father favored her.

In his eyes, she could do no wrong. Why would he attack her?"

"What if she was about to betray him?" I interjected.

She turned to me in confusion.

"What if she was about to divulge secrets about his businesses? Perhaps something even corrupt?"

Matilda's mouth had formed a small "o" in dawning astonishment. Her silence was rather telling. Not only did she stop insisting her father would never have harmed Miss Whitlock, but she also didn't deny the possibility that some of her father's business methods might be unethical.

Before she could recover, I pressed her on another point. "Your brother. He is the one person who has openly admitted to loathing Miss Whitlock. He called her deceitful and a liar. Do you know why?"

"I have heard him say that as well," she professed. "But I've never understood why." Her brow furrowed in chagrin. "He doesn't confide in me, his little sister."

Trevor turned his head back toward the window, but not before I caught sight of his bitter frown. Did he know something about Jemmy's accusations or was he thinking that "deceitful" and "liar" applied to Matilda?

"We'll be confirming your story with Mrs. McClintock." Gage crossed his arms, gazing down at Matilda sternly. "So if you'd like to revise any of your claims, now is your chance."

"No. Everything I've told you is the truth." She glanced toward Trevor, whose face was still averted, before adding ruefully, "This time."

"Then, stay where we can find you," he directed her as he shifted away from the door. "We may have more questions for you."

She nodded forlornly, understanding this was her dismissal.

I turned toward my brother, wondering if he wanted company or to be left alone. Gage seemed to think it was the latter.

"Are you coming?" he asked, holding the door to our suite open for me.

"Yes," I said. But I couldn't leave without at least arching up onto my toes to press a kiss to Trevor's cheek. He surprised me when he halted me by lightly grasping my arm. His lips curved into the facsimile of a grin, but it did not reach his eyes. I knew he was trying to reassure *me*, and that almost broke me.

He chucked me under the chin. "Go on. We'll talk later."

I smiled as bravely as I could and did as I was told.

Gage was still waiting, and he wrapped his arm around me, tucking me close to his side as we left the suite.

CHAPTER 21

Foolish lass!"

Those were Mrs. McClintock's first words to us after we explained what Matilda had already admitted. She tipped her head back to look at the ceiling, as if seeking divine intervention, and then shook it. So tightly was her iron gray hair secured that not even a tendril moved.

"I believe she was afraid you would be blamed," I explained.

She turned away, muttering to herself.

While still tidy, the butler's sitting room was far more austere. A single worn and faded armchair sat in the corner with a blanket draped over its back. Next to it stood a lamp and a table holding a book of military history. The floor was covered in an old rug which had likely graced the floor of one of the bedchambers abovestairs before being replaced.

We had instructed McClintock to sit, leaving myself,

Gage, and Bree standing over her. Not that she seemed in the least intimidated. Sunlight filtered into the room from just a single small window high on the wall, so we'd turned the lamp on, casting almost a halo around her head.

"Can you confirm Matilda's story? Did she ask you to dispose of the bottle of vitriol?" Gage pressed.

"Aye," she grumbled with a sigh. "Smuggled it in her portmanteau, the numpty eejit. She's lucky it didna burn a hole through her garments, the bag, *and* the carriage."

"Did she tell you why she'd brought it?" I asked, curious what she might say.

"Nay," she said slowly, clearly trying to guess whether Matilda had told us herself. "She kept that tae herself. Especially after I scolded her."

Gage spread his legs and crossed his arms, settling into a more comfortable position as he coaxed her for more information. "And what did you do with the bottle?"

"Ye canna just toss acid oot or dump it in the rubbish bin. So I tucked it away on the shelf in the laundry room until I could think o' what tae do wi' it." Her voice turned wry. "I s'pose that's when someone saw me wi' it." She sank deeper in her chair, her head tilted in thought. "And I s'pose that's hoo the killer kenned where tae find it."

Gage's brow lowered in displeasure. "You knew the killer used that bottle of vitriol?"

She shrugged. "I guessed they did, for 'twasn't there when I went tae look for it the next day."

"And yet you didn't say anything?"

McClintock stared defiantly back at Gage as if she found this to be a stupid question. "I ken what you'd think."

His eyes glinted angrily. "I *think* your remaining silent only makes you and the Birnams appear *more* guilty."

She scoffed. "They've naught tae do wi' it other than Miss Birnam's daft decision tae bring it."

"Then you didn't inform Mrs. Birnam what her daughter had done?" I inquired.

"And cause the lass more grief?" She frowned. "Nay."

"What about the other staff? Mr. Paget and Mr. Simpkins?"

"Paget's got his hands full wi' Mr. Birnam. As for the other . . . bah! He's useless." She tilted her head. "Though he was in the laundry, was he no'?" It was clear from her narrowed eyes that she was wondering if he was the one who'd tattled on her. "So maybe he already kenned. But no' because I told him."

I joined Gage in his skeptical scrutiny of the maid, trying to decide if I believed her. She *seemed* to be telling us the truth, but she was also unequivocally loyal to the Birnams. Had Matilda not confessed, McClintock would never have betrayed her confidence, perhaps even to the grave. Because of this, I doubted she would tell us anything that reflected poorly on any of the Birnams. Jemmy's valet seemed to be the exception, but I sensed he was a relatively new addition to the household, and the fact that McClintock seemed to think he exposed her first might have accounted for her attitude.

"We ken ye didna like Miss Whitlock," Bree spoke up, stepping forward. "What we dinna ken is why."

McClintock's pinched lips communicated that she didn't like being questioned by a member of the staff, and a younger one, at that. However, when neither Gage nor I objected, she condescended to answer. "Because she thought she was better than she was. Struttin' aboot like a crow in the gutter. She nettled my mistress somethin' fierce."

In other words, because she upset Mrs. Birnam, she upset her.

"How long have you worked for Mrs. Birnam?" I asked.

She arched her neck proudly. "Nearly twenty years."

"Then you were there when Miss Whitlock came to live with them the first time."

Her scowl returned. "Aye. I'll admit, she was sweet tae begin wi'. But she forgot her place."

"Is that why she was sent away?"

But she was too canny. "I'm sure I dinna ken."

I turned to Gage, signaling I was finished. We were going to get nothing from her that the Birnams wouldn't want her to say.

"What about the other guests and their staff?" Gage queried, attempting a different tack. "Have you noticed anything suspicious or out of the ordinary? Have any of them indicated they were previously acquainted with Miss Whitlock?"

McClintock tipped her head back as if the answer was written on the ceiling and then lowered it to shake her head. "Nay." She suddenly leaned forward. "But if you're askin' me, she must've arranged an assignation wi' the wrong man and got no better than she deserved. Why else would she be in that part o' the house at such an hour?"

Clearly, McClintock did not know the person Miss Whitlock had arranged to meet was *me*. Her self-righteous condemnation left a bitter taste in my mouth.

"You may go," Gage dismissed her, not bothering to hide his contempt for her and her closing remarks.

She sniffed, wrapping her wounded dignity around her like a cloak as she strode toward the door.

Once she was out of earshot, he softly urged Bree, "Follow her."

She nodded, understanding the assignment. He wanted to know where McClintock went and who she spoke to. If she knew anything, human inclination would be for her to warn anyone else involved.

"I take it you trust her as much as I do," I said as Bree departed.

"Which is to say, not at all." Gage glowered at the door they'd passed through. "Except . . . it's so nonsensical . . ."

"It might be true?"

He heaved a sigh, rubbing a hand over the back of his neck. "We know from multiple sources that she put a bottle on the shelf in the laundry, and that it was almost certainly filled with oil of vitriol. What we don't know or cannot prove is who then retrieved the bottle. It could have been McClintock. It could have been one of the servants who saw her put the bottle on the shelf. Or it could have been someone else. Someone who found it, though this seems doubtful. Or someone that McClintock or one of the witnesses told."

"Yet only two witnesses admitted to seeing her with the bottle, and they and McClintock denied telling anyone," I pointed out, joining him in his frustration.

"Except Lord Milngavie. Remember Mr. Armstrong told us that it was his employer who exhorted him to tell us what he'd seen."

"True. But I was under the impression that Mr. Armstrong had only recently informed him. And Milngavie's reaction doesn't seem like that of a man who is guilty of anything."

"No, it doesn't." He reached out to turn down the lamp. "It seems far more likely that one of the others lied. After all, it would be in their self-interest to do so."

"But how are we going to figure out who?" I fretted, tired of the lies and evasions we so often encountered.

"I don't know." Gage pulled me toward him, resting his hands on either side of my waist. "But we will. We always do."

I was glad at least one of us felt confident.

A chime sounded from the clock hanging on the wall. "Oh, goodness! Is that what time it is? I need to change Mr. Birnam's dressings."

"I'll come with you." Gage's eyes narrowed. "I've a few questions I'd like to put to Mr. Birnam."

"But if you're going to rile him," I warned, "please wait until I'm finished rewrapping his hands."

He agreed, escorting me up two flights of stairs to Mr. Birnam's bedchamber. It was Birnam himself who called out for us to enter, Paget being nowhere to be seen. This was surprising given the valet had been hovering near his employer's side ever since the archery attack the day before. Birnam was seated and waiting for us, and judging from his pugnacious scowl he was already aware of some of the afternoon's revelations.

"I expect ye tae release Mrs. McClintock at once," he ordered. "It is utter nonsense tae think she or my wife had anythin' tae do wi' Miss Whitlock's death. Whoever claimed he saw her wi' vitriol must o' been lyin'."

I gathered the supplies Dr. Clarke had left while he finished this diatribe, directing Gage toward a chair across the room with a nod. "She's already admitted to it," I informed Mr. Birnam evenly once he'd fallen silent.

His head reared backward in shock. "Then ye must have . . ."

"But it was your daughter who brought the vitriol to Bevington Park," I continued, placidly interrupting him as I arranged the dressings, scissors, and ointment on the table between us. "Mrs. McClintock was merely obeying her request to dispose of it."

He made a sound as if he'd swallowed his own tongue. Perhaps I was disobeying my own admonition to my husband not to rile the man, but really, he'd started it with his tirade. And it wasn't as if his accusations could go unanswered. He would never have stood for it.

"I'm sure Mrs. McClintock is already attending Mrs. Birnam," I finished, reaching for his left hand to begin unwinding the dressing."

"Matilda . . . ?!" He seemed at a loss for words, so I tried to supply the answer I thought he sought.

"I'm not sure where she is. We finished speaking with her perhaps half an hour ago."

"She said she brought the vitriol?" He seemed stunned.

"Yes." I watched his face carefully as I continued to unwind the dressing. "That surprises you."

He blinked as if waking from a trance, anger snapping in his eyes. "O' course it does!"

I focused on my task, waiting to see what he would say next.

"Did . . . did she say why she brought it?"

I looked up to meet his eyes, noting the pain and remorse and uncertainty swimming in their hazel depths. The gold ring at the center was all but swallowed by his pupils. My movements slowed as I felt a pulse of recognition. Miss Whitlock's eyes had been very similar.

But many people had hazel eyes. Matilda did, I recalled. Perhaps I was confusing hers with my memory of Miss Whitlock's appearance.

It was clear Mr. Birnam was asking me more than his daughter's reason for bringing the oil of vitriol, and I wasn't about to answer him. Not when that *would* rile him. Instead, I opted for a deflection. "You'll have to speak with your daughter about that."

He fell silent, watching me as I worked. If his hands ached, he didn't show it. But then, he was already aggrieved by the disclosure about Matilda. More than I would have expected, to be honest. I would have thought he would come to her fiery defense. At least, more so than he had for his wife's maid. I wanted to ask Gage what he thought of this, but I couldn't do so without alerting Mr. Birnam.

"Matilda also told us you directly received some threats on your life?" I prompted, opting to change subjects until I'd finished with his hands. Technically, Matilda had informed Trevor, who had informed us, but the result was the same.

"Aye." He seemed unconcerned by this.

"Why didn't you make that clear to us?"

"Because threats are just part o' the business. I get 'em all the time." A deep furrow formed between his brows. "I told her no' to worry."

I'd finished unwrapping his hands and now they were both laid out before me, flushed an angry red, particularly where the outer layer of skin had sloughed off.

"I need to examine them before I reapply the ointment,"

I explained, steeling my stomach for the task. "I'll try not to hurt you any more than necessary."

He gave a short nod.

Carefully grasping his hands, I turned them this way and that to get a better look, and pressed them in a few areas as I'd seen Dr. Clarke do, testing the blood flow, particularly to the tips of his fingers. His hands were stiff from pain and the days of trying to hold them immobile. However, after a few seconds I realized this stiffness wasn't only caused by the recent injury. Some of his fingers appeared to lack the uppermost joint, as if the distal and middle phalanx were fused.

I straightened in shock as the realization that I'd also seen *this* before struck me. The blood drained from my face and extremities.

"What?" Mr. Birnam demanded, looking from me to his hands as I abruptly released them. "Is there something wrong? Is the tissue dyin'?"

"Do we need to send for Dr. Clarke?" Gage asked from across the room behind me.

"She was your daughter," I accused, finding my voice.

CHAPTER 22

Portia Whitlock was your daughter," I stated with even more conviction, as half a dozen thoughts flickered across Birnam's astonished face. I could tell he was considering denying it, thinking of displaying outrage instead, but my firm expression must have persuaded him it would be useless. The anomalies in the bone structure of their hands coupled with their unique eye color were too much to ignore.

His shoulders slumped. "How did you know?"

This was too much of an admission for Gage to remain impartial. "Portia Whitlock was your daughter?" he repeated in disbelief as he moved nearer to us. "And you didn't think to say anything about it until my wife figured it out?"

Birnam made no response to this charge, though he seemed relieved that it was finally known. I gave my husband a stern look, glancing at the chair perpendicular to ours in a not-so-subtle suggestion that he take a seat. He complied begrudgingly.

I picked up the unguent to begin applying it. "Obviously *you* knew. And I assume Ellie Whitlock knew."

"Aye." He didn't attempt to deny the fact that they'd had an affair.

My voice was sharp with disapproval. "What about your friend—her husband?"

But if Mr. Birnam had ever felt any guilt over what he'd done, he didn't display it now. "If Clive knew, he never said."

I shared a look with Gage, both of us still struggling to grapple with the ramifications of this discovery and what it meant for our inquiry and the potential motives of our suspects.

I wiped the extra ointment from my fingers on the dressing before beginning to wrap his hand, starting at the center of his palm. "And your wife? Did she know?" Given Mrs. Birnam's treatment of Miss Whitlock, I suspected I knew the answer, but I waited for him to confirm it.

"Aye. She figured it oot a few years ago."

"Just before Miss Whitlock was sent away?"

He lifted his gaze to my face, and I glared at him in challenge, waiting for his response. "Aye."

I shook my head, for his dejected tone of voice grated on my nerves. He was not the victim here. And it sounded like his poor decisions had wounded almost everyone around him. "Have you told Jemmy and Matilda that they have a half sister?"

"Nay. They dinna ken." His voice hardened. "And I dinna want them to."

I eyed him with scorn, finding it difficult to believe he didn't think either of them had grasped the truth. It would explain Jemmy's animosity toward her. It certainly cast new light on Matilda's declaration that Portia had been like a sister.

"I think you're naïve," I told him baldly, surprising him, before returning to my task. "Miss Whitlock—*your daughter*—deserves justice. And we cannot promise the truth won't become known—if it isn't *already*."

"So you weren't her lover," Gage said, earning a glare from Birnam as he sorted through the implications. "When you decided not to find her a husband immediately and instead to hire her as your secretary, you were what . . . trying to spend more time with her?" Gage tapped his finger on the table. "Did *she* know who she was?"

He hesitated, making me look up as I finished with his first hand. "Aye." He seemed almost confused by this. "She kenned even before I told her."

"So her mother told her," Gage guessed.

"She must have."

That or Miss Whitlock had figured it out on her own. Either way, I didn't see that it mattered.

"And you weren't playing matchmaker with Miss Whitlock and your son," Gage mused.

"I already said I wasna," Birnam protested as I began wrapping his second hand. I'd wound the dressing around several times, concentrating on getting the tautness and spacing even, before he added, "I had someone else in mind for her."

There was something in his voice that alerted me to the fact that this wasn't an idle remark, and when I lifted my gaze, it was to find him watching me carefully. It took only a few seconds to realize what he was hinting at.

Dismay trickled through me. "Do not tell me you're talking about Trevor."

When he didn't respond, this all but confirmed it.

"But he's been courting Matilda. And he loves her," I argued in alarm and distress. "And she loves him!" Yes, they'd recently quarreled, and that may have changed matters, but that didn't alter the events that had led to this moment.

Birnam was unmoved. "Your brother misconstrued the situation. Wi' Matilda's bonnie face, her sweet nature, and my fortune, she needn't settle for anythin' less than a title."

I stiffened in affront at the notion that any girl would be "settling" if they married Trevor, and I must have inadvertently tugged on the dressing, for Birnam winced. Perhaps I should have apologized, but I didn't, thinking it was less than he deserved. "You were never going to accept his offer for Matilda's hand, were you? You were misleading him all along."

Gage joined me in my disapproval, scowling at the man. "For shame, sir. Trevor St. Mawr is the finest of men. Matilda would be only too fortunate to have him as a husband." He shook his head. "That was poorly done."

"No worse than you leading on Paddington's daughter," he countered snidely.

Evidently, he'd heard the gossip speculating there would be nuptials between my husband and Lady Felicity Spencer, or he'd asked someone to dig up what he could about all of us before coming here, for that was old news. Lady Felicity had wed someone else over a year ago, and rumor was that she was quite content with the way things had turned out.

"I never led Lady Felicity anywhere," Gage responded

evenly. "And she knew it. If there was any misunderstanding, it was between our fathers."

"Well, I've since made matters plain tae Mr. St. Mawr. If he continues tae delude himself, that's no' my fault. Lady Darby, really . . . ?" he scolded when I yanked the dressing too tight again.

"Say that again?" I exchanged a glance of misgiving with Gage. "You told my brother? When?"

"The evening Melbourne and the others arrived. A few hours before Portia was attacked." His head tilted back as he leered at me almost menacingly. "Suspicious timing, that. Maybe ye should be investigatin' your brother."

My blood rushed to my head in a mist of fury. How dare he suggest such a thing!

Gage rested his hand over mine before I could deliberately tug on the dressing. "Careful, Birnam. I wouldn't be issuing veiled threats if I were you. Particularly until she's done *tending* to your *wounds*."

My heart pounded and my mind spun, grappling with the hurt, confusion, and yes, fear that flooded me. For if Trevor had known that Birnam wasn't going to let him wed Matilda, that he wanted him to court Miss Whitlock, why hadn't he said anything? Why had he concealed it?

He must have realized it could have bearing on our inquiry. Did he not trust that we would examine this with equanimity? Or did he genuinely have something to hide?

While my thoughts unraveled and I fumbled through completing Birnam's wrapping, Gage kept his head. "Did Miss Whitlock know of your intentions?"

"Aye," Birnam grunted. "I told her that afternoon, shortly before dinner."

No wonder she'd seemed so uncomfortable at the table. What must she have thought when he'd told her? She must have been able to see the way Trevor and Matilda felt about each other. Given that, it was doubtful she would have welcomed this revelation.

Was that what she'd wanted to speak to me about privately? I supposed it was possible. But why would she have been so afraid of being overheard? For certain, such a revelation might besmudge a few reputations if it became known, but that was not enough to warrant outright fear.

"And Matilda?" Gage asked as I secured the end of the dressing.

Birnam sank back in his chair, perhaps realizing his answer could create trouble for his younger daughter. "I told her before we left Twizel Hall." His estate in the Borders. "I didna want her tae become too attached tae the notion o' marryin' St. Mawr and joinin' your family."

Yet he expected her to come here and pretend, knowing all the while that he would never consent to the marriage, that he intended Trevor to wed Miss Whitlock. It was beyond heartless. It was outright cruel!

I could only imagine how distraught Matilda must have been. Had she expected she could convince her father to change his mind? She must have. For it was still abundantly clear to me how she felt about my brother.

This was what had prompted her to bring the vitriol. In her grief and anger, she'd reached for the tool she'd seen others use to lash out and sway events in their favor. I only hoped she'd been honest with us. That she'd never truly intended to use it. That she'd stopped herself before it was too late.

I left the supplies on the table and pushed myself to my

feet, too disgusted with the man before me to remain a moment longer. All of the empathy I might have felt for him for losing his daughter Portia had been subverted into revulsion at the way he'd treated Trevor and Matilda. Not to mention the manner in which he'd lied to us all.

Gage soon followed, catching up to me as I stalked back to our bedchamber. I'd hoped I might find my brother still there, but he was gone. The hour was later than I'd realized, and Bree and Anderley were already preparing our evening clothes for dinner. But I was wound too tight to dress, pacing back and forth across the sitting room as I grumbled to myself. When our maid and valet entered to see what the disturbance was, Gage informed them of everything we'd just learned. Their exclamations of shock and disapproval were at least satisfying.

"He came here under false pretenses," I protested, pivoting angrily back in the direction I'd come. "He *and* Mrs. Birnam, because I don't believe for a second that she didn't know his plans once he told Matilda." I flung my arm out, pointing at the door near where Gage, Anderley, and Bree stood as I passed by. "I only invited them because I thought Trevor was on the verge of asking for Matilda's hand and that her father would accept. I only asked them here—risking my father-in-law's *wrath*—because I wished to smooth the way for the couple and show them what a worthy suitor Trevor is. *Not* to grant Birnam access to your father's political cronies for his own means. *Not* to break my brother's heart!" My voice cracked and I stumbled to a stop, clasping a hand over my mouth to hold back the sob that threatened to escape.

Gage came to me then, wrapping his arms around me so that I could bury my face in his chest. I wanted nothing more than to weep all over his waistcoat, but I was afraid that if I started, I might not be able to stop, and we would have two dozen guests downstairs awaiting our appearance in less than half an hour. So I gathered my tattered composure, squeezed the bridge of my nose, and inhaled a ragged breath as I forced myself to step away from him.

"I suppose we know now why Birnam was so insistent Miss Whitlock join us for tea and dinner," I quipped faintly. It seemed foolish now that I'd worried we were courting scandal by possibly allowing his mistress and his wife to dine with us, even though it was impossible that I could have guessed the truth.

"We'll need to speak to Mrs. Birnam again," Gage said, eyeing me in concern.

"And Matilda, *and* Trevor, *and* Jemmy," I added with a heart-weary sigh as I sank down on the edge of one of the chairs. I didn't want to consider my brother as a suspect.

"Anything to report on Mrs. McClintock or the others?" Gage asked Bree and Anderley.

"She went straight tae Mrs. Birnam," Bree replied. Which was to be expected, given she was her maid. "Hasna spoken tae anyone else, that I'm aware."

"Nothing to share about the other potential witnesses in the laundry," Anderley supplied. "Except that Mr. Simpkins looked rather cross when he returned belowstairs after being summoned to attend to the younger Mr. Birnam. A few of us attempted to get him to confide in us, but he remained close-lipped."

"Which I gather isn't typical for him."

Anderley shook his head. "That one's got tongue enough for two sets of teeth."

"Must've been given a good reason tae stubble it, then," Bree remarked.

Gage considered them both. "It would be interesting to know why."

Anderley grinned. "I'll see what I can do to loosen him up."

"Get approval from Bowcott first." His eyes narrowed. "And invite Mr. Armstrong, for good measure."

I turned to him in surprise. "Lord Milngavie's valet?"

He shrugged. "The more people, the less obvious it'll be. Ask Barnes as well." Philip's valet. "He'll prove a help. *And* he's got a strong head."

"He's a Scot," Anderley replied as if that explained his tolerance for strong drink.

Bree's gaze met mine before she looked to heaven as if seeking patience.

I smiled weakly.

"Come, m'lady. Let's get ye changed," she urged, ushering me toward the bedchamber while Gage and Anderley continued to plot.

Had I been able to come up with any plausible excuse to avoid dinner, I would have used it. But as hostess and investigator, pleading a megrim or an indisposition simply would not do. Not when I was supposed to see to the comfort of our guests and ensure justice was done for poor Miss Whitlock.

At any rate, it should not have been me who felt awkward sitting down to dine with Birnam and his wife and their daughter or even Trevor. *They* were the ones who should have felt trepidation about what Gage and I might reveal. While this could be said of Matilda, who struggled to hide both her misery and her unease, periodically darting glances at me, Gage, and my brother—glances I didn't know whether my brother returned because I was *avoiding* looking at him—the same was not true of Mr. and Mrs. Birnam.

Mrs. Birnam was as abrasive as ever, making her displeasure over everything known to anyone who would listen. However, it was Mr. Birnam who most disconcerted and flustered me. Considering everything we'd just learned from him and the scandal the information could cause, I'd expected at least compliance from the man if not some form of contrition for his previous behavior. Instead, he became even more tenacious in his initiative to dominate the conversation and bully the noblemen present to accept his opinion about the revisions to the Factory Act.

This was not well received by the majority of the table, particularly my father-in-law and Lord Milngavie who, true to his earlier promise to me, managed to temper his responses. I found that I was not equal to the task that evening of helping to suppress and redirect Birnam. At first, I was too shocked by the nerve of the man, and later I was too furious. He was clearly relying on our desire to shield the innocent from harm to keep us quiet when that should have been *his* concern. I wanted nothing more than to defy his challenge, but I couldn't bring myself to harm either the living or the deceased simply to spite him. Doing so could also prove to be detrimental to our inquiry, for we had not yet established who knew the truth about each aspect of the investigation. But I struggled mightily with the impulse to lash out at the man who had so wounded my brother in addition to his own daughters—Matilda and Portia.

I could tell that Gage was equally perturbed, though he

was able to verbally spar with Birnam without letting slip any of the secrets we were now privy to. I trusted he'd not yet spoken to his father about what we'd learned, or I doubted Lord Gage could have resisted upbraiding him, given the way Birnam continued to provoke him. It was almost as if Birnam had decided he no longer had anything to lose by being so unpleasant. Perhaps he expected us to ask him to depart, but we could not do so until Miss Whitlock's killer was discovered.

I also refused to be party to his machinations to separate Trevor and Matilda. At least, not until they themselves had come to some conclusion about the matter. At this point, I was willing to aid and abet them in making a dash toward the Scottish border so that they might be married over the anvil, so to speak. Of course, such an elopement was never ideal, but if my brother loved Matilda and wished to marry her, regardless of the consequences, I would help him see it through.

Unless one of them was a murderer.

I balked at the notion—particularly in regard to Trevor—but the facts still had to be wrangled with. They both had lied. They both had motive. They both might have had the opportunity if they'd discovered Miss Whitlock's intentions or followed her. Matilda had access to the weapon. None of this meant either of them was guilty, but it raised questions that needed to be answered.

Answers I feared. Answers that kept me silent even though it played into Birnam's hands.

CHAPTER 23

"Tell Mrs. Taylor that I trust her judgment should any other issues arise," I informed Bowcott. "That she needn't waste precious time waiting for my approval."

He had waylaid me on my return to the mauve drawing room after I'd gone upstairs to see to Emma. My daughter's schedule had been disrupted by our jaunt to the dower house earlier that day—had it truly been just hours before?—so I'd had to postpone her evening nursing. There were many details still to see to before the new guests arrived in two days' time, and with them came numerous questions.

"The same goes for you," I told the butler. "As does my order that you are both to seek your beds before the cock crows. I'll not have you run off your feet no matter how much work is to be done."

"Yes, my lady," he replied dutifully, though I knew they would both do as they pleased. He was humoring me.

I smiled knowingly and shook my head in fondness. At least, Jeffers and most of the dower house staff would be arriving the next morning to relieve some of the burden.

"Though if it's not too impertinent of me to say so . . ." Which meant it was *highly* impertinent, despite the gentle tone Bowcott used. "Perhaps you should take a bit of your own advice."

"I would if I could," I said with a sigh. "Though you might help me earn a temporary reprieve by standing here a moment longer and pretending to discuss some serious matter of household management."

He chuckled. "A hostess's work is never done, is it?" He gazed over my shoulder. "Even now, I see a young lady peering around the corner, waiting to assail you."

I glanced over my shoulder to find Matilda hovering near the entrance to the drawing room, darting looks at us while pretending to embroider. I wasn't certain I was prepared yet for another conversation with her, but if she was this anxious to speak to me, I decided I should hear her out.

I nodded to Bowcott resignedly and turned to make my way toward the chamber, where I was intercepted by Matilda before I'd even set foot inside. She'd peered furtively toward the other guests before setting aside her needlework and hurrying over to me. "Could I speak with you? Alone," she added, in case her intent should be unclear.

I gestured for her to follow me down the corridor to the right, entering the music room. This chamber was little used. My father-in-law had placed the Broadwood grand in the drawing room, leaving a pianoforte of lesser quality in this smaller space. It stood near the window next to a harpsichord. The drapes had not been pulled, allowing moonlight to spill across the instruments shrouded in their dust covers.

I considered returning to the corridor for one of the candles arranged across the console table adjoining the drawing room door, ready for the guests to light when they retired, but then decided moonlight might befit this conversation. Matilda worried the ribbon trim at the waist of her pale blue gown now washed gray in the light from the window between her fingers. She seemed to be waiting for me to speak, but rather than set the direction of the conversation, I elected to wait and see what she revealed.

She inhaled twice before finding her voice after the third attempt. "Have you spoken with Trevor?"

Even in my own preoccupation with avoiding my brother, I'd noticed that while polite, the pair had largely been eschewing each other's company. So I wasn't surprised when this was the first topic she addressed. "Not since earlier," I answered honestly.

She lowered her head, but not before I saw that she was fighting tears. I thought it was distress over Trevor's silence, but her next words proved me wrong.

"Father just told me . . ." She sniffed raggedly, trying to retain her composure. "He . . . he told me that Portia was my half sister." She looked up at me, tears glinting in eyes raw with pain.

I pulled a handkerchief out of my sleeve and passed it to her. "You didn't know?"

She shook her head, dabbing at her eyes. "I just thought . . ." She shrugged one of her shoulders. "He *wished* she was his daughter. But she already was." She frowned. "And she was my *sister*." She began to sob. "I always wanted a sister."

Watching her weep, I did not doubt the sincerity of her grief or the fact that it was twofold. That she'd lost a dear friend. Someone who had once been like a sister. Someone who had wanted to be close again, but whom she'd rebuffed at her mother's guidance. And now discovering that friend had actually *been* a sister, that she would never have the chance to remedy the situation and come to know her better.

"They all knew, didn't they? They all knew, and they lied to me." She glared at me—bleakly but insistently—daring me to lie to her, too.

"I don't know about Jemmy," I confessed. "And I imagine Portia was only allowed in your home on sufferance for her silence."

"Because Mother blamed her. Blamed her for Father and Portia's mother's indiscretion." She made a scoffing sound of disgust at the back of her throat as she turned away, resting her hands against the heavy brocade cloth covering the closed lid of the harpsichord. Her profile was limned in the milky light of the moon.

When she spoke again, her voice softened to a throbbing whisper. "Do you know what's the worst thing about all of this though? Father thinks I may have done it." She seemed to choke on the final words, having to swallow harshly. "He didn't say it outright, but I saw the way he looked at me. The way . . ." She broke off, shaking her head and leaving the thought unfinished.

She turned to look at me almost in challenge. "He promised to protect me." A promise she was now damaging by confiding this to me, but she appeared to know exactly what she was doing. "He said that while I was misguided in wanting to marry Trevor, he approved of my willingness to go to such extreme lengths to get what I want. But I'm not like that. I'm not like *him*!" Her facial features constricted in repulsion. "I knew packing that bottle of vitriol was wrong the moment my portmanteau was carried out of my bedchamber. I wanted to take it out, to take it back, but I couldn't get to it. And then I didn't know how to get rid of it without being seen."

It unsettled me to hear that Birnam's reaction to the notion that one of his daughters might have killed the other was not grief or anguish or anger but an endorsement of her ruthlessness, but I tried to focus for the moment on Matilda's actions. "He'd told you he wasn't going to let you marry my brother. That he wanted him to wed Portia."

She nodded, bowing her head in shame. "It seems foolish now, but I . . ." She broke off, dabbing at her eyes again. "I thought maybe if Portia wasn't so pretty, Father would forget his stupid idea. But then I realized that Portia's prettiness had nothing to do with it. That the problem was Father's determination that I have a title. But I don't want a title, Kiera!" She turned to plead with me. "I don't want any of that. Not if it doesn't involve Trevor."

"You love him?"

She blinked through her tears, holding my gaze. "I do. Please say that you believe me."

"I do," I answered honestly. She must have been in the deepest depths of despair to have contemplated such a reckless, terrible act. The important thing was that she'd stopped herself. That she'd not gone through with it. And I believed that, too. If anything, her reaction to her father's belief that she might have done it only further convinced me that she couldn't have.

"Will you tell your brother that?"

Looking into her imploring eyes, I was reminded of a conversation I'd had with Trevor more than two years ago while standing over our parents' graves. I'd been despondent after refusing Gage's first offer of marriage, believing that he wished to wed me for the wrong reasons. But my brother had tracked me down and made me see the truth about everything that in my fear and vulnerability I could not. If not for him, I might have missed out on all of the joy that marriage to Gage and motherhood to Emma had brought me. Perhaps it was time to return the favor.

Though it wouldn't entirely solve the problem, considering Mr. Birnam's insistence that Matilda wed a nobleman. But perhaps that was an obstacle to be faced at a later date.

"I will," I promised her.

Her shoulders slumped in relief. "Thank you."

I rounded the harpsichord and sat down on the wide ledge below the window, thinking we both needed a few minutes' reprieve before returning to the drawing room next door. Even now, I could hear the low hum of voices through the wall as well as one of the ladies playing a sprightly minuet on the Broadwood. But as the seconds ticked by, a new tension seemed to compress the air. I turned to Matilda, finding it scored across her brow and in the taut line of her mouth in the moonlight.

"She came to see me."

"Who?" I asked in confusion.

"Portia. She came to see me that night after I retired."

I straightened. "The night she was killed?"

Her swallow was audible. "Yes. She came to my room."

"When?" I demanded, struggling to hide my impatience.

"Sometime after ten, but before eleven. I . . . I don't know the exact time."

"Go on," I urged, tempering my irritation.

"She told me she knew about Father's plan for her to marry Trevor but that, even if he asked her, she wouldn't go through with it. That she couldn't. She said . . . she said she wanted me to know that."

The phrasing of this struck me as odd. "She wanted you to know. That's what she said?"

"Yes."

I could tell that this now struck her as odd, too, even if it hadn't at the time.

"Did she say anything else?"

"No. But then . . . I wasn't particularly welcoming." Her voice caught, indicating her regret.

I decided to try a different tack. "How did she behave?"

Matilda seemed flummoxed by this query. "I don't . . ."

"Was she happy, sad, angry . . . ?"

"Oh. Um. I suppose a bit sad. Her words were . . . sincere. I can see that now. She seemed concerned, worried even, for me. Or for herself." She frowned. "I'm not sure." She shook her head. "I should have asked questions. I should have tried to see beyond my own selfishness."

Though I was still aggravated with Matilda for keeping this from us, I couldn't allow her to stand there berating herself without saying something. "It sounds to me like Portia understood exactly how you felt. Understood and accepted it. Why else would she have come to see you?"

Matilda seemed affected by this, pausing in her self-recrimination to consider it.

"I'm more interested in why she felt the need to seek you out at *that* hour on *that* night to tell you."

Was it because she'd learned that Mr. Birnam had told Trevor that he would not be allowed to wed Matilda but that he could ask for Portia's hand? Or was there another reason for her urgency? A reason that led to her death?

Judging from Matilda's widened eyes, she grasped why I was asking, but she didn't seem to know the answer either.

In the end, I never returned to the drawing room that evening, for as Matilda and I were about to enter, I was intercepted once again. This time by my husband.

He greeted us both with a charming smile before addressing Matilda. "Might I steal my wife away?"

"Of course," she replied, her cheeks flushing.

It wasn't clear what she believed he was stealing me away for, but the manner in which she glanced back over her shoulder at us before disappearing into the room suggested it wasn't entirely proper. I found myself wondering what Trevor had been stealing her away to do.

Gage guided me away from the drawing room with a hand on my arm. "What was that about?"

"I don't know. But Matilda just told me something interesting." I relayed our conversation in the music room, keen to hear his impression of her confessions, while we made our way across the great hall and into the south corridor.

"Her father actually indicated he believes she's guilty?" He shook his head. "That's cold. And cruel. To both his daughters."

"Then you don't believe she did it?"

"No." He arched his eyebrows. "And neither do you."

I didn't dispute this, reassured we seemed to be on the same page.

He scowled. "But sadly, I think Birnam *is* capable of telling his daughter such things when he knows it isn't true, just to place her more firmly under his thumb."

It was my turn to be shocked. "You mean, you think he deliberately lied to her in order to better control her?"

"If so, it didn't work."

Because she'd directly confided in me.

"Do you think Birnam did it?"

His expression was troubled. "Let's just say, I'm not convinced he didn't."

I pondered this a moment before registering our surroundings. "Where are we going?"

His frown turned to one of annoyance. "Father wishes to speak to us."

"Now?" I asked incredulously, for it would leave our guests unattended.

"Yes."

I supposed there was a great deal Lord Gage didn't yet know, for there hadn't been time earlier to inform him of all the afternoon's discoveries. But there were also a great deal of people still to interview. Trevor, for one, though part of me was glad to postpone that confrontation.

"Were you able to speak to Mrs. Birnam?" I asked.

"She retired early," Gage reported. "And I think we should wait to speak to Jemmy until we find out whether Anderley is able to learn anything useful from his valet."

"The ball is in two days' time," I reminded him. And the day after, Lord Gage's political cronies were supposed to return to London for several important debates on the floor of the House of Lords, as well as their upcoming votes. Philip would be traveling down with them for the same reason.

"I know," Gage assured me as we reached the door to the study. "Don't fret, Kiera," he told me. "We must be close to the solution. We're just missing one or two key pieces of information."

All I could do was hope he was correct, for I would not be pleased with the alternative. And neither would his father.

CHAPTER 24

Lord Gage was far more satisfied with our report than I'd expected him to be. Though I suspected part of that satisfaction derived from learning that Birnam was less moral than he purported to be. Not that my father-in-law should cast any stones. He had also had an affair which had resulted in a child who had also fortunately been claimed by his lover's husband. In this case, knowingly. Lord Henry Kerr, Gage's beloved half brother, was acknowledged by the rest of the world as the youngest son of the Duke of Bowmont and no relation to the Gages. He would be arriving with our other guests on Saturday.

At any rate, Lord Gage had bid us to continue our investigation with haste. An entirely unnecessary command, for we would continue regardless and were making as much haste as possible. I was still grumbling about this under my breath when we reached the grand south staircase only to encounter Trevor descending.

His footsteps slowed as our eyes met, and I felt my heart still in dread.

"I was just looking for you," he said quietly before glancing about as if to see who might be listening. "We should talk."

He was right, but I also couldn't help but silently balk at the notion, fearful of the answers I might receive to my questions. I turned to suggest that Gage wait here, but he spoke first, understanding that this conversation was one that should happen between brother and sister.

"I'll see if Melbourne is interested in a game of piquet," he informed us before disappearing into the green drawing room.

I considered suggesting the library, but it adjoined the study where we'd just left my father-in-law. There was only one place we could be certain of not being eavesdropped upon, and this was not the time to risk it. "Our sitting room?"

He nodded and waited for me to join him on the fifth riser, offering me his arm as we climbed the rest of the staircase. Neither of us spoke until we'd reached the privacy of Gage's and my suite. I listened for any sound of Bree moving around in the adjoining bedchamber. I knew Anderley would be busy belowstairs trying to get Mr. Simpkins to talk. But if my maid was present, she was completing a quiet task. In any case, it didn't really matter if she overheard. Bree had been trusted with grave secrets before.

I had never favored strong spirits, but the burden of the day's revelations and those potentially to come weighed on me. So I went straight to the sideboard and poured myself a glass of Matheson whisky from Philip's distillery. After taking a single swig, wincing at the bite and burn as the "water of life" slid down my throat, I turned to offer Trevor a glass. He declined, remaining standing with his hands in the pockets of his trousers even as I settled in the chair closest to me.

"You've spoken to Matilda." This was less a question and more of a statement, leading me to suspect he'd seen us together.

I took another drink of whisky, trying to decipher his expression before I answered, but either I was too tired, the spirits were working too quickly to dull my senses, or he'd gotten better at hiding his feelings from me. "Yes," I confirmed. "But not before we spoke to Mr. Birnam this afternoon."

I knew I wasn't mistaken when I noticed the way his shoulders stiffened and his gaze turned watchful.

I swirled the remainder of my whisky in the bottom of the glass. "It seems Matilda is not the only one who has lied by omission."

Trevor did not attempt to deny this, but he did take a moment to gather himself as he rounded the settee and sat down facing me. He leaned forward, bracing his elbows on his knees. While he appeared wretched, he also looked relieved. "I didn't want to lie to you, but I'd not even come to grips with Birnam's refusal to allow me to continue courting Matilda and his . . . *preposterous* notion that I'd be content to offer for Miss Whitlock's hand instead, when you found her dead. I couldn't reconcile myself with any of it. And then I realized that the fact that Birnam had spoken to me just hours before her death could make me look guilty. Or that it could make Matilda look guilty, if she'd found out about it."

"The two of you didn't discuss it?"

"No." He stared at me, as if the answer might be written on my forehead. "Did she . . . know?"

I decided it would not break Matilda's confidence to tell him. Not when he'd also been informed. "Yes. Her father told her before they left Twizel Hall."

His head bowed. "I wondered. Especially after she admitted to bringing the vitriol." He scraped a hand back through his chestnut brown locks, making some of them stand on end. "But I didn't want to think that she could have done such a thing."

"If it's any consolation," I said, setting aside the rest of my drink, "I don't think she did. Attack Miss Whitlock, that is."

He almost looked afraid to hope.

"But you're right in that you deduced the real reason behind her packing that bottle of vitriol. However, she told me she regretted it almost from the moment she'd done so but was unable to dispose of it until arriving here. She swears she would never have actually harmed Miss Whitlock, that she could never have gone through with it."

"And you believe her?"

"I do." I leaned toward him. "She loves you, Trevor. And she let her despair over her father's actions temporarily cloud her judgment." My lips creased into a humorless smile. "I think we've all had moments when we've let our emotions cloud our judgment."

My brother seemed to recognize I was referencing my own previous mistakes, for the corners of his lips curled into an answering smile.

I grimaced, tilting my head. "Albeit to varying degrees." For I could not absolve Matilda of all responsibility for what had befallen Miss Whitlock. Matilda *had* brought the weapon which had been the cause of Miss Whitlock's demise, even if she hadn't been the person to use it against her. This was something I could tell she felt a keen regret for. "The *important* thing is that she almost immediately came to her senses and recognized what a horrific mistake she was making." I straightened, returning to the crux of our confrontation. "I do hope you would have eventually trusted me enough to tell me the truth."

Trevor's eyes glinted with regret. "I wanted to—numerous times—but I just couldn't find the words. I think I was deluding myself that if I pretended Birnam hadn't said them to me, then . . ." he spread his hands in a gesture of futility ". . . they wouldn't be true."

"Did he tell you that Miss Whitlock was his daughter?"

He sat bolt upright, frozen by surprise. "Are you in earnest?"

"Yes."

He blinked several times before exclaiming, "No! He . . . told me that she would also have a handsome dowry." He scowled in distaste. "As if that made the least bit of difference to me. But he never said anything about her parentage." His gaze trailed to the side as he seemed to grapple with the ramifications of this information. "Then that means . . . Good God!" His disgust was evident. "He was attempting to swap one sister for the other. What Matilda must have felt!" He turned back to me. "Did she know? That Miss Whitlock was her sister? Her half sister," he clarified.

"Not until this evening when her father told her."

He seemed appeased to hear this but then shook his head angrily. "Birnam has a lot to answer for."

"Yes, he does," I agreed, picking up my glass to drain it of whisky. "And the question remains to be answered, is he capable of filicide? Could he have killed Miss Whitlock either because she defied him or because he believed she was going to betray him?"

Trevor sank back into the cushions behind him, almost appearing bowled over by the implications. "I don't want to think so, but . . . his actions toward me and Matilda, the very fact that he still came here under false pretenses . . ." He gestured weakly with his hand. "I don't know if that makes him capable of murder, but it certainly puts his morality in question."

"And yet you still wish to marry his daughter."

He stared at me blankly.

"Trevor." I set aside my glass with care, attempting to organize my thoughts with the same precision. "You once pointed out to me that while you would not be marrying your in-laws, they would still be an important part of your life. You asked about how Lord Gage has affected my life. And while I still stand by my response that I would have wed Sebastian ten times over, even if things had not turned out well with my father-in-law, I have to take pause. Because for all of Lord Gage's faults and his efforts to keep his son and me apart, he was never suspected of killing his own child." I met his gaze evenly, trying to convey my concerns without alienating him. "So I ask, do you still want to marry Matilda, even knowing all of that, even knowing all of the obstacles?"

To my relief, he did not take offense, and he did not rush to answer, giving the question due consideration. Out of deference to this, I resisted the urge to expound needlessly, trusting he already understood everything that was at stake.

When he looked up at me to answer, I could tell he was both resolved and speaking from the heart.

"Yes. Even knowing all that. I love her, Kiera. My life is better when she's with me. And I . . . I can't imagine finding someone who better suits me. I want her to be my wife, to be the mother of my children."

I nodded in easy acceptance, for I knew my brother. I knew his heart. And if he believed Matilda was the bride for him and he was willing to brave any difficulties to make her thus, then I trusted he was right.

His face fell. "Though I don't know yet how we're going to convince her father to consent to our marrying."

"You may have to do something drastic," I cautioned him.

The proposition did not startle him, which told me that he'd already been contemplating it.

"Are you prepared to go to such lengths if necessary?" I pressed. "Even if it means forfeiting her dowry and gaining Birnam as an enemy?"

"Yes," he avowed, but then vacillated. "Though I would rather not have to resort to such extreme measures."

"Of course."

Trevor was an honorable man, so having to do something as scandalous as elope would manifestly conflict with his nature.

"But there's no need to resort to anything so extreme quite yet," I assured him.

Or so we thought.

Much as I would have preferred not to accost Mrs. Birnam again in her boudoir, the following morning she left us no choice. She didn't come down to breakfast, and she rudely ignored our request for an audience with her. As such, we had to resort to forcing our way past her maid, McClintock, and into her sitting room. When we then discovered Mrs. Birnam had locked herself inside her bedchamber, I had to threaten to retrieve the key from our housekeeper before she finally consented to join us. Though not without a great deal of complaining.

"And here, I'd thought I liked your family," she grumbled, flopping down on the settee where she'd been seated the day before. "Well, I'm afraid I shall have to withdraw my approval."

Gage and I shared a look of mutual disbelief. If the manner in which she'd treated us was meant to indicate approval, it was a wonder she had any acquaintances, let alone friends.

"We know your husband has withdrawn his consent for my brother to court your daughter. That he never intended to allow their union." My tone sharpened. "And we know you were also aware of it before you traveled here."

"Not until Matilda told me," she admitted, smoothing her aubergine-hued skirts. "And I must tell you, I was heartily disappointed. For I know my daughter is tremendously fond of Mr. St. Mawr. What's more, I like him." She scowled at us. "Or I did." She waved her hand as if to dismiss the matter. "But this is all beside the point. Jeremiah wants a title for Matilda, and your brother does not have one."

"Don't you get a say in your daughter's future?" I asked.

Her mouth twisted in scorn as she shared a look with McClintock, who stood off to the side. "What my husband wants, my husband gets." She fluffed and smoothed her skirt again. "Even me."

Sensing an opening to comprehend her better, I pushed for more information. "You didn't wish to marry him?"

"I had my heart set on someone else. Until Jeremiah persuaded my father otherwise. Then I obeyed my father and did what was expected of me." I couldn't help but wonder if she regretted this, particularly when she frowned, gazing into the distance. "I wanted something different for Matilda."

"What did you think of your husband's proposal that my brother marry Miss Whitlock instead?"

Her brows snapped together. "I thought that Mr. St. Mawr was too noble to agree to such a scheme." Her eyes narrowed. "No matter what wiles that girl used on him."

An accusation I'd seen no evidence of.

"We also know that Portia Whitlock is your husband's child," Gage declared.

Mrs. Birnam's eyes flashed with fire. "He told you, did he? Shared all the sordid details?"

"Hardly."

The twist of her lips expressed doubt. "What of it? He bedded that whore of a woman, who foisted the child on the man she cuckolded and then dared to do the same to me."

"You hated her," I realized.

"Of course I did. Would *you* enjoy daily looking into the face of the reminder of your husband's greatest betrayal?"

"But Miss Whitlock was not party to that betrayal," I argued. "She couldn't help the circumstances of her birth."

She scoffed. "As noble as your brother, aren't you?" She leaned toward me, her voice barbed with vehemence. "It didn't matter. Not when she was being wielded as a weapon, thrown in my face."

McClintock nodded in agreement.

"She could have married or sought employment elsewhere. She was determined to spite me."

"But could she truly have done those things?" I countered. "Your husband controlled her dowry and her fate."

"She had her mother's wiles, my lady. I'm sure she could have contrived something, had she wished to."

While I believed Mrs. Birnam was being unreasonable, I had to concede there was a grain of truth in what she was saying. Miss Whitlock might not have wished to marry yet or seek employment elsewhere. Not when she had this opportunity to get to know her father better and to possibly reconcile with her brother and sister.

But it had not worked out that way.

"Is that why you killed her?" Gage asked bluntly, evidently as tired of her acrimonious remarks as I was.

She huffed a scornful laugh. "Don't be ridiculous!"

"You hated Miss Whitlock," he persisted. "You'd managed to get rid of her once, but now here she was back, and ruining your daughter's life as well, being put forth as a bride for the man *she* loved. You knew about the oil of vitriol Matilda brought." He glanced at McClintock. "We're quite sure your loyal maid told you. She probably fetched it back for you. Or did you ask Paget to take care of it? After all, he also loathed her."

Mrs. Birnam bolted to her feet. "Lies! Lies and fabrications. I'm not going to let you pin this on me. I'm not going to let Mr. Birnam." She pressed an emphatic hand to her breast. "*I* have done nothing wrong. And I have nothing more to say to you." With this she whirled away, stomping off in offended dignity, her maid trailing after her. Apparently, we would have to see ourselves out.

"That could have gone better," I said once the door had slammed behind them.

"Maybe. Maybe not." Gage ushered me toward the outer door. "She clearly has a temper and a vengeful streak, and she did admit to hating Miss Whitlock."

"Yes, but none of that is proof she actually attacked her."

"No," Gage admitted in an undertone. "But it's a start."

CHAPTER 25

Our next step was to speak to Jemmy. Unfortunately, Anderley had gained nothing from his evening drinking with Mr. Simpkins except an aching head. Which meant either Jemmy's valet was better at minding his tongue than we'd hoped or he didn't know anything of use. Of course, his not knowing anything wasn't proof that there *wasn't* anything to know. Jemmy just might not have trusted him.

Whatever the truth of the matter, we had a number of queries to postulate to the younger Mr. Birnam. Except that he could not be found.

When the hour of luncheon had come and gone and he still had not appeared, I might have grown worried but for the fact that I'd since learned that Jemmy had been summoned by his father earlier that morning. I assumed that he'd revealed the same truth he'd informed Matilda of the previous evening and that Jemmy had not taken it well. Given my suspicions about what Jemmy had told me about Miss Whitlock's and his past, I could understand why.

If I were in his shoes, I could think of one place I might have gone to escape. I wondered if Jemmy had discovered it earlier in the week during one of his rambles and sought solitude there as well. So I requested that Bowcott have a picnic basket packed for me, and I set off through the woods. I might have asked Gage to join me, but he and Anderley were busy attempting to corner Paget again to try to extract further answers.

At the edge of the forest, beside a rippling stream, one of the previous owners had built a folly. The octagonal Gothic pavilion boasted tall windows on seven of its sides with a door on the eighth. It was topped by pointed arches like a crown, and ivy clung to the brick surfaces between the glass. Just outside, a small cascade had been created, directing the brook tumbling musically over the rocks.

As I rounded the bend, I could already see that my suspicions had proved correct. Jemmy was seated on the bench inside, gazing out at the tiny waterfall. It was clear from the way the muscles in his back turned rigid that he'd sensed my approach, but I rapped on the door nonetheless before pushing it open.

"I come bearing gifts," I said, hoping to circumvent any aggravation he might be feeling at my intruding on his seclusion.

He turned to see me holding the basket aloft.

"I thought you might be hungry," I added, passing him the basket before sitting next to him on the bench with my knees facing in the opposite direction.

He accepted my peace offering with a softly worded

"thank you," and then lifted aside the plaid fabric tucked over the basket's contents. There was a bottle of ale, a few slices of ham, a hunk of cheese, an apple, and two rolls of crusty bread.

I sat listening to the gentle rush and burble of the stream outside while he prepared himself a sandwich, all the while, eyeing me as if I was a snake poised to strike.

"Obviously, you're here to ask me more questions about Miss Whitlock," he muttered sullenly.

I turned to meet his dark eyes, thinking he would be a much more attractive man if his face wasn't perpetually sporting a sour expression. "She deserves justice, doesn't she?" I asked evenly. I tilted my head. "Or do you believe her life was expendable?"

His gaze dropped to the food in his hand, though I knew his serious contemplation was for my question and not the ham. "No. It wasn't expendable," he answered before taking a bite of the sandwich.

I allowed him to chew and swallow a few bites before posing my next query. "Your father told you the truth this morning. About Miss Whitlock being his daughter."

He stared mutely ahead.

"But you already knew, didn't you?"

His gaze darted to mine warily.

"She told you all those years ago before she was sent away. She trusted you. Or she noticed you exhibit the same biological anomaly she and your father do, and she thought that would convince you." I reached for his hand, touching the immobilized top joint of his fingers which caused him to hold the sandwich peculiarly. "But you refused to believe her. That's why you called her a deceitful liar."

His shoulders bowed. "I was so angry when she tried to tell me. I just . . . I didn't want to believe it." He glanced sideways at me, shame tightening his voice. "I was a little in love with her, you see. And here she was telling me I was . . . her brother." He choked on the words. "I . . ."

"You were confused and perhaps a little humiliated," I finished when he couldn't. "It's understandable."

He seemed surprised that I wasn't chastening him. "I suppose it was easier to think she was lying than to accept the truth." He frowned. "But I think part of me knew it anyway. And that unsettled me."

"Did you say anything to your father or mother?"

"Then? No." He shook his head fervently. "No, I didn't tell anyone."

He was too mortified to do so.

"I'm sorry, then."

His brow furrowed in incomprehension.

"For your loss. Miss Whitlock . . . Portia . . . was your sister, and it sounds like, at one time, a friend."

He turned to stare out the window toward the cascade, nodding numbly. His emotions were plainly still conflicted when it came to Portia, but one thing was clear: he was grieving. For what had been, for what he'd mistaken, and for what would never be.

"You didn't kill her, did you?" I felt certain I already knew the answer, but the question still needed to be asked.

He turned to look at me blindly at first, struggling to return to the present. "No. No, I . . . resented her. Resented what she'd made me feel. But I could never have physically harmed her. I couldn't." His gaze dipped to the sandwich forgotten in his hand and he scowled. "But you should know."

His dark eyes lifted to mine, stark with torment. "Father faked that archery attack."

I straightened. "You know this for certain?"

"I saw him pull the arrow from the lawn. I *watched* him fall to the ground."

"Did he know you saw?"

"I don't know." He glowered unhappily. "But if he did, he obviously counted on me keeping my mouth shut."

I touched his arm, drawing his attention back to me. "Thank you for telling me."

He nodded, his expression troubled. I wished I could reassure him, but I was afraid there were no words capable of that. And I needed to tell Gage what I'd learned.

I hurried back through the forest, keeping my eyes trained on the path before me, lest I twist an ankle on an exposed tree root. The sky was darkening with roiling clouds, heralding the approach of rain. Meanwhile, my thoughts churned with the possibility that Birnam had been the murderer all along. The prospect of it being a filicide was nauseating. When we confronted him, I could already envision his blustering denials.

Then I realized that the sound of shouting wasn't only in my imagination. Lifting my skirts, I hurried around the shrubberies lining the edge of the parterre garden to find Trevor had hoisted Mr. Thorndike up by the lapels and was screaming into his face. "Where did you get this?" When Thorndike's answer wasn't quick enough for his liking, he shook him before repeating himself. "*Where* did you get this?"

"I-I-I don't know what you're talking about?" Lord Gage's secretary stammered.

Trevor's outburst had garnered a crowd of spectators who looked on in shock and bewilderment. Among them was Gage, who pushed his way through as I approached from the other side.

"Trevor, what are you doing?" I demanded.

"I caught this . . . *cur* attempting to slip this piece of foolscap into my pocket."

Gage had managed to separate the two men, and now my brother brandished a rumpled piece of paper in the air.

"I was doing no such thing," Thorndike protested, which only drew more of Trevor's ire as he made another lunge at him.

"You were!"

"Whoa!" Gage yelled, separating the two men once again. "Control yourselves," he ordered. "And let me see that."

Trevor relinquished the paper to him but never removed his blistering glare from the secretary. Gage scanned the page before casting a look of misgiving my way. When he passed me the paper, I understood why. It was the missing note that Miss Whitlock had allegedly slid beneath Mr. Birnam's door on the evening she was attacked and killed.

"Both of you, come with me," Gage instructed Trevor and Thorndike. Trevor did so willingly, while Thorndike was more reluctant. I followed them across the garden and up the stairs of the terrace, clasping the note close to my chest. The guests stood in clusters, whispering to each other as we passed. Matilda, in particular, appeared worried. I wondered if Trevor had spoken to her since our conversation the previous evening.

Gage paused just outside the red saloon to issue instructions to Bowcott, requesting that Mr. Birnam and Paget be escorted to the study. Lord Gage already stood waiting for us at the opposite end of the great hall.

Once the five of us had gathered in the study with the door closed, Trevor let fly with his accusations again. "Where did you get this?" He gestured toward the paper I now passed to Lord Gage. "And why were you attempting to slip it into my pocket?"

Perhaps realizing that denials would do him no good when he'd been caught red-handed, Thorndike changed his tune. "Someone slipped it into *my* pocket. The one inside my coat. It must have happened while it was hanging in my office."

Lord Gage looked up from the missive to scowl at his secretary. "And rather than bring it to our attention, you thought to instead put it into Mr. St. Mawr's pocket?"

"I had already been accused of murder and knew I was on the verge of being sacked. I wasn't certain you would believe me." His response was not as deferential as perhaps it should have been, but it was nevertheless truthful. We probably wouldn't have believed him, for it strained credibility even now. However, there was one question we *could* address.

"The handwriting," I pressed my father-in-law. "Do you recognize it? Is it Mr. Thorndike's?"

The secretary protested, but we ignored him.

Lord Gage scrutinized the page, answering almost immediately. "No." He glanced at his desk, picking up another piece of paper and holding them both out for me to examine. "See?"

Gage and I stepped closer, comparing the two pages—one being the note to Birnam and the other presumably a sample of Thorndike's script. They weren't in the least similar.

Thorndike crossed his arms before him and harrumphed in affront as if this evidence entirely vindicated him.

"Return to your office," my father-in-law directed. "We'll discuss this later."

Thorndike sniffed but complied. I couldn't help but think his hours were numbered.

"Do you recognize the handwriting?" I turned to ask Gage and Trevor.

Both took their time perusing it but shook their heads.

"I don't believe I've ever seen Miss Whitlock's handwriting before," Trevor professed, indicating that he'd not yet grasped our suspicions that she might not have been the person to write it. None of us disabused him of the notion.

"What is the meaning o' this?" Birnam wanted to know after he and Paget arrived.

"Is this the missive that was slipped under your door?" Lord Gage thrust the paper out for him to see.

Rather than take it, a difficult task with his hands bandaged, he leaned closer, squinting his eyes to read. Almost immediately they widened in recognition. "Aye! I told ye there was a note, but ye didna believe me."

Gage turned to Paget, who still hovered by the door. "You told us that you saw Birnam pick up the note and set it on the desk, but you couldn't read it. Does this appear to be the same missive?"

"Noo, see here . . ." Birnam challenged, but Gage held up a hand, silencing him.

"It's a simple question merely meant to further validate your statement. Surely, you can have no problem with this."

Especially since Paget was bound to agree with his employer whether he actually recognized the note or not.

Paget inched closer, barely glancing at the paper before responding. "Aye."

Gage nodded. "Then will you please fetch us a sample of Miss Whitlock's handwriting?"

Paget looked to Birnam for guidance, who was eyeing my husband with dawning comprehension. "Do as they ask," Birnam confirmed. He waited until Paget was gone before speaking again. "Ye think someone else wrote it?"

"You tell us," Gage countered. "Does the script look like your daughter's?"

Birnam didn't flinch at his referring to Miss Whitlock as such in the present company, but his mouth did tighten in displeasure before he leaned close to examine the letter Lord Gage held out to him again. "I canna say for sure. But maybe? 'Tis certainly close enough tae fool me at a glance."

I wanted to ask him about what Jemmy had claimed about the archery attack, but I decided it would be best if we remained focused on the missive first. While the men discussed the matter—Trevor included, now that he was in accord with the rest of us—I took the paper back from my father-in-law to analyze its contents. It was short and, just as Birnam had portrayed it to be, a letter asking him to meet Miss Whitlock, but there were two discrepancies that leapt out at me.

"This missive asks you to meet her at 11:45," I pointed out to Birnam.

"Aye, but I didna return tae my room 'til almost midnight, so I went as soon as I could."

"But Miss Whitlock and I had arranged to meet at midnight."

"Maybe she wished to speak to Birnam first," Lord Gage suggested. "To explain why she'd asked him there."

This was plausible, but it still struck me as strange given my earlier interaction with Miss Whitlock in the great hall.

"And she asks you to meet her in the blue room." I gestured to the line in the note. "We were meeting in the office behind the morning room."

"You do have to pass through the blue room to reach the morning room and beyond, so maybe she thought Birnam wouldn't know where to go," Trevor offered.

Again, this was plausible, and the fact that no one else seemed to find these incongruities significant made me doubt my own intuition. But I still couldn't shake the feeling that these inconsistencies mattered.

Paget returned with a paper written in a neat, concise hand. Compared side by side, the letters matched the note in size, but not in the style they were formed. In fact, they differed enough that I wondered how Birnam hadn't recognized it. But it was at least possible that if he'd read swiftly without any expectation that it might have been forged, he might have missed it.

"Then who wrote this note?" Birnam demanded to know.

"Someone who wanted to lure you to the blue room," Trevor supplied.

The implication being, to kill him.

Birnam's features were thunderous, and while I might have been mistaken, I thought I detected at least a glimmer of genuine alarm in his eyes. "Ye said your secretary found it?"

"Yes, and he will be thoroughly interrogated," Lord Gage assured him. "But in the meantime, I think you should continue with the precautions you started taking after your attack on the archery field."

An attack his son had told me not an hour ago that he had feigned.

Birnam brandished a bandaged hand in Lord Gage's face. "Figure oot who killed Miss Whitlock, and do it quickly, or I may have tae take matters intae my own hands."

What exactly this meant, I didn't know, but he turned on his heel and stalked from the room with Paget trailing close behind.

"Are we sure Birnam didn't write that note to replace the one he allegedly lost?" Trevor queried once Birnam had gone.

"Let's just see." Lord Gage opened a drawer and removed a paper he'd clearly been saving for just such an occasion. I wondered where he'd gotten it.

But it took less than a second to apprehend that Birnam's handwriting looked nothing like the script on the missive. Birnam's scrawl—on a letter directed to Lord Melbourne—was chunky and uneven, while the missive was neat and precise.

"This doesn't preclude Birnam from having forged and planted the note, just that it wasn't written in his hand." Lord Gage looked to Trevor. "What does Miss Birnam's handwriting look like?"

Trevor's brow furrowed in displeasure, but he answered anyway. "Not like this."

There was a rap on the door, and Lord Gage called out for whoever it was to enter.

"Dr. Clarke is here to see to Mr. Birnam," Bowcott informed us.

I couldn't decide whether I was relieved not to have to perform the task of changing the unpleasant man's dressings or disappointed not to have a ready opportunity to question him again.

"Very good. Show him up," Lord Gage instructed.

I noted Trevor glide out the door before the butler closed it. I suspected he didn't wish to have his loyalty further tested by my father-in-law.

"Were you and Anderley able to question Paget?" I asked Gage before I lost the chance.

"Yes, and he was as closemouthed as ever," he said in disgruntlement.

"Not even your intimidation tactics worked?" I attempted to tease, but Gage's grave response sobered me.

"No. But he did let one interesting thing slip." His eyebrows raised. "He suggested that Birnam was in negotiations with Milngavie for Matilda's hand in marriage."

"Milngavie?" I repeated in astonishment, for I couldn't imagine a less likely match. "But he hates Birnam."

"That doesn't mean he hates his daughter."

We both turned to look at Lord Gage.

"Matilda Birnam is a pretty girl. And word is that Milngavie needs money."

"But at the expense of his integrity?"

He shrugged one shoulder. "Men have sacrificed more for less."

He wasn't wrong, but if Paget's claim was true . . . My stomach cramped. Poor Trevor. We'd thought there was time, but what if there wasn't?

Gage's eyes warmed with empathy. "There is one other thing you should both know. A pair of leather gloves was found tucked up on an overhead beam in the stables, and they'd clearly suffered some sort of damage from acid."

"Then there goes our supposition about Birnam," I replied. "For if he wore gloves, he wouldn't have burned his hands and wouldn't have had any reason to pick up the bottle after the fact to mask that."

"Not necessarily," Lord Gage cautioned, locking the missive as well as the sample of Birnam's handwriting away in his desk. "The gloves might also have been planted to divert suspicion. Or they might have nothing to do with Miss Whitlock's attack, perhaps being left there by a neglectful stable boy."

I groaned, earning myself sympathetic looks from both my husband and his father. "Then, let me tell you what Jemmy Birnam told me."

CHAPTER 26

After I'd informed them of Jemmy's confession about his father, I left both Gage men to debate the issue while I went in search of Mrs. Taylor and Bowcott. The next day, four dozen more guests were descending upon Bevington Hall, and I'd not conferred with either of the principal members of the household staff yet today to discover if they needed anything from me. Though I'd had little doubt, I was still glad to discover that everything was well in hand, as were preparations for dinner that evening.

I wanted to go directly to the nursery to see Emma, but I'd spent so much of my time the past few days on the inquiry that I'd largely neglected our guests. So I determined I should at least take a stroll through the public rooms to ensure that everyone was sufficiently comfortable and entertained. Most of the gentlemen were once again gathered in the green drawing room and billiards room for the afternoon.

The rumble of their voices and congenial laughter seemed to indicate they were at least satisfied.

Lady Brougham and Lady Lyndhurst were seated on the back terrace in the shade, enjoying the cooler weather that had been ushered in by the brief rain shower that had dampened the lawn while I was belowstairs. The clouds had since passed, and the afternoon sunlight made the water droplets sparkle so that the leaves and flowers seemed adorned with diamonds. I conversed with the ladies for several minutes while they continued their needlework before returning inside.

I found the mauve drawing room empty except for Alana and Lorna, who appeared to be enjoying tea and a cozy tête-à-tête.

"Kiera," Lorna cried upon catching sight of me. She patted the cushion beside her on the settee. "Come join us."

I gladly accepted the invitation, wishing I could remain for more than a few minutes.

"You look run off your feet," my sister declared, already pouring and preparing my tea the way I liked it.

I took the cup with a grateful smile before pressing a hand to my forehead. "I'll take that as an indication I look as ragged as I feel."

"No!" Lorna reassured me. "Just . . . a bit harried. And who can blame you?"

"I'm afraid I've been neglecting you, neglecting everyone," I said with a sigh.

"For good reason," Alana stated firmly. "I know we'll all sleep better once Miss Whitlock's killer is caught. That's your top priority. As for the guests, they're being well looked after. No one should be complaining. Now, drink your tea."

I did as directed, a bit confounded to hear my older sister defend my actions after all the times in the past when she'd bemoaned my taking part in these macabre inquiries. But Alana was nothing if not practical, and if the alternatives were having a locally appointed parish constable and his deputy investigate or allowing a murderer to walk free, she would choose me and Gage every time.

Lorna leaned forward, lowering her voice. "We've heard rumors. Is it true? Was Miss Whitlock truly Mr. Birnam's daughter?"

I knew I shouldn't have been surprised that this information had been spread—it was too scandalous to be kept quiet—but I was astounded, nonetheless. "Yes."

"That explains a few things," Alana remarked as Lorna shook her head sadly.

"Do you think that was the motive?" Lorna asked, aghast.

"We don't know," I hedged. "It seems to be a bit more complicated."

"But you'd rather not discuss it just now." Alana nodded. "We understand."

I wasn't certain that was the case, but I was grateful when they began to chatter about other things. It at least allowed me to bask in the semblance of normalcy for a few minutes while I drank my tea. In all the tumult and hustle, I'd had little time to anticipate the arrival of more friends and family the following day, but listening to them discuss who they looked forward to seeing elevated my own excitement. Then one of them mentioned Lady Bearsden, and I recalled Lord Strathblane's interest in reuniting with her after some years. Which made me think of his protégé.

"Have either of you observed anything noteworthy about

Lord Milngavie?" I asked them during a lull in the conversation.

"Other than his outburst after dinner several nights ago . . ." Lorna glanced at Alana. "No."

"He seems pleasant enough," Alana confirmed. "Though obviously he has a temper when riled. And he strongly dislikes Birnam." Her lips quirked. "But I do not hold that against him."

"Most wouldn't," I agreed.

So then why would he be negotiating to make Birnam's daughter his wife? Surely, there were other wealthy men eager to endow their daughters with large dowries in exchange for a title who were more palatable. Perhaps not *as* wealthy as Birnam, but near enough.

"What of his finances?" I queried, wondering if they'd heard something similar to Lord Gage and how widely his circumstances might be known.

"As I understand it," Alana began carefully, "he inherited a great deal of debt from his distant cousin along with the title. But he's also a sensible man and one accustomed to a more modest lifestyle, so he's not entrenched with the notion of being some great lord with dozens of castles and manors at his disposal. Philip said he's already sold a number of minor properties and is moving to parcel off some of the land from his central estate. He needs approval to break the entitlement on that land in order to do so, but Philip believes his case is strong and moreover practical, considering he didn't run up the debts in the first place. If approved, Milngavie should be able to recoup some of his losses and even expand the estate in the future with smart investments."

I was somewhat taken aback by the breadth of her knowledge until I realized: "Was that one of his goals in coming here? To confer with the other nobles and obtain their guidance on the matter?"

"And perhaps help influence the decision to allow him to break the entitlement in his favor?" Alana smiled. "Yes. Philip finds him to be a savvy fellow." Her voice turned wry. "And far preferable to the scapegrace who held the title before."

If all of this was true—and I had no reason to doubt Philip or Alana's word on the matter—then it made it even more perplexing that Milngavie would be interested in making Birnam his father-in-law.

Unless Paget had lied. I frowned behind the brim of my teacup. But why?

"What was that row between Trevor and Mr. Thorndike about?" my sister asked, harking back to the incident in the garden. "He seemed to be accusing him of something."

I finished my tea and leaned forward to set the cup on the tray. "Let's just say that Thorndike had something he shouldn't have and his excuse for doing so was less than satisfactory."

"He is a deeply unpleasant man," Lorna remarked almost offhandedly, her gaze focused on the delicate neoclassical frieze along the top of the wall. When this comment was met with silence as we waited for her to elaborate, she flushed and cleared her throat.

"How so?" I prompted.

"I just mean, you can tell how unhappy he is. That he seems to believe he's entitled to much more than he has, and he's frustrated by his inability to change that." She shrugged one shoulder. "Or that's how Alfie described it."

Gage's cousin wasn't wrong, and if anyone should recognize

this in Thorndike, it would be Alfie, for he'd exhibited similar feelings once upon a time. Feelings that I knew he was now slightly ashamed of. But Thorndike did not have the prospects Alfie had had. And meeting a man like Birnam, a man who had been born with even fewer prospects than Thorndike, who nevertheless had succeeded in ways that Thorndike couldn't contrive to achieve, must have only increased his bitterness and dissatisfaction. What I couldn't say was whether this had driven him to retaliate and what form this retaliation might have taken. But it was something to be contemplated.

Having finished our tea, Lorna and Alana elected to join me as I climbed the stairs toward the nursery, each of us eager to see our children. We spent a pleasant hour and a half in their company, despite Emma and Rory squabbling over a stuffed bunny, before we dispersed to dress for dinner. For once, I was running ahead of schedule and arrived in the mauve drawing room to find it empty. However, when I peered through the windows, I saw Lord Milngavie standing alone on the terrace, surveying the garden. I crossed into the red saloon and out the doors to join him.

As I drew nearer, I realized he wasn't scrutinizing the garden at all but rather a piece of paper. It was worn and creased, obviously frequently handled, and the brief glimpse I had of it seemed to suggest it was a list of names.

"Apologies, my lady," he exclaimed at the sight of me, casually folding the paper and tucking it away in the inside pocket of his coat. In his other hand, he clutched a cheroot he'd been smoking, and he glanced about, evidently uncertain what to do with it.

"No need for that," I demurred with a wave of my hand. "You couldn't have known I would appear."

"Perhaps not, but as I understand it, it's still an abominable habit to expose a gentlewoman to."

"I assure you, I've been exposed to much worse." I smiled. "I have a brother, after all, and numerous cousins, several of whom you shall soon meet."

During this declamation, he'd contrived to extinguish the cheroot and now straightened his appearance, smoothing his hair and adjusting his black evening coat. "I suspect you are merely trying to set me at ease, but I shall accept your kind assurances, for not to do so would be even more unforgivable."

I laughed. "My brother-in-law speaks highly of your intelligence, and I must concur. If you keep talking like that, you shall soon run circles around your cohorts in the House of Lords."

Milngavie blushed. "I'm flattered. I also think highly of Lord Cromarty. He's done much to help the laboring man and those whose livelihoods have been threatened by the clearances." His brow furrowed. "Much more than I can say of many who sit in Lords."

As he'd presented an opening of sorts, I seized it. "This may be impertinent of me to ask, but I think you will understand why I must." He met my gaze with interest. "Are you negotiating with Mr. Birnam for his daughter Matilda's hand?"

His head reared backward. "No, my lady, I am not," he stated firmly. "Though I think I understand how you might have been given that impression. Because Mr. Birnam did offer it to me."

It was my turn to stiffen. "When was this?"

His mien was sympathetic, evidently aware that my brother had aspirations to marry Matilda. "Sometime Wednesday afternoon, I believe. After the archery tournament. I turned down the proposition immediately." He grimaced. "Which may have been one of the reasons our discussion over port that evening grew so contentious."

"I suppose he didn't take your refusal graciously."

"No. Though my refusal has nothing to do with Miss Birnam," he hastened to add, lest I take offense on her behalf. "She seems like a lovely young lady, and I'm sure will make some lucky chap very happy. But . . ." His expression turned embittered. "I cannot align myself with Birnam. No matter what he offers in return."

I might have asked him exactly what those terms had been had we not at that moment been joined by Philip and Alana. Accordingly, our topic of discussion shifted to something more pleasant. But I couldn't help but continue to contemplate it, wondering if Birnam had offered the same thing to any of the other lords present. Baron Foley was still a bachelor, and Lord Melbourne and Lord Strathblane were both widowers. My anxiety for Trevor threatened to ruin my appetite and then the evening entirely.

It was with a great deal of relief that I finally retired, though then I had to face the realization that we had still not apprehended Miss Whitlock's killer. Gage took one look at my face when he joined me in the sitting room of our suite and called for Bree and Anderley to attend us. Then he bid us all to sit.

For a moment, none of us said anything, but simply gazed

at one another as if hopeful that someone else had had some sort of stroke of inspiration or epiphany. When no one offered either, Gage took charge again.

"Clearly, we are missing something," he surmised. "Or we're being distracted by factors that may or may not be related to the murder."

Such as Birnam's rejection of Trevor's courtship of Matilda. While my husband didn't say so, I could tell when he glanced at me that this was one of the things he was referring to.

"So let's return to what we do know."

I nodded, taking this as my cue to begin. "On the night in question, following dinner, Miss Whitlock pulled me aside as the ladies were adjourning to the drawing room. She then asked about my husband's reputation as a gentleman inquiry agent and requested I meet with her later in a more private location."

"Ye said her demeanor was frightened," Bree added.

"Yes. At the least, anxious and alarmed, but she definitely *seemed* afraid. Of what, I don't know. But her eyes kept darting around the great hall, as if someone might be listening to us. We parted ways, and she asked me to make her excuses, pleading a headache, while I returned to the other ladies in the drawing room."

"Who were all present?" Gage confirmed.

"Yes. Alana and Lorna both said no one left the room until later."

"And the only men who departed the dining room before we'd finished our port and joined the women were Jemmy, Thorndike, and Milngavie."

"Jemmy was allegedly indisposed," Anderley supplied.

"Yes, as several witnesses can attest," Gage said.

"And presumably went directly to seek a chamber pot. Milngavie claims he took the staircase off the blue room upstairs to gain control of his temper. And Thorndike crossed the opposite end of the great hall to return to his office and depart the hall for the evening."

Bree wrinkled her nose. "All of which may be true, but in terms of an alibi, they're no' verra good ones."

I had to agree. "Any of them might have lied and found a way to eavesdrop on me and Miss Whitlock. Or perhaps no one did. That's the trouble. We can't be certain Miss Whitlock wasn't simply allowing her fear to unnerve her."

"Irrespective, you made arrangements to meet Miss Whitlock in the blue room . . ."

I shook my head.

"Excuse me," Gage corrected himself. "In the office behind the morning room at midnight."

"It was out of the way and certain to ensure us privacy, and the hour was late enough that I figured my hosting duties would be complete," I said, explaining my reasoning.

"At some point . . ." Gage emphasized his words with his hands ". . . a note was slipped beneath Mr. Birnam's door, asking him to meet Miss Whitlock in the blue room at 11:45 p.m."

"However, Mr. Birnam didn't return to his room to read the note until, say, 11:55 p.m.," I recounted.

"So he was late," Anderley deduced.

"As was I. *Slightly*," I admitted. "But no more than two or three minutes."

"At which point, you reached the blue room to find Birnam standing over Miss Whitlock's deceased body." Gage pantomimed. "Birnam picked up the empty bottle of acid, burning his hands, and then dropped it again."

I pressed a hand to my chest. "I told him to go directly to the water closet through the morning room to rinse his hands. I then checked Miss Whitlock for a pulse and, finding none, went in search of a footman to send for you and your father, as well as Bowcott."

"Where did you find the footman?"

"In the library. I'd noticed him when I was making my way toward the morning room. In fact, he was the only person I'd seen."

"Neither footman on the main level confessed to seeing or hearing anyone except for a few men in the billiards room prior to you alerting them there was a situation," Gage emphasized.

"Not even me?" I asked in surprise.

"Not even you."

I frowned. "We speculated that the killer must have taken the staircase off the blue room in order not to be seen, but maybe we're wrong. If they didn't see me or Birnam or Miss Whitlock, then who else snuck past them?"

Bree tapped her chin in contemplation. "I think 'tis safe tae say that Miss Whitlock *did* take the blue room staircase, since 'tis directly off her room."

"But it doesn't really make sense for Birnam to have," Anderley mused. "His bedchamber is on the opposite side of the building."

"He told us he came down the north staircase," I replied.

"The oil of vitriol," Gage said, switching topics. "We now know that Miss Birnam brought a bottle that was likely the one used against Miss Whitlock. Several witnesses saw the Birnam maid, McClintock, place the bottle on a shelf in the laundry during late afternoon on the day in question. What we don't know is who later removed it."

Bree crossed her arms. "Seems tae me it had tae be a member o' staff. A maid or a footman or the like. Someone else woulda been noticed."

"Not necessarily," Anderley contended. "The staircase that leads up past the study and library is just around the corner. I reckon at the right hour, someone could slip in and out undetected fairly easily."

Bree tilted her head to acknowledge this. "Early in the evenin', most o' the staff woulda been in the servants' hall or kitchens, 'cept those waitin' on the family and guests in the dinin' room and drawin' room. Nay one woulda been near the laundry."

"Then that's probably when he took it." Gage sank deeper in his chair, running his index finger over his bottom lip in thought. "But how did he know about it? And what prompted him to take it?"

I worked at the fastening on my sapphire bracelet, having had enough of the way it had been irritating the sensitive skin on my wrist all night. "Was his intended victim truly Miss Whitlock or had he planned instead to attack Mr. Birnam? Don't forget the forged note."

Bree jolted forward. "But Birnam was late."

I stilled, picturing the missive slipped under Birnam's door in my mind. "He *was* late. And Miss Whitlock must have been early."

"Was the original plan to attack Birnam and leave him for Miss Whitlock and you to find?" Anderley ventured.

"Perhaps the killer even hoped Miss Whitlock would be blamed."

Or me. The words remained unspoken.

"But how did the culprit expect not to be caught? Or did he not realize that an attack with oil of vitriol is rarely lethal?" I was baffled. And so, it seemed, were the others, for at first no one put forth an explanation. Why would you attack someone so viciously, but use a method where the victim could later identify you? Had he or she expected to garner enough sympathy not to be convicted or to be given a light sentence? Or had he simply not thought that far through his actions?

"Maybe . . ." Anderley began but then hesitated to continue. "Maybe he had another means to finish the job if the acid didn't work."

"You mean, perhaps he had a knife or a pistol?" The tone of Gage's voice told me that he thought this idea held merit.

"Do we ken if anyone is carryin' a weapon? Anyone except you, that is." Bree was speaking to Anderley, but the same statement could have been said about Gage, for I knew he often concealed a pistol on his person. Even I had taken to tucking a Hewson percussion pistol in my reticule whenever I went out, though I had not done so here in my father-in-law's home.

"I would imagine a number of the gentlemen packed knives and pistols, though they might not carry them while in the house," Gage answered. "And of course, the armaments room is stocked with a number of rifles and assorted knives, but I'm not aware of any of them having gone missing."

"Paget is carrying a rather wicked-looking blade," Anderley supplied.

"So really, it could be anyone," I summarized, feeling my spirits collapse along with my posture.

"Perhaps what we need is sleep," Gage said, presumably after surveying all of our discouraged expressions, for I was not looking at him but the floor. "I'll assist Mrs. Gage," he told Bree before dismissing Anderley as well. "The two of you should also get your rest."

I heard them file out and then Gage took hold of my hand, pulling me to my feet. "Come," he said gently. "Let's stop thinking for a while."

"How on earth do you propose we do . . . ?"

I never got to finish my sentence, for his mouth captured mine. At first, I resisted, too exhausted and exasperated, but his gentle persistence lulled me into compliance and then eager participation as he tempted, teased, and coaxed me with his lips, his teeth, his tongue. He always had been difficult to resist. When finally we separated, my heart beat faster, and my worries had dimmed in the face of the needs now making themselves known throughout the rest of my body.

"That's how," he said, answering my unfinished question. His pale blue eyes heated with intent. "Distraction is what you need, Kiera. What we both need." He shook his head. "Or else I don't see either of us getting much sleep tonight."

He pulled me close again, exhaling a long breath. "So let's set everything aside for the moment and just take comfort in each other."

And so we did.

CHAPTER 27

Gage had been correct. A good night's sleep—and his thorough attentions—had helped immensely. I woke refreshed and with a renewed determination to unmask Miss Whitlock's murderer. Even though I was no closer to figuring out the conundrum of who had done it or why, I at least no longer felt daunted by the task before me.

Of course, it may have also helped that I had so many friends and family members I looked forward to seeing. We had asked our guests to arrive by four o'clock to allow them plenty of time to settle in and refresh themselves before the evening's ball. And to give our staff time to recuperate before taking up their duties for the ball. Naturally, the exception to this was the kitchen staff, who were already hard at work preparing the evening's meal when I stepped belowstairs after breakfast to confer with Lord Gage's French cook to ensure all was in order.

One of the first of our new guests to arrive around midmorning was Lord Henry Kerr, my husband's half brother. I had but a few minutes to chat with him before I was being swept into the arms of my Aunt Cait, Uncle Duncan, cousin Morven, and the rest of their branch of the family. Soon after, my dear friend Charlotte made her appearance, looking radiant, as always, on the arm of my cousin Rye. In a few weeks, they were to celebrate their first wedding anniversary.

Close behind them hobbled Charlotte's great-aunt, Lady Bearsden, escorted by one of our footmen. From the manner in which she clung to his arm, you would have been forgiven for thinking she required assistance managing the stairs. But although she was an octogenarian and carried a cane with a gold figurehead, I knew it was more the footman's handsomeness than her knees that kept her gripping his arm. The flush that had crested the young footman's cheeks only confirmed it.

"Kiera, my dear," she exclaimed upon seeing me, releasing the footman, who scurried back to his other duties. Her snowy white hair peeked out from beneath her bonnet. "I have been looking forward to this for ever so long!"

"The journey wasn't too much for you?" I asked, knowing it was no small feat for someone her age, no matter how youthful she seemed.

"Oh, fiddlesticks! I would have traveled twice as far, if need be. Now where is that good-looking husband of yours." Catching sight of him, her eyes twinkled with delight, and a flirtatious smile crossed her lips.

Amusement crinkled the corner of Gage's eyes. "Lady Bearsden, what a pleasure. Now our joy is complete."

She twittered as he bowed over her hand. "Now aren't you

incorrigible," she cooed. "Much like my Lumpy." Her much grieved late husband. "But far better looking, God rest his soul." Her gaze shifted to Lord Gage, who stood next to his son. "I suppose he comes by it naturally. You always did have the ladies eating out of your hand."

My father-in-law laughed as he made a show of bowing over her hand even more extravagantly than his son had.

Charlotte and I exchanged smiles, both glad to see her great-aunt in such good spirits. I knew she had taken ill in the late spring, and Charlotte had been worried about her slow recovery. However, Lady Bearsden seemed in fine form now.

"As I understand it, there's an old friend of yours already here," I told her. "He confessed delight at having the chance to reconnect with you."

"Oh?" She seemed intrigued.

"Lord Strathblane."

Her eyes lit with recognition. "Strathblane. Why, I haven't seen that old rascal in, oh, it must be ages." She glanced around her eagerly as if expecting him to appear. "It will be good to reminisce."

"*After* we've rested and refreshed ourselves," Charlotte said, urging her great-aunt deeper into the great hall.

"I'll show them up," I told Mrs. Taylor, seeing that no other carriages were queued or approaching. This would give me a chance to explain the distressing events of earlier in the week before the gossip reached their ears.

We'd just reached the south staircase when Lorna intercepted us, embracing Charlotte much as I had.

"The three hens are together again," Lady Bearsden proclaimed with a delighted click of her tongue. "Why, you three remind me of my own brood at your age. Oh, the mischief we made. Lumpy was forever shaking his head at our antics."

"Make," Charlotte corrected with an arch of her eyebrows. "You *still* make mischief."

Her great-aunt chuckled to herself, making Lorna and me turn toward each other curiously. However, Charlotte was tight-lipped, and Rye's expression seemed suspiciously blank.

"Well, we had a rather unfortunate event occur earlier this week," I began, knowing that at any moment I might be summoned away to greet another carriage full of arriving guests. But I didn't even make it past this sentence before being interrupted.

"Kiera," my brother-in-law called, emerging from the green drawing room where he must have been perusing the letter he held folded in his hands. Philip drew up short at the sight of the others, pausing long enough to greet them properly, before turning back to me. "I need to speak with you and Gage." The word *immediately* was implied in his tone.

"Of course." I hesitated a moment, realizing I couldn't leave my last statement unexplained. "Lorna, would you . . . ?"

She agreed, understanding I was asking her to do more than show them to their rooms. "Go on. I know where they've been assigned."

I clasped her hand gratefully. "Thank you. I'll see you all at tea," I called over my shoulder as I hurried after Philip.

"What is it?" I asked him as we made our way down the corridor past the library.

"When you mentioned the spate of acid attacks that have been occurring in Glasgow and elsewhere, I took it upon myself to write to my secretary in London to see if he had heard anything about them. As you know, Cowper always has his ear to the ground."

I nodded, recognizing that, in his position, Philip had to be made aware of the developments surrounding any number of subjects promptly, and as such he hired men like Cowper to keep him abreast of such issues.

"Well, he said that word is, a young woman had been attempting to make contact about the matter with my colleagues who have been involved with the revisions to the Factory Act."

I turned to meet his gaze in astonishment. "Miss Whitlock?"

"I surmised the same thing." His dark eyes were reticent. "Could that be what she wanted to talk to you about so urgently the evening of her demise?"

"That seems a logical assumption, doesn't it?" I replied as a sinking feeling filled my stomach. For if Miss Whitlock had wished to speak with a member of parliament about the Factory Act, and she'd been afraid to do so, then it was possibly because she had something to report that Birnam would not like. Perhaps something she'd learned during one of her visits to his mills and factories.

Philip and I found Gage and his father in his study. The windows there overlooked the front lawn and the circular drive where all of our guests would be arriving. We quickly informed them of the matters we'd already discussed as well as our own deductions. I could feel Gage's eyes on me, weighing and assessing how much this new information had rattled me, but I was determined to maintain my equanimity.

"Did your secretary mention which men she contacted specifically?" Lord Gage asked with a troubled frown.

"No. But I know that Strathblane is involved in the revisions," Philip said.

This surprised me, for he'd not seemed to express any interest in the matter whenever Birnam or someone else brought up the Factory Act. Was this a feint or was he trying to hide something?

Then Philip's voice turned wry. "Or he's supposed to be."

"You doubt it?" Gage queried.

My brother-in-law paused, seeming to choose his words with care. "Lord Strathblane is nearing eighty and he's noticeably slowed down. One can hardly blame him. But . . . rather than retire from the field, he seems to be relying more and more heavily on the work of his secretaries and protégés, and calling their work and opinions his own."

"Then if Miss Whitlock did attempt to contact him, you think her correspondence may not have been handled by Strathblane but a secretary or protégé?"

"We should still ask him," Lord Gage prompted, but his attention was then diverted by the cloud of dust presaging the arrival of another carriage filled with guests. "Later."

The opportunity came *much* later, in fact. Over tea. And by then, Lady Bearsden had remade Lord Strathblane's acquaintance. The two of them sat side by side on one of the settees in the red saloon, cackling like crows, appearing as if a day hadn't passed since they'd last seen each other. There was a decided sparkle in both their eyes which made me suspect they might not have *just* been acquaintances or even friends. Whatever the case, in each other's company they both looked a decade younger. And it was nearly impossible to divert their attention to other matters.

My smile had turned strained as I'd tried and failed for a

third time to get a clear answer from Lord Strathblane in regards to Miss Whitlock. Finally, I had to appeal to Lady Bearsden, pressing a hand to her arm. "My lady, please. I truly do not wish to intrude, but it is *important*."

Lady Bearsden seemed to recognize the pleading note in my voice that Strathblane had missed. "Miss Whitlock is the young lady who was killed in such a dreadful manner?"

"Yes," I gasped, glad that someone now grasped the seriousness of my query.

She turned to tap Strathblane in the middle of his chest with the fan she'd been wielding against the afternoon's warmth. "Answer her, Miles. Did this Miss Whitlock write to you?"

He rubbed the spot where she'd swatted him. "I'm afraid I wouldn't know, my lady," he told me with a shake of his head. "My secretary handles all my correspondence. Only shows me what I need to see. It's more efficient that way."

"Then he didn't mention her?" I pressed.

He shrugged. "Not that I recall."

"And she didn't try to speak to you here?"

"Nay." He tipped his head as if having a thought. "Though she may have tried to speak to Milngavie."

This made me still. "Why would she have done that?"

"My secretary passes some of my correspondence to him, as I've been training him up. Much like your father-in-law has your husband." He settled more comfortably, clasping his hands over his abdomen. "Milngavie got a late start to all of this. He wasn't raised to it like most. And I've been happy to help him."

"Is that the lad who inherited the Gale estate?"

"Aye. Your new neighbor, as the stork flies."

Lady Bearsden swatted him lightly with her fan again. "It's 'as the crow flies.'"

His eyes narrowed. "Nay. I'm pretty sure it's a stork."

I left them to bicker, circulating the room to speak to the other guests while keeping my eyes open for Gage.

It could mean nothing. Strathblane's secretary might never have received any correspondence from Portia Whitlock. Or if he had, he might never have passed it on to Milngavie.

But if he had . . . If he had, why hadn't Milngavie mentioned it?

This question troubled me more than I wanted to admit. And I suddenly had the rather strong suspicion that we had all been expertly misled.

For all my time spent living with Alana and Philip and the number of social events I had watched her host, I had failed to realize precisely how much effort went into them. Perhaps I'd simply not been paying attention, but I suspected this was more because my sister had purposely concealed the exertion required, even from me.

Whatever the case, this truth had now been laid bare. In the hours before the start of my first ball, I found myself like a soldier during his first battle feeling as if I'd been baptized by fire. The number of questions and requests which came my way, and the problems—both big and small—which needed solving were dizzying. I'd not understood why Bree had insisted she dress me at such an early hour, but I soon recognized her wisdom. Had I waited, I never would have found time to change into my ball gown. This would have been not only embarrassing but also disappointing because I actually liked my gown for the evening.

It being the height of summer, we'd settled on a midsummer's night theme, and so I'd ordered my gown to match. It was fashioned of indigo silk with a silver net overlay sprinkled with small glass beads that captured the light to twinkle like stars. Both the color and effect accented the lapis-lazuli shade of my eyes, making them shimmer "witch bright." For once, the descriptor I'd so often heard used to describe them—not always in a complimentary manner—did not sting when it came to mind. Much to my modiste's horror, I'd ordered the sleeves to be only slightly puffed, but not enough to require the usual padding and support garments strapped beneath the gigot sleeves which were so *en vogue.*

Coupled with the sapphire necklace and matching earrings Gage had once gifted me, the gown made me feel beautiful. And perhaps more importantly—at least, in this instance—competent. It certainly helped that everyone's reactions to my appearance—be it delight or admiration—seemed to make them more compliant to my decisions and instructions.

Unfortunately, this was not the case with Mr. Birnam, whom I'd sent a message to via a footman, asking him to seek me out as I'd not had the time to visit his chamber. I'd thought at first that he was merely being difficult, but when he failed to comply with standard precedence at the start of the ball, I realized he was actively avoiding me.

My father-in-law, my husband, and I were all positioned near the main entrance to the great hall in order to greet those who lived in the nearby vicinity who were arriving just for the evening's ball. The guests who were staying at

Bevington Park were supposed to process around to be received by us before entering the great hall where the dancing was to take place or the adjoining rooms where refreshments and other entertainments were being offered. However, the Birnams, undoubtedly at Mr. Birnam's behest, had ignored this piece of etiquette.

All of them but Matilda, that is, who Trevor escorted over at her insistence so that she could shamefacedly admit to her family's breach of protocol. I felt sorry for her, doing my best to reassure her that I knew the fault was not her own. In truth, I was relieved to see that she and Trevor seemed to have resolved their differences, though that did not change Mr. Birnam's edict.

Lord Gage, who had been relaxed and even complimentary of my appearance, now sported a crease between his brows that did not bode well for Mr. Birnam. "You said that you've been waiting for him to attend to you all afternoon?" he inquired, evidently having overheard me telling his son. Snapping his fingers, he summoned over a footman and directed him to fetch Mr. Birnam. One hoped Birnam would not be so audacious as to disobey such a request from his host in front of more than a hundred other guests.

"Perhaps I should send a footman to summon Mr. Armstrong much the same way," Gage leaned down to murmur in my ear.

I offered him a strained smile in answer to his quip. "No, I agree with your earlier assessment. Best to let Anderley handle it."

Though hopefully he would send word to us of what he'd uncovered soon.

We welcomed another round of guests, a baronet and his

lady and their daughter who were some of Bevington Park's nearest neighbors. When they'd progressed into the great hall behind us, we turned to find Birnam waiting impatiently off to the side.

"Ridiculous protocol," he blustered. "Ye already received us a week ago."

"Perhaps," I conceded, but was unable to keep the bite from my tone in response to his rudeness. "But since you're so eager to be a part of this world, you should understand that there is a certain way things are done. And while I don't always agree, in this instance it was a simple act of courtesy."

"I believe my daughter-in-law also requested the opportunity to speak with you earlier this afternoon and you ignored her." Lord Gage's voice was clipped and brusque but controlled. Our conversation would be inaudible to most beneath the strains of the orchestra floating down from the balcony at the opposite end of the room and the raised voices of the guests at the edges of the room watching the dancers at the center, but he was clearly still conscious of their presence.

"I'm tired o' cooperatin'," he snarled. "'Tis clear ye think a Birnam killed Miss Whitlock, and I'll no' help ye build yer case."

I couldn't help but notice that he'd not protested their innocence but merely avowed he wouldn't help us prove their guilt, but I didn't let this sway me from my intent. "I have a question that has nothing to do with that," I pronounced impatiently. "I need to know when you approached Lord Milngavie to offer him your daughter Matilda's hand."

Birnam glowered ferociously. "I ken ye wish tae help yer brother, but that is none o' yer concern."

"Oh, but it is . . ."

"I'll no' change my mind," he interrupted, grasping both sides of his dark evening coat as if about to give a speech. "Yer brother is no' the husband my Matilda needs."

I gritted my teeth, both in anger at his talking over me and at his dismissal of my brother simply because he had no title.

"Answer the question, Birnam," my husband warned, straightening himself threateningly.

"I'll no' be intimidated," he growled. "This is no' yer affair."

"Oh, but it is!" I snapped, stepping closer to his barrel-chested frame. "And if you actually cared one jot for your other daughter, Portia, you *will* answer me."

Birnam glanced from my face to Gage's and his father's before finally relenting. "The evenin' he arrived. Shortly before I spoke tae yer brother. I suppose that's what ye want tae ken," he snarled belligerently. "Weel, I never promised him a thing. He canna claim otherwise." With this he stomped off, not realizing he'd left me stunned for a different reason.

"He lied," I muttered to myself.

"Who? Birnam?" Lord Gage asked in confusion.

I turned to face them. "No. Milngavie. He told me that Birnam approached him about marrying Matilda on Wednesday, after the archery debacle and before their argument over port following dinner. But Birnam is saying they spoke Monday, not long after Lord Milngavie arrived." I shook my head. "Why would Milngavie lie?"

The sinking sensation which had begun earlier deepened, for I was afraid I knew the answer.

"Maybe he wished to spare your and your brother's feelings," Gage suggested, though I could see in his face that he was no more convinced of that than I was.

"Maybe," I murmured, turning to search the crowd gathered behind us in the great hall. Philip was conversing with Lord Melbourne beneath the bust of some ancient Roman while nearby Alfie was making Lorna and Charlotte laugh. Trevor and Matilda, and Lady Bearsden and Lord Strathblane were whirling about the room arm in arm—one couple more graceful than the other. I couldn't see Milngavie, but I knew he was there. And I suddenly felt an urgency to find him.

CHAPTER 28

I told Gage this, and while he didn't seem to feel the same necessity to locate Milngavie I did, he still conceded to my wishes. Deeming it was late enough in the evening that our absence from the receiving line would not be remarked upon, we left Lord Gage to greet any late arrivals and spread out to circulate among the crowd spaced throughout the various rooms of the manor. He set off down the corridor toward the green drawing room where card tables had been set up and the red saloon while I mingled with those gathered in the great hall.

Everyone seemed to be enjoying themselves, and part of me was relieved to see that Miss Whitlock's murder and the ensuing investigation had not dampened everyone's spirits. However, another part of me was rather saddened by how little Portia Whitlock's passing appeared to have affected the world. It seemed the lights should be at least a little dimmer, the joy just a bit more subdued. But then these people were not of her social strata. Most of them hadn't even known of her existence. I supposed it was foolish to expect any show of emotion.

I was gliding past a group of matrons surveying the dancers when I spied Anderley in the doorway. He was clearly searching the crowd for someone, and as I moved toward him, he nodded, stepping to the side out of sight. When I joined him, he was hovering near the entrance to the dining room.

"I finally cornered Armstrong," he said.

"What did he say?" I asked, conscious that Milngavie's valet might possess critical information about his employer.

"He swore he doesn't know anything about Milngavie's correspondence. That it's not part of his duties. But he admitted that he must have mentioned the bottle of vitriol McClintock left in the laundry on the same evening it occurred while he was shaving Milngavie before dinner." He arched one sardonic eyebrow. "I gather he's a chatterer."

"He's certain?"

Anderley straightened, sensing the earnestness of my request. "Yes. He swears he never spoke of it again until Milngavie asked him about it a few days later and instructed him to tell us what he'd seen."

Then Milngavie had known about the bottle of oil of vitriol before Miss Whitlock was murdered. He had known and when it had not come to light earlier had sought to misdirect us by having his manservant helpfully inform us of its existence and where it had come from—a Birnam staff member.

"Tell Gage," I directed Anderley, suggesting where he could most likely be found. "And then help us locate Milngavie."

He nodded, hurrying off while I returned to the great hall, intent on locating Lady Bearsden. I'd last seen her dancing with Lord Strathblane, but the music had since switched to a quadrille, and I did not spy either of them in the figures. Happily, I did spot Charlotte conversing with my Aunt Cait.

"Have you seen your great-aunt?" I inserted myself into their conversation to ask. They both turned to me in surprise.

"Kiera," Aunt Cait proclaimed, recovering first. "You're flushed, dear. Is anything amiss?"

"No, of course not," I replied with a forced smile that was probably far from convincing, not wishing to cause a scene. "But I do need to speak to Lady Bearsden. To ask her a question."

If Charlotte found my answers odd or stilted, she didn't let on. "Last I saw her, Auntie was headed out to the terrace for some fresh air."

"Thank you!" I exclaimed, striding off before I could be waylaid by anyone else.

Slowing my steps, I sauntered into the red saloon, finding a number of guests partaking of the refreshments laid out on the central table or scattered about the room engaged in discussion. I smiled at a number of them as they glanced toward me but avoided being drawn into any conversations. Exiting out onto the terrace, I heard Lady Bearsden's musical laughter coming from the right. Lord Strathblane passed me as I made my way in that direction, bowing shallowly as we crossed paths before continuing inside.

"Kiera, dear," the older lady proclaimed at the sight of me, gesturing toward the chair opposite hers at the wrought iron table. "Come sit with me for a moment. Miles has just gone to fetch me some more ratafia. You look flushed, dear. Have your hostess duties been running you ragged?"

I ignored her queries, but took the seat, leaning across the table toward her. "Lady Bearsden, you mentioned being Lord Milngavie's neighbor."

"Why, yes." She waved her hand in the direction her companion had gone. "Strathblane was just telling me what a bright future he anticipates for this Milngavie despite the disadvantages of his early life."

"Yes, though Milngavie told me he doesn't see them that way."

"Truly?" She seemed much struck by this, and I felt the pulse of irritation I imagined anyone born to less status or wealth must feel whenever the nobility assumed their lives were nothing but toil and tribulation, or perhaps somehow less worthy. But Lady Bearsden's next remark proved I'd misjudged her. "I would have thought that after what happened to his brother, he would feel quite differently."

"His brother?" I repeated, for Milngavie had said nothing about having a brother. He'd only mentioned his cousins to me.

"Oh, yes." She leaned across the table toward me. "It's quite tragic. He was injured in a terrible accident while working in one of the mills. And just eight years old!" She sat back, tapping her chin. "From what I recall, he died soon after."

My heart stilled at the tragedy of it, and then it began to race as all the pieces began to coalesce. "Who owned the mill?"

She blinked at the strident tone of my voice, forcing me to repeat my question.

"Who owned the mill where his brother was injured?"

"Why, I don't think I know." She turned toward an approaching figure. "But perhaps Strathblane . . ."

"Who owned the mill where Milngavie's brother was injured?" I turned to demand of him.

He fumbled the glasses he held, nearly dropping them. "The mill?" he repeated somewhat stupidly. "His brother? I don't think I know."

Rather than waste any more time trying to explain, I hastened back into the saloon, trusting they would forgive my rudeness later once I'd enlightened them. Once Milngavie learned we were asking questions about him, as he must inevitably, there was no telling how he would react. Particularly if his target all along had been Birnam.

Entering the house, I nearly collided with my husband. "Slow down, Kiera," he proclaimed, grasping my upper arms, lest I topple over. "What's the rush? Anderley already spoke to me. And just because . . ."

"It's Milngavie," I hissed, conscious of the eyes and ears surrounding us. Something in my tone must have alerted him to the fact this was no longer a supposition, for he ceased trying to dissuade me. I briefly explained what I'd just learned from Lady Bearsden, providing the context from my earlier tête-à-tête with Milngavie. "Why would he mention his cousins working in a mill but not his brother? Why hide that truth from me if there wasn't a very good reason to conceal it?"

Gage's brow had lowered in concern as he turned to survey the others in the room. "We need to find him." His gaze returned to mine. "But not cause a panic."

I inhaled a ragged breath, trying to slow my heart rate. "Right."

"He's not in the card room. Let's check the drawing room and the great hall again."

But after making a circuit of both, he was still nowhere to be found.

"Where could he have gone?" I asked, talking to myself as much as my husband. We had greeted him earlier in the evening when he arrived, but neither of us had seen him since. Could he have gone somewhere quieter? Perhaps the library or his bedchamber.

It was then that Trevor wandered over carrying two glasses of punch. "Have either of you seen Matilda?" he asked in evident confusion.

My stomach pitched.

"She was just standing under the balcony in the great hall waiting for me, but now I can't find her."

Gage sent me a speaking glance, letting me know he was entertaining the same fear.

"What?" Trevor demanded to know. "What is it?"

While Gage sought to explain about Milngavie, I searched my brain and our surroundings for inspiration. Though I'd ignored her at first, I took another look at Mrs. Birnam seated near one corner of the red saloon. She was watching us but trying not to draw our attention. Her gaze jerked to the side whenever I peered her way. I had to wonder why.

Trusting the men would follow, I approached the formidable woman. She turned to receive us with a sour expression, making it clear she did not wish our company. This I could ignore. It was the smug note hinted at in the corner of her lips that made my skin flush, and my chest tighten, making it difficult to draw a full breath.

"Mrs. Birnam, where is your daughter?"

She opened her fan to ply it before her, taking her time in answering. "I don't know what makes you think I'm answerable to you, but your continuous intrusions into my and my family's lives are tiresome." She waved the fan in dismissal. "Now, go away."

My heart rate spiked, her answer all but confirming my worst fears. "Where are Matilda and Milngavie?" I demanded.

She turned away. "That is none of your concern."

"It most certainly is," Trevor interjected, slamming the cups he held down on a nearby table, heedless of how their contents sloshed over their sides. "Because he killed Miss Whitlock."

This seemed to give her pause.

"Where is she?" Trevor demanded, his voice rising so that we were now gaining an audience. "I swear that if you don't tell me . . ."

"He took her out into the gardens."

Mrs. Birnam scowled at her son, who was seated a short distance away.

He rose to his feet to nod toward the French doors. "That way."

Trevor and Gage immediately began to move off in that direction while I trailed after them.

"My lady!"

I turned back toward Jemmy as he hurried toward me. I was anxious to be away.

His eyes were wide with worry for his sister. "It was Milngavie who told me about that folly."

I grasped his arm in gratitude, for it was a large garden, and with night having fallen, it was dark beyond the lanterns which had been lit nearest the house. "Come with us," I urged him.

He hesitated for a moment but joined me as I scurried through the doors out onto the terrace. Our footsteps pounded down the steps after Gage and Trevor, entirely heedless of how much attention we were now attracting.

"He may have taken her to the folly," I explained to Gage once we'd caught up with him.

It was as good a guess as any, for I'd met him myself as he was returning down that path one morning. Though he might not have waited until he reached the folly to harm her. After all, the woods were dark, and each moment longer they were gone, the more at risk he became of discovery.

I supposed it depended on his intentions. Did he intend to somehow lure Birnam out here or was he simply planning to kill Matilda in vengeance like he had Miss Whitlock? The latter filled me with terror, for he might act more quickly. Indeed, the deed might already be done.

The very thought threatened to halt me in my tracks, but the knowledge that Matilda's fate lay in our hands kept my feet moving as I led them in the direction I prayed they'd gone. Gage peeled away to issue instructions to a footman, hopefully requesting he fetch reinforcements in the form of Anderley and possibly Philip and Lord Gage. By the time I'd passed the line of shrubbery, Gage had returned carrying two lanterns.

I glanced at him in question. "He'll see us coming long before we see him."

"Yes, but the sound of the four of us moving through the forest is already likely to alert him, and this way at least he can't sneak up on us in the dark."

I couldn't fault his logic, but I did wish I had my Hewson percussion pistol with me. It would have made a rather bulky accessory to my ball gown, it was true, but at least I wouldn't now be weaponless.

"Are you armed?" I asked, curious if at least one of us was prepared.

"Yes. It seemed . . . prudent." One corner of his lips curled wryly. "And regrettably, I was correct."

A loud cracking noise resounded behind us, causing Gage and me to whirl around. However, it was only my brother now wielding a sizable branch he'd apparently rent from a nearby tree. "Now I'm armed, too," he proclaimed with deadly intent, leaving me in no doubt that he would use it if necessary.

Jemmy eyed him with misgiving but then glanced about on the forest floor as if looking for a similar weapon.

Rather than respond, Gage and I turned to resume our progress. For what could we say? The woman Trevor loved was in danger. Of course, he would be desperate to protect her however he could.

"If Milngavie is nearby, he may have heard that," Gage warned me in a low voice.

There was no need to tell me, for I'd already had the same thought. My eyes peered into the woods surrounding us, trying to peel back the shadows crowded under its canopy to see what might lurk beyond. The only sound was that of our shuffling through the leaves and undergrowth and the crunch of twigs. The temperature had cooled considerably, and I found myself longing for a shawl to cover my bare arms and décolletage. The air was scented with damp earth and the stench of my own fear, for the nearer we drew to the folly, the more apprehensive I became that we would discover something dreadful. That we were too late.

Eventually, we neared the final curve in the path around which I knew the folly would emerge. I could already hear the faint trickle of the stream as it tumbled over the artificial cascade. At first, we could see nothing but the squat form of the building, but then as we drew nearer, the folly's windows caught the lantern light, and the outline of a figure emerged in the doorway. No, two figures. The second had an arm locked around the torso of the first, holding her back against him. In his other hand, he clutched a knife to her throat.

CHAPTER 29

We stumbled to a halt as the seriousness of the situation became clear, then slowly began to advance again, not wanting to provoke Lord Milngavie into pressing his knife into the tender flesh of Matilda's neck. Her eyes were wide with terror, her chest rising and falling rapidly beneath his arm, but she didn't dare speak. Meanwhile, Milngavie's face had transformed into a twisted mask of rage.

He scanned us as we approached, his eyes flashing with fury. "Where's Birnam?"

Jemmy began to step forward.

"Not you," he snarled. "The old man. Where is he?"

None of us spoke, and neither did I turn my head, not wanting to take my eyes off the enraged man before us.

"Did he send you in his stead? Too cowardly tae face the consequences o' his own crimes!"

"Obviously, you sent him a message," Gage ventured.

"Aye. And it seems once again, he canna be trusted tae follow directions." In his wrath, his accent had slipped back into his native Scottish brogue. "Or perhaps he doesna care for even his ain children," he sneered in Matilda's ear.

"Then *you* slipped that note under his door," I accused, attempting to draw his attention away from panic-stricken Matilda.

"O' course, I did!" he brashly retorted. "And none o' the rest o' this would've happened if he'd simply done as he was told."

"Then the oil of vitriol was intended for him." Weaponless as I was, I decided the best thing I could do was keep him talking while the men tried to formulate a plan. If Gage could draw his pistol undetected, he might attempt a shot, but he was just as likely to hit Matilda as Milngavie from this angle and distance. They needed to come up with a different strategy, preferably without alerting Milngavie.

"Listenin' tae him continue tae deride the Factory Act over dinner, espousing his ain goodliness and it bein' unnecessary when all the while he works children tae the bone, carin' not when they become mangled in his machinery, castin' 'em aside as dispensable."

"Children like your brother."

If he wondered how I'd found out about that, he didn't show it. "Aye! And the twenty-three other children who have been maimed and injured in Birnam's mills and factories."

My eyes widened in shock, and I realized that was what the list of names written on that paper had been. The one he'd tucked into his pocket before dinner last night.

"Aye, I keep their names wi' me. Tae remember." His jaw tightened. "Tae remind me o' the justice none o' 'em received."

I felt a pang of empathy for those children and their families, and even for Milngavie, whose intentions had probably started out as noble. But over time, they'd become twisted with anger, just as his face twisted now with disgust.

"But listenin' to Birnam, I realized he didn't feel even an ounce of remorse or responsibility, and that he was never goin' tae see the error o' his ways. So I decided I'd have tae show him myself."

"You *did* overhear Miss Whitlock and me talking," I deduced. "And you decided to take advantage of it."

He shrugged and the knife must have bitten into Matilda's skin for she squeaked in alarm. Trevor surged forward, and I had to hold out an arm to stop him, lest he drive Milngavie into taking drastic action.

"I needed a way tae draw Birnam oot, and you provided one."

"But wasn't Miss Whitlock intending to inform on him?" I asked in confusion. "Wasn't she trying to report infractions at Birnam's mills?"

"She had her chance," he sneered, making me frown in confusion. "Or didna ye ken she met wi' me earlier that afternoon? We'd arranged it. I ken she visited his mills and factories, so when she tried tae contact Strathblane, I thought she had evidence tae give. But rather than denounce him, she tried tae defend him. Told me some sob story aboot how he'd taken her in as an orphan and all the care he'd shown her," he muttered in a mocking tone before growling. "So he's got compassion for the orphaned child o' his friend but no' all the factory children he exploits and mangles!" Evidently, he'd not heard the rumors that Portia Whitlock was Birnam's daughter, but I didn't know that it would have made a difference. As long as in his desire for revenge he'd harmed someone who mattered to Birnam.

Out of the corner of my eye, I could see Gage attempting to draw his pistol from his waistband at the back of his trousers and sought to keep Milngavie focused on me. "So you threatened her. That's why she was so uncomfortable seated next to you at dinner. That's what she wished to speak with me privately about." She'd feared for herself and perhaps Birnam.

But for once he didn't outright agree with this statement. "I dinna ken exactly what she wished tae say tae ye. I was willin' tae believe I'd shocked her intae growin' a conscience and she intended tae expose Birnam for what he was. But then she arrived before Birnam, and I couldna let her warn him." He shook his head. "She should have done the right thing. She should no' have gotten in the way."

It was clear he felt no guilt for what had happened to her. Just as he intended to feel no guilt for what happened next.

"Let's hope he mourns you more than his orphan," he told Matilda, beginning to back into the folly with her.

We were out of time.

"Milngavie, stop! You don't have to do this," I pleaded. "Matilda is innocent. She has nothing to do with her father's mills and factories."

But he was no longer listening. Whatever his intent was, he was through talking.

We surged forward. Trevor with his makeshift cudgel and Gage with his pistol charged to the front. We heard glass breaking at the back of the building, and I recalled the precipitous drop down to the cascades below. By the time Jemmy and I entered the folly, it was to find Milngavie on the ground with Trevor standing over him and Gage leaning out the broken window to peer down at the rocks.

My heart was in my throat and I thought I might be sick, until Gage turned back toward us with an evident look of reprieve. He gestured toward the wall, now open to the air, and I stepped closer to see what he already had.

Matilda looked rumpled and shaken, but she was alive, having been caught by some combination of Lord Gage and Anderley, who now lay crumpled in a heap, partially in the stream and partially along the little-used path workers used to perform any maintenance to the cascade. They appeared damp and bruised, but overall unharmed.

I collapsed against Gage's side, and he did his best to support me despite still cradling the lantern and pistol. Jemmy, likewise, seemed relieved. Then I remembered my brother.

He was panting, still standing dazed over Milngavie's insensible form. His cudgel hung by his side as he stared down at the man now bleeding from a head wound. Evidently, Trevor had floored him.

I gently touched his arm, though it took several attempts at saying his name to gain his attention. "She's alive." He blinked at me, making me repeat myself again. I glanced down at the tree branch. "And I think you can put that down now."

He dropped it at my urging and then moved toward the window to see for himself that Matilda was safe.

Locating the knife now discarded on the floor, I took the precaution of kicking it away from Milngavie, lest he regain consciousness, and knelt down to examine the wound. It was bleeding profusely, but the blow didn't seem to have cracked his skull. His pulse was strong, and he would no doubt survive. Though he would suffer from a crushing headache for several days. It was less than he deserved!

Recognizing that we needed to stanch the bleeding, I retrieved the knife and turned away to lift the skirts of my gown in order to cut away a portion of my linen undergarments. Then, careful to avoid the pool of blood forming beneath his supine form, I pressed the cloth to his head.

A short time later, those below had made their way around to the path outside the folly. Trevor and Jemmy rushed out to meet them while Gage ushered one of his father's footmen inside.

"Let him take over that," he told me.

I passed the duty to the footman, knowing he would care for him until we arranged to have Milngavie carried up to the manor where Dr. Clarke, who was already in attendance, could examine him. That Milngavie would be placed under lock and key and guard went without saying.

Gage passed me his handkerchief so that I could wipe what blood I could from my hands. Draping his arm around my waist, he joined me in the doorway, observing the warm reunion. Poor Matilda was crying as she clung to first her brother and then Trevor. Lord Gage looked on indulgently, his evening clothes damp and soiled. I had never been so happy for him to make an appearance.

But then he had to spoil it by turning to us with a sardonic lift of his brows. "Waited until rather the last minute to solve this, didn't you?"

I could only sigh resignedly, allowing my head to slump sideways against Gage's upper arm.

When Birnam arrived, blustering, "What on earth is the

meanin' o' this?!" I simply closed my eyes, allowing the rest of them to explain.

The upheaval caused by the events at the folly might have threatened to ruin the evening's enjoyment, but in the end, they only seemed to heighten it. The villain had been caught, and Matilda—the damsel in distress—was fussed over and cosseted and ultimately chose to return to the ball after changing her gown. She remained close to Trevor's and her brother's sides, while the other Birnams remained conspicuously absent.

Lord Gage also returned to the ball after a change of garments, now hailed as a hero, never mind that Anderley was just as responsible for saving Matilda's life. And none of us would have been there to stop Milngavie's nefarious plans if it hadn't been for Gage's and my deductive work and Jemmy sharing such crucial information. Regardless, we let Lord Gage have the accolades. Gage and I had no need of them, and we would be sure Anderley was aware of our gratitude.

Lord Milngavie eventually regained consciousness, but he was through talking to us. Instead, he insisted upon being transported to London, where he would plead his case to his peers.

"He's well versed in the privileges afforded to noblemen," Lord Gage told us the next morning as we stood before the window in his study, watching Milngavie be loaded into a carriage under guard. "In fact, I daresay he was counting on them. After all, he'll be tried in the House of Lords where every detail of what he knows about Birnam's business dealings will be aired during the trial."

"Do you think he'll be acquitted?" I asked in shock. For all that Milngavie had reason to despise Birnam, he'd still savagely killed a young woman who, no matter how misguided, had almost certainly just been trying to protect her family.

Lord Gage frowned, clasping his hands behind his back. "I doubt he'll walk free, but there is a definite reluctance to hang noblemen. It might set a dangerous precedent. It's more likely he'll be punished some other way. The severity will depend on whether he can convince them that death was not actually intended when he planned to attack Birnam and threw acid on Miss Whitlock instead. He'll also need to explain the timing and if he intended to see Miss Whitlock or you . . ." he turned to look at me ". . . accused when you ultimately stumbled upon Birnam."

"But if Birnam had survived the attack . . ."

"*If*, Kiera, *if*. Then I suppose he hoped your and Miss Whitlock's arrivals would at least muddy any evidence against him."

I contemplated the cruelty and dastardliness of these intentions, if in fact that's what he'd planned. For two young ladies to be the first to find Birnam's burned and scarred figure and for us to face suspicion.

"And the note he slipped into Thorndike's coat pocket?" I queried.

"No doubt a feint. An attempt to divert suspicion to someone else," Lord Gage explained. "He must have learned we'd questioned him."

It had been a relief to discover we hadn't been wrong in believing Thorndike wasn't responsible for the note, though that hadn't been enough to save him from being released from his position with Lord Gage. Even now, he was likely traveling by mail coach back to London.

The carriage door outside was slammed shut, and then the exterior guard climbed up beside the coachman, a rifle draped across his lap.

"Whatever the result," Lord Gage continued, "Milngavie will attain what he sought."

"Birnam's reputation exposed and ruined," Gage supplied.

It was no more than he deserved, particularly since it was unlikely he would face any jail time. Not when all the mills and factories utilized the same equipment and practices. The most that could be hoped for was that he would be fined and that the scandal might spur the passage of the revisions to the Factory Act and future changes in the laws.

But while I was glad that Birnam would at least face *some* sort of punishment, I also couldn't help but think of all the innocent people who would be hurt, including his own children.

"His denunciation isn't all bad," my father-in-law pronounced cryptically as he turned away from the window.

Gage and I glanced at each other before following his father over to the sideboard where he poured himself a brandy. It was clear he had more to say but intended to draw the moment out.

"What does that mean?" Gage finally prodded him as he lowered his glass.

"Well, now that he's facing ruin, there are few noblemen who will wish to align themselves with him. And those who will are naught but fortune hunters and scoundrels or worse.

Or so I reminded him." He rounded his desk, sinking down contentedly into his chair. "At this point, he should count his lucky stars if Mr. St. Mawr still wishes to wed his daughter."

I stared down at my father-in-law in astonishment before impulsively skirting his desk to embrace him.

"Oof! Careful. Girl, this is good brandy." He held his glass aloft lest I spill it, but I could tell, despite his scolding tone of voice, that he was pleased both to have astounded me and by my affectionate display of gratitude.

I pulled back. "Does Trevor know?"

"As of about an hour ago when I told him to be certain of himself, yes."

I pressed a kiss to his cheek before dashing off to find my brother. My husband's grin and Lord Gage's chuckle followed me out the door.

After a quick search of the house, I spied Trevor and Matilda through the French doors of the red saloon out in the garden. But before I could step a foot outside on the terrace, Alana stopped me.

"Wait, dear. I think they wanted a moment alone."

Heeding her advice, we stood side by side, watching from a distance as our brother bent down on one knee and asked the woman he loved to be his wife. It was evident from both of their reactions that she'd said yes. And just as evident when they began climbing the steps to the terrace to find us waiting for them, happy tears in our eyes, that we knew precisely what had occurred.

We embraced them each in turn, congratulating them and welcoming Matilda to our family.

"We aren't going to rush the engagement," she explained

in answer to Alana's question about when they hoped to wed. Trevor smiled warmly at her, content with her answering for them. "My mother's health has been in decline, and the shock of these latest events certainly hasn't helped. Jemmy and I think a trip to warmer climes might be good for her."

It would also allow them to escape the worst of the scandal that was about to erupt over their father's past and his business practices.

"I can tell you're surprised," she continued. "Particularly considering my mother's behavior over the past week. But I know that she loves me." She turned adoring eyes toward my brother. "And she'll be both relieved and delighted to hear I've become betrothed to Trevor."

After everything Mrs. Birnam had revealed to us of the matter and her own marriage, I could be convinced this was true.

"And what can I say . . ." Matilda shrugged. "She's my mother. She needs me. It's my turn to tend to her." She held out her hand as if just remembering something. "Oh, and don't worry. I haven't forgotten his lordship's garden." She grinned. "I have several ideas for it."

I was tremendously proud of Matilda for showing such grace and maturity, and I knew in that moment, beyond a shadow of a doubt, that she would make both a marvelous wife and a wonderful sister-in-law. If Trevor could wait until the next year to call her his bride, then who were we to argue.

Gage and I would have plenty to keep us busy in the meantime. Including an unexpected summons from our roguish friend, Lord Marsdale. Even though he had been anticipating his old and infirm father's death for some time, when it finally occurred, he feared the cause was far from natural, and that it related to a recent discovery he'd made in his scholarly pursuits. Gage and I soon found ourselves with not only the riddle of a murder to solve, but also an almost two-hundred-year-old royal mystery to decipher. A puzzle that someone was determined remain unresolved. And they were willing to go to dire lengths to ensure it.

ACKNOWLEDGMENTS

With the completion of each new Lady Darby novel, I pinch myself, feeling overwhelmed with gratitude. That I get to keep writing this series with these characters I adore; it feels like I will never grow tired of them. That readers continue to want to read about them and their adventures. That I have such a stellar team at my back—both personally and professionally—helping to make this possible.

All my love and thanks to my family. In particular, to my husband—my Gage. And to my children for their excitement, hugs, and support. And my parents for the love they've poured into me my entire life.

Heaps of gratitude to my incredible publishing team. To my agent, Kevan Lyon, for her excellent guidance and steadfast encouragement. To my editor, Michelle Vega, who seems to be able to read my mind at this point and always helps me find the words, or better words, to express what I'm trying to say. To all the incredible staff at Berkley for all of their expertise and outstanding contributions, including Annie Odders, Elisha Katz, Katie Ferraro, and so many others.

All my appreciation to my friend, floral artist Chelsea Meighen, for helping me finesse the floral arranging scene so that I didn't embarrass myself with my ineptness. (Any mistakes remaining are my own.) I'm also so grateful for Cara Welch, who won the right to name a character in this book through the Malice Domestic Auction. She named the character Ann McClintock.

Many, many thanks to all of my friends and extended family for their continued love and support, including my siblings, in-laws, aunts, uncles, cousins, and the ladies in my Moms Group. And thank you to my readers for loving Kiera and Gage and crew almost as much as I do.

And finally, thanks and praise to God, from whom all blessings flow, for granting me the wonder and the will.

Photo by Shanon Aycock

Anna Lee Huber is the *USA Today* bestselling and Daphne Award–winning author of more than twenty novels, including the Lady Darby Mysteries and the Verity Kent Mysteries, as well as *Sisters of Fortune: A Novel of the Titanic* and the anthology *The Deadly Hours*. Her novel *A Perilous Perspective* was included on the 2024 Indiana Author Awards shortlist. She is a summa cum laude graduate of Lipscomb University in Nashville, Tennessee, where she majored in music and minored in psychology. Her novels have been translated into multiple languages, and she is a member of Mystery Writers of America, Sisters in Crime, and International Thriller Writers. Anna currently resides in Indiana with her family and enjoys reading, singing, doing crafts, and traveling when she's not hard at work on her next novel.

VISIT ANNA LEE HUBER ONLINE

AnnaLeeHuber.com